Claire

A Novel

Gene B. Goodwin

ISBN: 1-4348-6946-6

Prologue
Friday, October 19

The little girl shivered from the cold she felt throughout her body. The darkness enveloped her; so dark, her hand was unseen in front of her face. It was a darkness that protected her, but now the coldness alerted her mind to danger. Where was she? Where was she going? Who was she? Did she have a name? A smooth and hard surface greeted each step the girl took with bare feet. After taking several steps, the girl noticed something to the right. It was a very faint light; a speck really. It appeared to be far, far away, but finally, she had a point for reference; a place to go. She began shuffling her feet across the floor of the darkened space toward the speck in the darkness. As the girl approached, the glowing light grew larger and certain features became clearer within her mind. She saw eyes that sparkled and a smile across the mouth. Suddenly, behind her and to the left another light appeared. She turned to look at the new image and an odor quickly filled the air. It was an acrid smell; repulsive, yet recognizable in her mind. The first glow of light on her right became clearer the closer she came. It was comforting to the girl. The little child had been drawn to the light. As she moved closer, the face took definite shape. It was a man's face. A loving face, a strong face and a face she somehow recalled from another place and time, like it had always been there. Then another face appeared from behind the loving face. Had it had been hiding, waiting for her to get closer? She didn't like this face. But, it too was known. From behind her, the second light was creeping nearer. As the smell filled the girl's nostrils again, she swung around to come face to face with the horrible, glowing, features of a being; red, piercing eyes and an open mouth reeking of the odors that now filled her head. She turned with a jerk to run toward the wonderful loving face, but she was held fast in the grip of the terrible entity behind her. The ugly face was now close to hers, breathing hard; with gurgling and grunting sounds coming from it's mouth. She tried to scream, but she couldn't. The girl wished for the loving face she had seen to come rescue her, but it had disappeared along with the other unkind face. She was alone with this creature, who tormented her. Inside of her head, she screamed for the monster to go away. Then, as fast as it came, the monster's face went away. The girl was alone again in the dark. She felt safe in this darkness. Again, she retreated into the comfort of the blackness, never realizing the tormentor would return to her memories.

From the second floor window with the sill and shutters covered with ivy, the cool rain obscured the faint outline of someone staring through the window. A thin and frail girl was sitting silently in a rocking chair with a checkerboard padded back and seat, hands folded across her lap, eyes focused at the window; the place she had been for the last three months. But, she did not notice the rain or the soothing sound of the drops beating against the glass. She did not notice the drab window with the faded curtains or anything from the outside world. She was not even aware she was in that particular room or seated in a rocking chair. Claire was lost in her own silent world, deep within her mind; a condition the doctors had not been able to unravel.

A hard pelting afternoon rain fell across the grounds of the old hospital, drenching the fallen autumn leaves. It was cool and winter was not far away in the mid-south. Rolling Hills Mental Hospital was built back during the 1940's in Tipton County, Tennessee with taxpayer's money to help treat soldiers returning from World War II. During the 60's the state government turned over all management operations to a private group of doctors and investors looking to make long term profits caring for state indigent patients. It had never had a profitable year since the transfer. Only a few patients remained confined to Rolling Hills. Claire Richards was one.

Eleven year old, Claire Elaine Richards had been brought to Rolling Hills three months earlier, right after her parents decided to end their marriage. The divorce had been finalized in September. Claire didn't even know and no one had bothered to tell her; they felt she wouldn't understand. Claire hadn't spoken a word since arriving. In fact, she hadn't spoken a word to anyone in over 6 months. All the doctors who had examined Claire during the past had little hope left trying to communicate with her. They were no closer to an accurate diagnosis today than they were when she was first admitted. Claire's parents had offered no possible reasons for her condition, although her father had his suspicions without solid proof. Day to day care at Rolling Hills seemed to be the last resort for Claire. Because of the long-term expense for treatment, the divorce and work pressures that were requiring more and more of her Dad's free time, visits with Claire were becoming limited and far between.

Claire was tall for her age, close to 5'4", blonde-hair and the only child of two successful parents. Her father was Cliff Richards, a 37 year old senior investment consultant for Merrill-Lynch Securities in Memphis, TN. Claire's mother, Marlena Richards was 35-year-old corporate lawyer for International Paper Company; a workaholic mother. Claire got her beautiful blonde hair from her mother. Marlena was tall too, nearly 5'10", with a short cropped corporate business style haircut.

Claire grew up, never experiencing the true love a mother and daughter should share. As she grew, Mae was always there for Claire, helping with homework from Briarcrest, the private school for the affluent, bandaging the skinned knees, playing dolls in the afternoons, having tea parties on the patio or deck and reading stories at naptime with hugs before sleep. Mae was a wonderful substitute mother and Claire loved her dearly, but it was not the same. Something was missing. Miss Mae, as Claire always called her, was a middle-aged black woman, who had 4 children of her own to raise. The Richard's paid her quite well for her services, much more than the average housekeeper. Mae's husband had left after the second son, Mae lived in the inner city of Memphis where most of the lower income families could afford housing and she would make the daily journey to the Richard's home in her worn out, 86 Chevy Malibu. Cliff had promised her a newer car after she worked for them at least a year, but failed to live up to that promise when the time came. He conveniently forgot, but Mae never did and never mentioned it to him.

Sometimes, Grandma Katie filled that 'mother' void for Claire. "Grammie" as Claire called her, was Marlena's mother, Katherine Wilmont. Grammie would visit Claire at least twice a week. Marlena and her mother could almost pass as sisters. They looked so much alike and Katie, as everyone called her, held her age well. Just in her early 60's, Katie filled in nicely for Marlena with one difference. She loved Claire dearly, and Claire could feel it. Claire was extremely close to her Grammie. They would go on the outings and picnics while Dad was out of town. Even Mae would tag along sometimes. Katie never understood how Marlena could not love this child the way she should as a mother. The job came first and Marlena was building her career fast, a child was just in the way, especially this child. Katie had always wondered what difference there would have been if Claire had been the boy that Marlena yearned for so desperately. Would her career path have taken the turns they did?

Now, all that was behind her in the past. Claire sat motionless in the little wooden rocker, facing the window, rain sprinkling in spatters against the pane. This had been Claire's room for the past three months. Not very spacious, just a double bed, 4 drawer chest and a couple of wooden chairs for the visitors that might drop in from time to time. The empty, dingy white walls were in need of new paint or fresh wallpaper. In the corner opposite the only window in the room was the bath with a door missing it's handle, a small room with just enough space for the required fixtures. Next to the bathroom was the even smaller closet, where only 4 multi colored cotton shirts and 3 pair of faded jeans hung, never worn. One pair of yellow Nike tennis shoes was all that was on the floor of the closet. Claire was normally dressed in the blue-striped hospital gowns that tied in the back, which she was wearing this afternoon. It was almost visitors' hour, even though she was always oblivious to any conversations around her. She would always sit motionless in whatever chair she might be placed. Claire's eyes would always remain straight ahead, rarely moving and never looking at anyone directly. She was safe in her dark place.

Marlena had not been to see Claire since the first day her child was admitted to Rolling Hills. She didn't understand what sense it made, to simply come and watch the girl stare into space. She had more pressing schedules to keep, the divorce was almost final and she could finally get on with her life. Cliff, Claire's daddy, could have this child. Cliff was there every Saturday and Sunday, when he was in town. He talked to Claire and she would stare out into space. Mae tried to get visitation rights, but was refused because the hospital policy stated visitors must be family only or have written consent from a family member. Because he was out of town when Claire was admitted, Cliff was not aware of the visitation policy, but Marlena had been informed the first day. She couldn't justify, in her mind, wasting time filling out additional hospital paperwork and forms, just for a maid.

Grandma Katie had been to visit a couple of weekends when Claire first entered the facility, but left for a previously planned and extended retirement vacation cruise with William, her husband of 40 years. She hated so much leaving Claire and thought seriously of taking her with them on the trip. The hospital doctors convinced her that Claire would be best served at the hospital. Katie was unmoved, and was sure they only wanted Claire there because of the large monthly fees they were billing Cliff. Katie relented and left behind her precious granddaughter.

Katie and William returned from their cruise around the Mediterranean Sea and all the ports of call in between; Greece, Italy, Morocco, Spain and southern France. For many days Katie's thoughts were back in Rolling Hills, in that drab little room and her delightful grandchild, who had locked herself into a stupor that no one could seem to break.

Comfortable in the darkness of her mind, Claire sat quietly gazing at the rain. The sun was finally coming through and the rays reflected between openings in the clouds, like God's magnificent fingers spreading across the earth. The walkway to the visitor's center was directly below and to the left of Claire's bedroom window. It was almost visiting time. Claire was getting a visitor. It was Grammie, coming to see her little granddaughter after weeks on a cruise with her husband. Grammie had not seen Claire in at least three months, but hidden in the back of her mind, she had never forgotten her. As Katie walked slowly up the long sidewalk to the entrance to Rolling Hills, she looked in the direction of Claire's window. She saw Claire sitting in her little rocking chair, like always, staring through the window, so Katie stopped, closed her umbrella and lowered the hood on her lined parka. The rain had stopped. With a big broad smile on her face, she raised her hand high that it might be clearly seen and waved at Claire. Then she blew her a kiss, something they had always done when she would visit her at home, before all this happened. Claire would always catch the kiss and blow her own kiss back, so Grammie could catch as well.

Claire's vision had not been affected by the trauma and she was still able to see as clear as when she was admitted to the hospital. All of a sudden, the darkness, which had held her tight all these months, began to fade from black to light. When her eyes blinked, the real world slowly came into focus. Her static stare slowly dropped to meet the sparkling eyes and smiling face of her Grammie. A single tear appeared in Claire's blue eyes. Her normally straight or frowning full little lips, changed to a delicate but definite smile. With one wave of a hand, Grammie had finally reached inside Claire's secluded dark world and touched that little heart she loved so much. Grammie was coming to visit and Claire was feeling happy inside. She was coming out of her black world and was becoming alive, again.

Chapter One
March 24
6 months earlier

Today, the Richard's household was in total chaos. It was Saturday and Claire was turning 11 years old. One of the very few times the day for her birthday would actually occur on the same day she was born.

In the backyard on the patio next to the in-ground pool, streamers and balloons were hung in many designs and patterns. The tables were decorated with pink flowers over bright yellow tablecloths. Along each of the 3 tables were matching folding chairs, each with a single helium filled balloon carefully tied to the back of each chair. Party favors and refreshments were laid out in perfect order along the serving table. The chocolate cake with yellow icing was still inside in the kitchen. Mae was holding that for the last minute.

Claire was still upstairs in her bedroom looking through enough clothes to fill a small boutique in a strip shopping center. Most of her outfits contained the color yellow somewhere on the garment. Yellow was Claire's favorite color of all time. After throwing several pairs of jeans across the bed and different shades of yellow tops, she decided on the perfect combination for her party.

Cliff was in route home from the office after a last minute meeting that had been arranged on Friday the day before; always an important meeting, always on Saturday with no regard for families or personal lives. He phoned home from the car to let Mae know he was on the way and not to start without him.

Marlena was upstairs in her room, making some phone calls of her own. There was a new meeting to schedule for Monday at 10 in New York. She needed to book a flight out of Memphis International on Northwest. They have 3 direct flights daily to the northeast. She would get the earliest; 6:30a.m. This party was an inconvenience, a mistake, an event she would rather not attend. Every year on this day, Cliff and Mae would plan an elaborate party for Claire and let her invite all her friends from the neighborhood and school. No fewer than 20 attended these celebrations. Marlena simply tolerated them and their rowdiness.

Marlena picked up her white remote phone from the cradle and dialed the airline. "Hello, yes I need to book a flight from Memphis to New York JFK for Monday the 26th, 6:30am. . . . . Yes I'll wait."

She completed the transaction with the Northwest agent and flashed the phone to get another dial tone.

She dialed another number and waited for the answer.

"Hey, it's me. Are you still coming by later? . . . . I made the arrangements. . . . . . OK, see you then."

She pushed the end button and placed the phone back in the charging cradle. Marlena turned her attention back to the mirror on the dressing table, staring for a few seconds at her reflection. She was still quite stunning for a woman of 35 years. Her figure had remained trim, no sagging in the wrong places. She managed to work out occasionally and keep off the unnecessary fat. With the help of special oils and other magical creams, she displayed fewer wrinkles around the eyes than most women in her age group. She was a beautiful woman without makeup, but she still preferred a little Mary Kay to enhance the look. She completed dressing in dark blue cotton slacks, double-pleated in the front, with a lighter blue long sleeve satin shirt. She chose a white belt and white casual shoes.

Cliff pulled his BMW into the triple garage next to Marlena's Mercedes convertible and went directly through the house to the back door and into the yard. Mae was finishing up with last minute touches on the table decorations.

"So, Mae, where is everyone?" he said.

She looked up from her chores. "Well, you're not late, Mr. Cliff. Miss Claire is ready, waiting in the living room for her guests to arrive and Miss Marlena just came down a few minutes ago. She's in the kitchen."

He leaned over and spoke softly, "What kind of mood is Marlena in? You know how she hates these birthday parties."

"Well, as best as I could tell, she is in pretty good spirits, or maybe she got into some good spirits on her own."

Cliff laughed, "You crack me up, Mae. That's why I've tolerated you for so long"

He gave her a gentle hug and walked across the brick patio to the deck that stretched across the back two-thirds of the house. Huge red clay pots decorated the railings. Marlena's only passion outside of her work was her plants. The deck and yard were dotted with her handiwork. Of course, she did have a landscape artist who provided services on more than one occasion, sometimes working late into the evenings.

He went through the double sliding doors leading to the great room at the rear of the house. The gourmet kitchen was to the right. Marlena was seated at the corner white French provincial breakfast table with some files open and papers spread across the top of the table. A tall glass with gin and tonic was placed on an orange and white coaster. Cliff just shook his head in disgust.

He sat opposite her. "Are you so backed up, you have to do this today?"

She lay her pen down and looked up at her husband. "Yes, I do. I have a meeting in New York on Monday and I have too much to complete before then. I will be working most of the day and maybe tonight, too. And when you refer to 'Today', yes I am aware of what today is and you know that I think too much is made of a birthday."

"Do you plan on making a calm presence or a scene for Claire?"

She glared at him. "I'll surprise you, OK?" She downed the last of the gin and tonic, handed Cliff the glass. "Fix me another, will you, Hon?"

Cliff took the glass in protest and went to the bar in the great room to prepare another. With a smile of contempt, Marlena watched him leave and continued with her work.

He delivered her drink and went to find his birthday girl. Claire was waiting in the living room on the sectional sofa. None of her friends had yet arrived, because no one was ever early. She looked up from her teen magazine to the smiling face of her dad. Claire jumped up and ran to his waiting arms.

"Daddy, I'm so glad you're home. I was afraid you would miss my party."

"I would never miss your party, Tweetie." Cliff had always called her Tweetie since she was old enough to walk. Maybe that's why she loved the color yellow so intensely. She wanted to always be daddy's Tweetie bird. He lifted her off the floor and gave her a big hug and kiss.

"No one is here, yet. They should be here in a few minutes. Miss Mae has everything sooo ready. She always makes my parties special."

"How does it feel to be another year older?"

"No different than before. I guess my party will be about the same as before, just with all my friends, Miss Mae and you. I suppose Mom will be working as usual. Why does she hate me so much, Daddy?"

They sat back on the couch, Claire sat on Cliff's lap and he held her close. "She doesn't hate you, Tweetie. She just has lots of work to do. Her job you know. Remember, I have lots of work to do, too."

"Yeah, but you always find time for me. She never does. And when she does, it's only for shopping or taking me to the doctor, you know just 'have to' things."
She snuggled deeper into his hug.

"Is your Grammie coming? "

"I hope so. I invited her last week. I think Grandpa Bill is coming too."

The doorbell rang twice and Claire jumped off her Dad's lap to open the door for her first guest. Surprise, there were three smiling girls waiting for her, each carrying a perfectly wrapped gift. Claire never really was demanding when it came to presents. She generally managed to get all the 'things' she wanted during the year, like most of all her friends who were coming today. Giving gifts at birthday parties was merely a required trinket you bring when you attend.

Trina Oakland, Allison Davidson and Janey Caldwell were dragged through the security door into the entry way. Claire hugged each one as she accepted their generous gifts, placing the boxes on the table by the front door. Cliff decided Miss Mae might need his help with something, so he said hellos to the young ladies and left for the patio. The girls ran off to the great room to chat and giggle about boys. More guests arrived and the party was in full swing. Everyone now gathered on the patio around the beautifully decorated tables.

The doorbell rang again, this time Mae answered. "Well, hello Miss Katie. How are you feeling today? And Mr. Bill, glad to see you sir, hope you are fine too!"

Katie hugged Mae as she entered with Bill behind, "Thank you Mae, we are just fine. How about you and your wonderful children?"

"Oh, I am doing the best I can. I get around. The kids are growing faster than I can afford to buy new clothes. But they're alright."

Bill sniffed the air and looked at Mae, "Is that fresh coffee I smell, Miss Mae?"

"Yes sir, your nose does not deceive you. It just got done brewing. I suppose you will be wanting a cup?"

"You betcha!"

They all went into the kitchen. Marlena had cleared her paperwork from the table and joined the crowd on the patio, but chose to sit at the patio table, away from the noisy children.

Katie told Bill, “You enjoy your coffee, Hon. I’m going to see the birthday girl.” She laid her purse on the breakfast table while Bill made himself comfortable in the first chair. Katie went to the patio door and outside.

No sooner had Katie opened the door, when Claire looked up from her conversation with her friends. “GRAMMIE!” She jumped from her seat and rushed to the waiting arms of her grandmother.

“I’m so glad you came. My party would never be the same without you.”

“You say that every year, precious.”

“But it’s true every year, too.”

Katie laughed and wrapped her arms around Claire and held tight. “Grandpa Bill is inside.” She whispered in her ear.

Claire looked up into Katie’s eyes and smiled from ear to ear. “He is? Oh, I’m so glad. Did he quit his job or something? He never gets to come to visit that much. Where is he?”

“He stopped in the kitchen for a minute to have a cup of Mae’s great coffee. Why don’t you go say hello to him.” Katie unwrapped her arms from around Claire.

Claire said, “I will.”

She ran to the kitchen door and into the kitchen. Katie spotted Marlena sitting alone at a white ornamental iron patio table. She was still nursing the fresh gin and tonic Cliff had prepared earlier. She sat in the chair next to her oldest daughter.

"Marlena, you know that you shouldn't be drinking out here. Especially in front of all these other children. And it's Claire's birthday."

"Yes please remind me of that. And I will drink whenever I choose, mother."

Katie looked down and slowly shook her head, "Honey, I don't mean to pry. I just wanted …"

"Yeah, you want me to be a perfect daughter and mother to Claire, just like you and I were? Let me see, how many nights were you gone on your business trips when I was growing up? How many birthdays did you miss? Guess the apple doesn't fall far from the tree, huh?" she picked up her glass and downed the rest of her drink. "I'm going to fix another, you want something?" Marlena got up and went inside leaving Katie sitting alone.

Cliff was helping Mae with final details. By now all the 10 and 11 year old friends had arrived. They were huddled together around the pool near the diving board deep in meaningful 5th grade conversation about boys, boys and more boys.

Claire looked up and watched her mother jerk the back door open and stomp in the house. She was not hurt by her mother's actions; she was accustomed to the attitude, the coolness. She never even noticed anymore how much her mother drank. Claire just wanted for once to have her mother take part in a birthday or any event that involved family and friends. She was always busy, always on the phone or leaving for another trip to New York or Chicago. Just one time, Claire wanted her mother to hold her close and tight, like Grammie does.

Allison noticed Claire was staring at the house, "Claire, what's wrong? Are you OK?"

"Yeah, everything is as it always is. Let's go, I think Miss Mae has the tables ready. " She got up and announced, "Come on guys, let's have cake."

All the kids left the pool area and each one found a seat around the party tables. Allison sat to Claire's right who always sat at the head of the table.
Janey sat opposite Allison. Janey and Allison had been Claire's best friends since they were 5 years old. Janey's family lived next door and Allison's house was across the street. The neighborhood was very stable. Homes rarely were put on the market on their street. Most families were longtime residents.

Allison had just turned 11 the month before and Janey's birthday would not be until June 5th. They were completing the 5th grade at Germantown Elementary. Claire had been transferred from Briarcrest and placed in the county public school after their last move. All of her new friends attended Germantown Elementary.

Cliff grabbed a cushion deck chair and sat next to Claire. Miss Mae was bringing out a huge single layer cake, yellow outside and chocolate inside and decorated with yellow, blue and pink flowers. "Happy Birthday Claire" was meticulously scrolled across the middle of the cake. Mae placed the cake with 11 lighted yellow candles in front of Claire. Cliff started the traditional song and everyone else chimed along. Bill had joined Katie, placing his arm around her, both smiling at their precious granddaughter, singing along.

Marlena stood silently in the kitchen staring at the party through the breakfast nook window. "Yeah have a happy birthday, daughter." She whispered sarcastically to herself.

Claire was smiling, looking into everyone's eyes and they sang just for her. She noticed her mother standing in the kitchen window and saw her turn and leave. Claire lost the smile, just for a second or two as she watched the back door, hoping her Mom would join them. No such luck. The party went on without her.

Marlena placed her empty glass in the sink and went down the hall past the living room on the right and through the great room into her office. She sat down in the burgundy leather executive chair. Her desk was dark mahogany. A Compaq Presario computer sat to the left side. Stacks of folders of work to be done covered the front half of the desktop. The walls on three sides were lined with dark mahogany bookshelves, filled with a complete law library. On the top shelf there were a few murder mystery novels by James Patterson and a couple of novels by Stephen King. She had a business phone installed several years ago with three incoming lines. She made two calls; one to verify her flight on Northwest to New York on Monday and the other was to a close friend who owed her a favor.

Marlena left the office and stopped by the bar in the great room. Her hand was on a clean glass ready to fix another one. No not now, she needed to be clear headed the rest of the day. She went out to watch the party.

It did not take too long for 18 hungry girls to finish off the cake and 1 gallon of French vanilla ice cream. Mae was clearing the tables with Cliff and Katie's help. Bill had accepted the responsibility to gather all the gifts and goodies from the house. Claire eagerly opened the first gift. Marlena watched from the shade next to the house. Claire noticed her mother watching but did not acknowledge her presence.

Cliff saw Marlena sitting alone and said to Katie, "I think you and Mae can handle things from here on."

Katie looked into Cliff's eyes and noticed he was looking in Marlena's direction. She said, "Yes we can handle it. Go sit with her Cliff. Talk to her. Maybe you can get through to her. This precious little girl will be grown and gone before she realizes it. I know too well."

Cliff hugged her and said, "I know. I wish things could have been better between you two. You had a career too. It'll all work out."

Cliff walked up to Marlena, "Can I join you?"

She looked at him and rolled her eyes. "Well, this is your place too."

"What's wrong, Marlena? Why have we grown so far apart? Your daughter is growing up and you're missing her life and the love she has to offer." he said as he sat next to her.

She snapped, "She's your daughter, remember that. I'll do what ever is necessary as *the mother*, but don't expect lovey-dovey hugs and kisses. I never was taught, so just drop it."

She started to get up when Mae came through the door, "Mr. Cliff, there's a call for you."

"Thanks, Mae. I'll get it in my office." He turned to Marlena. "Sit back down, and we still need to talk. Maybe after the party." He left.

Cliff had converted a spare downstairs bedroom into his personal office. He didn't need the elaborate décor that Marlena required. He only needed a simple oak desk with a hutch, two 4 drawer file cabinets for investment prospecting data and a small beige couch with matching chair. An oak table with a lamp separated the chair from the couch. Line one was blinking on his phone. He sat in his black swivel chair, picked up the receiver and pressed the button.

"Hello, this is Cliff Richards."

Katie handed Claire the last gift. This one was from Allison and she was squirming with anticipation. She couldn't wait until Claire opened it. Claire had wanted these for so long and no one else had bought it.

Claire looked at the card on top and read that this gift was from Allison. She looked at her best friend and smiled. Allison was ready to tear open the paper for her. "Hurry up will you."

"OK, I will."

Claire sensed Allison's anticipation and was slowing working at the paper on the package, just to tease her friend. Suddenly, Claire ripped open the gift. It read Nike on all sides of the box. Claire's eyes opened wide. She looked at Allison.

"Is this what I think it might be?"

Allison's grin gave it away, "Just open the box."

Claire tore off the top and peeled back the tissue paper. Inside were the newest of the Nike line of tennis shoes. This particular pair came in a brilliant yellow color, all leather, with white soles and white and yellow striped laces. Claire screamed. She had wanted a pair of these since first seeing an ad in Teen-Age magazine. Nike began marketing Nike Brights in brilliant solid colors just last month. The yellow shoe was the prominent pair in the magazine ad. Others colors were bright red, lime green, sky blue and tangerine.

"Oh, Allison, thank you so much. Look everybody. My cool new Nikes."

Everyone gathered round Claire as she tossed off her old tennis shoes and slipped on the yellow Nikes.

Cliff returned to the party and sat next to Claire. She showed him her new shoes and when she looked into his face, she could tell.

She said, "You're leaving aren't you?"

Cliff lowered his head and spoke softly, "Yes, Tweetie, there's a man in Jackson who wants to meet with me this evening. It's a big deal if I can land it. "

"They're always big deals, Daddy." She turned away.

"I'll be back tonight. No spending the night. We'll just have dinner and I'll try to get this account. Then I'll be home before you go the sleep."

"Well, you're gonna do it anyway, so I don't know why you told me."

"I love you, Tweetie bird. I'll see you tonight." He reached over to give Claire a hug and kiss good-bye. She jumped into his arms and held tight.

She whispered in his ear. "You better be back tonight, like you promised."

Marlena was sitting with her father at the patio table under the awning when she noticed Cliff talking with Claire. She had a sly smile in the corner of her mouth, while not missing a word her father was telling her about his own business deals.

Katie was helping Mae clean the gift wrappings and trimmings. The girls had rushed off into the great room to watch videos and talk.

Cliff returned to his office, closed the door, made another phone call and began loading his briefcase with some essential papers. He clicked the on-off button on his computer monitor and pointed the mouse to the Internet Explorer icon. He loaded his email browser to check for any important opportunities that he might miss while he is out. There was nothing but the usual junk email from every vendor trying to sell something plus one message from his office assistant. He saved that one and deleted the rest. One check of the weather for Jackson at weather.com and he was ready to leave. He picked up his cell phone on the table by the couch, flipped it on to check the battery level. Phone power was enough, besides he had a car adapter just in case.

He passed through the room of kids out to the patio. Marlena and her father were still seated under the shade talking about the topics of the day. He looked at his wife. "I will be out until this evening. I'm meeting a potential in Jackson. Will have dinner there."

Bill looked up, "Good prospect?"

"It could be. If it turns out the way I'm hoping, I could buy that new Lexus I've been wanting."

Marlena smiled and said, "Well, good luck. Shall I wait up?"

Cliff leaned over to kiss her good-bye. "I won't be late. 10:00 o'clock the latest. Keep Claire up for me."

"Well, I think she is spending the night at Janey's, so they'll be up real late. You can see her there, I suppose."

Cliff shook hands with Bill, thanked him for coming to the party and left through the kitchen to let Katie and Mae know of his plans. He went into the great room to give Claire another bye kiss, then out the front door to his BMW.

Marlena remained with her Dad on the patio, chatting about anything and everything. Katie had finished helping Mae with the party clean up and had gone to check on the little girls before she joined Marlena and Bill. Marlena was explaining details of a case she recently had been assigned when Katie approached. She quit talking and greeted her mother with a nod. Bill rose to offer her a seat and a kiss on the cheek. There was always love and affection between her parents. Marlena peered over the top of her new gin and tonic glass, watching the adoration her parents still felt for each other. That same recurring resentment was building inside of her, again. She couldn't explain it, but the sight of mother triggered an emotion that she couldn't control. She recalled how her mother, an important corporate lawyer herself, but now retired for 8 years, had traveled endlessly on the job. Marlena was always left with a relative, usually her grandmother. The old woman could barely get out of a chair much less take care of a child. Katie was the last of 6 children and her mother was 45 when Katie was born. Grandma Betty finally passed when Marlena was 15.

Marlena's life was following a similar blueprint with her own career and her own daughter, but she was blind to it. Katie finally came to the reality that life was speeding by on a chariot after Claire was born. She saw in Claire all the wonderful joys she did not experience with Marlena and she had become angry with herself for all the missed times she could have had with her own daughter. The career came first, always. Bill was away many nights and week-ends with his business dealings, but occasionally found some time to devote to Marlena as she was growing up.

After Claire was born, Katie would visit as often as possible, taking her to places like the zoo, the park or the ice cream store. Mae would gladly come along, just in case she was needed to help with the child. Marlena was normally on the phone or at the office and rarely went along or saw need to go. The less she had to deal with Claire, the better it was for her. Katie retired the year Claire turned three years old. It was the best decision she had made for her personally, only 60 years old and still in good health, ready to get involved and travel. Her company offered an attractive retirement package and she could not turn it down. Bill was only 2 years older than Katie and planned to work until he was at least 65; maybe longer. He had tapered down on the business travel considerably in the past year, which was the main reason he was attending Claire's birthday.

Mae was carrying her purse, preparing to leave. "Ms. Richards, I'm leaving now. Remember, I will be on vacation next week."

"Yes, I remember. You have fun and please be back on time the week after." Marlena never even looked up.

Katie sat next to Bill, "Sweetie, I think we need to be going, I have a few chores to do. We need to stop by Kroger and Walgreen's. And your cleaning is ready; we'll need to stop there, too."

"OK, but I was just getting comfortable. "

"Dad, you go ahead", Marlena leaned over and put her hand on his arm, "I have some calls I need to make and about an hour more of paperwork before I have to pack for my trip on Monday."

"Alright, sweetie", Bill said as he rose and leaned to give Marlena a kiss on the cheek. Katie was already up and didn't bother to kiss her daughter, too many years of not expressing love. She just said polite good-byes and left to find Claire.

Marlena grabbed her father's arm and held tight while she watched her mother enter the house. He looked into her eyes, "What's wrong, sweetie?"

"I don't know, I guess Mom gets to me some times. She didn't bother to give me a kiss good bye like you did. I can't remember the last time she did." Marlena took another drink.

"She never has been a close mother has she? What about you and Claire?"

Marlena just looked at Bill from the corners of her eyes. She could not see the similarity in her relationship with Claire as it was with her mother. "I care about Claire. I'm just so busy all the time."

"Yes, I know, just like your mother. "

She ignored the comment, "Dad, don't leave yet."

"I need to, sweetie. I have errands to do myself. See you in a week or so. I'll call you from LA and you can let me know how your meeting in New York went." He gave Marlena another kiss on the check. She grabbed his neck and hugged tightly and Bill returned her embrace. Marlena was so much like Claire when it came to the love of her dad.

Katie found Claire and her remaining two friends, Janey and Allison, in her bedroom, going through the gifts for the third time. Claire jumped from her queen-size bed and leaped into Grammie's waiting arms.

Katie kissed her many times, "You know, you're getting a little bit too big to be jumping on your old Grandma?" She held Claire tight.

"No, I'm not. I'll never get too big for you, Grammie"

"You're right precious, I'll never get tired of you. Grandpa Bill and I must be going now and I wanted to tell you bye."

"Please don't leave, not yet."

"We have to darling. I'll be back Monday, OK?"

"Well, I guess. Anyway, I think we're going to spend the night over at Janey's tonight instead of here. Mom has lots of work or stuff to do and she don't want to be disturbed." Claire gave her Grammie one final big squeeze and kiss on the cheek.

She sat back on the bed next to Janey. Katie went to the bedroom door and turned to blow Claire a kiss. Claire caught the imaginary kiss and blew one back to her Grammie. This was a ritual they had begun when Claire was old enough to understand and they have never failed to blow each other a kiss when one had to leave. Katie loved Claire so much.

Cliff was just passing the Canada road exit, when his cell phone chimed. He picked it up from the holder and clicked the answer button. "Hello!"

"Hi", "No, I'm on the way. Just passing Lakeland. Should be there in about 12 minutes." "No, no problems" "OK, see you then!" "Yeah, me too!"

He clicked off the phone and returned it to his holder on the center console. His speedometer read 70. He had the cruise control activated, so he punched the accelerate button until he hit 80. Traffic was not heavy this late afternoon, just the normal 18 wheelers.

Claire was packing a few clothes, a night shirt, pair of blue shorts and blouse to match and some personal items in her overnight bag, when Marlena lightly knocked on the door and came on inside the room without waiting for a response. Janey and Allison had already left a few minutes earlier and had said their good-byes to Claire's mom downstairs. Claire stopped what she was doing, closed the bag and sat on the bed. Marlena looked at the array of shirts, shorts and jeans laid out across the bed. Some socks and underwear were mixed in the pile. Claire had always been thorough when planning any trip, whether she would be gone for one night or 2 weeks. She packed accordingly and packed well.

Marlena was standing just inside the room, holding the open door said, "I'm going to be very busy the rest of the evening and don't wish to be disturbed. Do you have everything you will need for your sleep-over?"

"Yes, mother." Was Claire's cold reply.

"Well, don't stay up too late and don't give Janey's mother a hard time."

"I never do, mother. We'll be alright."

"OK, see you tomorrow." She left the room, closing the door softly. No hug, no kiss, not even a good-bye; just a *see you tomorrow*. Claire sighed and began clearing her bed of items she would not be taking. She put everything back in its own drawer or container. She finished packing, set her bag on the floor and threw herself across the bed, lying on her stomach. Claire wished her Dad did not have to leave today, but he would be back late in the evening. Maybe she could come over to kiss him goodnight. Mom would probably be asleep or still working in her office, so she wouldn't notice.

Claire looked at her phone on the night stand by the bed. She sat up and reached for the receiver. She was going to call her Dad. He must be still driving and could talk to her for a while. She held the phone, not sure whether to dial his number. What if he got mad? But, he wouldn't be mad, he would enjoy the company. Claire punched in the numbers to her father's cell phone. It began to ring.

"Hello?"

"Hi, Dad. It's me. Where are you?"

"Hi sweetheart, I'm about 20 miles past Lakeland. I've gotta stop for some gas. Didn't check before I left. Is the party over?"

"Yeah, everybody went home. I'm finished packing and fixing to go to Janey's house. The sleep over is there. Mom needs quiet. Dad? When are you gonna be home tonight?"

"I suppose around 10 or 10:30, if everything goes OK. Why?"

"I just wanted to get a hug and kiss before I go to bed."

"You just count on it. Where is your Mom?"

"Downstairs in her office I guess. She said she didn't want to be disturbed tonight. You know work and all. I don't believe she thinks she has a daughter; just someone to put up with."

"I know Claire, she works too much. I think I do too, but I don't think you're just someone to put up with. I love you very much!"

"I know Daddy, and I love you very much, too!"

"Well, my exit is coming up. You have fun at Janey's and I'll come over when I get home so I can get my night kiss."

"You better. See you later. Bye"

"Bye, Tweetie"

Claire hung up her phone, jumped from the bed, grabbed her bag and ran down the stairs and out the door. Not even so much as a *see ya* to her mother. Marlena never saw her daughter leave the house, but the slamming door was a good indication she was gone.

Marlena had been sitting at her desk, papers scattered in an organized mess across the top. With a gin and tonic in one hand, she reached for the phone and dialed the number from memory. It rang on the other end.

Marlena spoke softly in the receiver, "Hey, it's me. About 20 minutes OK?", "See ya, bye."

Chapter Two

Cliff pulled into the right lane of Interstate 40 to get off at the Brownsville exit. Claire had been in his thoughts the past few miles and he was ignoring KIX106 on the radio. They wanted the 10th caller for a pair of tickets to see Faith Hill and Tim McGraw at the FedEx Forum, Memphis's premier concert hall. He slowed down to the stop sign at the end of the exit ramp and flipped the blinker to make a left turn. About 3 miles further up the road there was a small restaurant. It was his planned stop. Traffic was non-existent. This was strictly rural country, the old Jim Walter white siding homes high on the hill with acres of soy beans or cotton within a stone's throw. Then the typical weathered barn sat near the fields always looked liked it had seen much better days on the farm. The little restaurant sat back from the highway, small faded sign out front, 'Charlie's Fine Foods'. Under that a hand written sign featuring 'Fried Green Tomatoes – 3.95'. Cliff never had acquired the taste for fried green tomatoes. Red tomatoes on a sandwich or hamburger were alright, but not green.

Only two cars were parked in a gravel filled area, old Charlie used for parking. Cliff recognized the red Pontiac Firebird. He pulled his BMW next to the Firebird. He got out, hit the auto lock on the key ring and went to the front door of Charlie's. The music from the corner jukebox was playing an old Merle Haggard tune, "Silver Wings".

Charlie was sitting on a stool behind the counter where everyone went to pay their bill at the cash register left over from the 70's. He looked up from his morning newspaper and nodded his head toward the tables scattered in no particular pattern, "Jes, sit where ya want, son. Maylene will be with ya in a minute." He went back to reading the sports pages of the local newspaper.

Cliff looked around the mostly empty restaurant. An older couple, probably local residents out for their usual lunch date, sat in a window booth, each with a huge slice of apple pie and ice cream waiting on the table. The little gray-haired woman was just finishing a plate of vegetables. The older man slowly sipped from a cup, probably coffee.

An old Philco window air conditioner, mounted in the wall of stained pine paneling, hummed and blew cool air across the room. Charlie must have forgotten the season changed. It was quite comfortable. Only two windows were in the restaurant, draped with red and white checkered curtains that looked like they were left over from the 50's. The checkered-cloth covered tables in the center of the room remained empty and cluttered with left over plates, glasses and silverware from customers, long since gone. He guessed Maylene was the only employee on duty, which probably made her the busboy and more likely the cook, too.

In the booth in the far dark corner of the restaurant with an ancient movie poster of Elvis 'Love Me Tender' barely clinging to the wall, he saw Kimberly McClain waving him over. Cliff waved back and headed to the booth. Only one red citronella candle lit the table. Kimberly was Cliff's assistant investment consultant from work. She was instrumental on many occasions closing deals for Cliff, making him hefty commissions. He never failed to acknowledge her efforts, always with praise plus cash. The soft glow of the light did not hide the fact she was quite attractive, in her late twenties with long brown hair, pulled casually in a pony tail today. She wore a button down collared white oxford shirt and blue shorts and she moved over allowing Cliff room to sit next to her in the booth.

Cliff sat next to her and leaned over and kissed her gently on the mouth. She returned the embrace. Cliff looked into her deep blue eyes and smiled. "Did you get it?"

Kim leaned back in the seat, "I couldn't find a thing on this Brandon Tarkinson. He doesn't exist, or it appears so. I checked all the known Business Journals and lists on the Internet. No luck. I searched Google, Yahoo and Northern Lights. His company does not have a presence on the World Wide Web. I tried all combinations of the name. I checked D & B. Are you sure you got the company name right, or his name?"

Cliff answered, "Tarkinson Builders, I'm sure that's what he said. He told me that his company had just completed a huge government contract, before the deadline and slightly under-budget. He got a hefty bonus from the state, 1,750,000 to be more accurate and he needed some seed money for his investment strategy." Cliff was concerned. Kim always was thorough when it came to background investigations. It never took her more than 2 hours to produce a complete profile package of any company or individual and she had at least 3 hours for this one. Cliff thought he didn't allow her enough time, after all this was short notice and she always knew details for searches days in advance. Still, in the back of his mind, he was wondering why a company, as large as Tarkinson's was suppose to be, did not have 'www' address on the Internet. All companies everywhere, small and large have jumped on the cyber-space band wagon, if no more than to tell the world who and where they are.

Kim sipped the last drink of coffee with International Delight Irish Crème, "I'm beginning to get a little suspicious, Cliff. What time are you suppose to meet him?"

"7:00 at O'Charleys off 40 in Jackson."

"Can you contact him?"

"No he said his cell was out and if any problems came up, he would contact me before then. He has my number."

"Well, I have my doubts."

Cliff looked at his watch. It was 6:00. He could be in Jackson in 30 minutes. "I guess I'll need to get going, soon."

"Not until you tell me how the party went. Did Claire have a good time?"

"Yea, she did. I hated to leave her. She called me just a few minutes ago. She sounded sad."

"If you had Marlena as a mother, you'd be sad too."

"I know, but there's very little that I can do. She needs a mother or someone she can relate to as a mother. I don't think Marlena will ever come around and realize what she's lost. Claire's grandmother is trying to fill in, and Claire loves her dearly, but she needs a full-time mom." He moved closer to Kim. "Kinda like you."

Kim's cheeks blushed slightly and moved closer into Cliff's arms. "Speaking of which, when are you going to make me Mrs. Cliff Richards?"

"Soon. I want this as much as you do, but I need to line up a few more opportunities, I'll need the extra income. Plus, I need to locate and retain my own attorney. After all I will be divorcing another lawyer. She'll get to pick from the crème of the crop, or the bottom of the barrel. Just depends on how you look at it."

They both laughed.

"Will she give it up easily, or will she fight?"

"I suspect she'll want a settlement of some kind. We both make good money. She won't take alimony, I know that. I doubt very seriously that she would want Claire. She would consider it 'good riddance'. And I won't ask her for child support, so we would pay our lawyers to handle the disbursement of our property and cash."

"She'll ask for the house, I'm sure?"

"Definitely. She didn't spend all that time landscaping and decorating, just to hand it over to me. No, I'll have to move out. You happen to know of any available space?"

Kim snuggled closer, "Well, it seems there is a vacancy on Briergate."

The double swinging doors to the kitchen opened and Maylene came through pulling a gray cart with plastic tubs filled with dirty dishes. She spotted Cliff sitting with Kim and parked the cart next to the salad bar. She shuffled across the wooden floor, pulling out her order pad, although she could remember every item on the menu and what every customer ordered. Rarely did she get it wrong. It was a talent she learned from years of food service. Maylene was a heavy woman in her mid to late fifties, hair put up in the style of the 70's and neatly covered with a black hair net. Her uniform was typical black with white stripes and a white apron with ruffles along the straps and around the bottom. From the stains on the apron, it was evident she was the cook and bottle washer.

Maylene eyed Cliff up and down, just checking out the new stuff. She smiled through tobacco stained teeth and smacking and popping a new stick of Juicy Fruit. "So what's it gonna be, sweetie?"

Cliff looked into blood-shot eyes, probably from last night's binge drinking with Charlie, "Just a cup of coffee for me and a refill for the lady?"

"Yea, Yea, I'm gonna get rich waiting on you two." She filled out an order, threw it on the table and stowed the order tickets in the pocket of her uniform next to a stash of soda straws and pencils. "Be right back." First she went to check on grandma and grandpa. At least they were eating food and they did leave tips.

Kim turned back to Cliff, "You have any idea what kind of investments this guy is looking for his money? Bonds? Stocks? Venture Capital?"

"Don't have a clue. He was not very clear, just that we would work out the details over dinner. But, after what you haven't found, I'm not at all sure that I want to go up there."

"Don't let that stop you. What if he is legit? A million seven will pay a nice commission. And don't forget, you'll need it."

Maylene was back, carrying a mug in one hand, the coffee pot in the other. She filled Kim's cup leaving a small amount of room for the creamer. She filled Cliff's cup and pulled a spoon from a pocket and placed it on a napkin with a couple of Half & Half creamers.

Cliff looked up into her eyes, the eyeliner was now beginning to fade and run down her cheek. She still chewed feverishly on the stick of gum, making the pops sound off with each chew. Only expert gum chewers can achieve a snap and a pop every time.

"Thank you, Maylene" Cliff said with a smile as he looked at her name badge.

She turned to walk away, she said, "Yea, whatever."

Cliff looked back at Kim, "I guess she's had a bad day."
Kim watched Maylene slam the coffee pot onto the burner, causing a spill. She just looked at the black coffee dripping onto the counter and continued on into the kitchen. "I think she has a bad day everyday, not just today."

She looked at Cliff, "OK, getting back to us, when are you going to leave Marlena and come live with me?"

"Soon, I have Claire to think about. I don't have a clue how she will accept this news. Something inside tells me she'll be thrilled to death for me and will jump at the chance to move out into a new place. So, I'll need to have a place of my own at first."

Kim pouted her lips. Cliff noticed and smiled. He leaned over to kiss her. "But who knows."

Cliff looked at his watch. It was almost 6:30. "I gotta go. Don't want to be late."

"Yea, I need to go too. Will you call me as soon as you know something?"

"Of course." Cliff leaned over and kissed her again, this time much harder. He wrapped both arms around her and held tight. Kim responded. "I don't know if you're gonna get out of here after that."

“Gotta go”, Cliff got up, reached for his wallet. He pulled out a ten dollar bill and laid it on the table. “Let’s see if this makes the day better for Miss Maylene.”

Kim scooted over and up from the seat. She took Cliff’s arm and they walked to the cash register to pay for the two coffees. Charlie was still engrossed in the latest scores. He looked up long enough to acknowledge they were standing at the counter. He glanced at the ticket Maylene had written, “Two coffees, that’ll be 2.48”

Cliff handed him a five and Charlie fished out the change from the open drawer, never bothering to ring up the sale. Seems Charlie did his own form of accounting. Maylene returned to the floor from the kitchen and went to clear the booth where Kim and Cliff had been sitting. Most regulars prefer the booths and she would always clear those first. She saw the ten lying under the half-filled coffee mug. Her heart fluttered a little bit when she realized the money was for her. She turned quickly to see Cliff and Kim heading toward the door. Cliff held the door for Kim and as he did, he saw the stare from Maylene. He waved. She smiled and he could swear he noticed a tear making a new eyeliner track down her cheek. Cliff thought, *Looks like I made her day.*

Cliff walked Kim to her car, held her again and kissed one more time. Kim was nearly 5’10” and she fit comfortably in Cliff’s arms. She looked deeply into his eyes and for a moment said nothing. Then she whispered, “I love you, ya know.”

Cliff smiled and stared momentarily into her eyes, “I know, and I do love you, too.”

He opened her door and Kim slid in behind the steering wheel. She pulled the car key from her purse and inserted it into the ignition, cranking the Firebird. Cliff closed the door; she looked up and smiled again waving small finger waves as she backed up. Cliff watched as she drove out onto the highway and walked quickly around to the driver’s side of his Beamer.

Cliff had 30 minutes to get to Jackson. He would be there in 25.

Chapter Three

Claire ran across her front lawn past the iron bird bath her mother bought in Mexico last year. She had just finished talking to her father on the phone. She wished he was here with her now. Janey's house was right next door. Only a small row of boxwoods separated the property. Claire sprinted and leaped across the tops of the shrubs. Her new Nike Brights scraped the leaves. She stopped long enough to inspect her new shoes. Good, no stains or scratches. Janey's home was a blue country-styled two story with a wrap around porch; trimmed in white. The porch was lined with padded lounge chairs and several folding deck chairs with small tables next to each for those afternoon and evenings when they would sit enjoying a glass of lemon iced tea.

She ran to the front door, knocked once and went on inside. This was an accepted rule between the families. Claire, Janey and Allison were more like sisters and their parents treated each of the girls like they were their own children; all but Marlena. She always tolerated their presence, but never really accepted them. She would prefer they never come over, but she did give in to Claire and allowed her friends to come visit.

Amanda Caldwell, Janey's mother, was coming out of the kitchen. "Hi Claire, Janey and Allison are already up in her room."

"Thanks Miss Amanda." Claire said and she ran up the stairs to Janey's room down the hall, last room on the right.

Janey's room was typical 11 year old décor. Clothes and magazines were on the floor. Third Day and Creed posters and pictures covered every wall. Above her desk cluttered with school papers and books, which almost buried the Dell computer, she had one photo of Britney Spears. It had been autographed, "To Janey, Love Britney". She was lucky enough to get the autograph at Britney's only concert in Memphis. Janey and Allison were lying across the bed reading "Teen" magazine. Claire pulled off her back pack and tossed it on the chair at the end of the bed.

"What's up?" she asked sitting cross-legged at the foot of the bed.

"Nothing much." Janey said, "Did you call your Dad?"

"Yeah!" Claire replied sadly, "He said he'll be home by 10. I wish he could have stayed home."

Allison rolled over on her side and propped her head on her hand. "Where's he going?"

"He's gonna meet some guy about investing money. You know, like, just work stuff, like he don't do enough of that all week."

"And on your birthday, too! I'm sorry, Claire." Janey sat next to Claire and put her arm around her.

"That's OK, I know he's just trying to make money. It's his job."

Allison sat up at the head of the bed and noticed the new shoes Claire was proudly wearing. "Do you really like the Brights? I know that's your color."

"Oh my God, I am so excited; I couldn't believe it when I opened the box."

Janey said, "You didn't like my gift? "

"Of course I did, Janey. I've wanted that CD forever." She reached for her backpack and opened it. "I brought it over so we could play it tonight." Claire rummaged through the little red backpack pulling out clothes and toiletries. No CD could be found. She emptied the back pack.

"I must have left it on my bed. I'll go back and get it."

Janey said, “OK, but later. First, what’s the deal with your mother? Is she trying to win the ‘bitch of the year’ award? What’s with her?”

Almost any girl would gallantly defend their mother from a comment like that, but Claire had lived with the ‘bitch’ for the last 11 years.

“She’s always been like that. I keep hearing that it’s her job and she’s so busy, yada, yada, yada. Like the same old crap. It’s just plain and simple. She doesn’t want me around. I should have never been born. To her anyway.”

Allison slid off the bed and said, “Let’s go downstairs and watch a movie. Talking about Claire’s mother is too depressing.”

Claire jumped up too, “Yea let’s. I need to think about other stuff. At least until Dad gets home.”

Clouds had been building and the first flash of lightning lit up the sky followed by the distant thunder. The girls looked toward the window. Claire said, “I guess I better get that CD before the rain starts.”

Janey said, “Please do. I really want to hear it. You want us to go with you?”

“No, y'all pick out a good movie. I’ll be right back.”

The girls left the room and went down the stairs into the great room. Janey’s father was a big fan of electronics. There was a wall, floor to ceiling filled with every conceivable device made; VCR’s, Cassette Tape Player, Turntable, DVD player, CD player, Stereo receiver, Graphic equalizer, Sony Playstation II and X-box games with surround-sound speakers in every corner of the room. All this equipment framed a 60” flat screen HDTV. It was the perfect mini movie theatre. On the left side was a collection of recent DVD movies and video games. The right side held VHS tapes from years past. Claire and Allison often spent weekends in front of this screen watching the latest on Nick at Nite or playing Mario on the Playstation. Xbox games appealed more to Janey’s dad. Allison began with the DVD's, while Janey started with the VHS tapes.

Claire opened the front door and stepped out onto the porch. The sky had become dark with heavy rain clouds. Lightning flashes brightened the bottoms of the clouds defining their ominous shapes. Claire knew she only had a few minutes before the downpour started. She was thinking this would be a good night for a scary movie, like 'Halloween' or 'Nightmare on Elm Street'. Both were oldies but they had watched each one at least a dozen times before. Maybe they would choose 'Scream II'. Next to the front door, Janey's mom always kept an umbrella stand that held 6 blue and white golf umbrellas. Of course they matched the house colors. Claire grabbed one from the stand and held it close. The rain was coming soon. This would come in handy on the way back.

Claire decided to go back through the front door of her house. Her mother would be in her office at the back, next to the great room. Claire would be as quiet as possible. She would get the CD and sneak back out. Mom would never know she was there. Claire didn't want her to know. There was an opening in the shrubs near the back fence. Claire went through the opening, not wanting to miss the jump in the dark. She went to the porch steps just below the front door and stopped. She took one step at a time, very careful not to make unnecessary noise. She put her ear next to the door, listening for sounds that might tell her Mom was close by inside. Nothing. She turned the knob slowly. Thank goodness the door had not been locked, she had forgotten her key. The latch clicked and Claire stopped. A flash of lightning illuminated the porch. Claire instinctively ducked like she had been caught. The roar of thunder startled her. The storm was much closer. She pushed the door slowly and peeked around the edge looking into the entry way. The stairs were 8 feet away. All was quiet.

Claire slowly closed the door behind her. The wooden floor squeaked from her weight. She stopped and listened. She pushed the door closed until she felt the latch catch. Then she tiptoed to the stairs and up to her bedroom. Luckily the carpet was thick on the stairs and her room was opposite from where her mother was working. Her office was an add-on room with no rooms above.

Claire's door to her room was open. She closed it and walked slowly to her bed. Most of the gifts she had received during the birthday party were scattered among the clothes and magazines. She sat on edge of her bed and sighed when she noticed on the night stand a picture of her and her father when they vacationed in the Ozarks. Claire reached for the framed photo and held it close in a hug. *Dad, why can't you be here tonight*, she thought.

Several minutes passed, with Claire deep in thought. Another sudden thunder clap brought her back into the real world. She placed the picture back on the night stand and remembered why she was here; find the CD and get out. She moved every thing off the bed. Where was it? The bed was clear. Claire looked around the room. *Where did I put it?*

She looked at her desk and then the dresser. Both were neat and in order. The CD rack next to her stereo had not been touched. She didn't remember sliding it into the rack, but she wasn't sure, so she checked anyway. It was not there. Then she looked on the floor between the window and the bed. There, underneath the opposite night stand was the Eminem CD. She snatched it up and quietly headed for the door. She felt like she was in a Mission Impossible movie, sneaking in, grabbing the prize and sneaking out without being detected.

The rain had begun outside and the sound would cover her movements to the door. The thunder and lightning were now coming more frequently. Claire left the room and was half way down the hall when she realized the umbrella was still on her bed. She went back to get it. The hallway was dark. She could see the light from the downstairs entryway brightening the stairs. With her back up against the wall, she crept slowly to the corner of the wall of the stairs, not making a sound, even though the rain was falling more intensely now. Claire knew she would get soaked. Lucky she had brought 3 outfits in her bag. She listened for any sounds before heading downstairs. All quiet. She straightened up and turned toward the stairs, grabbed hold of the banister rail. Just as she was about to place her foot on the first stair, the doorbell rang.

Claire jerked back from the stairs and wedged her back up against the wall. She wanted to become part of the wall, like a decoration that no one notices. She slid down into a squat position, thinking that would make her more invisible. No one could see her. She heard her mother, humming a happy tune, coming from the back of the house to answer the door. She thought, *Oh great, I'm going to get caught.* She leaned over just far enough for her eye to see the door. From her vantage point, she also had a clear view into the living room.

Marlena opened the door and smiled broadly at the visitor. "I thought you'd never get here."

Claire moved closer to the floor next to the stairs, hoping she would not be seen. She needed a better view. The door opened and a man with long dark hair, mustache and beard came in. He looked familiar to Claire. *Who was this man? Where have I seen him before?* She thought. *Yeah, at Mom's office. She thought he worked there, but didn't know his name. She just wasn't sure.*

David Anderson closed the door behind him and shook the umbrella slightly and leaned it against the wall next to the door. Then Claire's heart began to beat so fast. Her eyes widened like saucers. Her mouth dropped opened. She wanted to scream. She wanted to cry and then she did. Marlena's arms swept around this man and held tight. He wrapped her in a tender embrace. Their lips parted and met. David was slightly taller than Marlena. The kiss lasted almost a minute.

To Claire it seemed like it was hours. She didn't want to watch, but the anger was building inside and she was almost reached a boiling point. She wanted to run down the stairs and kick this intruder between the legs real hard. Put him in the hospital for a few days. She even thought, briefly of the rifle her Dad kept in his bedroom closet. She could take him out with one bullet in the head, but quickly brushed that thought away. Her mother, how dare she do this; to her father while he's out trying to earn a living. At this moment she could not hate Marlena more. Claire pulled back and limply sat on the floor, legs spread out in front of her, with her back against the wall. Then the tears began to fall. She forced herself to not cry out loud, even though it would serve her mother right if she was caught in the act.

"What am I going to do? That bitch!" she whispered to herself through the tears. Her nose was beginning to run. The sniffles were coming. She wanted her dad so badly right now. She heard them go into the living room and began to talk. Claire leaned over again, this time in a prone position, far enough back into the shadows as not to be seen, but with a clear view of her deceitful mother and this horrible man.

Marlena was sitting on the sofa with David very close. "We have only a couple of hours."

David smiled at her, "Did he suspect anything?"

"Not a thing. He is so intent on *Making the Deal*; he would go anywhere, anytime to make it happen. Carl owed me. He made the call and Cliff jumped at the bait."

Claire's eyes opened wider.

David continued, "What's he gonna do when he gets to Jackson and no one shows up?"

"Carl will call him again, you know expressing his apologies and he would be contacting him again soon. Of course that will never happen."

Claire was fuming. She almost jumped up from her hiding spot to confront her lying mother, but decided to wait. Maybe she should wait for the opportunity to leave unnoticed. Will she tell her father? She didn't know.

David got up to get a drink from the bar. He asked, "Is the kid tucked away?"

"The KID?" Claire softly said. "Who the crap does he think he is calling me *the kid*."

Marlena answered, "She's staying next door. We won't be bothered by her."

"Won't be BOTHERED by her?" Claire was mad. To say she was pissed off would be an understatement. Claire continued to spy on the adulteress mother and her lover.

David took one sip of his Chevas on the rocks and sat close to Marlena. He put his arm around her and pulled her close. Their lips locked. Marlena's hands were moving up and down his back. David's hand found her thigh and stroked her gently, inching higher and higher. He unbuttoned her blouse and removed it, leaving only Marlena's blue Victoria's Secret bra. When he reached around to unsnap, Claire closed her eyes. She was in total shock. She couldn't watch this, not her mother and this strange man make love right on their family sofa. She slowly and quietly crawled back to her room. She climbed onto her bed and cried softly, thinking only of her father. The rain was pouring hard now. That was good, she could cry out loud and know one would hear. Her mother would not even care. The sounds coming from downstairs were drowned out by the falling rain on the bedroom window. Lightning brightened the room and Claire stiffened waiting for the thunder clap.

Claire sat up and reached for her phone. At first she wanted to call her Dad, tell him what's going on here in their home, but she decided against it. Instead she punched Janey's number into the phone. She guessed, Mom would be too busy to hear a phone call.

Janey's mother answered. "Hello?"

Claire spoke just above a whisper. "Miss Amanda, this is Claire. I came over to my house to get a CD. It's raining too hard. I'm gonna wait for it to die down before I come back over."

"OK, is your Mom still there?"

Claire cringed. "Yes, she is."

"OK, we'll wait for you before we start the movie."

"OK, bye." She hung-up the phone and lay on the bed. The clock on the radio flipped over to 6:55. She cried softly. Part of Claire died that night.

Cliff was already at O'Charley's sipping a glass of ice tea. He had asked for a table for two and left Brandon Tarkinson's name with the hostess at the front door and to please direct him to the table when he arrived.

Carl Weathers worked in the IT department at the International Paper along with Marlena and David Anderson. It seems Carl had a slight problem with gambling down at the Tunica casinos. Marlena had bailed him out a couple of times, so he owed her. She came up with this plan to confuse Cliff and get him out of town on Friday. Carl checked his watch. It was almost 7:10. Cliff should be at the restaurant and wondering why his client was running so late.

He punched in Cliff's cell number into his phone. Cliff answered on the first ring. "Hello, Cliff Richards."

"Mr. Richards, this is Brandon Tarkinson", Carl began.

"Call me Cliff, please."

"Fine, Cliff. I guess you have come to the conclusion, I'm not going to show up. I'm sorry, but some things came up that I couldn't get out of tonight."

"Is there any way for a later time tonight?"

"I'm afraid not. This will take most of the night. My wife was expecting me by 9 and I believe I'll be disappointing her too."

"Can we reschedule?"

"Sure, let me look at my calendar. I have some appointments in Memphis next week. I believe I can squeeze another meeting. Maybe we can have lunch."

"That sounds fine."

“I’ll give you a call Monday or Tuesday. Is this cell number OK, or should I call you at another location?”

“No, this number is OK. Thanks for calling. Sorry we couldn’t meet tonight, but I’ll be looking forward to meeting you next week. Are there any areas of investment you’re interested in? I can have a little research ready for you to consider.”

Carl thought to himself. *This guy is selling already.* “No we can talk next week. Thanks for your patience. Goodbye, Cliff.”

“Bye.”

Cliff clicked the phone off. He sat for a few seconds, beginning to get a little bit perturbed that he allowed this man to take him away from his little girl’s party for nothing. He thought of Claire. He had promised her that he would see her at Janey’s before she went sleep. He would keep that promise.

He picked up his cell phone again and dialed Kim’s number.

“Hello?”

“Hey it’s me. Mr. Brandon Tarkinson didn’t show. He called just a minute ago to cancel.”

“Cancel! Why?”

“Other pressing business I suppose. Anyway, he said he would call Monday or Tuesday to schedule a lunch meeting in Memphis.”

“Did you get any other details?”

“Tried, but he was still evasive.”

“Do I need to continue my research?”

“Yes first thing Monday. Right now I am going to see my little girl.”

"Well, don't forget about this little girl."

"Never."

"OK, will you call me tomorrow?"

"I did some thinking after I left you tonight. Some real hard thinking. What would you say if I told you that I wanted you and Claire to meet, soon?"

Kim's heart skipped a beat. "Are you serious? I would love that idea."

Cliff smiled. "I thought you would. I just haven't figured out how to tell her. We need to be alone. Maybe I'll take her to a movie and lunch tomorrow. I'll work our conversation around to her mother and how miserable she makes both of us feel. She'll agree I'm sure. I'll bring you into the conversation, just don't know yet how that will happen."

"How about, 'I'm in love with another woman'"

"Well, that's crossed my mind, but a little abrupt. Don't know how she would react. I hope it will be a good reaction to any news that she perceives as happiness for the both of us."

"You'll come up with the right words, I'm sure."

"I hope so. Anyway, I'll call you sometime tomorrow afternoon on your cell. I need to get out of here and back home. Maybe the words will come to me on the way back home."

"OK, I'll talk to you tomorrow afternoon. And if you want to buy me lunch too, just give me a ring." Kim laughed.

"You never know. Talk to you later."

"Love you"

"I love you, bye."

"Bye."

Cliff clicked off the phone and put it in his pocket. The waitress came over and he asked for a check for the tea. He gave her a $5.00 bill and told her to keep the change. Cliff left the restaurant and went to his car and headed west on
I-40 to Memphis and his precious Tweetie. He could see lightning ahead, brightening the horizon. He had no idea of the real storm ahead.

Claire rolled over and checked the time on her clock. It was only 7:30. The rain was beginning to let up. She had to get out of this house even if she had to climb out the window like a thief in the night. She heard the front door open. She jumped from the bed and softly crept down the hall to her last perch at the top of the stairs. When she peered around the corner, Marlena was just closing the door and walked back to her office, but first made herself a new gin and tonic. Claire listened closely. Her mom always closed the door. There, the definite click of the latch of her office door. At the same time, Claire heard the sound of the car door close and the engine crank. She waited a couple of minutes. She felt for the CD in her pocket and held tight to the umbrella.

She took the steps much faster than before. The door was just ahead. She reached for the knob and turned slowly. Out the door and onto the porch, fast as can be and as quiet as the mouse. Claire raised the blue and white umbrella and ran down the sidewalk, she noticed the yard was soaked. She had changed into her old Nikes. She did not want to ruin her new Brights. Claire ran all the way and up to the porch at Janey's house. She closed the umbrella and wrapped the Velcro strapped around the base to hold it together and placed it in the rack. She knocked and opened the door. Janey and Allison turned to see Claire run into the room.

Janey said, "We were getting a little worried."

Allison was looking suspiciously at her eyes. "Are you OK, Claire? You been gone for so long."

Claire sat in the recliner that was normally reserved for Mr. Caldwell. He was out of town on a business trip this weekend. She tried to hide her swollen eyes.
"Well, it's like raining real hard out there. I was just waiting for it to slow down some. It just now did. Let's just watch the movie OK?"

Janey said, "Whatever!"

Allison continued to stare for a few minutes and then directed her attention to the movie 'Scream' just now starting. Claire could sense Allison's look, but turned her face to the big TV screen. Allison could not help feel something was really wrong with her friend.

Claire sat quietly, staring blankly at the screen. Her mind was not on the movie or on her friends. She could only see her mother and David Anderson together on their sofa, disgracing herself and her family, deceiving her husband and breaking Claire's heart into a million pieces.

Claire longed so much for her mother to love her and treat her like a daughter should be treated. Someone to tell secrets with, someone she could tell about her first boyfriend, someone to hold in confidence about female needs and wants. Tonight, she lost all hope for that to ever happen.

When the movie ended, Allison went to Claire. She noticed that Claire had not moved more than two times during the first hour of the movie. She did not want candy, popcorn and soft drinks, although she was asked. Allison sank to her knees on the floor next to the recliner where Claire continued to stare at a blank screen.

She took hold of her hand. "Claire, are you OK?"

Claire didn't answer. Her eyes were fixed ahead. Allison was scared now. She patted Claire's hands. She thought she had gone to sleep with her eyes open. It was freaking her out.

"Janey, come here quick. Look at Claire."

Janey was carrying plates and glasses back to the kitchen and stopped by Allison. "What's wrong with her?"

"I don't know. Call your mother."

"I think she's asleep."

Janey put the dishes on the coffee table and grabbed Claire by the shoulders and began to shake. "Claire, wake up. Claire?"

Claire blinked and trembled. She looked at her two friends. They had frightened looks on their faces. "What's with you two."

Allison fell to the floor off her knees. "Are you nuts? You scared me to death. Did you know you were sleeping with your eyes open?"

Claire rubbed her eyes. They were dry and burned slightly. "No I didn't!"

"Yes you did, unless you were in like a trance."

"Well, I wasn't. Why?" Claire was concerned and still intrigued.

Janey picked up the dishes and headed to the kitchen, "You have been staring at the TV for the whole time the movie was on."

Allison added. "And you didn't want anything to eat, like you were not even here."

"Well, I guess I had things on my mind tonight."

Allison cocked her head and looked at Claire as she pulled the lever on the recliner to lower the foot rest.

Claire said, "I'm ready to go to sleep." But Claire looked at the clock on the mantle above the fireplace. It was almost 9:00. She had completely forgotten about her father calling when he got home and didn't really expect him until after ten. "But, my Dad! Did my Dad call?"

Allison had gotten up to help Janey tidy up. She said, "Nobody called."

Claire started to get up, but her legs had been stationary for so long they had gone to sleep. The tingle ran up and down her thighs and calves. She shook them as she walked out the sleep.

From the front of the house there was a knock on the door. Janey came from the kitchen and looked through the see-through peep hole. She shouted to Claire. "Claire it's your Dad. He's here!"

Janey unlocked the chain and opened the door. Claire shook her legs one more time and ran to the front door.

"Hi Mr. Richards" Janey said.

"Hey Janey, have you girls been having a good time?"

Claire didn't give Janey a chance to reply, she ran to Cliff and jumped into his arms. She wrapped her arms around his neck and held tight. "Dad, I'm so glad you're home. I missed you so much."

He kissed her on the cheek and set her back on the floor. She clung to his waist. "What's going on Tweetie? What's with you tonight?"

Janey said, "She's been in a trance all night."

He pulled Claire's face up to his. "What is she talking about, Claire?"

She buried her head back into her father. "Nothing, I think I might have fallen asleep watching the movie."

"And what's wrong with that?"

Janey said as she went back to the kitchen. "She had her eyes open the whole time."

Cliff turned and put his arm around Claire and began walking her into the Great Room. Claire was so glad to have her dad home; she almost forgot the horrible pain she had to endure. She almost forgot how much she had been hurt. Almost, but the memories were beginning to fill her head again, reeling throughout her brain, playing the disgusting scene over and over again. Stabbing the knife in her heart one more time. Cliff was speaking to Claire. She was not responding. He sat on the sofa, Claire remained standing.

"Claire, sit down."

She didn't move. She only faced forward and eyes fixed on a spot somewhere in her mind. Cliff grabbed her hand and shook. "Claire?"

By this time Allison and Janey had returned to the room. "She's doing it again ain't she?" Allison asked.

"Again?" Cliff was now shaking her shoulders. "Claire? What's wrong?"

"She was like this all night." Janey said. "Is she alright?"

"I don't know. Claire?" Cliff shook harder. Claire blinked her eyes and looked down at her father. She couldn't remember walking into the room. She sat down and cuddled next to her dad.

"What happened, Daddy?"

"It looks like you might have been sleep-walking. Are you feeling OK?" He put his hand on her forehead to check for a fever. Something all parents do when their kid acts funny or coughs too much.

"Sleep walking? I don't sleep walk." She snuggled closer.

"Well, you were doing something out of the ordinary. What did you eat tonight?"

Cliff wrapped her up in his arms and Claire fell asleep. This time for real and she was in a deep, dreamless sleep. Cliff gently picked her up into his arms and carried her home to her own bed.

Cliff looked in his bedroom and Marlena was asleep, probably from too much to drink again. He decided to sleep in the guest bedroom. With all the thoughts running through his mind about Kim and Claire, he couldn't sleep right now. Tomorrow would be a good day. He will take Claire to lunch and Kim will join them. What happens after that, he will just play by ear.

Chapter Four

Sunday morning rolled in early. The guest bedroom window faced the east and the sunshine at dawn was bright. Cliff did not close the mini-blinds before lying down and the glowing sunlight was covering his face. He squinted against the brightness and checked his watch on the nightstand. It was just after 6:00. He was sure Marlena was still sound asleep and he did not want to explain why he had slept in the guestroom. He couldn't take any of her sarcasm this morning.

Cliff got up and quickly made the bed, grabbed his clothes and headed for the bathroom off the hall for a shower and shave. He quietly went to his closet for a change of fresh shirt and jeans. Coffee! Yes, he needed coffee. This would be a good moment to spend alone at the kitchen breakfast table to read the Sunday paper.

He found the coffee filters and filled the pot to the Mr. Coffee machine. While the coffee began to brew, he went outside to retrieve the paper from the sidewalk, fully expecting to have a quiet morning to himself.

When he returned, Claire was sitting at the breakfast table, staring out the window into the back yard. She still wore the clothes from the night before. Cliff had no intention of waking her last night by trying to change her into pajamas.

"Tweetie, what's wrong? Why are you up so early?" Cliff sat next to her.

Claire turned to face her father, and Cliff saw a terrified and angry look suddenly appear across her face. "Why did you bring me HOME?" she shouted through gritted teeth.

Cliff was stunned. "You fell asleep, baby. I just brought you home to your bed, so you could get a good nights rest."

"But, I didn't want to be here!" she turned away.

"Why? This is your home."

"I just didn't, that's all. Why couldn't you have stayed with me over at Janey's?"

"Well, first of all, I don't live there and our house is just next door." He looked at her again, this time turning her head around to meet his eyes. "What's really wrong, Tweetie? I didn't like the way you were acting last night, like you were in a trance or something and now I see the mood you're in this morning? Did something happen to you that you need to talk about?"

Claire jumped and pushed his hand away. "NO! Nothing happened. Just drop it, OK?'

Cliff wasn't at all convinced, but now was not the time to pursue the truth. First he would get through lunch. Maybe she will open up after that. Cliff sat for a couple of minutes, just watching Claire as she looked into the new sunrise. The coffee maker beeped, announcing the completion cycle, so he pulled a mug from the cabinet and poured his first cup of java. He supposed the paper would have to wait for now, because he had to change his girl's attitude before lunch.

"Claire, would you like something to eat or drink?" he asked while he stirred the coffee.

Claire looked at him curiously. He almost never addressed her as Claire. It was always, *Baby*, *Sweetie* or most of the time *Tweetie*. She guessed she had hurt his feelings more than she realized. She idolized her father and to cause him pain was more than she could stand. Tears began to form in her eyes. She ran from her chair and latched on to Cliff with her arms securely locked around his waist.

Surprised, Cliff put his cup on the counter, lifted his little girl into his arms. Claire wrapped her arms around his neck and legs around his waist. She was sobbing, hysterically and she laid her head on his shoulder. Cliff carried her to the great room, moved the coffee table with his foot and sat on the sofa. Claire sat on her father's lap and softly cried while he stroked her hair and rocked her back and forth like he did when she was younger. He began to hum a tune that always came to him in times like this and Claire stopped crying. Something bad went down last night, Cliff didn't know what, but he could sense it in her trembles. Claire had never acted like this before now. She was not sick, but her emotions had been compromised and Cliff would bet that Marlena had something to do with it.

Claire remained attached to Cliff for at least 15 minutes before she spoke. "Daddy, I'm sorry for how I acted. I didn't mean to be so ugly to you."

"Baby, it's OK, but I'm really concerned about what's going on in that little head of yours. When you feel like talking about it, I'll be here. As a matter of fact, I was planning to take you to lunch today; just you and me. There are some things I want to talk to you about. Not about this, but something else that's been on my mind."

"What, Daddy?" Tears were ceasing as she wiped her eyes with the back of her hand.

"Well, let's wait until we go to lunch. So, where would you like to go? We can even make it an early date if you want, like 11:00 o'clock. And we can stay late, if you like. It will be your day."

Claire hugged him closer as she wiped her eyes. "I would like hamburger but I don't think you're talking about that."

"No, I don't think so."

"What about Applebee's. I like that restaurant." Claire was looking up into his face and smiling.

"OK, Applebee's it is. Why don't you run upstairs, take a shower and change into some clothes that don't stink." He held his nose with his two fingers as he turned his head away.

Claire laughed and hit him across the shoulder. "OK, so since it is still early, how about you taking me to breakfast, too?"

Cliff thought about 2 seconds. "You got a deal. I'd like some IHOP pancakes, how 'bout you?" He would rather not be here when Marlena woke up anyway. She would most likely get ready and bury herself in her office.

"Yeah, IHOP is good." Claire said as she jumped from his lap. "I'll get ready and be right back. You read some of your paper."

Claire ran up the stairs and into her room. She gathered some clothes and headed for her bathroom for a shower.

Cliff smiled and returned to the kitchen to retrieve his coffee and paper. He settled into the breakfast nook and had just finished his coffee and first section of the paper when Claire bounced in with a big smile on her face, dressed in a yellow blouse, jeans and her new yellow Nike Brights. He was so happy to see his little girl in such good spirits. He might begin the serious talk at breakfast. If all goes well he might possibly invite Kim to join them for lunch so Claire could meet her. He would just have to wait and see how the morning goes.

"Well, that was fast! Why can't you be so quick on school days?" Cliff smiled as he stood and folded the paper.

"Take me to breakfast everyday and I might." She returned his smile.

"Fat chance!" He laughed and folded the newspaper and rinsed his coffee cup at the sink and placed it on the drain board.

They left the house arm in arm heading for the garage. Traffic was light this morning. It was just after 8:00 and the church crowds had not yet hit the roads. The drive to IHOP was short and the restaurant was not crammed full of the sinners in for some eggs and pancakes before they redeem themselves at the local Baptist church, so they were seated right away.

The waitress came by as soon as they were seated; 'Ruby' was the name on her pin attached to the uniform. Ruby was a fiftyish lady, red-headed with freckles, a little over-weight, but most waitresses were around here. “Good morning, y’all, what can I get you to drink?” she smiled at Claire and gave Cliff the once over.

Cliff smiled at her and said, “I’ll just have coffee. What do you want, Tweetie?”

Ruby looked again at Claire and smiled, thinking ‘What a sweet Dad he is. His little Tweetie’.

Claire replied without hesitation, “I’ll have a large chocolate milk and orange juice, please.”

Ruby jotted the order on her pad of order blanks and left to pour the drinks.

“What are you having this morning?” Cliff asked.

“Most definitely, pancakes ”

Ruby was back in a second with coffee and orange juice and set them on the table. “Chocolate milk is coming up sweetie. Are y’all ready to order?”

Cliff ordered for both as Ruby wrote it down on the order form in ‘waitress speak’.

Claire started fiddling with the salt and pepper shakers, then rearranging the syrup dispensers. Cliff just watched her for a few seconds, thinking of how he was going to approach this subject with her today. He had to tell her about Kim; about his decision to leave her mother. Claire would have to understand or he will have to make her see that a life in torment with Marlena is not what he needs or deserves. Claire needed a mother-figure in her life, too. Someone who would take the time to listen and be with her. Claire is changing from that little girl into a young woman. She needed the guidance of another women and Kim would be that woman.

Cliff peeled off the paper cover on the Half ’n’ Half creamer and emptied it into his coffee. As he stirred in some Equal with the spoon, he looked at Claire. "Tweetie, what was going on this morning? I know something was wrong and I want to help. I can't stand to see you hurting inside like that. So, please tell Daddy what's wrong with his Tweetie."

Claire shifted sideways in her seat and stared out the window and mumbled, "I don't want to talk about it." She wouldn't look at her father.

"But, you were so upset about something. Did your mother say something to you that hurt your feelings?"

Claire's heart jumped in her chest and nervously shifted again. Cliff had seen this before. Obviously, he had stumbled onto the problem, but was going to have a hard time bringing it to the surface. Claire had acted this way last year when Marlena had embarrassed Claire in front of all her friends at the movie theatre. Claire had forgotten her money and Marlena had to make a special trip to the mall to deliver the cash, but she made such a big deal from the incident and belittled Claire for being inconsiderate, stupid and irresponsible. Claire never enjoyed the movie after that and her friends were conspicuously absent the next couple of weeks. They wanted nothing to do with Claire if it meant being around the 'wicked witch of the west'. Claire remained in her room for two days after that, crying. Cliff could not get her to respond to him until a week later. He reprimanded Marlena for her callous disregard for Claire's feelings, but she just shrugged it off and insisted that he take care of it next time.

Cliff reached over and took her hand that was on the table and held it between both his. "It is your mother, isn't it?"

She didn't answer or move. She looked out the window, watching the Sunday morning traffic as it drove by. Maybe there would be a wreck and he would drop the subject.

"Sweetie, whatever problem you are having with your Mom, it will not go away until you talk about it. I'm here to listen. You know I love you very much and I will understand, whatever it is."

The traffic continued up and down Germantown Parkway, while Claire watched with tear-glazed eyes; she remained still and silent. Without turning her head from the window view, she pulled back her hand and placed it in her lap under the table.

Rudy dropped by with Claire's chocolate milk, noticing the upsetting mood with Claire. "Your order will be out in just a minute or two. Everythang OK? "

Cliff looked into her eyes and she smiled her waitress smile, "Just fine, thanks."

Claire turned around facing her Dad. She lifted the glass of milk and took a big sip. Tears had begun to coat her eyes like this morning in the kitchen. "I'm sorry, Daddy, but I can't talk about this right now. It's between me and Mom. We will work it out somehow and someday. I'm OK, she didn't hurt me or humiliate me again like she has done before. "

"But, Tweetie, I hate to see you so upset."

"Daddy, just forget about it OK? Let's talk about other stuff. When are you going out of town again?" Claire was insistent.

Cliff sat silent for what seemed like an eternity to Claire and sipped his coffee. He stared at her as she drank the milk. He took a deep breath and realized this conversation is going nowhere. She was not planning to divulge the problem with Marlena; not today or tomorrow, but in her own time.

"I have an appointment at the office in the morning, but I don't leave for Atlanta until Wednesday."

"When will you be back?" she said with sadness and returned her stare out the window, as if Cliff was abandoning her.

"Just 'till Friday. Maybe we can go to a movie together Friday night. What about that?"

She quickly replied, wiping her eyes with a napkin, "Can Janey come, too?"

"Sure, I don't mind sharing, .. YOU."

Claire laughed. Cliff was helping her, for the moment, to forget the terrible things her mother had done to upset her so much.

"OK, you promise not to be late and don't come up with any excuses to get out of it. I couldn't take it"

"I wouldn't dream of it."

Ruby came out of the kitchen with a tray loaded with steaming pancakes, sausage and eggs. She placed each plate in front of Cliff and Claire. "Here ya go sweeties. Y'all enjoy. Let me know if I can getcha something." She tucked the tray under her arm and tore off the check from the order pad and laid it upside down on the table edge closest to Cliff.

Cliff and Claire added all the required extras like salt, pepper, syrup to their meals and ate silently for a couple of minutes. Cliff did not want to drop what had happened to his daughter; it was really bothering him and upsetting to Claire, but she was hard-headed and he knew it.

He thought he should bring up Kim, but how? What reaction would Claire have, especially in this mood? Would she cry? Would she understand or would she stomp out of the restaurant, mad as hell at her father for letting her down, too? Claire continued to eat her pancakes and sausage.

Cliff put down his fork and held the coffee cup. "Claire, you remember when I told you there was something I wanted to talk with you about?"

Oh no, there it was again. He was calling her by her given name. This was serious and she stopped eating and looked directly at him. "Yeah, Daddy, I remember. But I thought we were doing that at lunch."

"Well, I figured this was as good a time as any."

She looked at her father with a curious intensity.

Cliff was gathering his thoughts. This had to be done slowly and with a well thought out plan. Can't just blare out, 'I am in love with another woman and I want to divorce your mother'. He was anticipating the worst reaction from Claire and yet he was hoping for the reaction that would favor this decision. The best way, sometimes was never the easiest.

"Tweetie?" he started.

Good he's back to calling me Tweetie, Claire thought as she smiled and took another bite.

"I know you're not stupid and you're old enough to understand the ways of the world. We spoke to you about sex and the changes that you would experience in your body a long time ago."

Claire lowered her eyes and became a little flushed. She cut her stare to other patrons next to them, just to make sure they weren't looking.

Cliff continued but acknowledged she was uncomfortable. "So..I hope you will understand what I am about to tell you."

She sat up a little taller in the seat.

"You know, how much I love you and I would do anything I could do that would make you safe and happy. I would give you whatever you need and spend as much time with you as I can. I would die if I ever lost your love. But ..", he stopped to sip his coffee.

"But, I have a problem with your mom, too."

Claire's eyes widened. What does he know?

"Ever since you were born, your mom has changed. We were very much in love and spent all available time together. But as time went by, we grew apart. She had a career and I had mine. We had little time to spend together, let alone spend quality time with you. Over the years, we became distant with each other. We didn't live as husband and wife. We only existed as a couple, becoming distant more and more. The only glue we had that kept us together was you. At least, you were the only reason I've stayed."

Claire was confused, yet she understood.

"Your mother and I are no longer compatible. We actually only tolerate each other and someone has to make the first move. I can't let things stay like this. It is not fair to me, to your mom, or especially to you. The love we had is gone."

"What, Daddy? Are you and Mom getting a divorce?" Claire's eyes began to water again. "You're not going to leave me there? Don't leave me, Daddy!"

Cliff took her hands in his, "Baby, I am NOT leaving you. That's the main reason I wanted to talk. Yes, I want to get a divorce from your mother, but I want YOU to come live with me, where ever that happens to lead us. Who knows, maybe Marlena would be willing to move out of the house instead of us. Then you could still have your room and friends next door."

"Daddy, I don't want to move. But I don't want you to leave me. Don't leave me at home alone with her. I hate her!"

Cliff sensed the resentment. The problem from yesterday was resurfacing in her head and heart. But to say she hated her mother. What did Marlena do? "Sweetie, regardless of where I go, you will be sure to go with me."

Claire looked at the window again and spoke to the glass reflection she saw of her face. "When are you getting the divorce?"

"That's the problem. I haven't even approached your mother with this. Based on her attitude toward me the past several months, I don't suppose she is apt to object. As a matter of fact, she probably will jump at the chance to free herself and make a new life with someone else. I suspect she has been doing that already."

Claire trembled inside at his words and stared deeper into her reflection. *If only you knew, Daddy, if only you knew.*

"Please, don't be upset, Tweetie. I just want you to face the fact that your Mom might be having an affair with someone else." Cliff paused. "You do know what I mean don't you?"

Claire turned back to face her father. "Yes, Daddy. I know what an affair means."

"Well, I have suspected for a long time, but I was not mad or upset. Like I said, your mom and I have drifted apart. We have no more love for each other, like a married couple should have. I would have left a long time ago, but you kept me in place. You were my glue that held me back."

Ruby came over with the coffee pot to refill Cliff's cup. He thanked her added more cream and sweetener. He was stalling. Kim had to come up in the conversation. Claire had to know about her. She had to accept her as Cliff's new love and possibly as Claire's new step-mom.

"Even though, I believe your mother has been starting a new love life with someone else, I want you to know again, that it does not make me mad. I'm sure you don't care what she does. You two have never gotten along as well as you should have. What I'm trying to say, is that I found someone else, too. I found a new woman to love."

At that comment, Cliff stopped, sipped his newly poured coffee and watched for Claire's reaction to this news. Claire looked into her near empty glass of chocolate milk, with the brown coating still clinging to the side. She turned her head to look again at the traffic moving down the street. She made no sound, no acknowledgement of what she just heard. Cliff studied her face, her expression; something that would tell him how she felt about this news. It was bad enough to bring up an idea that Marlena was having an affair, but to admit to his daughter that he was indeed fooling around was another thing to consider.

Claire continued to absorb the news. As she eyed her reflection a smile appeared across her lips. Cliff noticed immediately. He screamed in his head 'Thank you Jesus. She does understand. She approves, I hope'.

Claire turned again, head down slightly with eyes turned toward Cliff, the smile still across her mouth and growing larger. "What's her name?"

Cliff sighed. He sank a mile in his seat. What a relief he felt. All the pressure he put himself through, for the past year, trying to come up with the right words to say to his beautiful little girl, that would not hurt her or alienate her from him and she accepted his decision. She was not mad. She was not offended or hurt; in fact she seemed to be happy about what she just heard. At least, in Cliff's heart, he thought she was thrilled.

"Her name is Kim." Cliff replied "Are you having a problem with this, baby?"
He was smiling back at her.

"No, Daddy, not at all. Ever since Mom has been so mean to me or at least as long as I can remember how she has been, I have wanted to leave myself. I even thought about running away one time."

Now Cliff's eyes widened. "Really? When was this?"

"A long time ago, I don't quite remember when. How old is she? Where does she live? How did you meet her? When can I meet her?"

Cliff was flabbergasted. She was desperate for info. She wanted to know all about Kim. And she wanted to meet her.

"Hey, slow down."

"But I want to know."

"OK, you know I was really worried how you would act. I wanted to tell you sooner, but I was unsure. Are you sure, you're alright with this?"

"Daddy, face it, Mom is a bitch, and you deserve better. I deserve better."

Cliff's mouth dropped open as he gave Claire a disapproving look. What could he say to top that? "Well, her name is Kimberly McClain. She's 28 and works at my office. As a matter of fact, she works for me on all my accounts. She didn't always, the general manager moved her into my department last year."

"What does she look like? Is she pretty?"

"Yes, she's very pretty. She has long brown hair. She's a little tall, but I always went for the tall ones, you know. She's got blue eyes and she likes to run, so she's pretty fit."

Claire giggled.

"—and she wants to meet you, too."

"She really does? When did she say that?"

"When I left for Jackson yesterday, you know, to meet with a prospect? I had Kim meet me on the way with some details about the man I was supposed to meet. I decided it was time to get you two together. She was a little bit nervous at first, but she has always wanted to know you, really. Actually, she was planning to come by and share desert with you and me; that is, if the conversation between you and me went OK. But now, since we're talking about this at breakfast, maybe she can have lunch with us. What do you think about that?"

"Yes, that is exactly what I want too. I like her already, just knowing you care about her. Do you love her?"

He paused for a second before answering, "Yes, baby, I do."

"Are you going to marry her when you get rid of Mom."

"Don't say it like that, she is your mother, and don't ever call her a bitch again." Cliff spoke softly, smiled at Claire and she returned the grin. Then they both broke out into laughter. The couple at the booth behind them turned to see what was happening.

Cliff calmed down, "Well, Kim and I have talked about it, but first things first."

"You have your cell phone, don't you?"

"Yeah, why?"

"Call Kim. Wake her up if you have to. I want her to have lunch with us. Really, I would like her to get dressed and come on down here, right now. I want to meet the lady who has made my Daddy so happy."

Cliff couldn't believe what was coming out of Claire's mouth. She couldn't wait to know Kim and he was not going to deny her the opportunity to do just that. He pulled his cell from the snap attached to his belt. He punched in Kim's number. It was not too early and Cliff knew she would be up by now. She always rose before 6 and ran at least 3 miles before studying the latest Wall Street Journal over a couple cups of coffee on her balcony overlooking the community lake. Kim answered on the second ring.

Claire picked up her fork and tried to resume eating the remaining pancakes, but her appetite had gone. She tried to give her father the privacy he needed, but she strained to hear without seeming to pry.

Cliff turned in the seat, where his voice was directed away from Claire, like he had something to hide. He spoke softly, "Hey, you're not going to believe what's just happened. It's Claire. We are at IHOP having breakfast and we had our talk, the talk we wanted to bring up with her. She really wants to meet you. She even asked me to call you, now."

"No, I am serious. Are you dressed? Forget that, of course you are. You up to having a little coffee and meeting a young lady."

" .. OK, we're at the IHOP on Germantown Parkway. You're close, can you get here quick? "

"Make it 5 minutes. OK see you in a minute. OK, Bye. Love you, too." Claire smiled as she forced another piece of sausage into her mouth. She put down the fork. She had enough. Cliff motioned at Ruby as she was delivering a new order to the customers at the corner booth. Ruby paused and leaned in Cliff's direction, "What can I get cha, sweetie?"

Cliff moved his coffee cup to the center of the table, "I have another lady coming to join us in a couple of minutes, can you bring over another cup of coffee and a raspberry Danish and maybe a little more coffee for me? Claire you want some more milk or juice?" She shook her head. Ruby confirmed the order and continued with her chore.

Kim was ecstatic. As she ran through her apartment, she nearly tripped over the ottoman as she tried to place the cordless phone back into the charging cradle. For the past year that she and Cliff have been romantically involved, she had hoped that this day would come. Claire was the missing piece of the puzzle, she was the prize, and she was the direct way to a complete life with Cliff.

She had known all along that Cliff wanted desperately to take their relationship to a more permanent level, but he had been so unsure what Claire's reaction would be. This phone call could be the answer she needs for her and Cliff to build a life together; with Claire, too. '*He said she wanted to meet me.*' She thought as she took one look in the mirror on the wall.

She grabbed the keys to her car from the end table by the door and rushed out into the morning sunshine for the second time today. She was wearing her usual jogging shorts, Grizzles' T-shirt and Nike shoes.

No time to shower and change because this was a pivotal moment in her life. This was going to turn the tide.

Her car was locked and she fumbled with the key to unlock the door. The IHOP pancake store was just 3 blocks away. She would be there is less than 5 minutes, but it seemed like an eternity. She fastened the seat belt, cranked the engine and put the car in reverse almost hitting another car passing behind her. Finally, she was out of the parking area and onto Germantown Parkway, heading north toward the restaurant.

Claire was unquestionably quieter and Cliff watched her closely with great anticipation. He didn't miss one twitch of her mouth; the darting of her eyes came through the door. Claire knew from her Dad's description that she would recognize Kim the second she walked through the glass door. She wasn't disappointed when Kim reached for the handle, Claire's heart jumped in her chest. She looked at her Dad with a big smile, "That's her isn't it, Daddy?"

Cliff saw the approval in Claire's eye, "Yes, it is, sweetie." He slid off his seat and walked to meet Kim. He kissed her gently. She had already found them and was smiling at Claire who patiently waited to be introduced. They stopped arm and arm at the table. Claire was looking tenderly into Kim's face, who was beginning to let the emotions of the moment get the best of her. Tears were forming and starting to trickle down her cheek. Claire jumped from her seat and latched onto Kim's neck like she had known her for her whole life. They both were crying now. Cliff looked around, not wanting to draw a lot of attention to this wonderful first meeting. He eased himself into his booth and motioned for Kim and Claire to sit as well. They sat together and continued to just stare and hug each other.

Cliff smiled as he spoke to his daughter, "Claire, I want you to meet Kim."

Claire did the polite thing, what you're suppose to do meeting someone for the first time, she held out her hand. Kim looked down at the invitation of a handshake and looked into Claire's eyes. Claire said, "Glad to meet you Kim." smiled broadly then proceeded to grab hold again in a bear-hug embrace. As they cried and held each other tightly,

Kim looked at Cliff with such love, who by now had realized that he should have done this a long time ago.

Kim turned to Cliff, "Cliff, she is just more beautiful than you have ever told me." Turning back to Claire and holding her hands, "We have so much to talk about, you and me. We might even let your Dad join us, too."

Claire giggled.

Kim said, "Your father has told me everything about you, but to finally meet you, I just don't know what to say."

"Well, considering I didn't know about you until 20 minutes ago, I guess I have a lot to ask too." Claire replied with her incessant smile.

Cliff had nothing to say. His dream was coming true, finally. Marlena never crossed his mind. She did not exist at this moment. Kim and Claire never noticed when Ruby delivered coffee and Danish. They were engaged in such an intricate conversation that only those of the female sex could comprehend. They were jumping from one subject to the next, one topic to another and back again to one previous. Cliff heard this type conversation before. He called it 'spaghetti'. It was all jumbled up, but there was an order and it made sense to the ones consuming it.

Kim noticed the coffee and roll, "Ohhh, thank you for ordering me something. I was getting hungry. Claire have you finished? I'll share this with you"

"No, I had plenty." Addressing Cliff she said, "Daddy, can we spend the whole day together, just you, me and Kim?"

Kim's heart filled with joy. So did Cliff's. This was just too easy; all too simple. Something must not be right. It is not supposed to happen this way. He reached to take Claire's hand. "I can't think of a better thing I would want to do today."

They spent the next hour at IHOP, finishing breakfast, along with some more 'spaghetti' and a little more coffee. Cliff took the check to the cashier and paid the bill with his Visa card. He left Ruby a little extra for being patient, understanding and he hoped discreet. They headed back to Kim's apartment with Claire riding in the car with her new best friend. It was a glorious day, a day Claire would take with her always tucked away in her mind for that special moment when she can recall her happiness and contentment. They spent the rest of the morning and into late afternoon at Kim's home, talking, sitting by the pool enjoying cookies and cokes and talking more. Before the day was out, Claire knew more about Kim than Cliff could have hoped to know and Kim found what she had felt all along, she truly loved this little lady called Claire. She couldn't wait until the day she became Mrs. Kimberly Richards and the loving step-mother to Claire.

Chapter Five

Marlena was accustomed to sleeping in late most Sundays, especially when Cliff was out of town or had left early for the office to catch up on last minute details of the current deal he was working. The house was exceptionally quiet this morning. She had showered and changed into shorts and a casual matching white blouse. She slipped on her tennis shoes before heading to the kitchen for some breakfast and hot coffee. She noticed the dirty dishes in the sink and assumed Cliff had taken Claire somewhere, which was just as well for her. She wanted to be alone this morning. Maybe they would be gone for a long time, long enough for her to make some plans for the week; the sort of plans that did not need little ears nearby.

She fixed herself some coffee and dropped two pieces of bread into the toaster on the counter. She had to watch the figure. Cliff's day planner was left on the breakfast nook table. While the toast warmed and turned a golden brown, she retrieved the book and flipped open the pages to the current week activities. Cliff always left his planner in such easy places and Marlena always took advantage of the situation. She wanted to know where he was, but not really caring what he was doing. She had plans of her own.

The coffee was good and she prepared toast with butter and strawberry jam. She grabbed the cordless phone off the wall and sat at the table with Cliff's book.

She read to herself -
Monday, he's in the office all day.
Tuesday, leaves for Atlanta in the afternoon
Wednesday, Thursday, in Atlanta
Friday, home by 6:00

Marlena pressed the talk button on the phone and dialed a number.

"Hey, you been up long?"

"It looks like Wednesday is good for us."

"Yeah, she will be at a friend's house to spend the night, I'm arranging it........"

"You'll meet me at the same place as before?"

"OK."

She paused, "Love you, too. Bye."

She hung up the phone and reached for her address book on the shelf behind the table. She looked in the section marked 'C'. She turned on the phone again and dialed Amanda Caldwell, Janey's mother, then waited.

"Janey? Is your mother at home, please?"

Janey recognized her voice and made a face into the phone, then after composing herself she said, "Yes, hold on Mrs. Richards."

Marlena was surprised that Janey knew her voice. Amanda Caldwell picked up the phone. She liked Marlena as a neighbor, but she didn't consider her a close or personal friend. She had heard too many stories from Janey about how Marlena treats the girls when they are together at Claire's home.

"Hello, Marlena, how are you?"

"Fine, Amanda. It seems like the only time we get to chat, is when I need a favor." Amanda rolled her eyes back and thought *Again.* "Sure, no problem, what can I do to help you, Marlena?"

"I was looking at my schedule and I am out of town Wednesday and Thursday this week and Cliff is out until Friday. I know I am imposing on you and I really am in debt to you already, but can you allow Claire to sleep over on Wednesday night? Normally my mother would, but she and Dad have left for an extended vacation."

Claire was never an imposition to her family and Amanda never felt indebted to the likes of Marlena. "Of course, she can stay with us. What time do you expect to be home on Thursday?"

"Oh, no later than 3:00 for sure. I am so grateful. Just let me know what I can do for you, please."

"There is nothing you need to do. Claire's company is just fine."

Now Marlena rolled her eyes. "Great, I'll let her know as soon as she gets home. She and her Dad left out early this morning. Don't have a clue where, but thanks again for your kindness. Bye-bye."

She clicked off the phone just as Amanda was attempting to offer her good-bye. Amanda held the phone in her hand as if it was going to speak. She thought how rude of this woman. But Claire was always welcome. In fact, she wouldn't care if Claire just moved in permanently. Janey would love it and she had always wanted another daughter.

Marlena finished eating her toast and jam while reading the front page of the paper that Cliff had left on the table. She drank the last sip of coffee and put the plate and cup in the sink. Someone would wash them all later, but not her.

It was already after 11:00 and work was waiting. She went into her office and began another Sunday of legal mumbo jumbo. After all, this was her career, the life she chose over being a loving mother and wife. This was all she wanted. At least until Wednesday.

The afternoon had flown by and evening was settling in fast. Claire and Cliff hardly had noticed the time, but it was nearing 7:00. Cliff was on the couch next to Kim with his arm around her shoulder and Claire was lying on the floor snuggled into a huge blue and white pillow. They were watching a special on E!, featuring Jamie Lynn Spears.

Cliff looked at his watch and gasped, "Wow!! I didn't realize how late it was. Hey, Tweetie, we need to get home. It's late."

She ignored him. Jamie was talking about her life before Zoey 101 and she couldn't miss it.

"Claire??"

That got her attention. "What, Daddy? "

"We need to go. It's getting late, almost 7:00."

"That's OK, We don't need to go. Let's stay here. I don't want to go home."

Kim snuggled in a little closer to Cliff, "I like the way she thinks, too."

"Me too, but I do have to get to work tomorrow and so do you and she has school. Although I don't believe Marlena has even missed us today, we do need to make an appearance."

"Yeah, of course. Will you talk to her tonight?" Kim whispered.

"I'll see how the atmosphere is at home. Sometimes she is in a good mood, that's if she hasn't had too much to drink."

"Well try, please. I want this to happen and happen fast. Claire and I are meant to be mother and daughter and God knows she needs me as much as I want and need her. You know, this has been probably the best day in my entire life."

"Yeah, me too. Claire is so relaxed around you. We will have to plan another outing one evening this week. I mentioned to Claire that I would take her to the movies Friday when I got back from Atlanta and she could take a friend. Now, I was thinking of Janey, but maybe....."

"Hey, sweetie.." Ignored again. "....Claire, turn around and look at me, will ya."

Claire stopped staring at the television and sat cross-legged facing Cliff and Kim. "OK, What?"

Cliff smiled at his precious little girl. "Remember earlier today we talked about going to the movies Friday night and you could bring a friend?"

"Yeah, you're not backing out now? Are you?"

"No, but."

"OK, then I want her to be my friend." She pointed and smiled at Kim and Kim returned the adoring smile and look at Cliff like, 'I told you so'.

Cliff was dumbfounded, "Well, that's what I had in mind too! I guess we just think alike, don't we Tweetie."

Claire jumped up and slid onto Cliff's lap and wrapped one arm around Kim's neck and the other tightly around her Dad. She softly said, "Can't we stay a little longer, pleassssseeee?"

Cliff gave in to her sweetness, "OK, but just 30 minutes more. Take all these glasses into the kitchen, OK?"

Claire dutifully slid off his lap and gathered the glasses scattered on the wooden end tables and coffee table. Kim nudged closer to Cliff and he held her with his hands caressing her face, then kissed her tenderly. Claire never missed it either. From the corner of her eye, she saw the moment between her Dad and future mother. She smiled so broadly. Her heart was filled with such joy, it was about to burst. She had never felt so wonderful in her entire short life. This was going to be great. Her father would be happy and she would have someone that she would be proud to call 'Mom'; NO, 'mommy'. She loved Kim so much right now. She didn't want this day to end.

When the 30 minutes was gone, Cliff and Claire said so long to Kim with lots of hugs and kisses and promises to call in the morning.

Kim had asked Claire to memorize her work, cell and home numbers, because she expected to hear from Claire after school on Monday without question. Claire learned the numbers and assured Kim they would talk tomorrow and maybe tonight if that would be alright. Kim said it was OK and Cliff nodded.

On the way home, Claire never stopped talking. "Can we go back over to Kim's tomorrow night? "

"I don't know, Sweetie."

"But, Daddy, I want to see her, tomorrow and every day."

"I know, but I have to work tomorrow and I leave for Atlanta Tuesday. You've got school."

"Can I stay with Kim while you're gone? She's not going with you is she?"

"No, and no you can't stay with her. That wouldn't be right. I have to come up with a plan to talk about this with your mother."

"She's not my mother!" Claire huffed. "Well, I don't want her to be."

"Tweetie, don't be mean. I agree, she has not been the best, in fact she has been pretty mean herself, but. . . . "

"Yeah, she *is my* mother."

"Right, I hope you will give her some respect."

"For what? She never gives me any."

Cliff couldn't reply to that, she was right. Marlena had never shown any respect to Claire that Cliff had ever witnessed.

"Besides, she is not going to be my mother much longer."

"Baby she will always be your mother .. "

"No she won't, I don't want her to be. She is nothing to me. She's a bitch."

Cliff looked at Claire. "Claire, you know what I said about that."

"I know, Daddy, but she doesn't love me and I definitely don't love her."

This really hit Cliff between the eyes. He was totally shocked, yet not really. His voice became low and soft. "You have no love at all for her?"

Claire faced forward and folded her arms across her chest, just like a pouting child. "No! I hate her. She means nothing to me. If she died tomorrow, I wouldn't care. I wouldn't even go to her funeral. She can just rot."

Cliff didn't realize how deep the resentment was for Marlena. He was determined to find out soon.

They drove the rest of the way home in silence while Claire stared out the passenger side window at the late afternoon traffic driving on Germantown Parkway. Cliff didn't know if she was mad at him, herself or just disappointed to be going home. He pulled into the driveway and pressed the garage down opener switch on the overhead console of his car. They went inside through the kitchen door entrance from the garage. Claire ran up the back set of stairs and into her room. She supposed her mother would be locked away in her office and she was absolutely right. Marlena had spent the entire afternoon, oblivious to anything and anyone. She was preparing for Monday's workday.

Cliff picked up his day planner from the kitchen table and dropped the car keys on the counter by the door. He looked at the phone hanging on the hook and had the strongest urge to pick it up and call Kim, just to say good-night. Instead, he walked through the great room and down the hall to Marlena's office. The door was closed as usual, but he tapped quietly with his fingers.

"Yes" came the muffled reply to his knock.

He already had the handle and went inside. "We're back!" No need to volunteer anything. She was a lawyer after all.

"Well, good for you. A father daughter kind of day? I hope you had something to eat, cause I am not fixing anything." she said with some sarcasm.

"Yes, we grabbed something. Claire is upstairs. I have some work to do before tomorrow. I leave for Atlanta Tuesday and would like for you and me to have a talk Saturday."

She looked up from the stack of papers scattered across the desk. What was on his mind? She moved a pile of documents that covered her own planner. She flipped opened to Saturday in the current week. "Saturday looks OK. What'd you want to talk about? Am I mistreating Claire again?"

Cliff's heart jumped. His temper almost got the best of him, but he calmed down first. Count to 5, take a breath. "No, that's not what I had in mind, but since you brought it up, have you been mistreating our daughter again?"

"Cliff, don't bother me, please. We'll talk. I might just have a few things to say too." She waved him out of the office.

Cliff backed out of the room and flipped her a salute, which she never saw. He closed the door behind him, turned around with extended arm he flipped her the *bird*. Why had he tortured himself all these years? Claire's acceptance of Kim was phenomenal. If only he had introduced them last year, he and Kim would be married and settled by now.

He went upstairs to talk with Claire. Her door was slightly cracked open and he clearly overheard her speaking to someone. She must be on the phone, normally a common event in the life of a pre-teen girl. He listened long enough to realize, Claire was on the phone with Kim. He knocked lightly and the door slid open. Claire lying on her back across her bed, with her legs crossed and one arm wrapped in a coil of telephone cord. She waved at him and pointed to the edge of the bed.

"Well, I better go, Daddy is here. I'll call you tomorrow after school." Claire spoke to the phone.

"OK, Bye" she hung up the phone, sat up and hugged her Dad.

"Who was that?" he asked.

"Kim!"

"Let's be careful calling Kim from here, OK?"

"Mom never uses the house phone. She always uses her cell. Why don't you get me a cell phone and then I can call Kim anytime I want."

"I don't think so, and your Mother does use the house phone. Just make sure she's not home, first. I do!"

Claire smiled. "Dad, what are you going to do?"

He turned to face her and held both hands. "We are going to talk, Saturday. I'll get everything worked out then. I need some time to get my thoughts together and make sure I say what needs to be said and make it clear to her that YOU are coming with me and not staying with her although she would prefer it that way."

"You got that right. I wouldn't stay with her for nothing."

"Can you wait until then? Just stay out of her way, stay off the phone with Kim and concentrate on school. We can go out tomorrow night when I get home. Maybe we can catch a movie and then afterwards we can go for a hamburger. And if Kim happens to come by at the same time, I suppose that would be alright with you?"

"Yeah, that would be good. You'll arrange that right?"

"Sure will, but I have some work to do before tomorrow. You just hang out, watch some TV, call Janey or whatever you want to do. I'll come in and say good-night later."

"OK, I love you so much, Daddy!" she jumped up into his lap and wrapped her arms around his neck.

Cliff hugged her tightly, "I love you too, sooooo much, sweetie. You are very precious to me." He kissed her on the cheek and left her on the bed. He went
back downstairs into his small and simple office to work out some details for Monday. Kim would do more research on Brandon Tarkinson. He didn't want this one to get away.

Around 10:30, Cliff closed down his computer and loaded all the papers back into the leather briefcase on the edge of the desk. There were no extra lights left on downstairs, so he assumed Marlena had already gone to bed. Good! He preferred not to speak with her again tonight. He was thinking about sleeping in the guest room again tonight. Claire was still awake, watching Nick at Nite on her TV. She had already showered and was in lemon colored pajamas under a yellow cover sheet.

"Hi, Daddy!"

"Hey, Tweetie. I'm going to bed now. I have to leave early in the morning, so your mother will have to get you to school, OK?"

"I guess I don't have a choice."

He leaned down to kiss her good night. "Turn that off by 11:00 OK?" He pointed to the television.

"OK, I will. Nite Daddy."

"Sleep tight, sweetie. I'll call you tomorrow when school is out."

Cliff left and closed the door to Claire's room. He started down the hall to his own room and stopped. He turned and went back into the guestroom. This would be better for him.

Chapter Six

Monday morning came fast and with a loud bang. A strong, violent thunderstorm had preceded a low-pressure system blowing in out of Arkansas and Missouri. Claire jumped straight up when then the thunderclap rocked the house. She never saw the lightning. Wiping the sleep from her eyes, she looked at the digital clock on her nightstand. It was 6:30am. Cliff had already left and Marlena was up, showered and just putting on her eyeliner when the thunder roared.

Claire grabbed a new set of jeans, yellow blouse and some undies before heading to her personal bathroom for a shower. Marlena was already in the kitchen drinking coffee while reading the morning paper Cliff had left on the table. Claire was humming when she bounced into the kitchen, but quickly stopped when she saw Marlena at the breakfast table.

"Are you ready to go?" Marlena asked.

Not *'Hi, how are you'* or *'Did you sleep well darling'* or *'I missed you yesterday'*. No, it was just *'Are you ready to go?'*

"Yes, I'll get a cereal bar or something to eat on the way." Claire never looked at her mother.

Marlena looked up from her paper. "Oh, by the way, I am going out of town Wednesday and Thursday. I know your Dad is out until Friday, so I asked Janey's mom if you could spend the night Wednesday. You will go there from school."

Claire just looked at her as she returned to the paper, like what Claire might have to say didn't matter. The deed was done; what she said goes. "Fine!" Claire remarked curtly as she opened the box of strawberry Pop Tarts. "Let's go then."

The ride to school was quiet, other than the rain hitting the car and windshield wipers keeping time with the song on the radio. Claire kept her eyes on the road to the right and nibbled on the pop tart; she really didn't have an appetite. Marlena watched the traffic as she drove. Claire couldn't wait to get out when the car pulled to the drop-off curb at Germantown Elementary School. Without saying a single word to her mother, she snatched the umbrella from the back seat, pushed the button to open it and darted down the sidewalk into the building.

Cliff kept his promise and took Claire and Kim to a movie, even though Claire and Kim had spent at least 2 hours on the phone on Monday afternoon. Afterwards, they had pizza. They were becoming the best of friends and their love for each other was growing by the minute. Cliff sometimes felt like an outsider when they were together. Cliff managed to give Claire a ride to school on Tuesday morning but was gone by the evening. She missed him terribly. By Wednesday morning, Claire had devised a plan. Her mother was going to be out of town for 2 whole days. Dad was out of town until Friday. The house was going to be empty and she had a key.

After school, Janey's mom occasionally gave Claire a ride home from school. Today, Claire explained that her mother had cancelled the trip and would be home after work. Amanda had no reason to not believe what Claire was saying, so she didn't argue or insist that Marlena confirm. Claire and Janey giggled and talked secretly all the way home and agreed to call each other later.

Claire's plan was to clean up anything in the house that needed cleaning, prepare some pasta and veggies and invite Kim over for supper and a little chit-chat. She ran up on the porch, unlocked the door with her key and went inside, locking the deadbolt for security. She punched in the alarm code on the keypad hanging on the wall and threw her bag of books on the chair in the entry.

'OK, what to fix' she thought walking into the kitchen. *'Maybe I need to call Kim first and find out what she likes.'*

She grabbed the phone from the charging cradle hanging on the wall and dialed Kim's work number, from memory of course. Kim's voice mail came on.

"Good day, this is Kimberly McClain and I will be out of the office on business until Monday. If you wish to speak with my assistant, please press 101 now or you may press 0 for the operator to be connected to someone else. Thank you and have a glorious day."

'Oh no' Claire was screaming inside. *'This can't be happening. She went with my Dad? Maybe I should call his cell. No, he would know I wasn't at Janey's.'*

She hung up the phone without leaving a message after the beep. She went to the breakfast table to sit and think. She looked around. It was completely and deliciously quiet, except for the hum of the appliances and air conditioning unit. Who's to say she can't stay home all by herself. Thoughts of the movie "Home Alone" popped into her mind. At first, she was reminded of the bad guys trying to break-in and rob the place, but that was just a movie. It could never happen here in real life. This adventure would be fun. Maybe she should call and invite Janey over for supper, but she might tell her mother, who would force her to come spend the night at their house anyway.

Claire was alone and the time crept by so slowly. She spent most of the afternoon watching TV and playing video games. At one point, she thought of homework, but decided that it could wait until later. She was getting hungry, but what to fix? Eating alone would be no fun. She didn't want to prepare a big meal just for her. Claire went into the kitchen and looked long and intently into the refrigerator. There were a few can Cokes in the cooler shelf on the door. She pulled one out and set it on the counter. What to eat? Leftovers? Not many to choose from. She looked in the meat tray and found a package of Hormel sliced ham. Some pickles, lettuce and tomato with a spoon of mayonnaise and she had herself a nutritious sandwich. She pulled a bag of potato chips from the lower cabinet, the snack cabinet, and went into the great room to watch Wednesday night television and enjoy the peace and quiet.

Marlena and David had left work early and were finishing a delicious seafood dinner at Owen Brennan's restaurant, just a couple of blocks from the office. She always enjoyed a long and leisurely meal with a few drinks. Actually a few too many. They had talked about going to Alfred's on famous Beale St. for some quiet music and a few more drinks. David was a good driver even when he had consumed more liquor than he should have. He knew better, but Marlena definitely could not drive. He paid the tab and they left for blues alley in downtown Memphis.

Claire was watching "Scream" on USA Network, when the cordless phone lying on the sofa next to her rang right at the moment when the masked guy was about to stab the girl again and again. She screamed and jumped, but then laughed as she picked up the phone and punched the 'TALK' button. She realized at that moment that it was a bad idea to answer the phone. She wasn't supposed to be here if her mother or dad called, but why would they call. What if Janey's mom was calling? What if?

"Hello?" Janey's voice sounded from the receiver.

Claire relieved now spoke, "Oh, Hi Janey. You scared the heck out of me."

"Well, how could I do that, I'm not even there?"

"Never mind. I'm watching Scream on TV and then the phone rang right next to.. just forget it. So what's up?"

"I just wanted to know what you're doing. "

"Nothing, just TV. What about you."

"Nothing. I'm just bored."

Claire was quiet. Should she tell Janey about what happened tonight?"

Janey asked, "Are you there?"

"Yeah. Hey, if I tell you something, will you promise... I mean really promise not to tell anyone, especially your mother?"

"Tell me, I promise."

"You swear?"

"Yes, I swear now tell me."

Claire gathered her courage and told Janey, "My mother is NOT here. I just told your mom that she was not going to be out of town so I could stay home by myself." Claire wasn't going to mention Kim. Only her and Dad were to know about that, she promised and she was keeping her word. "I just wanted to be alone."

Janey asked, "Can I come over?"

"I don't know. What if your mother comes over to get you or something? What if she calls?"

"Oh come on, she's busy watching her TV shows and won't bother."

"I don't know."

"Come on, please."

Claire relented, "OK, just for a little bit. You just make sure your mom doesn't find out. I shouldn't have told you anyway."

"Be there in a sec. Bye" Janey said and hung up.

David managed to make the trip to downtown Memphis without incident. Alfred's was not busy; it never was on Wednesday evenings. The local band 'Steve, Steve and sometimes Dave' were playing their usual seventies rocks sounds. They were a favorite among the regulars. Marlena needed a drink, but more than that, she needed to visit the ladies room. They found a table next to the bar and David ordered two gin and tonics while Marlena left for the powder room. They spent the remainder of the evening, listening and drinking. Near midnight they decided to drive back to Marlena's for some passion and just plain ole good sex.

Janey and Claire had a wonderful time alone, giggling and talking about boys. No one bothered them, no phone calls; no killers attacking from the backyard - just two friends sharing quality time. Janey helped Claire pick up plates and glasses, empty chip bags and candy wrappers. They straightened the pillows on the sofa from the pillow fight they had earlier. Janey ran for her house, while Claire watched her, just in case the killer they missed spotting was still around.

Claire realized, when she looked at the clock and it was nearly 11:00pm, that her homework was still in her backpack and incomplete. Oh well, maybe she can get to it later, or maybe she will get up earlier and do it. She turned off all the downstairs lights and headed for her bedroom. She was tired. In her bathroom, she slipped on her yellow satin pajama shorts and matching top. She brushed her teeth and flossed. Then she brushed her hair several strokes and got into bed. She left the light on in her bathroom for her peace of mind. The room was a bit warm, so she lay on top of her cover sheet hugging her pillow. Within 5 minutes, she was sound asleep and dreaming about a life in the country with Kim and her Dad.

David's driving was exceptional for a drunken man behind the wheel, but he managed again to get from one side of Memphis to the other without killing himself or anyone else in the interim. He was lucky and he knew it. One day he was not going to be so lucky. Some well-trained police officer would spot him and notice the weaving and erratic driving was the sign of a drunk behind the wheel. He would go to jail, have a day in court and probably get slapped with a fine and a tap on the wrist with a warning about any future incidences would mean stiffer penalties. He parked the car in the driveway, just barely missing the closed garage door.

Marlena was 2 sheets to the wind. No maybe 4 sheets would better describe her drunken condition. After David parked, she fell from the car when the door was opened. She laughed hysterically as David attempted to help her back on her feet. They both stumbled and staggered up to the side door of the house. Marlena tried, but failed to insert the key, so David took the key and opened the door. They made it as far as the sofa in the great room when Marlena tripped on her own feet and landed face-first on the cushions. She broke out in laughter again and pulled David down on top of her and kissed him hard on the mouth. He responded.

She pushed him off, "Will you go upstairs in my room and get our little package in my nightstand? I don't think I can make the stairs. I'll kill myself." She had always referred to the lubricated Trojans she kept on-hand as the 'little package'.

"Alrighty, then." Slurring his words as he staggered to his feet.

David stumbled nearly falling and busting his head on the table next to the sofa. Finding the stairs in the dark, he grasped the handrail, tightly, pulling himself one step at a time up to the top. Marlena had completely passed out before he touched the first step.

He staggered and finally found the top stair. He walked softly, weaving and wagging. He stopped when he saw the light from Claire's bedroom reflecting in the hallway. Was someone home? He had no clue. David walked slower as he approached the room. The door had been left open halfway and the light from the bath illuminated the room with a soft glow. He looked into the room. He saw a figure lying across the bed. It was Claire, but, in his condition, he didn't realize this was Claire's room or who this was on the bed. She was uncovered lying on her stomach. The satin shorts she was wearing had worked a little higher on her body, exposing more of her backside and the delicate yellow panties she wore. The satin top had been pulled up displaying a budding young woman. Claire was developing faster than most of the girls her age. David stared. He moved into the room, getting closer; much closer than he should. Claire moved and he froze. She moved one leg up higher, giving him a better view than before. He turned, frightened, ready to leave, but he continued to stare.

Beads of sweat formed on his forehead. He moved closer. He was within inches of the bed, now. His shadow from the bathroom light fell across her delicate young body. He stared through bloodshot eyes. He reached to the front of his trousers. He was aroused. Carefully and quietly, his pants were lowered and he reached for her satin shorty PJ bottoms. Within seconds he tore off her clothes, flipped her over and was on top of Claire, pounding away, destroying her life.

Claire awoke with such pain, a pain she had never felt before. Suddenly, she saw this face, this man; a hairy face she thought she recognized, close and ugly with a breath reeking of liquor. Waking so quickly from a deep sleep, it took a few seconds to get her bearings. She thought at first that this was a terrible nightmare, a bad dream and that she would wake up in a minute; just to try and forget it. But, she realized that this was not a dream. She was being violated in the worst way. There was a man, a horrible creature on top of her, doing something to her that she had only talked about with Janey. She started to scream and scream loudly, but a hand quickly covered her mouth and nose. She could barely breathe. David continued destroying her life. She wanted her Daddy to save her, but she couldn't call out to him. The rapist was relentless. Claire tried so hard to fight him off, but he was stronger, even as drunk as he was, he held her tight.

She could only watch his eyes, watch as he pushed himself into her over and over again until it was over for him. She watched; she cried and finally, she went away to a safe place. She became limp all over, not moving, no longer fighting him, no longer resisting. She just wasn't here anymore.

David grunted and pulled himself up from the bed, reached for his pants and ran down the stairs, stumbling twice. Claire didn't move. She lay quietly on her bed, listening to sounds echoing from the house below. The outside door in the great room opened and closed quickly. A car engine cranked and she heard the car drive away, squealing tires as it pulled into the street. Claire blankly stared at the ceiling of her bedroom. She laid there for at least another 30 minutes before she even moved the first muscle. She was so scared he might return.

First, she looked at her open bedroom door. She quickly sat up, gathered her ripped bed clothes and walked slowly into the bathroom. She closed the door, locked it and pulled off her remaining clothes and hid them all in the lined trash can under the paper and soft drink cans. No one would find them. Reaching for the stopper, she placed it in the drain hole and turned on the water full force. A nice hot stream of water filled the tub and Claire slowly eased her body into the warmth and comfort, sitting and staring as the water ran. She filled the tub as far as allowed and turned off the faucets. Shampoo and soap were in the usual places and she instinctively reached for the Dial soap. A wash cloth was draped over the small towel bar on the side of the tub enclosure. She lathered the cloth and washed. She washed and washed until most of the bar soap had been used. She lathered and rinsed her hair several times. Afterwards, she lay back against the ceramic tub, lost in another world, another time. This world was one that was too bad to live in or remember. She remained in the tub until the water became room temperature. It was almost 2:00am. Claire suddenly sat straight up, pulled the plug from the bottom of the tub, pulled herself up and dried off. She found a clean set of underwear and pajamas. She dressed and began stripping the sheets and covers from the bed. She was fast and furious at the work. She rolled the bed coverings into a small round ball and pushed them into the laundry shoot located in the hall just above the laundry room downstairs. Claire found a fresh set of sheets in the linen closet. Not yellow, just plain white and she never noticed. She never made a sound. She never cried out. Her facial expression remained the same, static and lost.

Claire completed the bed, went to the door, closed and locked it. She turned off the bathroom light and went to her bed. She lay down, pulled the covers up to her neck and stared at the darkness of her room. A calmness and quiet fell over Claire, she began to drift away to a place where no one could hurt her again; a place she could feel safe. Her eyes became fixed in a stare; unmoving, unreachable. Not a stare that can be broken with a loud noise or with a quick slap on the face, but a stare with pain, with the look of a lost soul. She had been tragically violated, something so horrible, that she refused to remember it. It would be blocked from her mind. The full moon had risen and the light from her window reflected on the face of a girl who was living somewhere other than here in this room. She remained that way for another hour before her natural body functions allowed her to sleep. Her eyes finally closed.

Marlena woke the next morning in the same position as she was from the night before. Her head pounded with the pain of a hangover. Her eyes squinted at the morning sun beaming through the sliding doors to the back yard. The pain was greater when she moved, so she tried not to move. Finally in a sitting position and the dizziness subsiding, she looked at the clock as the readout changed over to 9:12. "Oh, shit" she muttered. "I'm going to be so late."

She looked around trying to figure out why she was in the great room and where she had been last night. She did remember having dinner with David, but after that it was a blur. She's been drunk before, but this one was too much for her to handle. She finally realized that she might have a drinking problem. She struggled to her feet and headed for the kitchen to find a dose of Excedrin and some strong coffee. The bottle of pain reliever was in the drawer next to the silverware. Only two were left. She normally took three on occasions such as this. That would have to do. She filled a glass with enough water to swallow the tablets. As she was finishing the last drink of water, Cliff came in the back door. He stared at Marlena, almost snickering at her appearance.

He looked down at her, "Looks like you had a good one last night?"

She cut a sneer at him, "Shove it."

"Thought you were out of town?" he asked.

She turned and balanced herself on the sink counter. She pushed the hair hanging across her face up and onto the back of her head. She watched Cliff as he went to the table to lay the morning paper down.

"You want some coffee?" he asked getting the coffee pot from under the Mr. Coffee machine.

She dropped her hands to give herself a push off from the counter. "Yes and make it strong. And, I thought you were out of town until Friday."

"Well, I finished faster than I thought. I left early this morning and drove all the way. Claire at school?"

"I don't know, I suppose. She stayed with Amanda last night. I guess she took them to school this morning."

Claire's mind heard a familiar voice. It was a voice she yearned to hear; a voice only her Daddy could make. She opened her eyes from the natural sleep. She could see and she could breathe, but she could not speak. She could not think or reason as she used to do. Claire was gone. Only a window to her mind remained; her eyes. The voice of her father brought her back into the world in which she refused to live, but it was the world where her Daddy lived and the beast lived in Daddy's world too. She lay still in her bed and stared into space; into the space of her new reality.

The coffee was ready and Cliff poured them both a cup and joined Marlena at the breakfast table. She reached for the coffee and took a careful sip without adding her usual cream and two sugars. Cliff watched her as he fixed his own and took the first drink.

Cliff said, "Are you OK? Forgive me for saying so, but you do look worse than I have seen you before after a night of drinking."

Marlena moaned and lifted the cup for one more drink. "No, I'm not." She reached for the sugar and creamer and dumped a portion into her cup.

"Is there anything I can do?"

"Yeah, get me a new head." She said as she stroked her temples with her fingers.

"Well, you've had a few too many before. This looks like the worst."

"Tell me something I don't already know."

Cliff held his cup with both hands and drank silently.

Marlena looked up at Cliff and he was watching her intently. He was thinking of the times they had spent together, but years ago. A time before Claire was born, when they talked for hours over coffee. Marlena almost cried, "I have a problem, Cliff. I think I'm an alcoholic. No, I know I am and I'm scared. I don't know what to do."

Cliff put down the cup, ready to move next to Marlena, to give her some comforting words, and the phone rang.

"It's probably my office, wondering where I am." She put her head on her crossed arms. "Tell them I'm on my way. Make up something."

Cliff reached for the phone and pressed the button, "Hello?"

"Yes, this is Cliff Richards."

"She's not sick, at least not that I know of, she stayed with a friend last night."

"OK, I'll check into it."

He hung up the phone and looked at Marlena. "Claire never made it to school…."

Cliff reached for the phone directory and looked up Amanda's number and dialed.

"Hello, Amanda, Cliff Richards….."

"Fine.. Amanda, the school just called and said Claire never made it…"

"Where did she go? ……."

"Here? Are you sure?"

"I'm sorry, of course you are. Let me do some checking. I'll let you know."

"Ok bye."

Marlena, for the first time in Claire's life, had a concerned look on her face, even through the hangover. "Where's Claire?"

"I don't know. Amanda said that Claire told her you weren't going out of town and that she wouldn't have to spend the night there. She was staying here with you."

"Well, I never told her that."

"I didn't say that you did. I just want to find our daughter."

He jumped up from his chair, knocking it over into the floor and ran to the upstairs hallway. He reached Claire's bedroom door and found it locked. He
knocked and knocked hard. "Claire? Claire are you in there, sweetie. Come open the door." He knocked again and again calling out Claire's name.

Finally he ran into his bedroom to get a hairpin that Marlena uses to hold back her hair when she puts on makeup. It was just the right size and diameter to insert into the emergency lock release hold on the opposite side of Claire's bedroom door. Cliff ran back down the hall and fell to his knees and pushed the blunt end of the pin into the hole. The lock clicked and he turned the handle. Almost afraid to go inside, he slowly opened the door. He first saw his daughter lying peacefully in her bed. She looked asleep, but then he saw she was awake. He went inside to the bed and sat down beside her.

"Why didn't you answer me, sweetie." He looked into her eyes. Cliff watched and saw no movement in her eyes. He waved a hand above her head. He snapped a finger.

"CLAIRE!!! CLAIRE!!! What's wrong baby?" He was yelling as the tears swelled in his eyes. He grabbed her and pulled her limp body to his and he held her. Claire could hear him and she wanted to speak, but she would have to come back to the beast's world. She wasn't ready for that.

The Excedrin had done its job and Marlena managed to make the stairs. She was standing in the doorway when Cliff screamed out Claire's name. "What's wrong, Cliff." She ran to his side. "WHAT'S WRONG WITH HER CLI…." She never got his name out before the back of his right hand knocked her off her feet. She stumbled and fell grabbing her cheek. "What did you do that for?" she was crying.

"WHAT DID YOU DO TO HER YOU BITCH!!" he was screaming at Marlena.
She backed up, in fear of another attack. "I didn't do anything to her. For God's sake, Cliff I didn't even know she was here."

Cliff held tight to Claire and rocked her, stroking her hair. He looked at Marlena on the floor rubbing the reddening cheek and moving a little further from his reach. "How do I know that. YOU don't even know what you did. You were too drunk to even know what you were doing. I've seen you that way before."

Marlena cried because she knew it was true. She didn't remember last night. Did she come home and find Claire here and do something to her as punishment for disobeying her or was she already like this. Marlena never remembered coming home so how could she remember Claire. Claire wasn't supposed to be here. She was supposed to be at Janey's house last night.

Cliff continued to comfort his child, "Go call 911. You can do that can't you?" he spoke softly and deliberately. Marlena shook her head in the affirmative and crawled until she reached the door where she pulled herself up to her feet. She ran down the hall to her bedroom and phoned the emergency number. After explaining the situation to the person on the phone, she ran back into Claire's room. Cliff was still holding her gently in his arms and singing to her softly. For the first time since she was born, Marlena was genuinely concerned about her daughter. She pulled the chair that was at Claire's computer desk and moved it close to the bed.

Softly she asked, "Cliff, what can it be?"

"I don't know, but I'm sure it had something to do with you, even though you don't have a clue because you were too drunk."

Marlena dropped her head into her hands and began to sob. Cliff was not moved.

He continued to stroke Claire's hair, her arms hanging loosely at her side and her face pressed against Cliff's chest with eyes wide open and drool falling from her lips. Cliff looked at Marlena with contempt, "When Claire and I were out on Sunday and even the night before, I sensed something was very wrong. She was in some sort of trance even that night. I didn't understand. On Sunday, I asked her what was wrong, but she refused to answer. When I asked if YOU did something she clamed up, wouldn't look at me. That told me right there it was you. I don't know what, and you, more than likely don't know either because you're drunk most of the time, but I know you did something." He turned his attention back to his little girl, holding her closer.

Marlena just looked at him. She couldn't answer and she couldn't defend herself. He might be right. The squeal of the siren grew louder as the ambulance approached the neighborhood. When the orange and white vehicle stopped with blue lights flashing, many neighbors were coming out of their homes. The attendants pulled the gurney from the back of the ambulance and wheeled it into the house. Marlena was at the door to let them in and direct the men to the upstairs.

Claire was taken to the Emergency room at Methodist Hospital in Germantown. The doctors first tested Claire for drugs that might be in her system and found none. All the medical tests revealed nothing that might cause the stupor which was affecting Claire. She spent several days in a private room at the hospital. Cliff decided to bring in neurologists and psychiatric specialists, who only determined that Claire was affected by an unknown trauma and had regressed into her mind to ease the pain of reality. Claire's condition never changed over the next 3 months. She was fed with a tube and her body was beginning to wither away. Her body forced sleep at different times of the day, but her condition remained the same. She was finally admitted to Rolling Hills where she remained until now.

Chapter Seven

Friday
October 19
Rolling Hills Mental Hospital

Katie waved at her precious granddaughter sitting quietly in the window overlooking the grounds. She never saw Claire looking back at her. Katie opened one side of the double-door entrance and walked into a magnificent domed entrance, like those found in better museums. An attendant was seated at a desk just to the right of the entry doors. She smiled at Katie as she approached the desk.

"I'm here to visit with Claire Richards."

The small gray-haired woman turned the sign-in log around for Katie to fill out. "Just write your name here, dear. Claire is just upstairs in room 6. She hasn't changed, though."

"I figured as much, but I want to see my granddaughter just the same."

"Yes, I have 3 of my own." She looked down at the log when Katie was finished.
"Thank you, Katie is it?"

"Yes, that's right"

"Just up the stairs over to your left. At the top, go down the hall and turn right. Room six is at the end of the hallway." She pointed to the staircase.

"Thank you so much, I've been here before." Katie stated, walked to the stairs, climbed and turned right. The door to room six was open and as she approached, she saw the back of Claire's head sitting quietly in her chair; the way she had sat for so long. Katie's heart broke every time she visited. She missed the vibrant smile and perkiness of her beautiful granddaughter. Katie tapped on the door and went inside. The clouds had given way to more sun and the light shone through the window. Claire sat still continuing to stare out into the world she once knew.

After storing her purse and umbrella, Katie pulled a chair that had been left next to the bed and sat down to Claire's right, but facing her allowing the sun to brighten Claire's face. She didn't want to miss a single expression. She was close enough to lift one of Claire's hands and she smiled, trying to think of anything to say that hadn't been said before.

"Well, hello my sweetie. I'm so glad to see you. I really missed you while Grandpa Bill and I were gone on our cruise."

Katie usually would ramble on about anything in her previous visits. The doctors told the family that familiar voices and faces would sometimes spark a nerve in these types of cases; so she talked.

"Would you like me to tell you about it?" Katie paused. "I thought you would. Well, your grandpa and I left Memphis for a cruise around the Mediteranian Sea about 6 weeks ago. It was a long cruise and the ocean was so wonderful and cool. We stopped at many places, maybe some that you have studied at school. At night we would have so much to eat and then we went to many, many shows that they had on the ship. Your grandpa really needed to get away. He has worked so much. "

Rising from the chair, Katie walked to the window to marvel at the brightness that comes after the rain. She continued to speak to Claire. "Your grandpa needed a vacation almost as much as I did. He loves you so much he...."

"Grammie?" Claire softly spoke in a scratchy tone from a throat that hasn't uttered a word in six months.

Katie stopped and quickly spun around to see that Claire's beautiful eyes were focused on her own. She ran to her little Claire and fell to the floor. "Claire, my precious, you spoke."

Claire followed her with tearful eyes and looking around the dingy room. "Where am I, Grammie?"

Tears were falling from Katie's red eyes. She wrapped her arms around Claire and held her tight. "Oh baby, we thought we lost you forever."

"Where did I go? Where's Daddy? What is this place?"

"Hold on baby." She reached into purse to retrieve the cell phone Bill had given to her. She never liked it and rarely turned it on. It was just in case an emergency came up on the highway or whenever she needed help. This was one of the best times she could think of to use it. She flipped it open and pressed the on button. Now, how did that salesman tell me to make a call?

"I'm calling your Dad, right now!" Katie dialed Cliff's cell phone number. At least she had memorized his number, and then she held Claire's hands in hers. Tears continued to fall. Claire was simply confused, unaware that six months of her life was lost to her. Maybe that was for the best. Maybe she needed the healing time.

Cliff pulled the phone from the belt clip and answered on the second ring. "Hello?"

Katie's voice was shaky. "Cliff" she couldn't speak between the sobs of joy.

"Katie? Is that you? Are you all right?"

She composed herself a bit more. "I was visiting, Claire..." she lost her composure again.

"Katie? Did something happen to Claire? KATIE?" He began to shout.

Katie looked at Claire and softly whispered, "It's your Dad. Talk to him." and to Cliff she said, "Hold on Cliff, talk to someone here."

Just the sound of that worried Cliff. His heart raced faster. What had happened to his Claire, his Tweetie?

Katie handed the cell phone to Claire. She looked at it and then to her Grammie, who encouraged her to speak. Claire put the phone to her ear, "Daddy?"

The sound of Claire's voice coming through the phone weakened Cliff's knees. An explosion of emotions flew through his body. The cup of coffee he was holding slipped from his hand, covering his suit pants and new shoes with hot coffee when it hit the floor of his office. He reached for his desk, holding on with one hand while moving to his chair to sit.

"Daddy? Are you there?" Claire asked again.

Cliff could not hold back the tears. He sobbed uncontrollably into the phone. "Claire? Is that really you, baby?"

"Yes, Daddy! I'm a little frightened. I don't know where I am. Grammie is here, though, but I don't know this place."

Cliff wiped his eyes on the sleeve of his shirt. "Just hold on Tweetie, Daddy is coming right now. It will take a little while for me to get there but I will be there real soon, I promise. You visit with Grammie until I get there OK? Then we'll explain everything."

"OK, Daddy, but hurry, please!"

"I will baby. Let me talk to your Grammie for a second."

"OK." Claire handed the phone to Katie. "He wants to talk to you, Grammie. He's coming to get me."

Katie took the phone and walked across the room that would allow a little more privacy. "Cliff?"

"Katie, for God's sake what happened?"

"I don't know, Cliff. I was telling her about our trip, you know, just talking like I've done many times before. This time, she spoke. It was like she just woke up. Cliff, she doesn't know anything, at least I don't think so."

"Please, keep her company. Keep her talking. I am on the way now. It should take me about 45 minutes to get there. See if a doctor or nurse is around, too." Cliff rose from his chair while he continued to speak and walked to the door. "I will call a few people on my way. Do you know if Marlena might be home?"

"I don't know, but I have her cell number. Hang on I'll get it from my purse." Katie retrieved the purse she had hung on the back of her chair. Claire watched in wonder as Grammie rummaged through the bag.

"Here it is. 555-4322. I don't know the area code, but I guess it is the same as all of Chicago."

"I know it. OK, let me talk to Claire again."

Katie handed the phone back to Claire. "Daddy wants to talk to you."

Claire took the phone. "Yes Daddy?"

"Baby, I am almost to my car. It will take me about 45 minutes to get to you. Just have a nice visit with Grammie until I get there, OK?"

"OK, Daddy. Are you bringing Kim?"

Cliff stopped. After all this time, she still remembers and wants to see Kim. Telling Claire that he and Kim are already married will be easy, yet hard because she will not understand what has happened to her. "No, Tweetie. She will see you later when I bring you home, OK?"

"Alright."

"OK, see you soon. I love you, Tweetie. Bye."

"I love you, Daddy. Bye."

She clicked the talk button on the cell phone to turn it off. She held it for a few seconds, just staring. She handed the phone to Katie and looked sadly into her grandmother's face. "Grammie, what is the place? Why am I here?"

"Baby, it is kind of a long story." She pulled the chair closer to Claire's and took her hand. "You have been here for quite a while now. You've been sick."

"I don't remember being sick." Claire was puzzled.

"Well, it wasn't sickness." Katie thought for a second. "Do you know what it means to be in a coma?"

"Yeah, have I been in a coma?"

"It was like that, but you have been more in a trance than in a coma. It's hard to explain. Maybe we can wait until your Dad gets here. Would you like to get cleaned up and change clothes?"

Claire looked down at the ragged gown she had been wearing daily for over six months. "Ugh. This is so horrible. Where are my clothes?" She started to stand, but her legs were so weak, she fell back into the chair.

"Whoa! What's up with me, Grammie? I can't stand up."

Katie stood next to her and put one arm around Claire's shoulder and the other to help lift her. "Here baby, just lean on your Grammie. You need to walk around a bit, to get some circulation back into your legs. They haven't had much exercise lately."

Claire held on tightly to her grandmother as she took small steps around the room. She was panting with exhaustion after only 5 minutes. Katie helped her back into the chair.

Katie asked, "Would you like some water? Maybe I could also get you a cool wash cloth and you can wipe your face."

"Yes, that would be nice."

Katie went into the small bathroom and rinsed the only wash cloth she could find. She grabbed the towel and looked at the clothes hanging in the open closet. The same yellow outfits that were left six months ago still hung neatly on the bar. She grabbed a blouse and pants. She pulled a chair even closer and laid the clean clothes over the back of her chair. "Here, let me wash your face, baby."

Claire closed her eyes as Katie ran the cool soft cloth over her face. It felt good. "Grammie, I want to take a bath. I feel so dirty in this thing I have on. Can you help me."

"Sure I can. You wait here. I'll start some water." Katie returned to the bathroom. The tub really needed a good scrubbing itself, but that would have to wait. She plugged the drain and turned on the faucets until a nice warm stream filled the tub.

Claire had found some renewed strength and managed to get to her feet and walk half way across the room when Katie came back to help her. "Well, it looks like you are getting a little better. Do you need my help getting in the water?"

"I don't know. Just be by in case." Claire walked the rest of the way to the bathroom on her own. Slow steps, but on her own. Katie closed the door and waited on the bed. The hospital gown was easy to remove. Claire had some trouble with her undergarments, but she finally was able to step into a warm bath. Something she had not done so long now, but she had no clue how long. Claire leaned back with her head resting on the back edge of the tub. Grammie had left the wash cloth on the edge of the tub. She found the soap, lathered the cloth and gently washed away all the pain from her weak body.

"Claire are you doing OK?" Katie called from outside the door.

"Yes, I'm fine."

“I am going to the nurse station, OK. I’ll be right back. Don’t try to get out by yourself until you know I’m back in your room.”

“OK. I just think I’m gonna lay here a while anyway.” Claire closed her eyes.

Katie left and hurried back down the stairs to the nurse attendant that helped her sign in earlier. The lady was busy with charts and listening to a small radio on the table behind the desk. The elderly lady had a name badge on, ‘Gladys’ was neatly embossed in the center. Katie had never noticed it before. “Excuse me, Gladys? Is there a doctor or nurse on duty, today?”

“Why yes ma’am, there is a doctor on today. Dr. Stanley Wilcox, I believe. Is something wrong?” she asked inquisitively.

“No, everything is right. My granddaughter is awake and speaking. Can you get the doctor?”

Gladys dropped her pencil. “No!! Praise God! That precious child. Yes, dear, I’ll find Dr. Wilcox right away.” The little woman slowly rose from her chair and walked into the hall leading to what Katie assumed were offices for staff and doctors.

“I’ll be back in the room. Please tell him to hurry.” Katie turned and hurriedly walked to the stairs.

Gladys was picking up speed and turned to wave Katie on. “I will dear. Go tend to that child.”

Cliff had already run two red lights and exceeded every speed limit on his way out of Memphis. His mind echoed the sound of his little girl’s words, spoken for the first time in months. He slowed down the car, allowing reason to take over. If he was pulled over for a traffic violation, that would only add more time to the trip. He pulled the cell phone off his belt and dialed Kim's number. She had left the day before for a three day business trip to Atlanta. She answered on the third ring.

"Hey Sweetie, what a surprise" as she saw Cliff's name on the caller id.

Cliff was getting choked with tears again. He couldn't speak.

Not hearing a reply but hearing the muffled sounds of sobs, she spoke again with concern. "Cliff are you alright?"

"It's Claire." He blurted out.

"Oh, God! What's wrong?"

"She's awake, baby. She's awake and talking."

"Oh my God, when?"

"Katie was visiting and she just woke up out of her trance and starting talking, but Katie doesn't believe she knows anything that has happened."

"Where are you, Cliff?"

"I'm on the way. I'll be there in about 30 more minutes or so."

"I'll catch the next flight back."

"Please do! She was asking to see you, baby. She remembers you!"

Kim's heart was overjoyed and her eyes filled with tears. "Oh, Cliff, I wish I was there now. I'll cancel everything that I have going today. I should be able to catch the 5:10 back to Memphis. Maybe earlier. My car is at the airport. Call me when you get there. I want to talk to her."

"I'll call you as soon as I know something. I love you so much. Hurry home. We got our Claire back."

"See you later today. I love you, too. Bye!"

"Bye sweetie."

Cliff was just approaching the Millington city limits. He knew he had to call Marlena, but what would he say? How would she react to the news her daughter is alert and talking after being trapped for 6 months in a stupor that hopefully, now the doctors can unravel. Would she greet the news with great joy, or would she accept it as one of ridicule and callus disregard? After all, she never did care for Claire as she grew up. Cliff retrieved the phone from the center console between the seats and dialed the number that Katie had given him earlier. Four rings and the answering machine picked up on the call.

" . . . . . . and if you leave your name and number we will return your call as soon as possible." The message ended. Cliff thought that Marlena sounded much more pleasant on that tape. Much like the woman he married many years ago.

The beep sounded. "Hi . . . . . Marlena, this is Cliff. It's kind of urgent we talk. It's about Claire. Call me tonight after 7:00. Bye."

That was quick and easy, but Cliff was concerned the message might cause panic. But again he reminded himself that this was Marlena and he was talking about Claire, the little girl she had no love for as she grew. The little girl she ignored and forgot too many times; the child who looked to her mother for guidance and got none. Anyway, he will get more details about Claire's condition when he gets there and speaks with someone on the medical staff. He looked at the clock on the dash. About 20 minutes more.

Katie was waiting on the bed when Claire opened the door to the bathroom. She had managed to get her clean, well not so clean, clothes on by herself. Holding onto the doorframe, she waved to her Grammie for help. Katie jumped quickly to her feet and grabbed Claire just as she was about to fall. She led her to the bed and sat her down. Katie picked up Claire's legs and moved them onto the bed.

"Claire, you almost fell. Are you OK?" Katie asked as she sat on the edge of the bed.

"I was just a little dizzy, Grammie. I guess I got up too fast."

"Well, you just lie here for a few minutes. I spoke with the nice lady downstairs, Gladys was her name. She is finding the doctor so he came come check you out. You know you're quite a celebrity around here." Katie was holding Claire's hand.

Claire lifted her finger and curled it backwards, signaling Katie to come closer. She wanted to whisper. "Grammie, I looked at myself in the mirror a minute ago. I'm so skinny. What happened to me?"

Katie smiled and patted her hand reassuringly. "I know you are my precious. How about we start putting a little more on those bones." She reached for her purse and pulled out a Snickers bar. Claire always liked Snickers and Katie managed to bring a fresh one every time she visited, just case in this day came.

Claire tore into the wrapper and took a huge bite. She didn't realize how hungry she was.

"Slow down baby. Take it slow." Katie said with a smile.

Claire chewed and swallowed the first and managed to only take a little second bite. "Grammie? " she said with muffled mouth. "Where am I?"

Katie looked down at her hands, searching for the right words to tell an 11 year old girl that she is in a mental hospital and six months of her life had passed by. She looked at Claire while she pulled herself up and leaned against the back of the bed.

"Dizziness gone?" Katie asked.

"Yeah, a lot better. Tell me what's going on."

"What is the last place and events that you can remember?"

"I remember my birthday party when you and Grandpa Bill came over with all my friends there. Then Daddy had to go to Jackson for a meeting and I spent the night at Janey's. And . . . . ." Just then she recalled the night she went back home for something and her Mom and some guy made love on the couch; right there in their home. Claire was silent.

Katie looked a bit worried. She thought for a second Claire might be slipping back into a trance. "Claire?"

Claire snapped at the sound of her name. "Oh, I'm sorry, Grammie. I was just thinking of stuff I did. Yeah, I spent the night at Janey's and Dad came home late and he took me home cause I fell asleep. I was so mad at him. I remember that, but the next day he took me to Ihop. And I met .. . . ." She stopped again, thinking very hard about meeting Kim for the first time.

"Claire, go on."

"OK." Claire was unsure if she should tell her Grammie about Kim. Maybe she already knew anyway. How would she approach this? "Grammie?"

"Yes"

"Did you know that Daddy was in love with someone else?"

Katie looked very surprised, but not at the news her granddaughter had sprung on her, but the fact that she even knew. She smiled at Claire and stroked her still wet hair. "Yes, dear. I knew."

"It was Kim right?"

"Very right. How do you know this, Claire?"

"Because Daddy and I had breakfast with Kim on that Sunday. And then we spent the whole afternoon together. I remember how happy I felt. Grammie, I know Mom is your daughter, but she never made me feel as happy as Kim did. I'm glad Daddy found Kim. He deserves her." She dropped her head, still going over the memories in her brain.

"Is that all you can remember?"

"Yes . . . . well other than I was alone most of the week until Daddy got back, but I don't remember him ever getting back. That's just it. So what is this place?"

"This place is called Rolling Hills. It's a hospital for patients who need long time care."

"Long time? Grammie? Claire paused. "How long have I been here?"

Katie's eyes met Claire's. "3 months here, but you have been like this for the last 6 months"

Claire began to cry soft tears and Katie held her close. She stroked her hair while rocking her in her arms. Claire's head was tucked deeply into the folds of her grandmother's embrace. Softly she asked, "What day is this Grammie?"

Katie continued to caress Claire's hair. She looked briefly out of the window, noticing the bright yellow, orange and brown leaves remaining on the trees. Laying her cheek against Claire's head, she whispered, "Its Friday, October the 19th."

Claire remained quiet, content to be held by her Grammie and wiped the remaining tears from her eyes.

Cliff hurriedly parked the car. He was feeling a sort of nervousness that couldn't be explained, like the first time he was meeting his own daughter. What would he say? How could he explain why she was here? He crossed the grounds, ignoring the sidewalks and taking the steps to the front door two at a time.

Gladys was back at her reception desk, reading an old Reader's Digest. Cliff nearly busted the door when he pushed it open. Gladys looked up from her book, took off the reading glasses. "Why Mr. Richards. So nice to see you. I guess you've been told the good news about Miss Claire."

"Yes Gladys, thank you." He said quickly while rushing to the stairway.

Gladys raised a hand to try and get his attention, "The doctor is on the way in Mr. Richards. He'll be here in about 30 minutes I suppose." Then she mumbled quietly to herself. "And I guess you never heard me. No one ever hears me."

Cliff walked quickly down the landing to Claire's room. The door was open and he noticed Katie sitting on the bed holding Claire. He stopped at the opening of the door and noticed that Claire was wearing her own clothes. She looked so frail, so thin. With unhurried steps, he went into the room. Katie noticed him out of the corner of her eye. She smiled and lightly rocked her head as a motion to come over. She placed her two fingers under Claire's chin and lifted her face to meet her father's own smile. Tears were already flowing from Cliff's eyes. In an instant, Claire saw the all too familiar face she had only carried in her mind for so long. She wanted to jump up and run into his arms, but the strength was gone from her body. She could barely manage to stand with Grammie's help.

Cliff ran to her and lifted her so tenderly into his arms. He hugged her with all the love a father could give his daughter. She wrapped her arms around his neck, kissing him on the cheeks over and over again. She was crying and laughing at the same time. Cliff sat on the edge of the bed and held her on his lap. Katie pulled a chair from the other side of the small room and sat next to them. She watched with an adoring heart at this moment. A moment everyone had been dreaming would happen. She thought of Marlena and how she should be here, too.

Through the tears and laughter, Claire said, "Daddy, I want to go home."

He laughed out loud, wiping his face on the sleeve of his shirt. "You got it, Tweetie. And the sooner the better."

Katie said, "We need to wait for the doctor to come in. Gladys called him. He was at home."

"I know" Cliff said looking at Katie. He lifted Claire from his embrace and looked into her swollen eyes. "Can you wait a few more minutes? We have to let the doctor check you out first. I promise you one thing, I won't be going anywhere."

"Do you know what happened to me, Daddy?"

"No, baby, we don't. We have always prayed that when you woke up, you could tell us."

"What's been going on for the, what . . . last six months or more?"

Cliff faced Katie, looking for support. She said while shrugging her shoulders, "Tell her everything. She'll find out anyway."

Claire said looking at Cliff, "Tell me what, Daddy. What's happened? Is something wrong with Kim?"

Cliff smiled. She had never forgotten Kim, even through all the trauma and half-comatose trance for six months. How would she react at the news he had to share?
He lifted her from his lap and placed her on the bed next to him. He searched for the words, for the correct tone of voice; words that were comforting and understanding.

"First, " he began with a slight tremor; "Your mother and I have been divorced for several months, now. Claire turned away and looked out the window. Her mother was not a favorite topic. Cliff continued, "She has re-married and moved to Chicago." He waited for a response, but none came. "And Kim and I got married."

At first, Claire didn't believe she heard right. She turned quickly to face her father.

"You what? You and Kim?" she said shaking.

She wasn't the least bit concerned that her mother was no longer around. She always wanted her to leave. "You and Kim are married?" She could not have smiled any broader. She grabbed her Dad's neck. "You're not kidding me are you, Daddy?"

Cliff was beaming, "No, I'm not kidding. Kim and I were married almost 3 months ago."

"Oh, Daddy, I'm so happy. Where is she? Why didn't she come? Does she live at home with you or did you get a new house?"

"She's in Atlanta. I called her on the way up here. She cancelled all her meetings and is catching the next flight back to Memphis. She should be home later tonight and yes, she lives in our house. Your Mom didn't want the house or any part of it."

"Oh, her. That's only right"

"Aren't you at all concerned about your mother?" Katie asked. "Aren't you interested in what has happened in her life? She's different, you know."

"Grammie, you know how she was, how she always treated me. I know she didn't love me. She never did. Even when I was born. It's the best thing that's happened in my life. I'm sorry, but it's the way it is. You were more a mother than she ever was."

"I know, baby. But, you know, she has changed a lot since you have been here. The most important of the changes, she has quit drinking and she has found a church that she really likes."

"Good for her."

There was a tap on the door frame. A tall man, early 50's, slightly graying hair, dressed in blue jeans, Adidas Running shoes and pull-over T-shirt. Dr. Wilcox came into the room, walking to the side of the bed. "I understand we have a patient that finally woke up."

Claire looked into an unfamiliar face, even though the doctor knew Claire very well. She said, "Are you the doctor who is going to check me out? "

"Why yes I am, Claire." He said sitting on the bed next to her. "By the way, I have been in to see you every week for a long time now, and you know this is the first time I can really meet you. How are you, Claire, my name is Dr. Wilcox." He held out a hand to shake.

Claire hesitantly held and shook the doctor's hand. "When can I leave Dr. Wilcox?"

"First, let me examine you, but on first appearances, I think you're going to be just fine." He said as he opened the medical bag and removed the stethoscope.

Dr. Wilcox worked gently and swiftly. He sensed the urgency that Claire was expressing to leave the hospital. He could find no abnormalities and Claire was in good health except for the loss of some weight, but he was sure she would take care of that very soon. "Well, Claire, I'm afraid I can't find a reason to keep you here and that you're OK to go home. I suppose I won't see much of you anymore after today, but maybe your Dad can bring you back for a visit?"

Claire smiled, "I don't think I would like that, but thank you anyway. Maybe you can come visit us."

"Now, that I would like. Can I please have a hug?" Dr. Wilcox reached out and Claire jumped from the bed and hugged him around the neck. Then she ran to Cliff who was waiting with Katie by the window where Claire sat for so many months.

Katie immediately began gathering Claire's remaining belongings for the trip home and told Cliff she would take Claire's possessions to his car. She was leaving before them to get the house ready. Cliff spoke briefly with Dr. Wilcox about final arrangements for the charges to be sent to his office and further treatment in Memphis. The walk through the hospital halls was so strange to Claire. She had never seen the first room or never met anyone on staff, even though they all knew her by name. Gladys got up to greet them when Claire reached the bottom of the stairs. She was almost in tears because of the wonderful news. Claire was just glad to be leaving. The ride home was non-stop chatter between Cliff and Claire. She had been filled in on all developments in everyone's life, all except why Claire was in the condition she had been for the last few months.

Cliff tried Kim's cell number several times, but assumed she was out of range or already on the plane heading back to Memphis. He wanted Claire to hear her voice.

Chapter Eight

The house was so familiar to Claire, so warm and inviting. She visually took in all the fall colored trees, the remaining flowers, and the row of hedges that she would jump when going to Janey's house and there it was. She wondered if Janey was at home. She should call her right away. Maybe she had a clue what happened. No one else did. Cliff pulled into the driveway and parked next to a car Claire had never seen before; a red Miata convertible with a beige top. A million memories were flooding through her mind, the birthday party, the sleepovers, and the pool and.. Suddenly she cringed. A bad memory broke through, a memory of a cheating wife and mother. She wondered if this house would always conjure up those nightmares and thoughts. She shivered. Cliff was holding her close with his arm gently wrapped around her and he felt the twinge in Claire. He sensed uneasiness in his daughter. He gently pulled her closer to his side, trying to reassure her that she was safe now; no one would hurt her here.

Cliff pulled into the garage and pushed the button to open the trunk. He got out and removed the bags Katie had packed at the hospital. Claire was a little apprehensive about getting out; like just she was learning to walk all over again. She felt a little unsteady. What feelings were going to fill her mind and body by coming back to this home she loved so much?

Cliff opened the garage entrance to the kitchen and dropped the bags next to the stairs and turned around to pick up Claire, who was just now coming into the kitchen. He pulled her close and said while spinning around, "Welcome Home, Tweetie. I have missed you oh so much." He carried her into the den and sat with her on the sofa facing the fireplace.

"What would you like to eat, just name it and we'll get it. Even if it's from China, I'll have it flown in." he hugged her again. She just giggled. She felt comfortable with her Daddy. He was her protection, her rock and mentor. She cherished him.

"Can we just have Mickey D's. I have been craving a Double Cheeseburger for about the last hour."

“You bet, and large fries and apple pies too. We’ll supersize it, too.”

Katie was upstairs getting Claire’s room freshened up when she overheard the conversation and chimed in as she walked down the stairs, “I hear that someone wants food from McDonald’s. I could go for a Big Mac myself, how ‘bout you Cliff? I’ll buy.“

“Well, since you put it that way, make it 2 Big Macs and a Double Cheese with fries and pies all around. You’re going to get it, too?”

Katie replied, “You bet. Give you and Claire a chance to catch up.” She grabbed her purse from the table and headed for the door.

Claire said, “Grammie, is that your red car out there?”

“Yep, sure is! It was a gift from your Granpaw. What’d ya think? Am I too old for it?”

“Naw, just right I would say.” Claire smiled.

Cliff smiled and said, “Take your time Katie and be careful.”

“Will do.” She blew Claire a kiss and went through the back door.

Cliff turned to Claire, “Would you like to go up to your room and look things over? Maybe take a shower before Grammie gets back?”

“No, I took a bath at the hospital, but I would like to go up to my room. Just want to make sure everything is still in place.”

Holding up two fingers, Cliff said, “Scouts honor, nothing was removed from the premises your majesty.”

Claire hit him on the arm. “Well, let’s go anyway.”

They both got up and headed to the stairs. Cliff grabbed the bags and followed Claire who was already near the top of the stairs. Her room was just down the hall. She could see the door was closed, maybe been it had been like that for 6 months or more. She felt stranger the closer she got to her room. What was wrong? She stopped suddenly, staring at the closed door to her room. Feelings welled up inside. Feelings she didn't understand.

Cliff nearly ran her over. He placed the bags on the floor next to the hall bathroom door. Claire remained motionless while staring intently at the opening to her old room. He dropped to his knees and looked straight into her face. Her eyes were fixed. She continued to stare.

"Oh, God! NO! Not again! Claire, what is it baby? What's wrong?"

In a voice that was Cliff had never heard before, Claire softly said while still gazing at the closed door. "I don't want that room anymore. I want another one." She turned and walked back downstairs leaving Cliff sitting on the floor of the hall in a daze, thinking to himself, *What just happened here*?

Marlena opened the back door of her home in Chicago, put the mail she was carrying on the kitchen counter and tossed the keys to her car in the catch-all box next to the canister set. The answering machine light was blinking 3 times indicating several messages were waiting. The messages would have to wait because she needed some caffeine. Since Marlena had quit drinking alcohol, she had switched her needs to Diet Cokes. She pulled a glass from the cabinet and filled it with ice. Opening the coke from the refrigerator, she filled the glass as she sat at the kitchen breakfast table. One huge sip seemed to satisfy her need at the moment.

She tossed her shoes by the door to the great room. She would pick them up later when she went upstairs for a bath. She stared at the blinking light on the answering machine next to her in the bookshelf. David would be one of the calls. He always calls with some excuse for being late, but she knew he was stopping at Butler's Bar to have a couple of drinks, just to wind down. Oh, God how she remembered those days back in Memphis. Daily AA meetings were a must for Marlena now. She could not make it through a week without sharing and listening to other recovering alcoholics. As hard as she tried, David would still not admit that he had a serious drinking problem, but she continued to ask him to come with her just one time.

She finished the glass of soda with one large swig and put the glass on the table. She pressed the play button on the blinking machine. The first message sounded through the small speaker. It was as she suspected. It was David.

‘ Hey! It’s me. Our meeting this afternoon lasted longer than we thought. I have a few more notes to complete before I leave. Be about an hour or more. See ya later.’

“Yeah, right!” Marlena said as she stared out the back window.

The next message was from the vet, reminded her that Max, her cocker spaniel, needed to come in for his shots. Marlena made a mental note to call in the morning.

‘Hi . . . . . Marlena, this is Cliff. It’s kind of urgent we talk. It’s about Claire. Call me tonight after 7:00. Bye.’

Marlena’s eyes opened wide. She turned with a jerk and looked at the machine like it was going to continue and explain what she just heard. Her heart began to race and she felt flush. She looked at her watch. It was only 6:30. What was wrong with Claire? Cliff sounded anxious and a little nervous. Maybe Claire had gotten worse or even …… She couldn’t bear that reality. Many more thoughts raced through her mind. Most were not good. To hell with waiting until 7:00, she reached for the phone and dialed Cliff’s number in Memphis.

In utter confusion, Cliff just watched Claire walk away. She seemed very coherent and alert. She sounded definite about finding another room, but why? What was wrong with her old room? Cliff left the bags on the floor and returned downstairs and found Claire sitting on the sofa in the great room. She was hugging the blue throw pillow close to her chest while she slowly began to rock back and forth. Cliff eased onto the couch next to her and put his arm around her shoulders. She leaned closer while tightly clutching the pillow, still staring at the space across the room. He stroked her hair with a loving father's embrace.

Softly he said, "Claire, can you explain what you meant by…."

The phone rang and startled Claire.

Cliff pulled her face gently toward his. "I'll be right back." Then he kissed her nose tenderly. "Don't go anywhere." She smiled and continued to rock with the pillow.

The phone rang a fourth time by the time Cliff picked up the receiver. "Hello?"

"Cliff, thank God you're home!! What's wrong with Claire?" Marlena sounded so scared.

Cliff paused a second. "Claire is home, Marlena."

Through the tears starting to fall Marlena shouted, "What!! When? Is she really OK? Has she said anything?"

"Get a hold of yourself. Katie was visiting this afternoon and Claire just starting talking again. Other than a little thin, she seems to be alright."

"What does she remember?"

"Nothing. At least not that she is telling. But I honestly believe her memory of the events that caused this will come back sooner or later."

"Has a doctor looked her over?"

“Yeah, one of the staff doctors at the hospital and gave her the OK to leave, but I am taking her to get a physical next week and will find a psychologist to get some therapy started soon.”

“Can I talk to her? Please!”

Cliff held the phone and looked at Claire sitting on the couch. She was too fragile at this moment to allow her to speak to Marlena.

“Cliff? Please?”

Cliff cleared his throat. “I don’t think that would be a good idea right now. She just got home and you and I both know that you may be the cause of her coma in the first place. Not that you remembered it anyway, but if she heard your voice, it might do something to her. I couldn’t deal with that right now.”

Marlena’s tears fell on the phone. “I know. Cliff I’m so sorry. If I could change things with her, I would.“ She paused. “But, I was never the mother to her that I should have been. I’m so afraid that all this was my fault.”

Cliff was not going to argue the point. “I just wanted you to know that she was out and her recovery to a normal life is beginning.” He could hear the sobs through the phone. “It will be alright, Marlena. I’ll tell her that you called. If she has any desire to speak with you, we’ll call back.”

Marlena had pulled a box of tissues off the bookshelf. She sighed deeply. “Cliff, I understand. You might not believe this, but I have been praying for her everyday. I truly miss her. I screwed up her life, your life and my own. I am trying very hard to get my life in order first, because I don’t want to be left out of her hers. Even if it just a little piece of her life. Please talk to her for me.”

“How’s David?” Cliff said trying to change the subject.

She paused. “About the same. I am not ready to give up on him yet. I have been clean and sober for 160 days now. David will not listen.”

"I respect you for what you're doing. Keep after him."

"Is my mother there?"

"No, she went to pick up some food for Claire. You want her to call you when she gets back?"

"Yes, please."

"Well, I need to get back to Claire. I promise I will tell her you called."

"OK, tell her I miss her." A pause. "No, tell her that I prayed for her. She wouldn't believe I missed her." Marlena thought another couple of seconds. "Well, just tell her I called. I think she would never believe that I actually pray."

"I will, bye"

"Bye, Cliff" she said and then hung up the phone. Marlena put her head on her crossed arms and began to cry uncontrollably.

Cliff hung up the phone and stared at Claire as she rocked herself slowly on the couch. He could only imagine she had done just this same thing at the mental hospital when she was alone in the dark. She needed this to comfort her when she felt stress or tension. She did the same when she was a toddler. He went to her side and lifted her slim, lanky body onto his lap. He pulled her head on his shoulder and rocked her as he held her tight. He began to sing some old lullaby he sang when she was an infant. Claire giggled. "That's really bad, Daddy."

Cliff smiled, but continued to sing. And Claire let him. She felt so safe in his arms. He was her protector from all the bad things. He was the only one she could count on.

The phone rang again.

Cliff thought to himself, '*Marlena, not again!*'

Claire jumped off his lap and tossed the pillow aside and lay her head on the armrest. Cliff went into the kitchen to answer the phone.

"Hello?"

Kim beamed into her cell phone. "Hey honey, I'm at the airport. I guess you're home. Is Claire doing OK?"

Cliff smiled from ear to ear. "Yes and we tried to call earlier, where were you?"

"I got the first ride to the airport I could. Things seem to fall into place at the right time. I got the first flight and before I knew it I was home. Can I talk to Claire?"

Cliff looked at Claire lying on the sofa and smiled. "You wanta talk to Kim?"

Just the mention of Kim's name totally flipped Claire's mood. She jumped to her feet, nearly falling to the floor as she rushed for the phone. Cliff held out the phone as she ran past snatching the receiver from her dad's hand. He could only smile as Claire leaned against the kitchen counter and began her conversation with her much loved stepmother. He thought for a brief moment how much Marlena had missed raising this adorable child. Cliff returned to the great room and sat on the sofa. He could not believe how well Claire had accepted Kim. Claire needed a mother in her life and Kim was going to fill the position quite well.

Claire and Kim continued to talk for the next 20 minutes while Kim waited on her luggage to appear from the plane. Katie had returned with a sack of hamburgers and french fries and setup the kitchen table with plates, napkins and of course ketchup. Cliff joined her at the table.

Katie sat next to Cliff and began emptying the sacks of food. She said, "I assume that's Kim on the phone?"

Cliff smiled, looking at Claire immersed in conversation, "Yes she is. By the way, Marlena called a few minutes ago. She wants you to call her."

"Did she speak to Claire?"

"No I haven't told her she called. I was waiting for the right time. We both know how she feels about her mother. I don't want to rush her into the past quite yet."

"I agree, but she needs to be told. Marlena is trying to change. She's made remarkable progress."

"I know she has and she deserves a better life. I want her to have contact with Claire, but I want that to be on Claire's terms."

Katie only nodded.

"Katie, there was something that happened earlier that I'm a little baffled over. When Claire and I were going upstairs to put her things away and get her room ready, she just stopped in the middle of the hall and froze in place. Then she said she wasn't going into that room. She wanted another room and then she just turned and came downstairs. At first I thought she was having like a relapse or something. I got real scared. What do you make of it?"

Katie looked concerned and thought a second. "Have you talked to her about it?"

"I was going to, but Marlena called and then Kim. She seems normal now, even better than before all this happened. I can't imagine why she acted that way or said what she did. Maybe I need to go through her room again. We haven't really done anything to her room since she has been gone."

"Let's talk to her together when she finishes with Kim." Katie offered.

Chapter Nine

The smell of opened hamburger wrappers and french fries was too much for Claire to resist. She said her good byes to Kim until she got home and sat next to her dad at the table. Katie had already made a place for her with the Big Mac and fries pour out onto a plate. Claire tore into the burger like a starving tiger.

Cliff looked at Claire and smiled. "Well, what did you and Kim have to talk about for so long?"

Mumbling through a mouthful of fries Claire said, "Nothing much, just talk. She'll be here in about 45 minutes. I can't wait! "

"Me too!" Cliff said and then looked at Katie and paused. "Your mother called a while ago." He watched her reaction. Claire acted as though she didn't hear him. She continued to eat.

"Claire, your mother called to check on you." He said again.

"I heard you."

"I told her that you could call her if you wanted to talk."

"Yeah, like that's gonna happen."

"But Claire ......", Cliff started to say, but Katie put her hand on his arm, and her eyes let him know it was alright and not to pursue it at this time. Cliff nodded in agreement.

No one spoke for a minute. Everyone, especially Claire, was enjoying their burgers. Cliff looked first at Katie and then put his burger down on the plate. He looked right at Claire and asked, "OK, which room do you want?"

Claire looked at him like he had lost his mind. "What do you mean, which room? Is there something wrong with my old room? You didn't clear it out did you?"

"No, but upstairs a while ago you said you wanted a different room."

Claire stopped eating and stared right at Cliff. "No I didn't. I haven't even been upstairs yet." She finished the last bite of her Big Mac and wiped her mouth with a napkin from the table.

Cliff was dumbfounded. He turned to look at Katie. She just shrugged her shoulders and took another bite of her burger. He wasn't going to push the issue, just yet. He would discuss this with the doctor in the morning. He watched as Claire finished her meal. She was so thin and pale. He knew that she would regain all her strength and weight in no time, but he was concerned that her mind had changed.

Marlena stepped out of the shower and reached for a towel hanging next to the door. The hot stinging pulses of water helped her feel somewhat better. After all these years of rejecting and ignoring the child she gave life to, Marlena was beginning to experience remorse for the decision she made to come to Chicago and marrying David. She truly loved him, but his refusal to accept help and attend the any AA meeting was causing her to rethink their relationship. She suggested he go to another session, but he refused to acknowledge that he had a problem. The thought of losing Claire had finally sunk in after she begun cleaning up her own life and quit drinking. She had developed a good friendship with several of the women who attend church with her. They prayed together quite often for Claire's recovery as well as Marlena's own recovery. In fact, her AA sponsor attended the same church. David refused to go to church. He was a non-believer and so far could not be budged from that belief. Marlena knew the first step was to help him see his problem with alcohol and get into treatment. Then he would think with a clearer mind and she could help him find a relationship with God.

With a towel wrapped around her hair, she put on her housecoat and lay on her king bed. The bedroom was dark and she didn't bother to turn on the lamp on the nightstand. The darkness soothed her and gave her comfort. Again the emotions from the news from Memphis filled her head and she began to softly cry. At this moment, she was feeling something in her heart, for the first time, something she had never felt during the past 11 years; she was missing Claire. She wanted so desperately to have a relationship with her daughter, but she didn't know how. She was never the mother she needed to be, nor wanted to be. Her career was first. Her love for Cliff had dissolved in a bottle of gin. She never felt love for Claire until this moment. It's too late, she thought, but yet there could never be a chance to mend this life with Claire while she was here so far away. She decided that Memphis was where she needed to be tomorrow. She had some time off coming from work. She would take it.

Marlena had made up her mind. She would fly to Memphis on the first available flight from O'Hare in the morning. David would have to understand. Cliff would not like it, but Claire was the one she must see. Claire was the one she wanted to reach out to. While grabbing for the phone, she pulled her purse from the nightstand and fumbled through it until she located the green address book at the bottom. United Airlines would have several flights throughout the day, just finding a direct to Memphis would be scarce since Memphis was a Northwest Hub and only 3 or 4 United flights flew into Memphis daily. She found the frequently used direct number to the United Reservations desk and punched in the number on the phone. She was surprised she didn't have the number memorized.

A pleasant voice answered on the second ring. "United Airlines reservations, how may I help you?"

"Hi, can you check for a seat available on the morning flight to Memphis from O'Hare?"

"Please hold", the voice said.

After several seconds, which seemed like minutes to Marlena, the kind voice reported, "Yes we have a first class only leaving at

6:42am and arriving at 9:30. All others are full. Would you like to reserve this seat?"

Marlena did not hesitate, "Yes, please book it." As a frequent flyer with United, Marlena had set up a special company account that contained all her data required to fly. She gave the pleasant person the account number and the transaction was completed within 3 minutes.

Marlena became apprehensive about the trip. What was she going to say? What if Claire refused to see her? What if Cliff refused? So many thoughts rushed through her mind. But, she was determined to rebuild, or actually begin building, a lasting relationship with her daughter, no matter what it cost.

David was her next call. She had to tell him the news of Claire's awakening. Regardless of what he said, she was going to Memphis. Nothing could stop her. She picked up the phone again and dialed David's cell number, hoping that he would answer and not ignore her when he noticed the name on the caller id.

Butler's was packed with the regular business men and women who would rather spend some down time tossing back a few shots rather than face the constant pushing and shoving trying to catch the next train to the suburbs. It was dark inside as usual with several cocktail waitresses busily moving from table to table collecting orders and tips. Only 2 stools were available at the bar and one was next to David, who covered his regular seat at the end, like Norm did on "Cheers". He had just finished his 3rd Jack and Coke and ordered another from Tony the bartender. Tony retrieved the empty glass and mixed the new drink and delivered to David, picking up the $5.00 cash David always paid; 4.00 for the drink and 1.00 for Tony. David was a good customer and Tony would take care of him. David lifted the glass and took one sip. He was already feeling the buzz from the first three. A familiar tune sounded from his coat pocket. It was the cell phone. He reached inside his suit coat and pulled out the ringing phone. He looked at the color screen revealing his home phone number and name. He knew it had to be Marlena calling to check up on him. He considered letting it ring or forcing the call to voice mail, but something told him that he needed to take the call.

David pushed the send button. "Hello?"

"David, its Marlena."

"I know, what's up. I'll be home soon."

"That's OK, whenever. I got to tell you something. Some good news."

David couldn't believe he was hearing right. She wasn't going to cuss him out because he was out drinking again. He tried to speak without the drinker's slur, but she knew what he was doing and he knew, too.

"Really? What's going on?" David said.

Marlena paused to find the words, "David..." another pause. ". . .it's Claire. She woke up and she's home."

David sat upright on the stool. "She what?"

"Yeah, she just woke up. She's going to be alright. Isn't that great news?"

"Yeah, sure, that's good news." David began to shift on the barstool. He moved the phone to his other ear. "Uhh, what has she said? Does she remember anything?"

"Cliff said he just got her home. As far as they know right know, Claire doesn't remember anything that happened."

"So, what is he going to do? Will she see a doctor?"

"I suppose. She needs to have therapy as soon as she can." Marlena paused again. "David, I hope I wasn't the cause of all this. I was so drunk the night before all this happened. I don't remember a single thing. I only remember waking up on the den sofa. I barely remember coming home."

David was beginning to sweat. The buzz from the Jack Daniels was quickly wearing off. He looked nervously around the room. "Where is she now?"

"She's at home with her father and my mother I suppose."

David was silent.

Marlena summoned the courage, "I'm going to Memphis in the morning. I've already made reservations."

David's eyes popped wider, "You're what? Going to Memphis, Why?"

"She's my daughter, David."

"Since when? You never wanted her."

Tears formed in Marlena's eyes, "Since I realized that I have been wrong the past 11 years, that I realized that I'm a mother of a precious little girl. That I want to be her mother and try to reconcile with her and at least be friends."

"You're dreaming Marlena. That'll never happen."

"Well, I'll never know until I try." She thought. "You could come with me, you know."

"And why would I want to do that. She's not my kid and if you stop and think about it, she's not yours either. You may have given birth to her, but from what I know about you, she certainly is not your daughter. At least as we know mothers and daughters should be."

Marlena began to cry again and through a tearful voice she said, "I'm going in the morning. I didn't expect you to go, but I hoped you would in some way, understand. But, I guess I was wrong. Are you coming home soon?"

David looked down at the last drink on the bar, "Yeah, I'll catch the next train out."

"I'll wait up, see you soon." Marlena hung up the phone and then dialed her office to leave a voice mail that she would be out of town on personal time starting tomorrow.

David held the phone for a few moments longer, caught up in pensive thought. He pressed the end button on his phone even though the connection had been severed when Marlena hung up. David had always been able to hold his liquor. Even though he might register over 0.10 on a Breathalyzer, he still could effectively drive with no problems, he could recall events from the night before. His mind was reeling back to a time in Memphis. He recalled a time when he and Marlena had been partying in the Beale Street bars and then back at home. Fuzzy memories were flooding his brain, some good, some not so good. It was going to hit the fan. He had to do something.

Tony came down to David. He watched his long time customer just sitting there. Something was wrong; he could tell. David was holding his glass just staring. "Are you alright, man?" Tony asked.

David jerked out of his memory trance and looked up into Tony's face. He looked at the glass in his hands, drank the last swallow and put the glass down on the bar. "Nothing, I'm OK... I gotta go." David slipped off the stool and left the bar for the train station.

Chapter Ten

Kim pulled into the driveway and parked her car next to Cliff's in the triple garage. She picked up her purse and left the luggage in the back seat, hurrying to the door. Claire had heard the sound of the car pulling up and had beat her to the door. They ran into each other's arms, crying, kissing and hugging one another. Cliff and Katie were wiping tears from their eyes as the two came into the great room. Kim was carrying Claire in her arms. She sat her on the floor next to Cliff.

"Let me look at you." Kim eyed her up and down. "We're gonna have to start feeding you young lady." She said teasingly.

"I know, I'm like skin and bones ya know." Claire said.

Cliff got up and kissed Kim tenderly and embraced her with a big hug. Claire watched with smiles ear to ear.

Katie rose and gathered the plates and glasses they had accumulated in the great room and placed them in the sink. She went to Cliff and Kim and gave them both a hug and said with a smile. "I'll leave you two alone, so you can begin some normalcy in your lives."

Cliff walked with Katie to the back door and told her. "Don't forget to call Marlena. Remember, she called while you were out and asked that you call her."

"I'll phone her on my way home."

"Good, thanks Katie for being there for me and especially for Claire. I don't know what I would have done without your help."

"You just take care of her, and yourself. I am only glad to do anything for my granddaughter. You have my number. Call me for whatever, OK? " she patted him on his arm and reached for another hug and kiss on the cheek.

Cliff opened the door for her and watched as she walked to her car. He waved and she waved back and he closed the door.

Kim wrapped her arms around her stepdaughter and held on tight. “Hey, why don’t we go upstairs and get your room ready and just lay around and do some good girl talk.”

Claire returned the hug and said, “That sounds like a great idea to me. I need to catch up on what’s been happening for the last 6 months. You know, the real stuff, because you know how Daddy is, he doesn’t remember anything.”

“Right, let’s go”, Kim said.

Claire looked at the back door, “What about Dad?”

“He’ll find us. But this is just girl talk. Men are not allowed.”

Claire giggled. “OK.”

They went arm and arm through the great room toward the stairs. Claire was dancing and skipping with joy in her heart. Kim was becoming a girl again while going up the stairs. She truly loved this child as her own. They reached the top step and began their dance down the hall toward Claire’s room. Claire looked at the door to her room. The muscles in her neck slightly tighten. She began to sweat, but didn’t notice. The closer she got to the door, the faster she began to breathe. Her heart was racing. Kim was totally unaware of the changes occurring in Claire. They reached the closed door. Kim reached for the handle and turned the knob. She pulled Claire into the room behind her. Kim ran to the bed and jumped onto the comforter, laughing and patting on the bed next to her. Claire stood still staring with little emotion; not at Kim, but at the bed itself.

Kim said smiling, “Come on Claire, jump on the bed. Let’s talk.”

Claire did not move. She stared. Kim became scared. “Claire are you OK?”

No answer.

"Claire!"

Claire lost all feeling and strength in her legs. She fell hard to the floor. Kim jumped from the bed and ran to Claire sprawled out on the carpet. Kim fell onto her knees and pulled Claire's head into her lap. Claire's eyes were still open, but she had the same look she had in the hospital. Kim patted Claire's face gently, trying anything to wake her.

"Claire wake up, honey!" Kim began to cry.

Kim screamed at the top of her lungs, "CLIFFF!!"

Cliff was coming in from the garage when he heard the shrill scream coming from upstairs. He quickly looked to see that Kim and Claire were no where downstairs. His adrenaline went into high gear and he darted for the stairs taking two steps at a time. He saw the door to Claire's room open and surmised they were in there. He ran for the door. Cliff saw Kim holding his daughter in her arms, rocking gently and stroking her hair. Kim looked into Cliff's eyes for answers, but none were to be found.

Cliff sat next to Kim and pulled Claire into his lap. "Claire, honey, Tweetie, can you hear me." She only stared at the ceiling of the room. He spoke but continued to comfort his little girl, "What happened, Kim?"

Kim was still crying, "I don't know, Cliff. We were coming up here to do some girl talk. She just froze up when she came into the room. I couldn't get through to her."

Cliff stood and lifted Claire into his arms. "I'm taking her into our room. Come on." He left the room carrying his limp child. Kim rose and followed while wiping the tears from her face.

Cliff laid Claire across his bed and sat next to her. Kim sat at the foot of the king bed. "Cliff, what happened? Do you know?"

Cliff watched intently at Claire's breathing. He looked into Kim's eyes. "Baby, she did something weird earlier when I brought her up here to put her bags away. She refused to go in the room. It was so strange how she said it. It was like it wasn't Claire talking, but someone else. In fact, when I asked her about it later, she never remembered that she had said anything. It was like she wasn't here when she went upstairs."

"Do you think there's something in her room that caused all this?" Kim said.

"Baby, I don't know. I just don't know. But I do know, she is not going back in there until we figure this out. I need to get her back to the doctors. We can't go through this anymore."

The trains were on time for a change. David exited the platform for his car, still worried about the situation with Claire. He knows something happened and he knows it was wrong, but the details continued to be fuzzy. Traffic was fairly light and he managed to get home from the train station in 20 minutes, which normally took more than 45 minutes when the traffic lights catch him. He parked his car in the space next to Marlena's in the double garage of their suburban home. She wouldn't be expecting him so early and he suspected that she knew all along that he lied about working late so often. The slight buzz he consumed at the bar wore off before the train pulled into the station, but his breath would reveal his drinking habit. He couldn't remember the last time he faced Marlena sober. For the first time, a thought rushed through his mind that he might have a problem with drinking.

He put the key into the slot on the entrance door and went inside. The kitchen table was littered with the morning dishes he forget to put away. There was an empty Diet Coke can left on the counter; a sure sign Marlena was home. He stopped briefly to shuffle through the stack of mail. He was stalling.

He could hear Marlena coming down the stairs. He went into the living room and noticed Marlena as she sat her black pull behind suitcase beside the front door. A look of confusion came over David's face. He looked at Marlena, who was surprised to see David home so early.

David put his hands in his pockets and softly said, "What's going on, Marlena. Are you leaving me?"

Marlena smiled and walked over to hug her husband. "No, of course not. Did you already forget that I'm going to Memphis in the morning?" She realized that he was probably wasted when she told him the first time and he just didn't comprehend what she had said. Her arms sensed tension in his body. "Are you OK?" she said looking up into his face. His eyes would not meet hers. He pulled away and walked over to the sofa and sat down.

"I'm OK. What time is your flight?" he asked.

"6:42 so I have to get some sleep. Did you want to drive me to O'Hare or should I leave the car in long term parking."

David was in deep thought.

"David, did you hear me?"

"What, Oh yeah, just drive yourself. I have an early meeting."

"OK, I'm getting ready for bed. You coming?" Marlena said as she leaned over to kiss David goodnight.

"In a bit. I'm gonna watch a little TV first" David said and reached for the remote control on the coffee table and punched the power button.

Marlena turned to walk back upstairs to her bedroom thinking to herself that his early appointment was more than likely with Jack Daniels. She felt so helpless to see David like this. She wanted him to see the light, like she did, but she had learned from AA that it only happened when the alcoholic would seek the help and admitted that they have a problem.

David stared at the TV screen, but it was clear his mind was not on the show.

Cliff gently stroked Claire's hair as she lay on his bed. He spoke to her softly, calling her name and whispering how much he loves her. Kim was preparing several damp, cool wash cloths from the bathroom to wipe her face. She sat on the opposite side of the bed and began to place a wet cloth on Claire's forehead. She held another cloth in her hand wiping her cheeks, eyes and mouth. Claire never moved.

Cliff pulled the wallet from his back pocket and retrieved the piece of paper where he had written the phone number for a doctor that was recommended by Dr. Wilcox at Rolling Hills. Laying the paper on the bed next to his leg, he reached for the phone on the nightstand and dialed the number. Several rings and the doctor's answering service picked up. "Dr. Robert Chandler's office"

Cliff rose from the bed and began pacing back and forth. "Hi, this is Cliff Richards. I need to speak to Dr. Chandler about my daughter, Claire. He was referred by Dr. Wilcox at Rolling Hills Mental Hospital in Tipton County."

"May I have your number, Mr. Richards and we will contact Dr. Chandler for you."

Cliff gave the person on the other end of the line his number and hung up the phone. He stood beside the bed and stared at Claire so helpless. He didn't know what to do. Kim continued to run the cool soft washcloth over Claire's face. She looked at Cliff and noticed his eyes were filling with tears. She reached for his hand and he took hers and kissed it gently. "Kim, I love her so much. I am so afraid that this nightmare is not over. It might just be starting."

"I know, sweetie. I love her, too. We'll get through this. Together."

Cliff picked up the phone again and dialed Katie's cell number.

Katie had just pulled into her driveway. She took the phone from her purse and hit the send button. "Hello?"

"Katie, Cliff." His voice was breaking.

"What's wrong, Cliff?"

"Claire is back into a coma. I'm waiting on the doctor to call back. It happened when she and Kim went into her room."

"Oh, no!"

"Kim didn't know what I had told you earlier. Now I'm more convinced than ever that something happened in her room that put her in this condition in the first place and I'm gonna find out what."

"Do you want me to come back over?" Katie was beginning to cry.

"No, not yet anyway. I want to speak to the doctor first. He might want her to go to the hospital ER. And if he doesn't call soon, I'll be taking her there myself."

"OK, but you call me no matter what time. I'll stay up until I hear from you."

"I will. Just say a prayer."

"You know I will. Now, you go watch over that baby. Bye, Cliff."

"Bye." Cliff hung the phone and sat on the bed next to Claire. He put her hand in his and gently began to massage the back of her hand with his thumbs.

Claire's mind was active. She felt like she was dreaming. She could hear sounds and feel sensations like she was there and yet she was seeing herself from the third person perspective. She heard a familiar voice; a voice she cherished and loved to hear. She wanted to hear more. Then she heard the soft and soothing voice of a woman. It was pleasing to her. She felt content at the sound. She felt safe. She blinked her eyes several times just to clear up the images that were so faint before. She realized that she was lying down. There was something wet on her face and someone was holding her hand, but she was enjoying the feelings. She first cut her eyes to her father. He was talking, but not to her. She looked at Kim and smiled. She pulled her hand from Cliff's grip, which startled him. He turned quickly to see her smiling face.

"Hi, Daddy. Why are we in your room?"

Kim and Cliff appeared to be in shock, but tears of joy exploded from their eyes and smiles reached ear to ear as they pulled Claire from the bed and embraced her long and with such emotion.

Chapter Eleven

The digital clock on Marlena's night stand flashed at 4:00am and the soft buzz aroused her from a dream. She opened one eye and looked at the time and rolled over to hit the switch. She laid back on the pillow staring at the dark ceiling thinking of the day ahead of her. She looked to her right and noticed that David was not in bed. Reaching for the lamp, she turned the switch and saw that the bed covers had never been disturbed. *He must have fallen asleep on the couch,* she thought to herself.

Without hesitation, she threw off the comforter and headed for the bathroom for a shower. Forty-five minutes later she was dressed, had her makeup on and hair styled in the normal business look she always used. She grabbed her purse and checked for keys, airline confirmation, credit cards, id and of course some cash. It was getting late and she needed to get out onto the interstate before the usual buildup of traffic, but it was Saturday and many commuters choose to stay home at this early hour.

Marlena turned out the lights and walked down the stairs and into the den. The television was still on and David was curled peacefully on the couch, covered with a patch quilt blanket. She leaned over to kiss him on the forehead. He stirred and opened his eyes at the touch of her lips. He rubbed his eyes, noticed the TV was still on and he looked at his watch.

David sat up and said with a yawn, "You leaving already?"

"Yeah, gotta get there to check in. You want me to call you from the airport to make sure you are up?"

"I guess. Are you sure you need to do this trip?"

"David, my daughter needs me."

"Since when", he said with a little sarcasm.

"Now that wasn't fair. I know I have never been the mother of the year, but I have changed and I hope Claire and I can form some kind of bond between us."

"Well, good luck."

"Thanks! Gotta go, bye." Marlena leaned in to kiss David, but he rose to meet her and held her tight.

"Remember, I do love you." He said softly into her ear. Marlena was a bit taken back. This sounded a lot like the old David she fell in love with.

"I love you, too. I'll call you." She said.

Marlena went into the garage, entered her Lexus and headed for O'Hare airport. She noticed the traffic was even lighter this morning than usual and she felt confident that the trip would be quick. Her mind gathered thoughts of Claire; thoughts of mistreatment, belittling, insults and ignoring. She was a bad mother. She didn't deserve this child, but her life had changed for the better and she wanted to change her relationship with her daughter.

David laid on the couch and pulled the covers up to his neck. His mind was going over and over the actions of that night in Memphis, trying to piece together the details, which were so fuzzy in his mind. David knew he was the cause of Claire's condition and he knew why, but entire night was like a dream. A dream that you always can remember, but the scenes are not very clear. It was like he was an observer to the attack and not the perpetrator. What will happen to him? Will she remember anything? Had she told anyone? What will Marlena say? What will Cliff do? Do I need a lawyer? The thoughts were bombarding his brain, uncontrollably. He had to do anything to get out of this. His career was important. His marriage was critical, though unstable right now.

David threw off the blanket and sat up on the sofa. He picked up the remote to the television and shut off the power. NBC's early Saturday morning news was just coming on the air. He rose and walked immediately and instinctively to the bar, reaching for a clean glass. He held the glass in his hand, staring for what seemed like minutes. This was the root of all his problems. Marlena was right. He realized the problems he had been experiencing lately have all been tied back to booze. He knew right then and there, he was an alcoholic. What a great time to come to this crossroad in his life, only to find the trouble now facing him cannot be solved by putting down the bottle. He needed a diversion, an escape from the true reality. He needed to bury his thoughts and actions in productive work. He was planning to finish a software project he started 3 weeks ago and today would be a good day to get it done.

David folded the blanket and returned it to the hall closet. He went to the bedroom he shared with Marlena and drowned his memories in a hot, pulsating shower. Within an hour, he was dressed and out the door driving to the train station for a short trip into the city and his office. He would concentrate on computer code today. While he waited for the train, Marlena phoned him from O'Hare, just as she had promised. Marlena noticed some tension in his speech and wondered if he had started the morning with a couple of Bloody Marys.

The morning sunrise filled the bedroom where Claire was sleeping. Cliff allowed her to sleep between him and Kim during the night. He had risen at 7:00 to make Saturday morning breakfast for the family. He liked the sound of that, the family. In all the years before, he never had a feeling of family with Marlena no matter how hard he tried to make it happen. Kim had completed his dream. Kim was finishing her run through the neighborhood and came in the kitchen door out of breath and hungry.

She dropped into a chair at the breakfast table and pulled off the blue headband. "How much longer? I'm starved."

"Just a few more minutes, the sausage is just finishing." Cliff said as he removed the last of the links from the skillet. "There's some coffee ready, unless you just want OJ or water." He looked toward Kim and smiled.

"I think water first, then some coffee." Kim said and went to the refrigerator to retrieve the bottled water she always bought. "Is Claire up?"

"I don't think, but I'll get her. You want to take a quick shower first?"

"Yeah, I think I need to, I'm beginning to smell myself." She said as she walked into the downstairs bath.

Cliff put the spatula on the counter and turned the burner off under the skillet. He wiped his hands on the red checkered apron he was wearing and climbed the stairs to wake Claire. When he opened the door to his bedroom, he saw that his precious child was snuggled contently under the floral comforter. The sunrays were beaming across her face from the window. She looked like the beautiful little girl he had always known. He walked over and gently sat on the edge of the bed, determined not to startle her from a dream she might be having. He stroked her hair and pushed it back tenderly over her ears. He was so proud of his daughter. He loved her so much, but he was in such great pain that he could not help her get over this problem. He could not be her rescuer; her hero. The best he could be was her Dad. The man who would give his life for hers in a heartbeat and the dad she could look up to for anything she needed. That was his best.

Cliff leaned in close and affectionately kissed her cheek and whispered, "Claire? It's time to get up." He kissed her once again.

Claire blinked her eyes a couple of times and strained to open them against the bright sunshine covering her face. She wiped the sleep from her eyes and sat up in the bed. "What time is it, Daddy?"

"It's almost 8:30. You want some breakfast. Maybe french toast or pancakes with sausage links. I'm cooking." Cliff took her hands in his.

"Sure." Claire said as she looked around the room. She was remembering staying in her dad's room all the night before, talking and laughing with him and Kim. Then they watched DVD movies until she fell asleep in the wee hours of the early morning. For the first time in many months, Claire had a feeling of security and safety. The horrible night 6 months ago was buried deep within her mind. She wasn't letting it out.

Claire leaned over and wrapped her arms around her father, "I had a great time last night. Can we do that again sometime?"

"You know it, Tweetie. Anytime."

Claire smiled with her head on Cliff's shoulder. It was the first time that nickname he gave her really registered in her mind. It meant more today. She felt love from her dad. She felt wanted and secure. She held him tightly.

Cliff pulled her away where they were face to face. "You want to shower first or come on down now? Oh, wait, Kim is in the shower right now so come down when you get ready."

"What are we going to do today, Daddy?"

"I don't know, we'll find something fun to do. Maybe a movie, but first we need to eat. So what is it French Toast or pancakes?"

"French Toast. We got any Texas Bread?" Claire said.

"I think so. And French Toast it is." Cliff got up and returned to the kitchen.

Kim finished the shower and came back into the kitchen in a white terry cloth robe that hung only halfway down her thighs. Cliff turned to look and whistled, "Now, that's what I'm talking about." She laughed and threw the towel she was carrying to the laundry room and hit him across the back. He laughed and reached down to pick up the towel and tossed it back to her. He cracked open several eggs into a bowl and began to whip them with a fork.

Claire came bounding into the kitchen running to embrace Kim as she came out of the laundry. Their arms tightly held each other for several minutes. Kim leaned over to kiss her cheek and Claire returned the affection.

Cliff turned to witness the reunion and said, “OK, ladies, take your seats and prepare for the best breakfast you have ever had.”

Kim and Claire giggled and took their seats next to each other at the table. Cliff completed the French Toast and served them hot with syrup and coffee or chocolate milk. They talked and laughed over every bite. Cliff was about to forget the terror of the night before. The phone rang. Cliff got up to answer.

“Hello?”

“Is this Cliff Richards?”

“Yes it is, did you want me?”

“Mr. Richards, I’m Dr. Anderson. My service says you called last night?”

Cliff turned so his back would be toward Kim and Claire. Kim noticed, but continued to chat with Claire. She figured that the call was about Claire.

“Yes, Dr. Anderson, this is concerning my 11 year old daughter, Claire.”

“Oh, yes. Stanley Wilcox called me yesterday about Claire. I was out of town yesterday and I told him I would get in touch with you Monday, but it seems you need me now. What seems to be the problem?”

“Did he tell you about her past condition?”

“Yes he covered that. Has she had a relapse?”

“Well, I don’t know. She seems to be fine right now. But twice yesterday when we were near her bedroom, she froze up. The first time she spoke very strangely and the last time while she was actually in her bedroom with my wife, she went into a trance like she has been for the last 6 months. I mean to tell you I was scared."

"I'm sure you were. And now you say she is alright or appears to be?"

"Yes, so far. I took her into my bedroom after she had the last incident. Eventually she came around and everything seemed normal. She doesn't remember ever being in her room or going into the trance state."

"Well, just on the surface, it appears she might be trying to suppress something traumatic. And again, without testing and questioning, it also appears as though her bedroom has a pivotal part in her trauma. Let me contact my administrative assistant this morning for her to schedule an appointment for you on Monday. I would like to see both of you together. Can she reach you at this number today?"

"Maybe my cell number would be better. We are planning some fun stuff for today. My cell is 555-4211."

"Ok, got that."

"Dr. Anderson, is there anything I should do before then?"

"In the event she becomes traumatized again, call me and get her to the ER at Methodist Germantown. Other than that, just watch her closely and if you have a spare bedroom, I would suggest you change her room."

"That was part of my plan anyway. Thank you for calling back so quickly. I'll be waiting for your assistant's call."

"Don't worry, we'll get to the bottom of this, as long as Claire remains coherent and alert. Goodbye Mr. Richards."

"Good bye and thank you." Cliff said and hung up the phone.

Cliff returned to the table and looked at Kim. Claire was busy finishing the last bite of her breakfast. It wouldn't take long to get her back to the same old Claire. Her appetite was certainly improving.

"Tweetie, when you finish, why don't you run up to our room and take a nice long shower. Kim and I will get you some clothes ready. We're going shopping this morning."

"Can I buy something from Macy's?"

"You can get whatever you need. I think it's time for a new wardrobe anyway."

Claire hugged Kim and jumped from her chair to hug her father. When she had left for the upstairs, Kim asked, "Who was on the phone?"

"That was Dr. Anderson. We have an appointment Monday when his assistant calls with the time." Cliff put his head in his hands.

Kim moved to the chair next to him. "It'll be OK. Claire is strong. We'll get through this and be better for it. What else did he say?"

"Well, it seems he confirms my suspicion that whatever triggered this is related somehow to her bedroom or something in it. He suggested a new room, which was what I had in mind all along."

"You talking about the guest room?"

"For now. We need to make it home for her. Make it hers. Make it yellow. So we shop."

"Hey, this is going to be fun." Kim said.

"Will you go into her room and get several outfits she can wear. We'll put them in our closet for now. I have a new blowup bed in the attic. We can use that for her in our room until we get the guestroom ready."

The guestroom was the first bedroom off the stairway. Claire's room was next with a full bathroom and then Cliff and Kim's Master suite. One smaller room was across the hall but was never used for sleeping. Claire had created a playroom there when she was younger, but had not used the room for quite awhile. Cliff considered this room as his choice, but realized that Claire's bedroom door was directly opposite. By using the guestroom, Claire would not have to pass her old room, subjecting her to possible setbacks.

Claire took her time getting ready. Kim had gathered many different combinations that she could choose and they both were having a great time. Cliff was finishing with the cleaning of the breakfast dishes. Cliff decided he would need some help with Claire. There was only one choice - Mae. When Claire went into the hospitals for treatment, the cost was more that Cliff was prepared for and he had a meeting with Mae. He explained the situation and she understood and accepted the fact that Claire needed his full attention and support. She told him that she would get by regardless. Cliff missed the warmth and compassion Mae gave to the family. He missed her. Cliff wiped his hands on the towel draped over the counter and picked up the phone. Somehow he remembered her number after all the time that had passed.

Cliff lifted the phone and punched in the number. Two rings and Mae answered. "Hello"

"Hello Mae, this is Cliff Richards."

"Well, bless my soul, how are you Mr. Cliff? And how is Miss Claire?"

"That's why I'm calling you."

"Miss Claire is alright, ain't she?"

"Yes, even better, she's at home."

"Praise the Lord! " Mae screamed.

"Mae, I need you back. Claire needs you. Please tell me you can work for me again."

"Why sure Mr. Cliff. I only been working at odd jobs since I left you. I hoped and prayed that one day you would call me back. Is Miss Claire OK, now?"

"Yes, she is fine so far, but she still needs to see a doctor."

"I understand. When would you have me start again?"

"Is Monday too early?"

"Monday is fine."

"Thank you Mae, you know I never forgot you in all this mess."

"Yes sir, and I never forgot Miss Claire, either. I miss her dearly."

"Do you have transportation?"

"Yes, I can get there."

"Thanks again. Mae. I'll see you Monday."

"OK, Mr. Cliff, I'll be there. Give Miss Claire a big hug from me."

"I will, bye Mae."

"Bye Mr. Cliff."

Cliff returned the phone to the cradle and feeling proud that some good things were happening in their lives. Cliff poured the last cup of coffee in the pot and sat down at the table to reflect on the day to come. He was planning to convert the guestroom into a girl's bedroom and he only had one afternoon to accomplish it. The phone rang.

Answering the phone Cliff said, “Hello?”

“Cliff, its Marlena”

“Hi Marlena. This is not a good time.”

“Why, what’s going on. Is Claire alright?”

“No problems, we’re just getting ready to go out.”

“I’m at the airport in Memphis.”

“You’re here?”

“Yes”

“Why?”

“I need to see Claire. Can that be arranged?”

“I don’t know. She is still pretty fragile. I don’t know what it would do to her.”

“Cliff, I’ve changed; changed a lot. I need the chance to make amends with her.”

Cliff was torn between the protection of Claire and allowing Marlena access to his daughter. She made it very clear that she wished to have nothing to do with this child when the divorce was finalized.

“Well, let me talk to her. Do you have a place to stay?”

“I’m going by Embassy Suites on Shady Grove. I called from Chicago. They have a room.”

“We’re going shopping this morning. After that, it’s up in the air.”

“OK, I’ll get checked in and get back with you later.”

"OK. You know Marlena, this is some serious shit going on here."

"Yeah, I know." She paused. "Cliff, do you think there is a chance for me and Claire to have some type of relationship that's good? Do you think we will ever be friends?"

Cliff thought and then said, "It's all up to Claire at this point."

"I guess you're right. I'll take what I can get. Will you help?"

"I'll try, gotta go, see ya Marlena."

"Thank you, bye Cliff. See you later." She said and then hung up the phone.

Cliff rushed to shower and get ready before leaving for the mall.

Chapter Twelve

Katie was rushing back and forth from the kitchen to the great room carrying trays filled with tasty snacks, veggies and various meat products. Mae had finished with vacuuming and dusting the tables and entertainment center. Janey was busy with some yellow streamers. Allison was in charge of paper plates, cups and forks. Charlene from Cliff and Kim's bible study group was in the kitchen making her famous onion dip while Amy, another member of their group, was filling another plate with homemade chocolate chip cookies. They were desperate to complete setting up of the welcome home party before Claire returned with Cliff and Kim from the mall. Time was crucial. The family should be pulling into the driveway any minute now.

Katie sat the last tray on the table with a yellow table cloth and she stopped to watch Janey. "It's looking real super, Janey girl."

"Thanks, I hope Claire likes it." Janey said.

"No doubt."

The kitchen door opened and Katie jumped. She wasn't expecting them this soon. She ran to the kitchen to find Bill coming through the door with a couple of sacks filled with chips and popcorn. "There's some 2 liter soft drinks out in the car." He said as he put the bags on the counter. He leaned down to kiss Katie once and headed back to his car for the other groceries.

Allison was meticulous at her table setting chore. She managed to make paper look classy. Janey had completed another run of twisted yellow streamers through the banister rail of the stairs. Allison sat on the sofa and pulled her knees up and wrapped her arms around them as she watched her friend.

Allison asked, "Janey, do you think Claire has changed, you know, like is she different? Like weird?"

Janey dropped the remaining streamers in the plastic bag of decorations on the floor and sat on the opposite side of the couch from

Allison. “What do you mean, weird? She’s our friend. She’ll be the same as always. Miss Katie said she was like real thin and needed some more weight, but that’s all.”

“But she was in like a mental place. Do you think she’s crazy?”

“No and I’m ashamed you even think so.”

“What if she don’t remember us?”

“She will. Let’s just finish this OK?” Janey said and left for the kitchen leaving Allison sitting alone in the great room.

Bill returned with the remaining items from the store. “Look who I found outside!”

Katie looked up to see Marlena following Bill through the door. Marlena seemed a little apprehensive entering her former home, but everything was so familiar. She dropped her purse on the counter as she had always done before when returning from work. Katie’s arms were open wide and Marlena did not hesitate running to her embrace. Tears were streaming down Marlena’s cheeks. Katie held her tight. Bill had placed the packages on the table with the others and joined in hugs with his daughter.

Katie pulled away and held Marlena at arms length, “Sweetheart, I had no idea you would be here so quick. I knew you would come, but why now?”

Marlena pulled a napkin from the holder on the table to wipe away teardrops from her face. “Mother, I couldn’t stay in Chicago. I need to be with Claire. Becoming sober has opened my eyes to so many things I have done that were wrong and the events in my daughter’s life that I have missed out on and I don’t want to do that anymore.”

Katie’s eyes widened as if to say, *Did I hear that right, my daughter?*

Marlena sensed her amazement. “Yes, mother, I did say my daughter. I find that even hard to believe myself. I must try and make amends, try to smooth out all the problems we had, try to convince Claire that I am not the same mother she used to know."

"You know she's not the same little girl either."

"I hope so, mom." Marlena said and sat at the chair she always used. Katie sat next to her.

Bill had moved over to the Mr. Coffee machine and was opening the canister to fill the filter for a new pot of deep roasted blend. "Anyone care for a bit of java?" He looked at Katie and then Marlena for an answer. They both declined.

Allison had come into the kitchen when she heard Bill enter the back door and make his announcement. She thought Claire had arrived, but was shocked to see Claire's mother in the room. Janey was sitting on one of the barstools at the breakfast bar with Amy and Charlene. They were talking among themselves and listening to the conversation that was going on across the room.

Turning with a surprise, Marlena finally noticed the additional people in the room. Mae had just entered after checking all the downstairs bathrooms for toilet tissue and soap and towels. "Why hello, Miss Marlena."

Marlena rose to greet her former housekeeper with a warm hug. "Oh, Mae, it is so good to see you. How have you been?" Mae backed up a step.

"I've been just fine. Mr. Cliff hired me back just today." Mae found it hard to accept the 'new' Marlena. Was this real or put on because she had seen both Marlena's before?

Katie finally realized her bad manners and walked over to introduce the others gathered in the kitchen. "Marlena, I apologize. I think you remember Janey and Allison, Claire's good friends"

"Best friends", Janey reminded her.

"Yes, best friends." Katie continued. "And this is Charlene Applegate and Amy Deerfield. They are in the same church bible study group with Cliff and Kim."

Marlena walked up to the women and politely shook their hands. Allison remained still on the stool and eyed her suspiciously. Janey was not bashful. "Hi Miss Marlena. Remember me?"

"Of course I do Janey. I hope one day you and Claire and I can spend some time together." Marlena was about to hug Janey, but pulled back for fear of what the child might feel. She recalled the many times that she had been so rude and indifferent to Claire's friends.

Marlena spun around to speak to Katie. "What is going on anyway? Where are Cliff, Kim and Claire?"

Katie rolls her arms to point to everyone in the room, "We're giving Claire a welcome home party. It was a impromptu decision and we are stretched for time. They have gone shopping and we expect them back any minute."

Marlena smiles, "Can I help?"

Katie leaned in closely and whispered to Marlena, "I don't know if Claire's mental state is stable enough for you to see her right now."

Marlena's eyes closed and tears formed at the corners pulling down a streak of mascara. She walked head-down to the kitchen table and sat down at the closest chair. She turned her back on the others in the room to hide her heartbroken emotions. Katie followed and sat in the chair next to her. She put her hand on Marlena's arm and smiled a motherly smile. "Sweetheart, you know as well as we do that Claire's problems may have been through your actions when you were under the influence." Katie couldn't bear to refer to her own daughter as a drunk. She patted her arm gently.

Marlena's eyes did not meet with her own mothers'. She pulled her arms close in to her chest to comfort herself in an embrace. "Mother, don't you know I have lived with that thought all these months? The idea that I could have hurt my own child was what actually sobered me up, made me realize that Claire was my beautiful little girl that I ignored and rejected even from the first day of her life. I don't expect to be accepted by her with open arms, but I would like the chance to see her every now and then and maybe begin a relationship that could start as friends and lead to something more. You of all people can understand this."

Katie didn't need to be reminded of her own faulty mothering skills. Careers always seemed to come before family. She never ignored or rejected Marlena as a child, but she was the absentee parent, with the housekeeper and relatives taking care of her girl. Only after Marlena was grown did Katie comprehend the loss of the affection from her child. She knew that those years missed as mother and daughter could never be recovered, but maybe she could repair the friendship as adults.

"Yes I do and I feel partly responsible for everything."

"Don't say that, Mother. You are not responsible for my actions. I have a lot of issues to deal with and Claire is my main concern right now. I would just like your support as my friend and as MY mother."

Katie began to tremble and tears fell freely. She reached for Marlena and held her tightly. They both cried softly exchanging 'I love you`s'. Everyone else had retreated to the great room and applied the finishing touches to the food and decorations.

Marlena looked deeply into Katie's eyes. "Can I stay? I need to see Claire."

"Will you do this then. When they get here, will you wait in Cliff's office while I spring this on Cliff first. I think he should make the decision whether or not you should see Claire. If not then .. Well, we'll cross that bridge when we get to it. Can you accept his decision?"

"I suppose. He did say he would speak to Claire and ask if she wanted to talk. Did he?"

"I really don't know. But, let's go see what we can do to help."

"Thanks Mother. Thanks for believing in me and standing by me."

They hugged one more time and rose to help the others with the party planning and setup.

David had spent the last two hours looking at the same programming code on his computer monitor. His mind was elsewhere. Saturday was a good day to work without the distractions of a regular workday, especially from the IT manager's constant barrage of requests for reports and statistics. Many of the tech employees chose to come in on Saturdays for that very reason and there were at least 10 programmers scattered throughout the cubicles on the IT floor. David's work space was located next to a bank of windows facing south providing him with a ninth floor view of the city; mostly buildings. Just in case of emergencies, there was a small pint bottle of vodka hidden in the lower desk drawer behind a rack of file folders. This qualified as an emergency and David had not drank since hearing the news from Memphis, but this crutch he was hiding deep behind his files was calling to him. Calling, begging him to take just one drink; just a little sip. He needed to take off the edge. He never drank during work hours before. He had always managed to tolerate the pain until 'happy hour' at Butlers. But today was Saturday. This was not a workday. He was doing this on his own. At least, that's how he justified fishing out the bottle from the file drawer. He held the vodka close in his lap. The walls of the cubicle were high enough to offer some privacy, but paranoia was creeping into his senses. First he looked out from the cubicle opening to insure he was alone and then David quickly unscrewed the top of the bottle, guzzling down half the liquid before stopping. He looked around again like he was expecting someone to come by at any minute to confront him with drinking on the job. He remained alone. The hot burning drink as it drained into his throat soothed David. He felt the tension ease. The pressure was relaxing. After recapping the liquor, he wiped the top dry on his jeans and quickly replaced the bottle in it's hideaway spot. The fuzzy memories kept creeping into his mind; haunting him, taunting him. He could see her face; the terror in her eyes. He could not stop. He recalled through the hangover the next day a call from Marlena about something happening to Claire; she was catatonic, not responding to anyone. Then he remembered the weeks that followed and the fights Marlena had with Cliff and then the divorce; hurried and fast. Claire remained the same; no change. Soon he and Marlena were married and he was relieved when she agreed with no hesitation to move to Chicago. He felt safe. No one would know what happened that night but him. Claire was gone.

He looked back at the screen and came to the conclusion that he would never get a single bit of coding done until he got some answers from Memphis. He looked at his cell phone lying on the desk next to his mouse pad and decided that Marlena must have arrived by now. He needed to know what was happening. Dialing the number of Marlena's cell, David looked again at the closed file drawer. *No, not yet.* He thought.

Marlena's purse was still on the kitchen counter when it began to chirp and beep. She never was into the fancy songs and cute tones many cellphone companies offered. Hers was a simple set of tones. It worked for her. Marlena was is a much better mood and had assisted with final decorations. She was sitting with Amy and Charlene on the sofa talking about church and bible studies they were each involved in at the moment. Marlena had become quite comfortable with the new found spirituality in her life. It was the only thing that kept her straight. That along with the support of the many AA group members and her sponsor. The beeping from the kitchen was unmistakably her phone. She excused herself and went into the kitchen.

She fished the phone from her purse before the 4th ring forced the call to voice mail. Noticing the caller id on the display, she pressed the send button and connected. "Hello, David."

"Hey. Just thinking about you. Wanted to make sure you got in OK."

"Yeah, made it OK. I'm here at the house now."

"How is Claire?"

"I don't know."

"What do you mean?"

"She's not here. Seems I walked into some party planning of my mother's. Claire has gone shopping with Cliff and Kim. So to answer your question again, I don't know. We expect them any minute."

The back door to the garage burst open and Janey came running in yelling "THEY'RE HERE!" Janey had been sent out to watch for the car.

Marlena quickly ended the call to David, "I gotta go, baby. They're here and this is a surprise party."

"OK. Hey call me later and let me know how things went."

"I will, bye." She pressed the end button before David could answer. She ran for the great room, catching Katie's eye and her head motioning to the office door. Marlena smiled and mouthed softly that Katie would understand, *I love you.* Katie understood and smiled back. Marlena passed through the office door and waited on the leather couch beside the massive oak bookcase she had special ordered; now empty. This used to be her office when she lived here.

David held the phone for a few seconds. Thoughts raced again through his head. What will she remember? What should he do now? The stress was too much. He closed his cell and put it in his pocket. He powered down the computer and filed away some documents in the drawer where his friend was waiting. He didn't disappoint him. He finished the last of the vodka, flipped off the lights under the overhead bins in the cubicle. He put the empty bottle in his pocket. He would dispose of it later. David left the building and headed straight for Butlers.

Claire led the way into the kitchen carrying a large plastic bag with Macy's printed on both sides. It was filled with new clothes, yellow of course. In addition to new clothes, Cliff had sprung for a completely new bedroom suite from Ashley Furniture. That order would be delivered on Monday. Claire's life was beginning again. Cliff was determined to take away any reminders of the past, although in his heart he knew she would have to face them before everything would get better.

The great room lights had been turned off and everyone was hiding in various spots around the room difficult as it was. Katie was ready, hand on the switch that would illuminate the overhead recessed lighting. Claire was first into the room with Kim close behind. Seconds later, the lights shone brightly and everyone popped out and yelled, "SURPRISE!!!"

Claire dropped the bag. With a startled look on her face, she looked at each one in the room; her friends, her Grammie and Grandpa Bill and a couple of ladies, she didn't recognize. They were all smiling broadly at her. Kim was just as surprised. Cliff had stopped briefly to drop the mail in the box for letters and bills.

Cliff said, "What's going on?" He looked at Katie. "Are you behind this?"

Katie bowed her head, "Guilty as charged, sir."

Claire ran to her Grammie and hugged her with all the energy she could muster. When Janey and Allison joined her, Claire screamed with delight and grabbed each one for a big embrace. It had been so long since she was able to be with her best friends. Claire looked into her grandmother's face, "This is so cool, Grammie. Thank you." She let her go and looked at how the room had been so carefully decorated. When she saw the table filled with food, she and her 2 best friends ran for the first serving. Kim joined them and introduced Claire to Amy and Charlene while Katie caught Cliff's attention. She motioned for him to return to the kitchen. He understood and she followed.

"Katie, this is so sweet of you to do this. Although I am not surprised."

Katie looked at Cliff with that, *we need to talk look.* Cliff sensed a problem. "What's wrong Katie?"

She pulled Cliff to the end of the kitchen counter, the farthermost spot from the opening to the great room. She didn't want ears to overhear. She held his hand and looked tenderly into his eyes. Cliff got nervous. "Cliff, Marlena is here."

"What, HERE?"

"Yes, she flew in this morning. She wants to see Claire."

"She can't."

"Cliff think. Marlena has changed……"

"I know that, you know I can't take that chance and let her see Claire."

"We can't protect Claire from everything. We haven't a clue what happened that night anyway. If Marlena was the cause, then don't you think it would be best to find out now."

"No, not now. What if she goes back into a trance again?"

"Cliff, I know. I'm scared too, but what if Marlena was not the cause. What if it is something medical that the doctors can't figure out. You would be denying her the opportunity to make amends with Claire."

"Katie, I want that more than anything, for Claire and Marlena. I'm just scared. Am I wrong to be over-protective?"

"No, but we have to have some compassion too."

Cliff was ready to cry. Katie wrapped her arms around him putting her head against his chest. "It will be alright. We'll be there for

Claire. We'll watch. If she appears to be falling back then we'll end it immediately."

Cliff thought as he looked out the window into the garden on the side of the house. "Where is she?"

"In the office, waiting to hear from me. Or you."

"We'll both go. I hope you're right Katie."

"I hope so too. I want Claire to be healed. I want my little granddaughter back whole again. We have 6 months of catching up to do."

Cliff looked at Katie. "I know you want this to be OK as much as I do. Thank you for your love and kindness. Claire is lucky to have you as her Grammie."

"No, I'm the lucky one."

"OK, you go into the office and let Marlena know what's going to happen. Make sure she understands that both of us will be in there with her. Any sign of problems and the visit ends."

"My thoughts exactly."

They both walked into the great room, with Katie heading for the office door while Bill gave her a nod of acceptance from the recliner and Cliff moved next to Claire on the couch. She had filled a plate with smoked sausage meat slices, cookies, veggies and ranch dressing for dip.

Cliff smiled at Claire. "This was a cool surprise party, wasn't it?"

"Yes, Daddy, this has been the best day so far."

"Well, your Grammie has another surprise for you too."

"What?"

“Just come with me.”

Cliff got up from the couch and Claire put her plate on the coffee table next to her glass of orange soda. Claire put her arm around Cliff’s waist as they walked toward the office door. When Cliff turned the handle and opened the door, Claire noticed her Grammie leaning against the huge dark desk. She ran to grab her grandmother, not noticing Marlena sitting on the sofa to the right of the door. She had flipped off the reading lamp and her outline was obscured.

“Grammie, this is the best day. Daddy said you had another surprise?”

Marlena fought back the tears. “Hello, Claire.”

Claire turned with a jerk and saw the figure sitting in the shadows of the room. Memories flooded her mind, filled her brain with the images of a treacherous mother; a cheating wife. Cliff was watching closely. His eyes never left Claire. He was looking for any sign of regression back to catatonic state she suffered for so long. Claire’s eyes could not lie. Cliff saw contempt. He noticed pain. He saw disappointment, but he thought he could see longing and desire. Cliff continued to watch for the signs. None came.

Marlena rose slowly from the couch so she would not frighten Claire. As she walked slowly toward Katie and Claire, she came into the light from the desk. Claire saw someone she had never seen before. This was not the same woman with the bloodshot eyes at 10:00 in the morning. This was not the deceiving and contemptuous mother she remembered. She saw eyes that sparkled with a new freshness; without the aid of alcohol. She felt warmed by a smile that was genuine and not faked. She saw a different mother than she remembered. But she still put up her guard.

“Hello, mother.” Claire said almost insulting.

Cliff thought to himself, *So far so good.* He looked at Katie and she nodded with her eyes.

Marlena approached slowly and reached for Claire's hand. Claire refused to touch her at first, but as she continued to stare into these eyes she had never seen before, she relinquished and allowed Marlena to hold both hands.

"Claire, I really don't know what to say."

"Say you're leaving."

"Well, I am. But first I wanted to see you. See how you are."

Again, Claire stared into this face that was so pleasant, so wonderful. Her guard remained. "OK, I'm here. I'm OK."

"Would you allow me a few minutes just to talk?"

She bowed her head down. "I guess."

Katie let go of Claire's shoulders and looked at Cliff. She was looking for his non-verbal approval to leave and let Claire react with her mother. Cliff agreed. He said, "Claire, we'll be out with the others, OK?"

Claire ran to him. "Don't leave me, Daddy."

Katie went to Claire. "Claire, it's OK. We're here."

Claire watched as they left the room. Marlena had returned to the couch and turned on the reading light, which only helped to enhance her face features. Claire noticed the difference. It was the face of a mother she never had known before and she felt more comfortable, at ease with her, although her inside guards remained at ready. She joined Marlena on the couch.

Everyone, including Kim, had been staring at the door in anticipation. Kim was totally in the dark about the situation occurring in the other room. Katie left the room first with a thumbs up sign to Bill. Kim just looked confused. She went immediately to Cliff after he followed Katie from the room.

"Cliff, will you explain to me what in the world is going on?" Kim said with some anxiety in her voice.

Cliff told her, "Marlena is in there."

"WHAT! You allowed this, but Cliff...."

"It's OK, I had many reservations when Katie told me. You know, I just found out too. Claire is OK. She didn't have any negative reaction when she saw her."

"Why is she here? What does she want?"

"She is just concerned about Claire, like we are. She arrived this morning, Katie said. I think Marlena needs this more than Claire does right now."

"I hope so. I can't believe she has the nerve.."

"It's going to be OK, sweetie. Let's let Claire make the choice to see her or not from now on. I was just concerned about the initial contact. I watched her close, Kim. She reacted different than I expected. Almost a calm, serene attitude, even though she did have some words that brought back the old Claire."

"Cliff, I don't know what I will do if she does anything to harm Claire in any way."

"Spoken like a true step mother." Cliff laughed and gave Kim a big hug. She laughed with him. "Let's get something to eat and go chat with Amy and Charlene."

"Good idea."

Marlena was uncomfortable to say the least. She shifted her weight from one side to the other, crossing and uncrossing her legs. "This is hard for me, Claire." She finally said.

"Why is that, mother?" Claire said.

Marlena clasped both hands together in her lap. She looked directly at Claire, who had not ceased staring at this new unfamiliar face. "Claire, I know I have been a bad mother to you all your life and I know there is nothing I can do to make up for the hurt and pain I caused you. But.." she trailed off and choked back the emotion building in her heart. "But, I was hoping that I might be able to start over. You know, at the beginning with you. I would like first to gain your confidence. I hope that your trust will come later. I want to try and be your friend and show you that I truly am not the same person you remember. If our relationship ventures past friendship, then that will be your choice. I will settle for just friendship."

Claire could not stop looking at this woman who gave birth to her so many years ago, yet forgot that she had a daughter or cared to acknowledge her existence. In the back of Claire's mind were all the times her mother belittled her and embarrassed her friends just for spite. All the times she thought only of herself and no one else. But those memories remained there, in the back on her mind. She was longing to learn more about this new woman.

The ever-present guard protected her when she spoke. "What makes you think I want to be your friend?"

"I don't know. I never gave you a reason in the past… before all this mess happened. I just want you to know that I have changed and tell you what I did to change my life for the better."

"I heard you got married again."

"Yes, but let's not talk about that now. Later, maybe. I need to convince you somehow that I am not the mother you grew up with."

"Mother, you have said that before. Alright go ahead. Tell me how you're different."

Marlena shifted again. She was gathering her composure. She picked her words carefully. "Claire" she stopped. "Claire, I'm an alcoholic."

"Tell me something new." The guard was at work again. Her guard was hard at work, protecting.

"That's the first thing I learned I must do. Admit I have a problem. Admit it to a group. Admit to God. Admit it to myself. I have a serious problem, but I haven't had a drink of alcohol in 6 months. In fact, I put it all down when….. Well, when you went into the hospital."

"That's good, mother. How long will it last? You being sober I mean."

"Forever, I pray."

"You pray? You never prayed in your life."

"You're right, but I have found a place for God in my life. I have been attending a church every Sunday. You might not believe this, but I was baptized 2 months ago."

"For real?" the guard went to sleep on that one.

Marlena smiled. For just a quick moment, she felt a connection. Claire was truly listening and responding and Marlena's heart was beginning to mend.

"For real. My AA sponsor got me going to her church. It's non-denominational, you know, not Baptist or Methodist or Catholic. Everybody can come. I liked it the first time I went. I felt welcomed, even with my problem. As a matter of fact, there were more people like me in that church than I could ever have imagined."

"Who's your AA sponsor?"

“Her name is Donna. She has become a close friend. She is also in a bible study group I attend once a week. They have helped me a lot.”

“You’re studying the bible? I would have never guessed.” Claire wanted to hear more. She pulled hers legs upon the couch; got more comfortable.

“Like I said, Claire, I have changed. I am a totally different person inside. I learned that I first need to love myself and then I can love others. I’m still working on the ‘love myself’ part. Too many bad things keep coming back to haunt me. The worst, I realized, was how I treated you while you were growing up. And now look at you, a little thinner than I remember, but still a growing young woman.”

“There is something that is different about you. I can’t place it, you just look special somehow.” The guard was on vacation for that one.

Marlena began to blush. “Why thank you. That was sweet. So am I making progress”

“Progress with me believing you?”

“Yes. That’s step one.”

“Well, you’re making it believable. I guess we’re making some progress.”

Marlena smiled. She wanted so much to pull this little girl close to her and show her that she had finally discovered the love she had ignored all these years, but she resisted the temptation. “Well, this is a good start. Why don’t we go in the other room. After all this party is for you and I certainly don’t want to take you away from it.”

The guard must have been asleep. Claire couldn’t believe her mother was thinking of someone instead of herself for a change. Maybe she had changed. They got up from the couch and walked to the door. Claire reached for Marlena’s hand and pulled back when the inside guard woke up.

Mother and daughter joined the party. Claire ran to her best friends to tell them about the talk she had with her mother. Marlena went directly to Cliff and Kim who were sitting at the bar stools talking over two cups of special blend coffee. Marlena's greeting was warm and cheerful. She held out her hand to Kim. Kim looked surprised. "You must be Kim. I am so glad to meet you finally." Cliff turned a bit red.

Kim took her hand and politely shook. "Nice to meet you as well. How did you think Claire was tonight?"

"I don't know. I think we made a little step forward in building a relationship. I only want a small part of her life. You have made great strides in giving her the mother she deserves and I will never try to undermine what you have done for Claire. I know she loves you dearly."

Kim was in awe. "Thank you, Marlena, for that confidence. I'll try not to let her down."

"Like I did?"

"No, no I didn't mean it that way."

"It's OK, I did and I admit my errors. I failed her and I failed Cliff." She looked at Cliff and then back at Kim. "You have made a great difference in both their lives. You're all a family, the family I could never provide. I am beginning a new life as well in Chicago. I just want to take my time with Claire. Make it all work out for the betterment of Claire. She needs our support now. I need her confidence and acceptance. I need her forgiveness most of all. One day I pray it will happen."

Cliff knew this was not the Marlena he last saw. This was more of a replica of the woman he married so many years ago. He liked the change. He went for more coffee in the kitchen, to find Bill pouring himself another cup.

"Bill, you better lay off that stuff. You'll never sleep a wink."

"Never has bothered me yet. So what do you think of Marlena, now."

"I don't know Bill. She sure is not the same woman I recall 6 months ago. She has a glow about her, don't you think?"

"Yeah, that's my girl. I think it looks good on her."

They returned to the great room. Kim and Marlena had gathered with Amy, Charlene and Katie to discuss women topics, while Bill and Cliff retired to the bar and talked shop.

Claire was sitting on the floor with Allison and Janey. Claire was bursting at the seams to tell Janey some secrets she had been harboring for months. She didn't want to hurt Allison's feelings by not asking her to spend the night. Claire just wanted her very best friend, Janey, to stay. She took the chance anyway. "Janey, can you spend the night with me?"

"Sure, let me call mom first."

"Allison, how about you?" Claire held her breath.

"I don't think so, Claire, we have to like get up early for church. You want to come with us. You and Janey."

"Maybe not so soon, OK."

"Sure, I understand."

The party continued for another 2 hours. Janey had called to get permission for the sleep over. She could run home later to gather some clothes. Amy and Charlene left first and Marlena told them she was so glad to have met hem and hoped they could talk again when she returned from Chicago. Bill and Katie left after big hugs and kisses. Allison's mother had dropped by to pick her up.

Kim, Cliff and Claire began clearing some tables. Marlena said, "Well, I don't know about you guys, but I had a great time. I must get back to the motel and let you get rested." Marlena left for the kitchen to gather her purse, followed closely by Claire. She looked lovingly at Claire and whispered as if she were telling her a secret. "Will it be OK if I call you tomorrow?"

Claire smiled and answered. "Sure. That would be good." Where did that guard go off to now. Claire forgot he was there to protect. Did he get fired?

Kim and Cliff joined them in the kitchen. Marlena opened the back door and waved to all. "Bye, Cliff, Kim. Thanks for allowing me to stay."

Cliff had an urge to pull her back, but resisted. "I'm glad you were here. Really."

"Me too." Kim said with a smile.

Marlena left.

Claire returned to the great room with Janey. "Let's go to your house and get your stuff. Then we can come back here. I got some stuff I need to tell you. About my mom."

Janey turned to look at her. She jumped up from the floor. "Let's go."

That night in the guest room, Claire told Janey everything that happened the night she saw her mother and that man make love on the sofa downstairs. Janey cried with her as Claire spilled out all the pain that had built up inside her all these years. Yet, even with prodding from Janey, Claire could not remember anything about that terrible night she had fallen into the deep trance. They talked well into the early morning hours. Claire and her best friend were getting to know each other better than ever before. This was a friendship that would last the test of time. Finally they fell asleep, side by side with the moonlight through the mini blinds covering their young faces.

Chapter Thirteen

Marlena drove her rental Ford Taurus into the parking lot at Embassy Suites on Shady Grove Road. Embassy Suites was always her favorite hotel when she traveled. The rooms were all suites, the service was excellent, the food to die for and of course there was the free happy hours. Marlena made it a point to avoid the patio area where many guests had gathered to chat and get a little bit tipsy before heading out to eat or return to their rooms.

Marlena walked through the automatic door from the drop off canopy and made her way to the first elevator just across the walk bridge that traversed the small indoor creek filled with fish of varying size and color. Her suite was on the 4th floor.

Upon entering the room, she tossed her purse on the first room sofa and sat in the matching chair. She kicked off her shoes and rested her feet on the coffee table. Recalling her meeting with Claire, she smiled to herself. She did love her little girl and only now did she realize what she had missed the past 11 years. She reached for her purse and retrieved the cell phone buried somewhere in the bottom. The phone was still on. She had 1 missed call. It was from David. She pressed in the speed dial combination for David's cell. He always left his phone connected, even when it was charging.

David answered on the second ring when he noticed the caller ID. "Hi. How's everything there?"

Marlena leaned against the back of the chair resting her neck and relieving a bit of the tension. "Oh, David, I think everything is going to be alright. Claire is very much alert. She hasn't remembered anything as of yet, but Cliff has an appointment with a Dr. Chandler on Monday. We had a good talk. I think I made some progress with her."

"You say she doesn't remember anything?"

Marlena could hear a definite slur in David's speech. He had been drinking again. She should keep this conversation short.

"Not yet. I am going to invite her for lunch tomorrow. We will talk more then. So what's been going on up there?"

"Nothing. I went in to work a little while this morning, but could not get focused. I guess all this is on my mind and you're down there."

"Well, I'll be leaving Monday. You think you can survive until then?"

"Sure. It'll be hard, but I'll manage."

Marlena paused.

"David? How much have you had to drink today?"

David didn't answer. She could hear his breathing.

Marlena persisted. "Sweetie, you can't hide it. I know. Remember I was there too."

Finally David spoke. "I know. I haven't had as much as you might think. . . . "

"And?" Marlena's simple question penetrated David's soul.

David was quiet.

"David? Are you there?"

"Marlena. . . . . . . uhh, I think I have a problem, uh . . . . a problem with alcohol." David almost broke down when he heard himself say those words.

Marlena began to cry. "Sweetheart, that's the first step. Keep saying it to yourself. I'm here to help you if you want."

"I hoped you would understand. I'm going to need you on this."

"More than you know. We'll get through this together."

"Thanks. I needed to hear that. Will you call me tomorrow after your lunch with Claire?"

"Yes I will. You get some sleep and remember what you told me in the morning. When you feel that addiction calling you, then you call me. Or if you want, call Debbie. Her number is inside my nightstand drawer."

"OK. . . . . I love you, Marlena."

Marlena choked. "I love you, too. Bye."

"Bye."

David clicked off the phone and reached for the bottle of Jack on the coffee table. He looked hard at the brown liquid inside the glass, calling to him, taunting him to take just one more drink. You know you haven't reached your limit for today. You're still standing. David reached for the top and screwed it down tight. He walked to the kitchen, open the trash can under the sink and dropped the new, half full bottle of Jack Daniels inside. After closing the lid, he stared for a few moments, unsure whether he was doing the right thing. He shivered at the thought of his past attempts at personal recovery. The shakes and tremors would always make him feel so helpless. Then there was the burning pain that was a reminder of his addiction. Relief was as close as the bottle was to his lips. He resisted. David walked away. He stumbled up the stairs to bed. At least he could sleep. Or could he? The foggy memories of that one night in Memphis were bound to haunt his dreams.

Marlena prepared for sleep. She had showered and slipped into a pair of comfortable pajamas. She didn't feel like going anywhere to eat so she had ordered room service. She watched local TV shows and news while finishing the burger and fries. Sleep was fast coming. Marlena felt so content. She was beginning a relationship with her only child and her husband had made the first crucial step in his recovery.

During the night a soft fall rain began to make its presence known. The light from the early morning filtered through Claire's new bedroom window. She had slept soundly with no dreams to disturb her rest. The raindrops lightly tapped on the window. Claire opened her eyes. The darkened room was strangely unfamiliar to her. She looked toward the sound of the rain outside. For a moment she was transported back to the mental hospital in Tipton County. She expected to see her Grammie walking up to the building, waving lovingly at her through the window. Then she saw this lump in the bed next to her move. Claire timidly reached for the covers and pulled back the comforter to reveal her best friend. Suddenly, every detail of the night before flooded her mind. She smiled and poked Janey on the shoulder to wake her.

Janey turned, rubbing her eyes of the sleep. "What'd you wake me up for? What time is it anyway?"

Claire looked at the digital clock on her side of the bed. "6:30, let's get up. I'm hungry."

"Hungry? Don't you mean you're sleepy. Let's go back to sleep." Janey said as she wrapped her arms around the pillow she was holding and turned her back to Claire.

"That's OK. You sleep. I'm getting up." Claire pulled back the blue comforter and jumped off the bed. After visiting the bathroom, she went downstairs to the kitchen to find her father at the table reading the Sunday paper and having a cup of coffee.

Cliff put the paper on the table when he heard Claire enter the kitchen. "Well, Tweetie, what are you doing up so early?"

"I don't know. I just woke up. Where's Kim"

"Believe it or not, she went to run, even in the rain. She just left 5 minutes ago."

"When will she be back."

"About 30 minutes. That's her normal routine."

"I'm hungry."

"You want me to fix you something?"

"No, I think I'll just get some cereal." Claire said as she went to the pantry for the box of Fruit Loops. She grabbed the milk from the refrigerator and a bowl from the cabinet. She sat with her dad at the table. He had left the paper on the table and began to sip his coffee as he watched his daughter.

Cliff was pensive, not sure whether to bring up Marlena with Claire, but he needed to know if her reaction was genuine and not faked just for his benefit.

He spoke softly. "So, what did you and your mom talk about yesterday?"

She ate noisily at her breakfast. "Nothing much. She just wanted me to know that she was an alcoholic, like I didn't already know that."

"You're right, but do you think she has changed any?"

"Yeah, she did seem different; a good different. So I guess that's good for her."

"Yeah, that's good."

"She's suppose to call me this morning."

"Really?"

"Yeah, she told me yesterday she wanted to."

"So, you OK with that?"

"Sure."

Claire put her spoon back into the bowl and gazed into her father's eyes. "Daddy, who did Mother marry?"

Cliff wasn't sure where this question was leading, but he needed to answer. "She married a man named David Anderson. They moved to Chicago right after the wedding, well after the marriage at the justice of the peace."

"Where did he come from?"

"What do you mean?"

"Where did Mother meet him?"

"He worked in the same office with her here."

Claire began to shudder. She was shivering. She looked frightened and Cliff quickly rose from his chair and ran to Claire. He put his arm around her. "Are you OK, baby"

Claire looked confused for a moment and then she was fine. She didn't recall her father running to her. Cliff looked at her face for any indication that she was regressing. She looked into Cliff's face smiling her little girl smile. "Sure Daddy, I'm OK. Why wouldn't I be?"

Cliff returned to his seat trying to calm himself down. He felt his blood pressure spike. "I don't know Tweetie, you just looked like you were cold for a second there."

"Oh, don't be silly. I'm OK."

Claire finished her cereal and Cliff returned to his paper. Janey came into the kitchen rubbing her eyes.

Claire turned to see her friend. "So, you got up after all. You want something to eat?"

Still rubbing her eyes, she plopped into a chair next to Claire. "No, not yet. I have to wake up first."

Cliff returned to the morning news while Claire and Janey moved into the great room to watch TV, when the door to the garage opened and Kim came in, soaked from head to toe. Her running shorts and T-shirt were clinging to her body. She reached for a dish towel hanging above the sink and wiped the wet from her face and arms.

Cliff smiled. "Got wet, did we?"

"Funny! I need a shower."

Claire heard Kim's voice and ran into the kitchen ready to grab a hug, but she hesitated and backed up. "You're WET!"

Kim laughed. "Well, that happens guys when you try to outrun the rain."

Throwing the towel on the counter, Kim rushed past Claire and Janey toward the stairs and up into the Master bathroom. Later she returned dressed in jeans and pull-over print shirt. She poured herself the last cup of coffee and seated herself next to Cliff. Janey and Claire had returned to the bedroom upstairs. Cliff and Kim spent a quiet time together until an hour later the phone rang. Cliff looked at the wall clock just above his head. It was just after 8:00am. He got up to answer.

"Hello?"

"Cliff, its Marlena."

"Hi, Marlena. Kinda early aren't you."

"Well, I couldn't sleep and I hoped you were all awake. Please tell me I didn't wake you."

"No, we've been up a while. So what's up?"

"I guess I need to get right to the point. I asked Claire yesterday if I could call her today, but I would like to take her to lunch if that's OK with you and, of course, if she will even go. . . "

"I don't know, Marlena. That might not be a good idea."

"Oh, please, Cliff. You or Kim can come along if you want. I just want to spend a little time with her before I leave in the morning."

Cliff thought quietly for a moment.

"Cliff?"

"Yeah, I'm still here. Alright, will you hang on a minute? Let me talk to Kim."

"Sure." Marlena said, but was thinking W*hy do I need permission from the stepmother to visit my child*?

Cliff laid the phone on the counter and walked to Kim who had been watching in anticipation when she heard 'Marlena'. He spoke softly. "Marlena wants to take Claire to lunch today. She said one or both of us could tag along. What do you think?"

Kim was torn between her love for Claire and Marlena's deep need to see her own child. Kim said, "I don't know. You don't think she would try something stupid, like kidnapping do you?"

"No, I don't believe that's her motive. She's leaving in the morning and wants to have time with her today."

"Where is she staying?" Kim asked.

"She said that she would be at the Embassy Suites. It's her favorite chain. Why?"

"Why don't you agree for lunch at the hotel and we will drop Claire off and pick her up. That way, at least, we will have some sort of control. What do you think?"

"Yeah, that would be OK. We can stop in at Salsa's and have our own lunch. How about that."

"Good thinking, Mr. Richards." He leaned over and kissed Kim.

Picking up the phone Cliff responded. "Marlena? I think that will be OK. Are you at the Embassy Suites now?"

"Yes. Why?"

"As long as you have lunch there at Grisanti's then we'll drop Claire off and you can call me to pick her up."

"Don't trust me?"

"No, not that. Just want to ease into things right now. After all she just got home 2 days ago."

"Sure, that will be fine. I'm sorry Cliff. I just feel so desperate to connect with her. Can I speak with her and I will make the invitation. Who knows, I might strike out anyway."

"OK, hold on." Kim had already bounded for the stairway to get Claire. They were coming into the kitchen. Cliff handed her the phone and returned to the breakfast table with Kim and Janey.

"Hello?"

"Hi, Claire. How are you today."

"Oh, hi, Mother. I'm doing fine."

"Claire, I was wondering. . . no I was hoping that you would have lunch with me today. Here at the hotel. I asked your father and he said he would bring you, if that's OK with you. . . . "

Claire thought about her conversation with Marlena the day before and also her talk with Janey the previous night. Claire needed to tell someone what was bottled up inside. Janey was there and she was her best friend. She would not judge or condemn her. Janey accepted her. If there was going to be a relationship with her mother, then she needed to meet Marlena at least half way. After all, her mother was not the same mother she remembered.

"Sure, Mother, that will be good. What time? I'll tell Daddy."

Marlena's heart jumped. "Oh good. How about 12:30. I'll meet you at the door. OK?"

"OK, see you then. Bye."

"Bye, Claire."

David had been up for an hour, had 3 cups of coffee and looked at the trashcan where he had tossed the bottle of liquor the day before. He was trying as hard as he could to resist, but the temptress was calling to him. *Just one drink, that's all you need.* He forced himself to look away even though the pain in his gut was aching for relief. He looked outside. The leaves were falling from the trees. There was a chill in the air. The cold front coming through today might even bring in snow flurries tonight. His elbows rested on the table and he laid his head in the palm of his hands. The memories of that night filled his thoughts. What had Marlena learned? What will the girl remember? He needed to know more. He needed answers. He got up and walked to the desk in the den. In the bottom right drawer, he kept an address book of friends he had left in Memphis. He never considered moving back into the south, yet he kept the book of close acquaintances. Never knew when he would need to ask a favor, but this seemed like this was one of the times.

David sat at the desk and pulled the book from the drawer. He leafed through the pages looking for the one person he believed could assist him. Page after page, he noted the lawyer, the policeman, the 'you work you ride' car dealer, a fellow programmer, the investigator. He stopped. Just the one he was looking for; Roger Dempsey, Private Investigations. David looked at his watch for the time. 9:30, that would not be too early. He pulled the phone close, took the receiver off the hook and dialed the number in Memphis.

After 3 rings someone answered. “Hello?”

David detected a child had picked up the phone. “Hello, I would like to speak to Roger Dempsey. Is that your father?”

“Yes it is”, came back a shy voice. “Hold on.”

A few seconds later, a man answered. “ Hello, this is Roger.”

“Hey Roger, David Anderson.”

“David?. . . . . My old drinking buddy, David?”

“Same one.”

“So where did you run off too? Haven’t seen you down at TG’s in ages.”

“Well, I kinda got married and moved to Chicago.”

“No shit? To Chicago? I didn’t think anyone deliberately moved to Chicago. So who did you finally marry? Anybody I know?”

“No, you don’t know her. Just someone I’ve known a while.”

“So what’s up? You didn’t call after all these months just to spill some good news on me about your nuptials.”

“You still doing PI work?”

“Sure, you need me to find somebody for you?”

“No, just watch someone. Pick up what you can.”

“OK, get me some details.”

It was nearly 12:00 and Claire had just finished dressing in a pair of the new faded jeans and a yellow blouse from Macy's. The new Nikes she received at her last birthday were still new. Fortunately, her feet didn't shrink when she did. She stood in her new bedroom and looked at her full figure in the long mirror attached to the closet door. She was amazed at the difference in her size. She had lost a lot of weight. She must weigh less than 100 pounds and with her height, she looked like a rail with clothes on. Time will change all that and today was the start. She was looking forward to spending some quality time with Marlena. Something deep within her was yearning for a connection between them; she just didn't know it. Cliff called to her from the bottom of the stairs. She glanced one more time in the mirror and grabbed her purse from the bed.

Kim was waiting by the car. She had been talking to her own mother on the cellphone, giving out some details of the weekend they had just been through. Cliff and Claire came through the open garage door and Cliff opened the driver's door and Kim got in on the passenger side after ending her call. Claire took the back seat. The ride to Embassy Suites was quiet. Kim, thinking of her role in all of this and Cliff concerned about a reoccurring episode might happen and he would not be there to help. Claire was concerned with the topics of interest that Marlena would want to cover. What would she say to her mother? What should she say? Tell the truth? Just ignore her feelings?

Cliff was on Poplar Avenue heading west when he turned right onto Shady Grove Road. The hotel was just one block north. He pulled into the street that separated the hotel from a shopping center and then left into the drive, which led up to the drop-off canopy that covered the entrance to the Embassy Suites Hotel. Marlena was waiting patiently by the door.

Marlena came to the car and opened the back door to let Claire out. Cliff exited his side and stood by the open door. He said to Marlena, "Hi. They busy in there?"

"No, looks light today, for Grisanti's that is." Marlena said as she helped Claire out.

“We’re having lunch at Salsa’s. Take your time. Just give me a call when you’re through.” He looked at Claire. “Have fun, Tweetie.”

“I will Daddy. Now you and Kim go have lunch.” Claire said waving him away and smiling at Kim staring through the tinted window.

Cliff returned to the driver’s seat, but waited as he watched them go inside. He couldn’t help worrying about Claire; how she would react to Marlena. He drove away as soon as they passed through the inner door.

The hotel was quite busy on this particular day. A special corporate lunch crowd had gathered at the opposite end of the cavernous first floor gardens. There was a convention gathering of businessmen who were milling about the tables which had been set up throughout first floor. A large buffet had been prepared for the group near the breakfast bar and happy hour pavilion. Grisanti’s was sparsely filled with the regulars in for Sunday morning brunch.

Claire waited silently as Marlena was approached by a cute, young woman with long blonde hair and a name tag pinned to her uniform, announcing that she was Ashlie. Marlena asked for a table for two in a non-smoking area. Ashlie led them to a booth for four near the back of the restaurant. At least there was a window view into the parking lot. Ashlie left the menus and announced the specials for the day, which she had memorized and really didn’t care if her customers were interested or not. She was just doing her job until she got off and went to her real life. Claire and Marlena remained in silence, neither one ready to begin a conversation without feeling awkward. They calmly studied the menus.

Finally Marlena spoke. “You see anything you like?”

“Maybe just a cheeseburger and fries”, Claire said as she pondered the other choices.

“That sounds pretty good.”

Silence reined at the table until Brenda showed up with pad and pencil in hand. Brenda was slim and short; a seasoned waitress to be sure. Uniform was all in place with not a single spot of spilled food dotting the front of her crisp attire. Order pads stuffed into the pockets of the jet-black slacks and extra pencils in the breast pocket of her long sleeved white blouse. Chewing incessantly on a stick of Juicy Fruit she asked. “You ladies ready to order, yet.”

Marlena looked at Claire. “Cheeseburgers?”

Claire nodded.

“OK, let’s have 2 cheeseburgers and fries. I’ll have Coke. What do you want to drink, Claire?”

“A coke will be fine.”

Brenda jotted down the order in record speed and in waitress shorthand. “Be back in a second with your drinks.” She left carrying the menus with her.

Marlena watched Claire for a moment, contemplating how to form the words. This seemed so strange, so foreign to her. She had never been at a loss for words in a courtroom, handling a deposition or cross examining a witness. She trained for that, yet she never trained to be a mother. This was so new to her. Claire was staring at a couple of older ladies three tables away, who were finishing a 2 hour gossip brunch. One’s hair was so white, it shimmered with a bluish sheen.

Marlena reached over the table and lightly touched the back of Claire’s hand. Claire didn’t repel from her touch, but turned to face Marlena. She smiled at her mother and put her other hand on top of Marlena’s.

Marlena started the conversation. “Do you feel as awkward as I do?”

"Yeah. We never did this before. You know, just you and me. Lunch."

"You're right and I'm so sorry that we never did. Maybe this can be the first of many lunches together."

"Maybe."

"Claire, you know what we talked about yesterday was not just me talking. I meant everything I said. I am not who you remember me to be. That woman and that mother is gone. The new improved me is here and I want to share a part of your life, even it is just a small part."

"I know."

Marlena paused. She had the words, but couldn't say them. Claire nervously looked around the restaurant. Brenda appeared with 2 cokes and straws. "Your order will be right out."

Marlena said, "Thanks!"

Brenda attended to her other customers, including the gossiping aged women with blue hair. Marlena welcomed the break, slight as it was it gave her enough courage to speak. "Claire, can I ask you something and will you be truthful with me?"

Claire looked into her mother's eyes and saw a wanting, a sincerity glowing back at her. "Sure and will you be truthful too?"

"Of course I will."

"Alright, then ask." Claire said taking a sip of her drink.

Marlena just dove in, head first. "Do you hate me for how I have treated you all your life?"

Claire turned away. She didn't want to answer.

"Remember you said you would be truthful. I need to know even if it hurts."

Claire returned her gaze back to those loving eyes. "Well . . . . I did. I guess I did before yesterday."

"Why yesterday?"

"Well, mainly you were different. I never saw you like that before. I liked it."

"But before that?"

"I hated you. I hated how you treated me and my friends, how you treated Daddy and I hated what you did." There she said it, without even realizing the words came out.

Marlena's eyes opened wide. She sat up straighter. "What, Claire. What did I do? I know I was mean to you and to your friends. And I was mean to your Daddy, too. But that was my alcohol problem controlling all that. But what did I do that hurt you so bad?"

Claire could have tolerated the attitude and the rejection of her friends all the years. She had learned to live with that, but what she saw that night, that night her mother made love to another man, right in their own house. That was an unforgivable act. Or was it?

Claire looked away. Marlena reached for her hand and held it in both hers. Claire did not pull away. Her mother's touch was soft and reassuring. "Claire, please tell me. I need to know the truth. I promise I will not hold anything back from you. We agreed to be honest with each other."

Claire pulled her hand from Marlena's grip and placed both hands in her lap. She looked into Marlena's face for a moment and then spoke. "Janey spent the night with me last night. . . . She's my best friend in the whole world. We talked for a long time; after midnight I think. . . . She was trying to help me remember stuff that I couldn't, you know. But

I couldn't so then she said for me to tell her about stuff I do remember, you know before I went into the hospital. So I told her everything."

"And what did you remember? What did you tell her?"

Claire took a deep breath. She looked out the window for words. Then she faced Marlena boldly. "I remembered my birthday party when Allison gave me these shoes." She held her foot out from the table so Marlena could see. "I remember Grammie and Grandpa Bill coming over and how glad I was to see him. I remember all the stuff I got. I remember Daddy leaving for a quick trip when I didn't want him to go. I remember going over to Janey's house to spend the night. Do you remember all that too, Mother?"

Marlena didn't know where this was leading, but she agreed. "Yes, I remember all that. Go on, tell me more."

Claire shifted in her seat. She started now; she couldn't stop. "I remember calling Daddy from at Janey's house and asking him to come home. I remember the rain and lightning and thunder."

Marlena was remembering too, but her experience she recalled was not frightening.

Claire continued. "I remember me and my friends getting ready to watch a movie and I remember coming home to get my new CD. I remember sneaking into my own house so I wouldn't disturb you at whatever you were working on." Marlena gasped. "I remember coming to the top of the stairs, getting ready to sneak back out when someone knocked on the door."

Marlena closed her eyes and put her head down. *Not this* she thought.

"Do you want me to go on, Mother?"

"No, please don't."

"But I need too. I need to tell you the truth." Claire paused. "I remember hiding by the stairway trying to think of a way to get out without being seen. I remember seeing some strange man come into our house and kiss my mother on the lips. Then I remember seeing something I never saw in my life."

Marlena covered her face with her hands. "Please, Claire. Stop!"

"I remember seeing some man and my mother . . .'do it'. . on the couch in my house; my Daddy's house. I remember how much I hated you at that moment. I remember thinking of how could you do that to me and to Daddy. I just wanted to die right there. I wanted you to die right there."

Marlena was crying quietly, hoping she would not attract attention of the other patrons in the restaurant, especially the busybody old ladies, but she could not stop. She reached for a napkin and wiped her eyes. Her mascara had begun to run.

Through continued tears she said to Claire. "Baby", Marlena choked back more tears. "I am so sorry. If I had known that you were." She looked directly at Claire. "I don't have a defense. I'm guilty. I'm so ashamed. I will never be able to make it up to you. Please, please forgive me, Claire." She covered her face and continued to sob.

Claire watched her mother. She watched with some satisfaction that she had inflicted a little pain of her own, yet she also watched with the great compassion she held in her heart for others. She sensed a burden had been lifted from her heart and mind. Relief rushed throughout her body. Did she forgive her mother after all that? Should she forgive her? All Claire knew was that the woman before her now, was not the woman she remembered on that particular day and night in her past. This was a woman and mother who was definitely feeling great remorse for the hurting she had inflicted on her innocent child. Claire slid across her seat in the booth and walked around to Marlena's side. She moved in close and pulled Marlena's arms away from her face. Marlena had a surprised look come across her face at seeing Claire next to her. Claire held her mother's hands in her own and looked deep into her Marlena's swollen and make-up blackened eyes. She spoke so softly. "Mother. . . .

.. Mom, I do forgive you. I know now that wasn't the real you back then. This is the real Mom."

At those words, all the guilt Marlena felt and all the pain Claire had felt, melted away in their tender embrace. Claire wrapped her arms around her mother's neck and Marlena caressed Claire's back. Both were crying now when Brenda stopped by with the cheeseburgers.

Sensing she was at the right place at the wrong time she offered. "Excuse me, should I come back later?"

Marlena and Claire released their grip on each other and Marlena reached for another set of napkins, handing one to Claire. She looked up at Brenda and smiled. "Sorry, just a great mother/daughter moment."

"Know what you mean. I've had them myself; got 3 girls of my own." Brenda said as she set the plates down and quietly backed away from *this particular moment*.

Claire and Marlena were smiling at each other. Claire took a napkin and helped clear some smudged makeup from Marlena's face. Marlena said. "So what happens now, do we start with this moment as a new beginning?"

Claire returned to her side of the table and pulled the plate close. She grabbed a single french fry and plopped it into her mouth. "Yeah, I guess. We can start new. As long as you don't turn into the other mother I hated again."

Marlena said. "As long as I have you to help me and God's willing, I will never be like that again."

"Is that man your new husband, David?" Claire ate another fry and sipped her drink.

"How did you know his name was David?"

"Daddy told me."

"Oh, OK. Yes, his name is David and that was him. Claire you do understand that your father and I were on the verge of splitting up anyway? Stuff like that happens in the real adult world. I pray you will never have to go through it when you grow up, but it is a part of life these days."

"Yeah, I kinda felt that was coming down. I met Kim after *that night.*"

"You did?"

"I wanted you to go away and let Kim be my mom. She loved Daddy and I told him to marry her."

"You did?"

"Yeah. I wanted a mother who would do stuff with me, and talk to me. And she did that the first time we met. You never did that. Maybe if you did, all this would never have happened." Claire said as Marlena's heart sank a little further.

"You're probably right. All this truly is my fault. As long as you can give me forgiveness and we can go forward with a clean slate, then that's all I can hope for. So can we agree on one thing between us?"

"What's that?"

"Let's agree that we will always be honest with each other. Don't hold anything back no matter how much it might hurt. I don't want anything to break up this start of our relationship. I want to be your friend. I want to be a mother to you. I will never take away or try to take away what you have with Kim. Kim is good for you. She deserves you more than I do. Maybe Kim and I can become good friends, too. I am just happy to have a fresh start. So do we agree?"

Claire looked at Marlena, then outside at a passing car. "As long as you don't change from how you are now. I want to be honest. I want to be your friend and I want you to be my mother too."

"Thank you, sweetheart. Thank you so much. I will try to show you the love I never did before. I will try to hold your trust and confidence."

Claire smiled at Marlena and she returned the smile. Claire reached for her cheeseburger and took a big bite. Marlena joined her. They spent the next 90 minutes eating and talking about plans for the future, plans for visits, shopping, favorite colors, food, boys, friends, Kim and Cliff, Grammie but they never talked about the past. Marlena paid the bill and called Cliff for pickup. She waited with Claire at the door until he and Kim pulled into the driveway. Claire turned to her Mom and wrapped her arms around her waist and held tight. Marlena gave her the biggest hug she could and kissed her on the cheek. Kim looked at Cliff in disbelief. Cliff was speechless. Claire released Marlena and ran to the car. She waved at her as she opened the back door of the car. Marlena waved back and stood by the door as they drove away. She smiled and returned to her room where she planned to call David.

On the ride home, Claire told them the same story she had told Marlena. She was planning to be honest and not hold back anything from her dad or Kim. They were flabbergasted at this revelation of the little girl. Cliff was now beginning to form some pieces to the puzzle in his mind. He was almost certain that these events might have led up to her psychological breakdown, but it was not the trigger.

When they arrived home, Claire was first out of the car. She opened Kim's door and helped her out. Standing before her, Claire wrapped her arms around her tightly. Kim looked at Cliff as he was rounding the front of the car. Claire looked into Kim's face and tenderly said, "I love you, Mommy." Kim could not hold back. She burst into tears and held tightly to her stepdaughter.

After a few minutes of tears, Kim looked at Claire. "What brought that on, sweetie?"

"I'm such a lucky girl. I have 2 moms. I have you, you're my Mommy and I have a mother who will be my Mom. I love you because you loved me first. And I love Mom because she loves me, now."

The rest of the day was spent relaxing at home; no visitors, no surprises, just Dad, Mommy and Claire.

Marlena called David from her room and reported the great news. David was excited for Marlena, but remained concerned for his own welfare.

Chapter Fourteen

Monday morning came in with a bang. A strong cold front blanketed the mid-south with drenching rain and falling temperatures. Claire was awakened from a wonderful dream by a tremendous thunderclap. Her eyes jerked opened and noticed another bright lightning strike brightening her room like it was noon in the middle of July. She covered her ears in anticipation of the loud thunder that would come next. She pulled the comforter from the bed over her head and tried returning to the dream she enjoyed so much. In the dream, she was with Marlena on the beach; just the two of them. They had been swimming in a deep blue lagoon, snorkeling for seashells. An umbrella covered their bodies from the bright sunshine, while they sat at a beach table. A dark tanned young man was bringing an order of cheese nachos and pineapple-orange drinks in a glass with the little umbrella on a stir stick. They were talking about a variety of subjects from school to shopping in Paris over the weekend. The more she recalled of her dream, the more she smiled. Her heart felt mended.

Claire lifted the covers far enough to see the clock on the night stand. It was nearly 6:30. Maybe she should get up. She couldn't go back to sleep with the storm coming through. Throwing back the comforter, she jumped from the bed and walked down the hall to the bathroom. She froze for an instant when she walked past her old bedroom. She felt shivers run throughout her body. A strange terror overcame her. Then it was gone. She didn't recall it after she entered the hall bathroom.

Cliff and Kim had been up for at least an hour. Kim was disappointed that the storm had forced her to cancel her usual morning run. Cliff was content to have coffee and read the morning paper.

Kim was opposite Cliff at the breakfast table. She had prepared a cup of hot tea for herself. "Would you like some breakfast?"

Cliff put down the sports page. "Not yet. I'll wait for Claire to wake up."

"What are we going to do about her school?"

"I guess we need to arrange a meeting with the principal. She has missed so much. I don't know if she will have to start over or just do catch up. Maybe we can hire a tutor to get Claire up to her grade level."

"I have a friend at work whose sister tutors in the home. At least, I think she does. Anyway, you want me to call her?"

"Maybe. Let's see what the school says we need to do."

Kim took a sip of tea. "I have a trip scheduled for next week. I'll have to leave on Sunday. Will you be OK?"

"I was thinking about taking a leave of absence. Maybe just 3-4 weeks; just until we get a routine down and Claire back into a normal life."

"We'll be OK. We have enough savings to cover."

"And Mae will still be coming in every day. "

"So far . . . ." Cliff looked up to see Claire enter the kitchen. "Well good morning Tweetie. Did you sleep well?"

She sat next to her Dad and pulled a juice glass from the tray in the center of the table. A pitcher of orange juice was half full. She filled the little glass and downed the juice. She needed something cold and tangy to open her throat.

"Yeah, I was sleeping real good until that thunder scared the stew out of me."

Kim said, "Yeah, me too."

Claire poured another glass and said to her father. "What are we doing today?"

"Your new bedroom furniture is being delivered today."

"Yeah, I forgot."

"And I need to go to your school."

"What for?"

"You've missed a lot of studies. All your classmates have moved on to the 6th grade. You never finished the 5th. What would you say if I got a tutor for you. You know to help you get caught up and then you can join your regular class."

"Can we do that?"

"Well, I hope your principal will understand."

"Mrs. Sherman?"

"Yeah, I suppose. Is she the principal?"

"Last I remember."

Kim rose from the table and gathered the scattered cups and glasses. "Who wants breakfast?"

Claire promptly threw her hand in the air. "I do, I do. French Toast please."

"OK, French Toast for you and Cliff you want the same or something more exotic?"

"That will be just fine."

Kim busied herself gathering the eggs, milk, butter, bread and the other necessary ingredients for her famous French Toast. The family sat joyfully at the breakfast table with Claire between her beloved Dad and her new Mom. Claire was extremely content.

Marlena was a bit nervous flying with electrical storms in the area. No matter how much the airline personnel at the check-in counter tried to calm her fears, she was apprehensive enough that she had considered canceling and flying later in the day or even tomorrow. She closely watched the repeating news and weather on the overhead televisions in the waiting areas. Her flight was not scheduled for departure until 9:30 and Marlena looked at the digital watch showing only 8:00. It appeared the worst of the storm had already passed. From the large picture windows she could see some clearing in the west. Maybe this would be a smooth flight after all.

The waiting area was filled with passengers this morning. Marlena was seated in a row of seats that faced the outside window. She always enjoyed watching the activity on the tarmac and if she happened to be at the right gate, she could watch the planes land and take-off. Seated two chairs to her right, a young mother was tending to a young girl with long blonde hair, who appeared to be no more than 2 years old. As she casually observed the loving way this mother cared for her child, she was reminded of the callus attitude she had for Claire when she was about that child's age. Marlena closed her eyes as tears formed. What would her life have been like if she had been in recovery sooner? This new relationship with Claire means so much to her now that the thought of drinking again had become the farthest thing in her mind.

She continued to watch and casually started a conversation. "You have a very adorable little girl there."

The young mother turned to the stranger and fellow passenger. "Why, thank you."

"How old is she, 2?"

"She will be in December. December 18th to be exact."

"What's her name?"

"Elaine. It's after my grandmother." The mother said smiling proudly at her child.

"Why that's beautiful. I have a little girl myself. She's 11 though. And her name is Claire Elaine."

"That's cool."

At that moment Marlena's cellphone in her purse began to ring. She reached for the bag under her legs next to the seat. She pulled out the phone and notice the caller ID, David. She excused herself with the mother and little Elaine. She turned to have her back to the other passengers.

"Hi sweetie. You at work?"

"No, I called in sick." David answered.

"Are you sick?"

"No. . . well, I just couldn't make myself get up."

"Are you hung-over, David? Did you fall back on your promise?"

"No, No. Honest, I have had nothing. Well, nothing last night. I went to bed after we talked. I actually threw away half a bottle of Jack."

Marlena was quiet for a few seconds. She stared blankly out onto the airport runways. She had to begin to trust David, even though he had tried many times before and failed. "Well, that's good, sweetheart. Maybe you should stay home today. Get some rest. Fix yourself a good breakfast and relax in front of the TV. Catch some soaps."

"Yeah, like I'll do that." David laughed.

Marlena smiled and said. "I should be home after lunch. Then we can talk. See you then. Love you."

"Love you, too. See you when you get here. Bye."

"Bye." Marlena snapped her cell phone shut, stared out the window and again checked her watch.

David dropped the receiver on the cradle of the phone. The cloudy memories and images bombarded his thoughts like an incessant hail storm banging on a tin roof of an old barn. He went to the kitchen looking for some Excedrin. It was there in the cabinet above the sink. He tapped out 3 tablets into his palm and flipped them in his mouth. Leaning over, he turned on the cold water tap and sipped enough water to down the pills. David stood motionless, staring at the door below the sink for what seemed to be an eternity. Inside the door, just inches away, still tightly capped and tucked neatly inside the trash was the answer to his problems. It called to him. It beckoned him to just reach in and take hold of that bottle. It can make the shakes and shivers go away in an instant with just one gulp. It can drown those haunting memories from his mind. David's head snapped upright and he covered his face with both palms. He began to sob uncontrollably, ignoring the searing pain in his gut. David turned and pulled several sheets from the paper towel holder. He wiped his face and felt ashamed for breaking down like a little child. He tossed the wet paper onto the counter and returned to his bedroom for a quick shower and clean clothes.

Claire had finished breakfast and helped Kim clean the kitchen. Her dad had left for her school to discuss Claire's catch up education. Kim left for work and Miss Mae had arrived an hour earlier to maintain the house. Claire had been given instructions to clean her new room before the furniture arrives. She was busy picking up clothes left on the floor from the night before. She threw those into a small pile next to the hall doorway. Throwing the pillows onto the floor, Claire pulled the fitted sheet from her bed and then the cases were removed from the pillows. She carried this bundle to the laundry chute in the hallway. When she pushed the sheets through the small door flap of the chute, Claire's mind flashed back to a hidden memory; of a time she had done this same thing before. She felt flush, dizzy and ready to faint. The door flap snapped shut as the laundry fell to the first floor. The sound brought Claire back into the real world. She opened her eyes to find she was bracing her body with palms flat against the wall. The feeling of pain and fright subsided and Claire went back to her room to gather the remaining dirty laundry. The memory never left her, like a bad dream that would wake you up suddenly, but wouldn't go away. As she tidied the room, she continued to think about the incident; trying to make some sense of it. She had finished cleaning the room, when there was a small tap on the bedroom door. It was Janey. Claire looked up and smiled when Janey pushed open the door.

"Oh, hi Janey. I'm so glad you're here." Claire ran to hug her friend.

"Well, I am like supposed to be in school, but I wasn't feeling to good this morning and mom let me stay home." Janey said as she sat on the edge of the bed.

"So you're OK now?"

"Yeah a lot better. I would rather be here with you anyway. Mom said I had to be home in like an hour. So what are you going to do today?"

"My dad went to school so he could talk with Mrs. Sherman about getting me caught up and all. I'm probably getting a tutor or something who'll help me with subjects I missed last year and this year."

"Then you can come back to school?"

"I guess. I do kinda miss it." Claire said as she sat on the bed next to her best friend.

Claire and Janey talked more about school and upcoming events when Miss Mae came knocking on the door informing the two that the men with the new furniture had arrived and that Janey's mom had called, wanting her home. Janey hugged Claire and ran down the stairs to the front door. The first of the many boxes were being unloaded onto the lawn, where the men would remove the furniture from the crates and carry them upstairs to Claire's room. Janey couldn't wait to see what it looked like and she knew there would be the color yellow somewhere on every piece.

As Janey walked to the sidewalk to her house next door, she noticed a blue Ford Taurus parked on the opposite side of the street, two houses down. She remembered this particular car from the day before; because it was not one she had ever seen on this street before. Sure, people who live here buy new cars all the time, but what felt strange to Janey was the fact that the last time she saw the car, there was a person sitting in the driver's seat and this time was no different. For some reason, she could feel eyes watching her as she walked up her driveway. She started to run and kept on running until she bolted through the front door. She ran to the window in the living room that faced the front yard. She pulled back the drapery from the edge, only enough to peer through at the blue Taurus down the street. The car was still there and the person was still there as well. Janey was bent over a chair staring out the window when her mother came in.

"What are you peeping at, Janey?" her mother asked.

"Oh, nothing. Claire's getting new bedroom stuff and I was just watching." She lied.

"Well, let me check your temperature again."

"Oh, mom!"

Marlena's plane arrived at O'Hare on time and without incident. The weather had been perfect for the flight. The terminal was exceptionally busy and Marlena knew her luggage would be late arriving at the baggage pickup; it always was when flying Northwest. She spotted a Starbucks Coffee sign and decided to stop for a cappuccino and rehearse her talk she planned to have with David later this afternoon. She had to find out all he might have remembered from the night Claire went in that state of unconsciousness. She certainly could not recall what happened. Though she had tried and tried to bring back those memories of that night, she barely remembered coming home. The night out with David was a blur. She only recalled visiting some of the restaurants on Beale St. The rest of her memories were a foggy dream.

Starbucks was a favorite stop over for travelers. She found it so amazing that people would pay 4 to 5 dollars for a cup of coffee; she being one of them. A cute young waitress took her order at the counter and rushed to get her coffee ready. Marlena stared at the planes landing. The sky was perfectly clear and she was lost in the activity when sweet thing returned with her order. Marlena pulled out a ten dollar bill and told her to keep the change. Marlena found an empty table by the window. She placed her purse on the empty seat and sat down. She took one careful sip and looked at her purse and pulled out her cell phone. She punched in the speed dial for David's phone. If he was out, then he would have his cell with him. It rang until the voice mail system answered. She pushed the off button and dialed their home number. David answered on the 2nd ring.

"Hello", David said with a muffled tone that told Marlena he had been asleep.

"Hey, sweetie. Did I wake you up?"

"Well, I guess I did doze off. Where are you?"

"Just got in at O'Hare. I'm waiting on my luggage. You know how long that takes. I'll get a cab."

"Sure you don't want me to pick you up?"

"No, I'll get a cab. We would probably pass on the interstate anyway. You been having a good morning?"

"Yeah, best I can."

"You still sober?", she asked boldly.

David paused.

"David?"

"Yeah...... but it has been hard to do. I don't know how you did it."

"It was real hard for me, too. It still is. That's why you need a sponsor. That's why you need to get into a group of other alcoholics. We all have the disease. We need to support each other."

"And you're going to be there with me?"

"All the way, baby. You can come with me to my group or we can find you one of your own. Sometimes it works better when we're not sharing with those we love. We'll talk all about that when I get home. I also want to talk about that night we went out when Claire was home and we didn't know. I am looking for some answers and maybe you can remember more that I did. So, make us some coffee and maybe some lunch. I'll be home in about an hour."

David started to shake. Sweat started to bead on his forehead. It was bad enough that he was already plagued with the memories, now he had to reveal what he knew to Marlena. He would have to lie. Would he be able to be convincing? Would Marlena be looking for signs? His mind was reeling.

"David? You still there?"

Her voice snapped him back. "Yeah, sure I'm here. What would you like for lunch? Soup? Sandwich? There's some leftover pizza."

"Oh, just surprise me. I'm a little hungry. Anything would be good."

"OK, I'll get on it. See you when you get here."

"Alright, bye. Love you." Marlena said.

"Love you, too. Bye."

Marlena closed her cell and returned it to her purse. She sipped her coffee for another 20 minutes and left for the baggage area. To her surprise, hers was one of a handful left on the rolling conveyor. She retrieved the bag and went outside to hail a cab.

David dropped the phone on the hook. He laid his head on the back of the sofa, staring at the vaulted ceiling. Marlena wants to talk about what happened that night. He had been trying so hard to forget those memories. He thought everything was alright with the girl; she didn't remember anything and that was it. He needed a plan. A plan that would be convincing to Marlena, yet not reveal his lies. Jack started to call him. "Davey? I'm still here. I can solve your problems for you."

David quickly covered his ears, shaking his head violently he yelled, "NO, NO. I will NEVER allow you to ruin my life. I did that to myself."

But Jack still spoke through his covered ears. "You know you want me back. I'm just a step or two away. Come get me, Davey!"

David stood up. With hands at his side, he turned to stare at the kitchen cabinet. His gazed was fixed on the door under the sink. He couldn't take his eyes off the cabinet door. It kept calling to his mind; taunting and humiliating him. The force was strong, pulling him closer to a breakdown. It took all his strength to resist the temptation.

"David, come get me. I'll make you feel better."

David was weakening and the burning in his gut was unbearable, but then the thought of Marlena gave him the courage he needed to break the hold. He turned to the stairs and ran up to his bedroom, two steps at a time. He could not go into the kitchen again. Jack was there. He was strong and David was weak. Marlena would have to understand why lunch was not ready. David lay on his bed staring at the ceiling. He felt the wetness trickling down his cheek. He closed his eyes tightly and began to cry.

Claire stood silently in the doorway of her new bedroom admiring the furniture the delivery men had just completed installing. They were paid extra to take down and move the existing furniture into an empty bedroom down the hall. Mae had let the men out the front door, making sure the empty cartons were reloaded onto their truck. She returned to Claire's room and found Claire lying on her unmade bed.

"Well, what do you think of all this, Miss Claire?" Mae asked.

"This is awesome, Mae. I just love it."

"Well, maybe we should get some linen on your new bed. Didn't your daddy buy some new sheets too?"

"Yeah, they're in the hall closet, I think."

Mae went into the closet and pulled the new sheet set from the top shelf. She returned to the bedroom and found Claire rearranging the desk and chair.

"I guess you weren't right with the way those men set you up were you Miss Claire?"

"I think I want my desk by the window instead. That way I can look out."

"Well, come help me with your bed. Then we can rearrange anything else you want."

Both Mae and Claire completed the bed in just a minute. Claire fussed with the pillows and checked the length of the yellow flowered comforter, making sure it hung the same on both sides and the foot. Mae had left for the kitchen downstairs and Claire stared intently at her bed. There was something missing; it just wasn't right. All at once the answer came to her. She needed the three small yellow throw pillows with white fringe along the edges that were left in her old bedroom. Without a second thought, Claire went into the hall and walked right up to the closed door of her previous room. She began to shiver but didn't know why. She thought this was just too silly, so she reached for the door knob and turned it. The door opened into the room and Claire stood frozen for a second in the door opening. The pillows were still on the old bed, which was now unmade except for the pillows she needed. After boldly taking the first step into the bedroom, Claire found the additional courage to hurry across the room and gather the pillows.

As soon as she got next to the bed, her mind began to swirl. The walls began to spin around her. Bright flashes of light, like an enraged thunderstorm opened up her memories. This was a bad place. She was so afraid of it. She immediately closed her eyes, hoping to block the memories that were flooding into her mind faster than she could analyze. Her eyes were tightly shut and were rolling furiously underneath her eyelids while trying to comprehend the blurry and shadowy memories that made little sense to Claire, but something was forcing her to see. A face appeared. An unfamiliar face came to her thoughts inside. She detested this image. It was horrendous. It was dangerous. She started to screech inside and collapsed onto the floor where she lay for what seemed like hours. Finally, she struggled to her feet and ran out of the room back to her new bed. She jumped onto the bed, pulling the comforter up and over her body; burying herself deep within the softness of the material. The thoughts continued to haunt her. She could not shake that blurry face from her mind.

Mae had returned to Claire's room to announce that the brownies had just come out of the oven. She saw the bed in disarray and noticed feet protruding from the pile.

"Miss Claire, are you in that mess on the bed?" Mae asked.

Hearing Mae's soothing voice, Claire threw back the covers, jumped from the bed and ran into Mae's arms.

"My, my missy, you are shaking something awful." Mae said as she stroked her hair. "What happened to you, child?"

Claire didn't say anything, but held her dear friend closer.

"Claire, what is it, now? You can tell Miss Mae"

With a stammer in her voice, Claire told her "I got scared."

"And what scared you, sweetie?"

"I was finishing making my bed and I thought my old throw pillows would look good on this bed, so I went into my old room."

"You know you shouldn't go in there."

"I know, but I was alright until I got inside. I started having flashbacks or something like that. I kept seeing this scary looking face. Well, it looked like a face. I got scared and I ran in here."

Mae continued to comfort Claire. "Well, you best keep 'way from that room. So are you OK now. Maybe you could use some brownies and milk."

"Yeah, that would be cool. Will you come with me?"

"Sure, sweetie, let's go."

They left the room arm and arm. When they passed the *bad* room, Claire held tighter to Mae, burying her face into her upper arm until they reached the stairs. They spent the next hour munching on delicious brownies and talking about happier times.

Chapter Fifteen

Marlena and David spent a quiet afternoon together. He admitted to her the struggle he had been facing and asked for her help. She phoned her AA sponsor and they met for a couple of hours over pizza at a nearby Chicago Pizza place. Many times Marlena tried to talk with David about the visits she had with Claire, but he always managed to take the focus off Claire and bring it back to him and his problems. Marlena soon dropped the topic of Claire and they spent a quiet evening at home, lying in bed and watching TV. David dozed off early and Marlena decided to call Claire and talk more about that night. She was making a good connection with her and she didn't want to lose that relationship she had begun. She quietly got off the side of the bed and went downstairs to the great room to phone her daughter. She left the TV on in the bedroom to help drown out any conversation that might drift upstairs.

She checked her watch and noted the time; it was only 9:00pm. Claire should still be awake. She made herself comfortable on the sofa and pulled the phone from the table into her lap. Feeling a bit nervous, Marlena picked up the receiver and dialed the long distance number to Memphis.

Claire and Janey were in a deep conversation that only 11 year old girls can have, when call waiting beeped. Claire excused herself and clicked the button on the receiver to switch to the new call.

"Hello?" Claire announced.

"Hi Sweetie, are you in bed yet?" Marlena answered.

"Oh, Hi Mother, let me get Janey off the other line."

"OK." Marlena was excited.

Claire clicked the same button again. "Janey, my mother's on the other line. I'll talk to you tomorrow, OK?"

Janey said, “I’ll call you when I get home from school. I wish you were back in school with me.”

“Yeah, me too. Bye.”

“Bye.” she said and clicked back to Marlena.

“I’m back, Mother. So what’s up?”

“Not much, I just wanted to talk before I went off to sleep. You don’t mind do you?”

“No, I’m kinda glad you called.” Claire said as she laid back on a stack of three pillows and pulled up her comforter over her legs up to her waist.

Marlena hesitated for a second and then spoke softly. “I wanted to talk a little more about that night if you will. I regret I was never the mother I should have been. I want to try and make some things right between us and that night is a blur to me. I feel so responsible in some way for what has happened to you.”

“Well, Mother, I really don’t know what more I could tell you. It’s all a blur to me too.”

“Start from the day when you got home from school.”

Claire thought for a minute, switching the phone receiver to her other ear. She pulled the covers up closer. Maybe for comfort or maybe for protection, she didn’t know. Those strange and un-nerving sensations were beginning to roll through her head again. She closed her eyes for a second or two, taking deep breaths.

Marlena sensed some anxiousness in the sounds coming through the phone line. “Claire, are you OK?”

Claire took a deep breath and said, “Yeah, I’m alright. I don’t know what’s been going on lately, but I’ve been getting these weird feelings that scare me. I see things.”

Marlena sat up quickly, "What, baby, what things?"

"Oh just lights and images mainly. Kinda blurry. I really can't tell what it is that's going on. I get real dizzy and sometimes lose track of time." Then she thought of the face. "And I see this face. Well, it looks like a face. That's the scariest part."

"Have you told your dad about this?"

"No, not yet. Miss Mae was around today when it happened."

"How often has this happened?"

"I don't know. I've been getting weird dizzy feelings for a couple of days, but I just figured it would go away. But this afternoon, was the first time I saw stuff that scared me."

"You need to tell your father. Tonight! OK? Has this happened since this afternoon?"

"Well, it kinda did just a minute ago."

Marlena realized at that moment Claire was regaining the tragic memories that had plagued her all this time. It had to be the answer. She understood that she had to be careful not to press the issue; don't make her remember until she was ready. Marlena was already planning a return trip to Memphis. She had to be there for her daughter.

"Baby, why don't we just talk about this another time? You should get some sleep. Maybe you'll feel better in the morning."

"I feel fine now, Mother. I just get these sensations that scare me every now and then. Right now I'm OK. And about that night, all I remember is that Janey and I spent a couple hours together over here before I went to bed. I brushed my teeth and hair like always and got into bed and went right to sleep. Next thing I remember was Grammie coming to see me in that awful place."

"Well, you get some sleep now. I'll see you tomorrow sometime."

Claire looked surprised. "You're coming back? Tomorrow?"

"Yes, I have to be there for you. I want to help you remember and then maybe I can regain my memories from that night too. I'll catch the first flight out in the morning." Marlena paused. "That is OK with you, isn't it Claire?"

Claire was smiling ear to ear. She really didn't want Marlena to leave in the first place. "Sure, I want you to be here. Is, uhh, David coming, too?"

"I don't know. Never thought about it. Maybe it would be good for him to get out of Chicago and visit some old friends there. He could use some cheering up. He's been in the dumps lately."

"OK, see you tomorrow." Claire said.

"OK, goodnight sweetie. I'll be thinking about you all night."

Claire smiled again. "Bye, Mom."

A tear formed in Marlena's eye. "Bye, sweet dreams." She hung up the phone.

Claire pressed the off button on the cordless receiver and laid it on her nightstand. She quickly fell back onto her pillows and jerked the comforter over her head. She wanted to block out the world for a moment. She never felt happier than at this time. A dream was finally coming true for her. Her mother liked her and she had another mommy to love too. She lay quietly under the covers, watching the lights of the lamp shine through the yellow fabric that made up the comforter. She smiled at the wonderful day she would have tomorrow. She reached up and wrapped her fingers over the edge of the covers and threw them off her head. Cliff had come up to say goodnight. The instant she saw his body at the end of her bed, she screamed. The images and lights reeled in her head, causing her to feel dizzy. She started convulsing. That horrible face appeared and was getting closer to her. She screamed again and again.

Cliff ran to her and pulled her into his arms, trying to hold tight. She thrashed and her arms flailed at her attacker. She resisted the binding arms holding her down. The image was getting closer. It was so ugly, so vile. It smelled. It reeked of whiskey, she was getting more and more signals. Her mind was clicking into overdrive. She was recalling the sensations. Cliff held tight. He noticed Claire's eyes had rolled back. Only the whites showed. She went limp. Claire resisted no more. Now the pain would not hurt her.

By this time, Kim had heard the screams and had rushed upstairs into Claire's room. She saw Cliff lovingly trying to contain the frightened little girl. He was crying. Kim ran to his side. Claire was beginning to calm down. The images in her brain were going back to their hiding place.

"Cliff, what's wrong? What's the matter?"

"I don't know. I just came in to say goodnight and she went berserk."

He started to rock her gently in his arms, stroking her hair. Kim could hear a soft humming song coming from Cliff, even though he was unaware he was singing to his child like he did so many years ago. It was automatic. It was a daddy's lullaby.

As suddenly as it started, Claire opened her eyes and stared at her father holding her so close. "Hi, Daddy. When did you get here?"

Cliff looked down at his precious child and smiled. Kim had climbed onto the bed next to Cliff. Claire looked over toward Kim. "Hi, Mommy."

They could only smile. Cliff lifted Claire from his lap and laid her back on the pile of pillows. He asked, "Do you know what just happened?"

Claire looked at Kim and then looked into her Dad's eyes. "I guess I had another one of those spells."

Cliff sat up straight. "Baby, what spells? What are you talking about?"

Claire sat up. "Well, it was like the one I had this afternoon. Miss Mae was here and she helped me."

Kim said, "Why didn't you tell us about this?"

Cliff said, "Tweetie, this is not good. We need to know these things."

"I know, Daddy. I was going to tell you later, but I never got around to it."

Cliff looked at Kim, "I'm taking her to the doctor tomorrow."

Claire jumped up, "No not tomorrow. Marlena's coming back."

Cliff looked surprised. "Tomorrow, but she just left today."

"I know, but when I was talking to her awhile ago, she said she wanted to come back tomorrow."

"You were just talking to your mother?" Kim asked.

"Yeah, she called me to talk about *that night*." Claire said as she made the image of quotation marks with her fingers. Then she paused and thought a second. "And that's when the images came back."

"Images? What images, baby?" Cliff asked.

"It's mostly weird, kinda scary lights. And then there's that face. It's really scary."

"Who? What face?" Cliff implored.

"I don't know Daddy. It's just some blurry looking face. I can't make out any details. It's just scary. And it stinks."

"Well, that settles it, let's get dressed. We're going to the doctor tonight."

"No, Daddy! I'm not going to a doctor now."

Kim moved closer and put her hand on Cliff's arm. "Sweetheart, maybe this can wait until morning. Maybe Claire can stay with us, in our room."

Claire looked at her dad and then to Kim's smiling face. Cliff looked at Claire and felt the love of 11 years pull at his heart. He reached for her hand and said, "OK, you win. I'll get the rollaway bed out of the attic."

Kim looked at Claire and then put her hand on Cliff's arm. "No sweetie, I think there's room in the middle of our bed."

Cliff dropped his head in defeat. He would never win with these two. He loved them both dearly. Cliff rose from the bed and turned his back toward Claire and placed his hands and arms down by his side. She immediately recognized the piggy back ride stance. She jumped out from under the covers and leaped on Cliff's back. He happily trotted out the door and into his bedroom. Kim followed. Claire fell asleep very quickly and was not bothered by recurring images and dreams.

The blue Ford Taurus was parked outside on the darkened street as before. The male driver was busily writing notes in a log book that he retrieved from the passenger seat. He made some final notations and removed a small pair of headphones from his ears and dropped them into a box in the back seat. He cranked the engine and drove away without lights on until he turned the corner.

Janey was not at all tired and after her conversation ended with Claire she sat on her window sill bench and listened to a few songs on her portable CD player while staring at the nighttime sky. Something suddenly caught her attention outside. She noticed the same car that had been on their street just the day before. She jumped up, ran to her closet and pulled out a pair of binoculars she used at concerts. The curtains were slightly opened, so she turned out all the lights in the room and opened the curtains further. She placed the binoculars up to her eyes and focused on the blue car parked on the opposite side of the street. The man inside was holding something close to his ears. He stared forward. He was listening to some headphones. Janey thought he might be listening to music too, but this was not right. He shouldn't be here. Then he started writing something in a book. Janey strained to see what he was scribbling out on the page, but could not distinguish any words. Then, he drove away.

Janey put away her binoculars and closed the window. She lay on her bed, making a vow to herself, that she would uncover this mystery. She would find how who this guy was and what he was doing on their street.

Chapter Sixteen

Marlena was all ready awake and on the phone with Northwest Airlines when David came into the kitchen for a morning cup of coffee. He glanced at Marlena sitting at the breakfast table and her cell phone held tightly to her ear. She had made a pot of fresh coffee and was working on her second cup. David reached into the cupboard above the dishwasher for a mug. He looked with desire toward the cabinet under the sink. Jack was still there. He knew it, but he felt he was getting stronger. Marlena was talking softly and he couldn't catch many words. He pulled out a chair and sat next to his wife. She was finishing her phone call.

"OK, thanks. Is the flight on time?" she asked the person on the phone.

David was taking his first sip of coffee and cut his eyes to Marlena. He thought, *Was she leaving again?*

Marlena hung up the phone, took another drink of her coffee and leaned over to give David a morning kiss. "I need you to do something for me."

"What? I gather you're leaving again. Do you need me to wash all the clothes?"

"No! But you're right, I am leaving again. What I need you to do is call in work and take a few days off. You're going with me."

"What? I can't take off any work. And where are you going?"

"You need some time off. Tell them something has come up, something personal that you need to go out of town for at least 3 days."

"Where, Marlena?"

"We're going back to Memphis. Claire needs me. She has had a breakthrough of sorts and I need to be with her."

David's heart almost stopped. He couldn't possibly return to Memphis. There's nothing but trouble waiting for him there. What had happened? Did the girl remember something?

David began to sweat, "Baby, I can't go to Memphis. I need to get into the office today. I'm behind as it is."

"I won't take no for an answer. You need some time off. It'll do you good to get out of town for awhile. We'll be at a motel and you can find some of your old buddies in Memphis to run around with. I'm not asking you to stay with me all the time. But I do want you to make at least an appearance at Cliff's house and meet Claire, Cliff and Kim. They do need that much."

"I don't know, Marlena. I need to work."

"If you don't call in, then I will. You are going with me and that's it. No more questions please. We leave this afternoon at 3:10. Now, drink your coffee and go pack."

David couldn't finish his coffee. He pushed back from the chair and went upstairs. Marlena could sense he was troubled, but she assumed his drinking problem was at the core of his uneasiness. She heard the bedroom door slam.

The morning sun illuminated the room as the rays from the window crept slowly onto Claire's face. She squinted when the brightness covered her closed eyes. Claire turned over and pulled the comforter higher to block the unwanted light. She only wanted to sleep. One eye was open and she noticed the clock on the nightstand. It was almost 8:00am. She struggled to recall what was special about today. Nothing came to mind. She closed her eyes again, intent to sleep a little longer. Her eyes popped open at the same time. She remembered. Her new school tutor was coming by today at nine.

Claire threw off the covers and jumped out of bed. Realizing she spent the night in her dad's bed, she ran to the closet in her new room and reached for a clean shirt and pair of jeans. A stop at her new dresser and she gathered a clean set of undergarments. She sure missed having a bath in her own room, but that was the old room. She would have to use the bathroom off the hall.

Cliff was completing his second cup of coffee and the morning paper, when Kim came in from a morning run. She wiped the sweat from her face with the towel she carried around her waist and she grabbed a bottle of orange juice from the refrigerator. Kim took one large drink and greeted Cliff with another kiss.

Cliff smiled, "Enjoy your run?"

Kim sat down and took another sip. "I wish you would start running with me again. You know I hate being alone out there."

"I will, I promise. I guess everything with Claire has me in a whirl. I just don't know what's coming next with her. I mean last night really scared the crap out of me."

"I know. It scared me, too."

"I heard the water running upstairs, so I guess she's up." Cliff added.

Kim picked up a piece of buttered toast that Cliff had prepared. "The tutor comes this morning?"

Cliff looked at his watch. "Yeah, she's supposed to be here at 9. It's getting late, so I guess I need to get ready myself."

"You know I have a meeting back in Atlanta tomorrow?" Kim asked as she placed her hand on his arm.

"I know. I wish you didn't but we'll manage."

David was hoping a hot shower would calm his nerves. He couldn't go to Memphis. There had to be a way to get out of this trip. He dreaded the moment when he would have to face this girl. What had she remembered? He was going to jail. He just knew it. His hands shook as he dried off with the towel. The burning deep in his gut started. He was beginning to feel helpless against the power. He sat naked on the toilet and doubled over, trying to squeeze out the feeling. As he lay limp over his legs, the unmistakable voice resounded in his ear. "Davey . . . Daaaaveyyy. . . I'm still here. Right where you left me."

David covered his ears, hoping to block out the sound. He shouted, "You'll not get me back!"

"Ohhh, but yes I will Davey. You are weak. I am so strong. You will do my bidding. You are mine forever. I am the master and you are my slave."

"NOOO!!"

Marlena opened the door and saw David sitting in his birthday suit on the toilet, curled up in a fetal position. "David? David? Are you alright?"

The sound of a familiar voice brought him back into the real world. He lifted his head and stared blankly at Marlena. His face was drenched with sweat and flush with embarrassment.

He wiped the towel across his face, "Yes, I'm OK. Just going through some personal pains."

Marlena said softly, "I understand. I'm here and don't forget that."

"I will."

Marlena closed the door and left David to get ready.

Cliff met Claire on the stairway. "Hey, Tweetie, are you feeling good today?"

"Sure, Daddy. Is Kim up?"

"In the kitchen." He said and Claire ran the remaining distance.

"Hi, Mommy!" Claire announced loudly as she entered the kitchen.

Kim smiled at those words. "Well, good morning to you my darling daughter. Did you sleep well?"

Claire retrieved her own bottle of juice and sat next to Kim. "If you're thinking I might have had some more weird stuff happen and visions, then the answer is no to that and yes I had a good sleep. Didn't wake up until the sun woke me."

Kim took Claire's hand in hers. "Baby, I have to go out of town this morning for Atlanta."

"No, you can't. We just got started."

"Well, I never finished what I started when your dad called me to tell me that you had finally come out of that coma. I need to do my job."

Claire hung her head, pouting her lip. "I know. I'm just selfish. Can I go with you?"

"It will be for only 1 night. I'll be coming back tomorrow night."

"Well, that's better, but I still want to go with you."

"I wish you could. Besides, you're going to be busy with the new school tutor. She is supposed to be here real soon."

"Yeah, I know. I'm kinda scared."

"You know the work. It won't be hard. You'll do fine." Kim patted her arm.

Marlena had showered and completed dressing. David was on the phone when she came into the great room. She went into the kitchen and poured a cup of coffee that David had just made. He had opened a package of white powdered donuts, so she grabbed a couple and placed them on a napkin. She returned to the other room and David was hanging up the phone. She sat next to him and placed the napkin with donuts on the coffee table. One sip of java and Marlena held the cup tightly in both hands.

She asked, "So, who was that?"

"Work." he said without looking at her.

"Did you make arrangements to be off?"

"Yes! And they didn't like it. You know, such short notice. But they believed my sad story."

"What story was that?" Marlena asked taking another slow drink of coffee.

"That I needed to go with you to tend to a sick relative."

"David! That's not nice."

"Well, it's not far from the truth, is it?"

Marlena shifted. "I don't know. Maybe."

David got up and took his empty cup into the kitchen and placed it in the dishwasher. He looked at the cabinet door that would reveal secrets under the sink. The trash was there. Jack was there. The burning started again. He doubled over and walked slowly back into the great room. Marlena didn't notice his condition. He tried and tried to straighten up; make a good appearance and not show weakness. He held on to the table behind the sofa where Marlena was drinking her coffee.

She turned to see David's face racked with pain and agony. She jumped from the couch and ran around to her husband's side.

"David? David, are you OK?" she held onto his arm, helping him to the sofa.

Holding his stomach, he replied in broken words. "I'm OK just having a bit of a spell. It's hard going through this cold turkey. I think I might lose."

"NO! No you won't! I'll be here for you. Lay down on the couch. Put you legs up. I'll get you some water."

"I don't need water. Just a little rest." His voice was tart and insensitive.

Marlena sat on the coffee table staring at David. She could feel his pain, too. It wasn't that long ago that she went through the same trauma.

David turned to face Marlena. " Baby, I don't know if I can get through this."

"Don't you say that! You will get through it and I'll be here for you."

Marlena held his hand. "David? You haven't taken a drink have you?"

He closed his eyes. "No, but I wanted to; real bad, Marlena. I'm scared it's going to get me. He calls to me."

"Who? Who calls to you?"

"Jack. He's hiding in the kitchen. He wants me to come get him." David was beginning to get delirious. His eyes were glazing over. His speech became slurred, almost like he was intoxicated.

At once, Marlena understood what he was talking about. "David, where's Jack. Where is he in the kitchen?"

David turned away. Marlena reached and pulled his face back toward her. She leaned over and spoke softly and lovingly. "David, where is Jack hiding?"

He dropped his eyes, focusing on the opening to the kitchen. "In the trash."

Marlena quickly rose from the table and marched into the kitchen. She stared briefly at the cabinet doors that were hiding the torturing demon that had plagued her David. She had strengthened herself against these demons, but she was still fragile and could be tempted. She abruptly stopped and placed her hands together. She closed her eyes and looked upward. Softly she prayed, "*Father, give me the strength I need to overcome this current obstacle in our life. I ask for Your loving healing and guidance for David. Ease his pain. Let him know that You love him. Let him know that I love him. Keep us strong. Keep us on Your path. In Christ's name.*"

Marlena opened her eyes and jerked the two sink doors open. The trash can was half full. She reached in and removed the container. There, hiding under a few wet paper towels and a rotten apple core, she saw the object of David's pain; a pint bottle of Jack Daniels. Very little was gone from the bottle. Marlena guessed it had taken all David had to throw away all that liquor. To make sure, she pulled the bottle from the bag and poured the liquid down the drain. After dropping the empty bottle back into the trash, she pulled the trash can liner from the plastic container and twisted the opening. A tie was on a small shelf under the sink. She fastened the bag closed and took the trash to the refuse box outside. Tomorrow was pickup day. She added a new liner and placed the can back under the sink. She returned to David.

David had sat up on the couch. She sat next to him. "It's gone. Are there anymore?"

David looked at her with trusting eyes. "No, I promise."

“Feeling better?” she asked.

“Yeah.”

“I have to pick up a few toiletries from Walgreen’s. Why don’t you come with me?”

“No, I’ll be alright. I think I’ll go back to bed for a little while.”

“You sure?”

“Yeah, baby. You go get what you need, I’ll be OK!”

Kim’s flight was scheduled at 11:45 and she busied herself getting ready. She would only need a change of clothes for one night. Claire was lying on the bed, watching while she completed applying her makeup. Cliff had driven to Kroger for a few needed groceries.

Claire heard the kitchen door open and Miss Mae called out, “Anybody home?” Claire ran down the stairs to greet her. As she reached the bottom step, the front doorbell rang. Claire stopped and went to the front entry. She peeked through the small narrow windows on both sides of the large double door. A smiling face saw her through the window. Claire smiled back and opened the door.

The woman on the porch was quite young, maybe mid 20’s, long brown hair and sparkling blue eyes. She was slightly shorter than Claire and appeared to be in good physical shape. She carried a large black bag draped over her shoulder and was wearing jeans and a yellow and white blouse. Claire liked her already.

“Hi, you must be Claire. I’m Casey Lynnfield. I’ll be your tutor for a few weeks.”

Claire opened the door wider and offered Casey entrance. “Hi, Casey. I like your blouse. It’s pretty.”

"Thanks. Did your dad tell you I would be here today?"

"Yeah, he did. I'm kinda glad too. I want to get back into school as soon as I can."

"Well, that's the plan. Where do you want to have class?"

"I guess in our great room. We got plenty of space and there's a desk that nobody uses. Come on in, I'll show you around."

They walked through the entry and into the great room. Mae was cleaning away the cups and glasses left behind. She stopped her chores and walked over to meet the new lady.

"Well, hello. You must be Miss Claire's tutor. I heard you was coming today. My name is Mae Watson. I kinda take care of my Claire during the day."

Casey reached out to take Mae's hand. "It's good to meet you, Mae. My name is Casey Lynnfield. Claire was just about to show me around the place."

"You go right ahead. You want some coffee, tea or soft drink maybe?" Mae asked.

"Coffee would be good, thanks."

Mae left for the kitchen and Claire gave Casey the grand tour of the downstairs; the important rooms being the kitchen and bathroom. Kim came downstairs and introduced herself to Casey. She kissed Claire goodbye and left for the airport.
Claire and Casey settled into the sofa to go over the first lesson plan.

Marlena had been gone for an hour and David was dozing peacefully in his bed. The phone rang, jarring him from a deep sleep. He reached for the receiver and pressed the talk button.

"Hello?" he said in a slightly groggy voice.

"David? It's me." The voice on the phone said.

David sat bolt upright in the bed, wiping the sleep from his eyes and drool from his mouth. "OK, what's up? Anything new?"

"Well, I installed the bug in the house like you suggested. It was difficult, but it's done. It cost more than you said, too."

"OK! So, what did you hear?"

"The girl's been going into some fits or something. I think she's having flashbacks. At least that's what it sounds like. She's seeing images in her head. Something sure scared the piss out of her."

"Oh, shit!"

"That's not good, is it?" the voice asked.

"No, it's not. OK thanks. Keep it going. I'll be in Memphis tonight. Against my wishes, but my wife is making me go back with her."

"Good, you can pay me the balance when you get here, right?" the man asked.

"Sure, sure. You still have the same cell number?"

"Yes. Call me as soon as you can. I'll be waiting. I suppose your wife will be visiting with the girl?"

"Yea, but maybe tomorrow instead. We won't get in until early evening."

"OK, you call me. I'm expecting my money! Your bill is a quite high and I'm running a little short of cash, if you know what I mean."

"OK, no problem. Bye!" David said and hung up the phone.

David jumped out of the bed and began pacing back and forth, forcefully banging his hands together. As he passed the night stand he swung out and hit the lamp shade, causing the lamp to fall across the bed. He could feel the tension building. He began to sweat. He sat on the bed, trying to calm his nerves. He returned the lamp to its place on the table. He put his head in his hands and rested his elbows on his knees.
He wanted a drink. He needed a drink.

Thoughts were racing through his head. *Did I hide a bottle that I forgot? This cannot be happening. He must have been mistaken. She must have been a bad dream or something. She couldn't remember my face. Where is that bottle?*

Suddenly, David heard the backdoor open. Marlena was back from the store. He couldn't let her see him stressed out; she would have too many questions. He jumped from the bed and hurried to the bathroom. Pulling back the shower door, he reached in and turned on the water. Quickly removing his clothes, he stepped into the shower allowing the force of the water to wash away the sweat and tension. The warm piercing water felt good.

Throwing the plastic bag from Walgreen's on the sofa, Marlena went upstairs to check on David. She heard the shower running in the bedroom bath. She opened the door slightly and announced her presence.

"I'm home, sweetie. You about finished, we need to get moving."

David faced the stream of water and held his head back. This is not going to go away, no matter how much he wished for it to vanish. "I'm just finishing. Be right out."

Marlena completed packing the last minute items into her bag and carried the luggage downstairs. David was getting ready, constantly searching for a way out and trying to calm the desire for a drink that was incessantly hitting him in the back of the head.

The ride to the airport was quiet. Marlena sensed a problem with David, but assumed it was his attempt to fight the alcohol. She remembered all too well her first days in the road to recovery. The flight departed on time and arrived a few minutes early. Marlena contacted Cliff and arranged a meeting with Claire for the next day. For now, she would spend a quiet evening with David.

Chapter Seventeen

Kim had taken the early bird flight from Atlanta to be with Cliff and Claire when Marlena returned. She had stopped at the Cinnabon shop at the airport to pick up a few of those delicious buns. Cliff had told her that Claire loved them and he usually picked up a few when he traveled. Kim checked her watch on the drive home. It was almost 7. Maybe she could surprise them. Cliff wasn't expecting her until that evening.

Parking the car in the garage next to Cliff's BMW, Kim tried to be quiet when opening the back door, but she found Cliff and Claire just sitting down to a breakfast of eggs and sausage. Claire looked up from her meal and shrieked a scream of joy at the sight of her step-mom. She raced around the table and grabbed hold tightly to Kim's waist.

Kim smiled and looked at Cliff, who was smiling too. "Well, I guess you missed me, huh?" she said to Claire.

"Yeah, we did. I thought you weren't coming home until tonight." Claire said holding on with both arms.

"I wanted to surprise you, but I see that I'm too late." She walked to Cliff to give him a hello kiss. "Hey, I bought us some Cinnabons. You up for one?"

Claire snatched the bag. "Are you kidding? I'll eat 'em all."

Kim moved a chair close to Cliff and poured herself a glass of orange juice. She took a sip, letting the coolness of the liquid soothe the dryness in the throat. She looked at Cliff. "Anymore sessions with Claire?" she whispered.

"No, everything is like normal. I'm taking her to a doctor today."

"You hear from Marlena?" Kim asked, sipping at her OJ.

"Yeah, she called last night after they arrived in Memphis."

"They?" Kim looked at Claire who was busily devouring another Cinnabon.

"She's bringing David with her. She wants Claire to meet him. Christ, Kim she needs to get to know Claire first. All I see this doing is confusing Claire more. She needs time to recover. She needs to see that doctor."

Kim responded, "Does Claire know that he's coming?"

"I haven't mentioned it to her."

Claire looked up with sticky icing covering her lips. "Mentioned what, Daddy?"

Kim looked at Claire and laughed. She was a mess. It reminded her of the times when she was little and got her food from ear to ear when she was learning to feed herself.

Cliff said, "I spoke with Marlena last night. She's already in Memphis. She brought David, her husband, with her too." He studied Claire's expression, looking for any sign of stress from the news.

Claire took another bite and said, "Well, I gotta meet him sometime. I guess today is as good as any. When are they coming over?"

"She'll call this morning to make arrangements." Cliff told her. He was a little relieved.

Kim said "Why don't you finish up here and get a bath and some clean clothes on. I think you still have a tutor coming by this morning. School work never stops."

Claire put down the bun and held on to her stomach. "I think I ate too much."

Cliff smiled and said "You might be right. You want a bicarb?"

Claire turned her eyes in the back of her head. "Nooo Daddy. I'll just go upstairs now."

Cliff and Kim watched Claire, holding tightly to her tummy, slowly get up from the table. She would be alright once the hot water hit her in the shower.

Kim rose and started gathering dishes from the table. She tasted a bite of eggs from Claire's plate before placing it in the dishwasher. Cliff carried his own plate and cup to the sink and went to the great room to read the morning paper. Kim had become very concerned that Marlena was returning so soon and this time with her husband. Was she trying to move in on Claire too soon? Claire was much too fragile at this point to introduce a new personality that might or might not cloud up Claire's recovery process. The previous episodes with Claire frightened Kim to the point she considered taking some time off from work as well. With dishes cleared from the table and ready for cleaning, Kim hurried up to her bedroom to change into something more casual before the guests arrived later.

Claire completed the shower and she did feel somewhat better than before. She had dressed in a new yellow and white striped shirt and white shorts. She located her new Nike Brights that Janey had given as a present on her last birthday. It only seemed like yesterday to Claire, but she realized that had happened more than six months earlier. The phone on the night stand rang. Claire was sitting on the side of the bed tying the laces on the shoes. She reached for the phone and answered. "Hello?"

"Hi Claire, it's Janey." her best friend said.

Claire laid back against the pillows of the unmade bed. "Aren't you supposed to be in school?"

"Yeah, but I'm not feeling too good, so Mom said I should stay home today. Besides I think I might have a fever. Well, I feel a little warm."

"You want me to come over. . . oh, never mind, my tutor is coming by this morning. Maybe after that."

"That would be nice. I need the company." Janey told her with a meek voice.

"Is your Mom still home?"

"For now. She's going to work in a few minutes."

"She's OK with you staying home?"

"I guess. And I told her that you and your dad were right next door. And Miss Mae will be there too, right?"

"Sure!"

"Claire, I need to talk to you. I've been seeing some strange stuff going on and I think it might have something to do with you."

"Me! What is it?"

Janey hesitated for a few seconds and took a deep breath. "A few days ago when I left your house, I saw this car, a blue car, parked across the street in front of Mr. Wallace's house. There was a guy in it and I got the feeling he was watching me as I went home. It was creepy. Then when I got inside my house, I peeked out the window to watch him. I think he was watching your house too."

"Why would he be watching us?" Claire pulled the comforter closer and tucked her socked feet underneath.

"I don't know, but it looked like he was writing stuff into a book or something. Like I said, it was kinda weird and kinda scary too."

"Did you see who it was?"

"No, but that was not the only time I've seen that car there. It's been here other times, too."

"Have you told anyone, like your Mom?"

"No, not yet. I didn't want to make anyone upset. But, I still think he's looking at your house all the same and I thought you should know."

"Should we call the cops?"

"I don't know, maybe. Maybe you should tell your dad first."

"I will. Right now."

"OK, I'm kinda tired. Call me when your tutor leaves. Maybe you can come over this afternoon."

"Yeah, that'll be fun. Bye."

Claire hung up the phone and scooted further into the warmth and softness of the bed covers. A feeling of fear began to overcome her. Who would want to watch her? Suddenly, Claire threw off the covers and leaped from the bed and ran down the hall in her stocking feet, nearly tripping as she turned to make the stairs. She ran as fast as she could, almost falling the final 3 steps. Cliff was on the sofa, quietly reading the morning Commercial Appeal's Business section. Claire jumped onto the couch and grabbed hold of Cliff's arm, jerking the paper from his grip.

Cliff recovered the loose paper and looked down at his child, quivering uncontrollably, while holding his arm like a vise grip. "Tweetie, what in the world is wrong?" Instantly, he recalled the blackouts she had been having. "Did you have another spell like before?"

She cowered and buried her face into his arm. "No, Daddy. Janey just called me and said she has seen some guy watching our house."

Cliff pulled Claire from his side and placed both hands on her shoulders, pulling her face close to him. "Where, baby? Where did Janey say this guy was?"
Cliff looked into her eyes and could sense the fear.

"She said he was in a blue car."

Cliff let her go and he ran to the front door, jerking it before realizing the dead bolt was still engaged. He turned the latch and opened the door. He stared up and down the street and saw no blue car. Not wanting to be alone, Claire found her way to Cliff's side again. "Are you sure Janey got that right? A blue car?"

"That's what she said. Is it there?"

"I don't see one. But you can bet I'm gonna be looking."

Kim was coming downstairs, dressed in a T-shirt and jeans. She looked at the pair with a puzzled expression on her face. "What's going on?"

Cliff closed the door and wrapped his arm around Claire's shoulders. We think there might be a stalker or spy in the neighborhood."

"A what?"

"Janey told Claire that she had seen a guy watching our house. Well, she thinks. I need to talk to her myself."

Claire jumped in front of him, "Janey's sick today Daddy. She and I are going to see each other this afternoon. You can come with me then, OK."

Cliff was not convinced he should let this pass, but he would get to the bottom of it before the day was over. When they returned to the great room, the phone rang. Kim took the call from the phone on the desk against the fireplace wall.

"Hello?"

Marlena beamed at the sound of Kim's voice. "Hi, Kim. It's Marlena. How are you? Hope I didn't call to early, but I couldn't wait."

Kim rolled her eyes and turned to face Cliff. She mouthed Marlena's name and pointed to the phone. Claire was still clinging to her dad and didn't see Kim's signal. She spun around on her heels to face the wall and spoke softly into the receiver. "Hi, Marlena. You just get in?" she asked, knowing the full story.

"No, we got in last night. Didn't want to bother anyone so we just hung out here at the hotel."

"We?" Kim asked the question so Marlena would have to explain.

"Yeah, David came with me. You know, my husband?"

"No I don't know him. But I am looking forward to meeting him." Kim said as Cliff walked up behind her. "Hang on, here's Cliff." She said and handed the phone to Cliff.

Claire had remained curled in a ball on the couch, so Kim went to be with her.

Cliff talked quietly for just a couple of minutes and hung up the phone. He was seated in the office chair at the desk. Kim and Claire were already staring at him, waiting for an explanation. "Marlena and David will be here for lunch. About noon, I told her."

Kim continued to hold Claire. "Do you want to order something in? Or maybe Mae can fix something good."

"I'll let you take care of that. Anything will be fine. I'm concerned about a possible stalker here on our street. I'm going to get with some neighbors and see if they have noticed a strange car on our street. Claire, is Janey still awake?"

"I guess. Her Mom is leaving for work. She's alone."

Cliff looked at Kim and at once they both looked at Claire. "She's alone? Claire, we can't let her be alone. Not after what you told us. I'm going over there."

Cliff said while the adrenaline pumped through his body.

Kim asked, "Does Janey's mom know about this?"

"No, not yet."

Cliff was on his feet in a second. "Well, I'm going over. Maybe I can catch Amanda before she leaves." Cliff said as he headed for the front door.

Claire was not going to stop her dad, or even try. She was frightened and she needed her daddy's protection, yet she felt safe with Kim beside her. They sat quietly for a few minutes before Kim spoke. "Hey, you need to get ready for your tutor."

"Do I have to? I really don't think I could concentrate on school after all this. And besides, we have to get ready for lunch."

"Well, I tell you what. I'll talk to your dad. I kinda agree. You won't learn much of anything today. Anyway, go put on your shoes and brush your hair and teeth. I'll be right down here."

Claire hugged Kim one more time and ran off to her bedroom. Kim sat quietly staring into empty space. Her mind was going over and over who would be watching their house. Was someone after Cliff for a bad business deal he might have been involved with; or was there someone mad at her for some reason. Maybe Mae's ex-husband was looking for her or maybe she got into some trouble and was afraid to tell Cliff. Then a frightening thought came to Kim. Was the stalker watching Claire? A million scenes flashed through her mind. Claire had been having these trances where she was faced with a strange and scary face. Did this guy in the blue car own the face that terrified Claire into such a frenzy? The more she concentrated on this guy in the blue car, the more terrified she became. There had to be a connection to this guy and what had happened to Claire. She couldn't sit here any longer, dwelling on unproven facts. She went into the kitchen to make plans for the lunch to come, which was another worry unto itself.

Claire had joined Kim in the kitchen later when they heard the front door open. Claire ran into the next room to see her daddy with his arm around a blanket wrapped little girl that looked a lot like Janey.

"Hi Janey. Sorry, but I told my dad like you said, but he went to get you. And I'm glad." Claire said as she came up to her friend.

Janey peered out from behind the blanket. "That's OK. Your dad called my mom on her cell and explained it all. He said for her not to worry about me, cause I will be here all day."

Claire jumped a little with excitement as she took Janey's hand. "Good, come on you can lie down in my bed until you feel better." Cliff handed Claire a small bag of clothes and personal items Janey had gathered before leaving. The girls went upstairs and life seemed almost normal for an instant.

Kim asked. "What did you tell Amanda?"

Cliff headed for the great room and Kim followed. They sat side by side on the couch. "I told her what I knew. She said she's seen the car, but didn't think much about it. She said thanks for watching Janey. She needed to work today. They're behind on something or other at her office." Cliff sat pensively in his own thoughts. Kim saw the concern on his face.

Cliff looked into Kim's eyes and asked. "Should I call the cops?"

"I would say yes, but what are you going to tell them? They need evidence of a crime being committed. Sitting in a car on the street is not a crime. No one has broken into our house or bothered us, or Claire."

"Well, you can bet I'll be looking for this guy. I'll get answers, you can count on that." Cliff forcefully told her. Kim had never seen this side of Cliff before. This was the natural instinct of a father who would defend and protect his child at all cost, while never thinking or considering the consequences.

Kim asked. "Cliff, what about Claire's tutoring for today, don't you think we should cancel? You know with all that has happened so far and it's not even 9:00."

Cliff laughed. "You're right. Let me call before she leaves home." So much had happened. He went to the desk and pulled out his name and address book to locate Casey Lynnfield's number. Kim walked to the kitchen and filled the coffee pot with water. She needed some caffeine. She filled the filter with a couple scoops of coffee and slid the holder in place; hitting the on button. Kim took a seat at the table. She was in another world of thought when Cliff came in to join her.

"I caught Casey just as she was leaving. She will call later tonight to verify for tomorrow's session." He told her.

"Good."

"I also called Kate and invited her and Bill for lunch, so if you haven't made food plans, then include 2 more."

"That's a good idea. I think they should be here anyway."

Chapter Eighteen

Mae had arrived for work as usual at 9:00am and begun her normal chores. Kim had asked for help with lunch planning and Mae was delighted to assist. Making food choices and party planning was much more enjoyable than washing clothes and cleaning up after messy family members. Kim had decided to serve a crisp salad with cherry tomatoes, fresh raw vegetables, grated cheese and sliced hard-boiled eggs, along with homemade deli sandwiches. She sent Cliff to Kroger to gather the necessary ingredients. Mae got busy decorating the table in the formal dining room off the kitchen's east side. The table would seat 12 when an extension leaf was added. She made sure the walnut table was polished to a high shine before adding the place settings. The final touch was a large bouquet of flowers in the center.

After Cliff returned, Kim and Mae prepared the trays for the meats and cheeses. Cliff also picked up a couple of frozen key lime pies for dessert. Katie and Bill arrived around 11:30. As usual, Bill was in need of coffee and Kim was ready for him. She had just made a fresh pot. He made a cup and sat at the kitchen table and was content to watch the preparation of lunch. He would provide the best service by being out of the way. At least, that's what Katie always told him. After hello's and hugs and kisses, Katie went upstairs to visit with her dear sweet Claire. They were all ready for a pleasant meal and enlightening conversation.

When Claire saw her grandmother, she ran to give her a big hug. "Grammie, I didn't know you were coming over." Claire said.

"I didn't either, but your dad called and invited me and your grandpa for lunch. I understand your mother is joining us too." Katie said looking at the child in the bed. "And who is this in your bed? This can't be Janey, can it?" Katie added.

Janey pulled the covers a little further from her face. "Yeah, it's me. I'm staying with Claire today. I'm sick."

Katie sat on the edge of the bed and placed her cool hand on Janey's forehead to check for fever. Mothers do that and so do grandmothers. After taking her hand away she said, “You feel a little warm. Have you been given any aspirin or Tylenol?”

“Yeah, Miss Mae brought me a couple aspirins a little while ago.”

Katie looked at Claire and said, “Are you ready for some lunch?” And looking at Janey she asked, “You feel like eating something?” Janey nodded yes.

Claire said, “Yep! Has my mother got here yet?”

“Not yet. You’ve never met David have you, Claire?” Katie asked Claire as she pulled her close.

“No, but I guess he’s OK. Mother likes him anyway, so I guess I can too.”

Katie smiled and patted her on the arm as she said. “That’s the right attitude. I know he’ll like you too.”

Traffic was heavy on Poplar Avenue when David and Marlena left the Embassy Suites. It was nearly noon and the normal Tuesday business lunch crowd was out in force. David turned east onto Poplar and continued to search his mind for a reason he could use to convince Marlena that he should not go to this meet and greet luncheon. It had been a terrible day and night since he last took a drink. The pain was almost more than he could bear. Occasionally, Marlena would look at him and see the same pain and frustration that she went through herself not so long ago. She did not feel she was completely recovered and many times that strong and uncontrollable desire to take that first drink would nearly overpower her. But, she would call Debbie Hawthorne, her AA sponsor for comfort and guidance. Debbie always came through for her. David had yet to find a sponsor, but he was ready. She had to get him to the first meeting. He had made the crucial admission that he had a drinking problem. Now, it was up to him to do something about it. Marlena was more than willing to provide encouragement and support, but she knew he must do this for himself and not her.

The drive was particularly silent until David came up to the first turn off Poplar. Inside he was a nervous wreck and he was sure Marlena could sense the tension building within his body. He moved into the right lane of traffic and flipped the signal on to make the turn. He started to shake, almost to the point he couldn't control the rental car. Quickly he pulled over to the curb. Marlena noticed the tremors, thinking that he was reacting to lack of alcohol. David held tightly to the top of the steering wheel; his knuckles were turning white. Slumped over onto his hands, he slowly and methodically began bumping his forehead against the wheel he gripped so firmly.

Marlena put her hand on his shoulder. "You OK?"

Without looking up David answered. "Marlena, do I really have to go with you? I can wait in the hotel and you can have a great lunch with your family. I just don't think I'm in the right condition to see anyone."

"David, you need to be strong. It's only been 2 days since you've had a drink. I can promise you that there will be nothing to tempt you at this lunch. And besides, you're my family, too."

David turned his head slightly and cut his eyes toward Marlena. If only she knew the real reason he was avoiding this meeting, she would leave him high and dry in an instant. He grunted softly.

"Would you like to get some coffee first or maybe a coke? It might help."

"Naw, I'll be alright in a minute, I guess."

For the next couple of minutes, they sat in the quietness of the car, with only the sounds of passing traffic. Marlena knew he had to work this out on his own. He knew this was going to be the hardest moment that he would have to endure. So many thoughts were racing through his mind, telling him what he needs to do and what he wants to do. If the kid does not react, then he would be home free, but otherwise he's dead. The night was still a blur to him, but he knew that what he imagined had happened; it really did happen. His nerves were shot. He wanted a drink so bad. For a split second, he seriously considered getting out of the car and walking to the nearest bar or liquor store, leaving Marlena behind with no explanation. Life was not too good for David at this moment.

He turned loose of the wheel and put the car into drive. Two more streets and they would be there. Now was the time to face the consequences of his actions; good or bad. He just didn't know which.

Mae was finishing the final preparations for the salads when she heard the car pull into the drive. Cliff, Kim and Bill were in the great room talking quietly; probably about some business deal. Mae called out, "Mr. Cliff, I do believe Miss Marlena and her husband are here."

By the time they came from the great room, David and Marlena were knocking at the kitchen door that led to the garage. Mae opened the door and greeted Marlena with a brief hug and shook David's hand as Marlena introduced him. Mae had never met David before and she didn't attended their simple wedding. David was feeling the tremors start; this time even more intense than before. It was hard to control his fear and Mae could hear a slight tremble in his speech when he said hello.

Cliff walked right up to David and extended his hand. David offered his hand and made they casual nods at each other. Marlena went to her father and wrapped her arm around his. "David, you remember Dad don't you?" They had only met once.

David went to her side and shook Bill's hand. "Sure, I do. How are you Mr. Wilmont. Good to see you again."

"No, please call me Bill. You can call my father, Mr.", Bill answered with a laugh.

"OK, Bill." David said with a tight smile.

Cliff pulled Kim to his side and introduced her. "David, this is my wife, Kim."

He shook Kim's hand as well and offered, "Yes, nice to meet you too. I've heard some nice things from Marlena about you."

Kim looked at Marlena and smiled. "Why thank you. Why don't we go into the other room. We can sit and chat for a minute. I believe Mae is about ready for us." She looked at Mae.

Mae went back to the salads and said, "Yeah, you're right Miss Kim, so scoot out of here and let me finish."

Marlena looked around and noticed Katie and Claire were missing. "Cliff where are Mother and Claire?"

"They're upstairs visiting with Janey."

"Janey?" Marlena asked.

Kim explained. "She was sick and we offered to let her stay here while her mother went to work." Kim looked at Cliff and he understood as well that Marlena didn't need to know the real reason Janey was their guest.

Cliff went to the bottom of the stairs and called out. "Claire, Katie, ya'll come on down. Our guests are here."

Katie jumped up from the bed and helped Janey slip on a housecoat. Claire was almost out the door, but turned to wait for her friend. Janey moved a little bit slow, but the time she spent in bed during the morning helped her gain some strength. Now she was hungry and looked forward to lunch. Claire took Janey's hand and led her down the hall to the stairs. Katie followed.

When they reached the bottom of the stairs, Marlena was talking with her dad when she saw her little girl come running. David, Kim and Cliff were busy in a conversation about David's job. Claire didn't see David at first. Claire felt comforting warmth when she hugged Marlena.

It was a feeling she had so longed for when she was growing up. Marlena reached under Claire's chin and pulled her face up to meet hers. She smiled and as she wrapped her arm around Claire's shoulder she said. "Claire, I want you to meet David."

At that instant, David turned around to face Marlena and the child coming toward him. Claire looked up into his eyes. David stared back at Claire. He saw it in her eyes before it happened. All at once, Claire broke free from Marlena's hold, knocking over a lamp on the end table. She began to back up slowly, her eyes never leaving David's. Katie was just coming off the stairway when Claire opened her mouth. Terror was burning in her eyes. She screamed at the top of her lungs. Everyone turned to look, but Claire continued to shriek in fright. She backed into Katie and Katie tried to hold her, but she pushed away screaming as if she was in terrific pain. Janey ran and cowered in the corner of the room. David's feet started to turn. She knew who he was. The truth was now going to come out. All the horrible pain he inflicted on this girl was tearing him down now into the lowlife he was. Claire could not stop screaming, she could not take her eyes off this monster. Those eyes she stared into, now came clear into her mind. Those dreams of the terrible face that haunted her so often at night, now came into clear focus. She screamed again and again. Cliff rushed to her side, fearing she was going through another spell that she experienced before, but she pushed him away and screamed again. Marlena was crying. Kim was crying, confused and didn't know what to do. The beast was here and he was here to harm her again. Claire could not control herself. All the memories of that night began to flood her mind. The pain, the awful pain was almost more than she could stand. This monster was the same one who came into her room and violated her in a most horrendous way. The stench of the liquor from his panting breath filled her nostrils and made her nauseous. She recalled in vivid detail the tearing of her night clothes from her body. She cringed at the remembrance of him thrusting himself into her. All the memories came back; all the memories that held her prisoner for so long. She fell against a chair next to the stairs. Tripping, she landed on her backside still screaming. Cliff went to help her. With a long thrust of her foot, she kicked him away, again. Everyone was looking from Claire to David. He was the object of her fright. He was the cause of her suffering. They didn't understand. David did. Claire did.

Without thinking, David quickly turned around and ran toward the kitchen and out the back door. Marlena called out to him but he refused to answer. She heard the car door slam and the car squeal away just as Claire screamed for the last time. She fell over in a faint on her side and silence finally filled the room. Everyone ran to her. Cliff lifted her in his arms and carried her to the couch. Marlena sat next to him. Kim shoved the coffee table away and sat on the floor at Cliff's feet. He held Claire close. Cliff was crying. Kim and Marlena were crying. Katie and Bill stood behind the couch. Katie held tight to Bill's arm. Tears were flowing.

Cliff was the first to speak. "My God, what was that all about? She was scared out of her mind at David. Why?"

Marlena answered. "They've never met, Cliff. I don't know."

Kim said as she held Claire's hand in hers and looked at Marlena. "Claire has been having some episodes lately, dreams if that's a better word. She has been seeing scary faces. Maybe this is another spell and David may have triggered it. We need to find him, don't you think?"

Janey managed the courage to come to see Claire, lying helplessly in her father's arms. "Mr. Richards, is Claire going to be OK?" she asked.

"I hope so, Janey. I'm going get her to the emergency room. She needs a doctor and she needs one now! Kim, you drive!"

"I'm coming too." Marlena stated.

Katie grabbed Marlena by the arm. "You can ride with us. You can try to locate David while we drive." she said as she gathered her purse. Bill was already on the way to the car.

Mae had been watching in horror as well. As Cliff passed her carrying a limp little girl he asked. "Mae, do you mind staying all day. Janey needs to be with someone. Her mother will get her later."

"Sure I will, Mr. Cliff. You get that baby to the hospital." Mae told him as Janey came into her arms for comfort.

Kim opened the door for Cliff. He was not letting Claire go. Kim ran around to the driver's side, jumped in and started the car. She backed out with a jerk and quickly turned the auto towards the street. Methodist Germantown Hospital was on Poplar, easily a five minute drive. She planned to make it in 3. Bill had pulled his car further back in the turn-around drive to give Kim room. He followed closely and when Kim turned right on Poplar, he knew where she was headed.

Marlena was in the back seat, frantically dialing David's cell number on her phone. He would'nt answer. She got his voice mail and left him a desperate message to return her call. She tried to convince him that this was not his fault. Katie reached over the front seat and took Marlena's hand. "Keep trying, dear. You'll get him soon."

Marlena looked out at the people in the passing cars on Poplar, hurrying back to and from their lunches and back to work. Maybe David was right. Maybe this was not a good time to meet Claire. Marlena began to feel the tension creep into her gut. She recognized that feeling she had so long ago learned to live without. She felt the burn; that call for relief. The only thing that would ease her pain was not in reach. She closed her eyes and tried to will the pain away. *I have to be strong for Claire. . . . . No, I have to be strong for me.* She thought.

David heard the ring of his phone as he sped toward south Memphis on I-240. He saw that the call was from Marlena. He ignored it by throwing the phone in the back seat. So many thoughts ran through his mind. No doubt, he had been identified. It was only a matter of time before the cops would be looking for him, not to mention Cliff and Marlena. He had to get out of town. His life as he knew it was over. His marriage, his job and most of all his sanity was going to slowly creep away. The first thing he needed to do was get hold of some more money. He had a couple hundred in his wallet. He could get $400.00 more from the ATM and maybe a cash advance on his credit card, but he would need several thousand to get away; far away. Mexico came to his mind. He took the Airways exit to search for an ATM machine. Any place would do. He found an Exxon gas station on the corner at the first intersection off the interstate. He whipped the car into a hidden parking space next to the outside restrooms and ran into the station. After getting the 400.00 from his checking, he took a cash advance of 400.00 more from his MasterCard. He walked backed to the car, trying to calculate how far 1000.00 would take him. He needed gas. No, he needed another car. This was a rental. He could be tracked down in this car. What was he going to do? David was scared. He couldn't go to prison. The thought of being locked up behind bars with other men; men who would destroy any man who had harmed children, burned in his soul.

Now the aching in his gut started. He knew the feeling well and he was going to obey. As David eased into the driver's seat and started to crank the car, he noticed the store in a strip shopping center next to the Exxon. Airways Liquor was open for business. Without a moment's hesitation, David jerked open the car and nearly ran for the liquor store. His eye caught the captions lining the massive shelving. He was looking for Whiskey. He was looking for Jack. Jack would be here. Jack would help him. Jack would make him feel better. Jack would make all this go away. He found his friend, waiting patiently for him to return. David could hear him say, *I knew you wouldn't desert me. I'm here now. I'll make it all better.* David gathered one party size and two quarts of Jack Daniels. He went to the counter and a well built, nice looking black woman, probably in her late twenties rang up his purchase. She looked him up and down, wondering why this good-looking white guy was in her store today.

"I guess you gonna be partying later on, huh sugar." She asked with a flirty smile and wink.

David noticed her name tag. "You don't know the half of it, LaToya, *SUGAR.*" He smiled back as he said with emphasis on the sugar.

Latoya completed the sale and packaged the liquor into standard brown paper bags. David handed her three twenties from his wallet and collected the change. As he picked up the bags and headed to the door, she said. "You come back anytime, Sugar, I'll be here." David turned and gave her a big grin and pushed the door open thinking to himself.

Yeah, bitch, I bet you will be. Maybe another time and another life, it would be good.

He was not even back at the car, before he pulled out one of the quarts, twisted off the top and turned up the end, draining a long stream of the warm, soothing, brown liquid. Instantly he could feel the tension subside. Relief was on the way. Getting caught in Memphis on a DUI was the last thing he wanted to happen, so he recapped the bottle and placed it back in the sack. He had to find a place to stay for the night. A place he could make plans. A place he and Jack could get reacquainted.

It seemed like hours since the attendants had taken Claire into exam room #4. Cliff and Marlena were with her. The doctor would only allow parents at this point. Claire was still unconscious and unresponsive. Cliff had explained her history and the most recent episodes. Claire was lying comfortably on a gurney with an oxygen tube directing air into her nostrils. A nurse was checking her vitals again. Blood pressure was normal. Pulse rate was a little high, but nothing to be alarmed over. Her pupils appeared normal; no dilation. Heart rate and breathing were good. Whatever threw Claire into this state was not clear to the doctor; the same diagnosis as 6 months ago.

The emergency room attending physician completed his exam. "Well, let's watch her for now. She appears to be comfortable and not in any distress at this time. Julie will check back every 10 minutes or so. Why don't you get something to drink, coffee or tea or soft drink. We'll page you if anything changes."

Marlena looked at this young doctor and thought of Doogie Howser an old TV show. "Thank you, doctor." And 'Dr. Doogie' continued on his rounds into the next exam room.

Marlena went to Cliff who had his head resting on the edge of the bed. "You want to get some coffee or maybe a sandwich?"

Cliff lifted his head without turning to meet Marlena's eyes. "No, I'll be alright. You go. I prefer to stay here with Claire."

Marlena headed for the door. She turned to look at Cliff, in pain over the suffering their child was enduring. If only she had been a better mother, maybe this would have never happened. But she couldn't blame herself. She needed to talk to God. Hospitals have chapels, she remembered.

As she passed the waiting room, Kim called out to her. "Marlena, over here."

Marlena almost forgot they were there waiting. "I'm just going for some coffee. There's no change. Cliff is going to stay with Claire."

Katie asked, "You want company?"

"I could use a cup, myself." Bill said.

"Sure, I'll meet you in the cafeteria. I have to stop off someplace first."

Katie looked curiously at Bill as they left for the cafeteria on the basement level. Kim decided to stay in the waiting room in case something came up. She was not much of a coffee drinker anyway.

Marlena found the chapel on the first floor near the front entrance. She slowly opened the huge wooden door, hoping no one was inside, but she didn't want to startle anyone in case there was. It was a beautiful room, decorated with white and yellow flowers; apparently artificial to cut down on cost. There were two short rows of wooden pews; four in all. The floor was carpeted with soft dark blue plush pile. Her steps were silent as she walked up to the four foot golden cross that hung at the front. Below the cross on the floor there were several thick and luxurious cushions spread around for users to kneel and pray if they chose to. She had never kneeled before the cross and prayed. Until recently, she had never prayed. This situation needed serious prayer. She set her purse on the pew closest to her and she eased down on a cushion directly in front of the cross. There was a small wooden rail where she folded her arms and looked directly into the cross. Tears formed in her eyes as she formed the words in her mind. She bowed her head and closed her eyes.

Softly she began. "God . . . Father, I am at a loss to understand what is going on here. My precious little girl needs you now more than ever. I need you more than ever. I've never prayed much before, because I didn't know you. So many years, I had another I worshiped. You helped me get rid of that crutch. Now I am asking for you to intervene in Claire's life. Help her through this. Help us to understand what is going on. Help David, Lord, because I know he's frightened and confused. Bring him back so he can help us understand what is going on. Give strength to Cliff, Father. He loves our little girl so much and I never saw that until now. Gives us your wisdom to carry out your will. Give us the answer we seek. Help us help Claire. Let your Grace shine on us today. . . . I ask in Jesus' name.

Marlena remained silent in a prayerful pose for several more minutes. Maybe the silence would bring her an answer from God. She left the chapel with renewed spirit and hope that Claire would quickly recover and life would again get back to normal. Slowly walking through the halls of the hospital, she began to concentrate on the night before all this happened. The evening was a blur because of her drinking and so much time had passed. She recalled her and David going to downtown Memphis for dinner and of course, drinking, but where they went was unclear. She remembered driving home and lying on the couch in the great room. What was different? She strained to bring up those hidden memories blinded by the liquor. She walked further until she reached the elevators. She pressed the down button. Maybe her mom and dad would still be in the cafeteria. She was getting hungry. As the door opened, she walked in and pressed the [B] button. The door closed and she closed her eyes. What happened that night? There was no answer. David followed her into the great room. They were going to make love. Or were they? The memories were getting foggy. This was going to be difficult. She rolled her neck to ease some of the tension building up. She trained her thoughts on that last night. What did David say? What did I say? Like a flash of lightning she remembered, she asked David to get some protection. That was a sure memory. It just popped into her head. She never recalled that before. She was absolutely sure this was fact. But we never made love. I woke up on the sofa. David was gone. The thoughts were getting clearer.

The elevator stopped at the bottom floor. While remaining in deep thought, Marlena left through the door and stopped suddenly. She looked up toward the ceiling and softly spoke, “No! It can’t be. You must be wrong or I must be. Please let me be wrong.” Marlena began to sweat. The cafeteria was just at the end of the hall on the left. She immediately found Katie and Bill, who had just finished tuna club sandwiches and coffee. She joined them and told of her recent intuition.

Cliff was sitting quietly in a chair next to the bed where Claire lay so still. Marlena returned to the exam room and went to him. “Cliff, can we talk a minute?”

He was almost dozing when she came in the room. He shook his head and looked first at Claire, who continued to sleep in her protective state. “Sure, what’s up? Did the doctor speak to you?”

“No. I need to ask you something.”

“OK what?”

“I went to the chapel to pray just a few minutes ago. I asked God to give us an understanding of this situation and help our daughter. I think he might have pointed me in a direction we have never crossed.”

“What are you talking about, Marlena?” Cliff was becoming agitated.

“When you first found Claire, we took her to various hospitals and had many doctors check her over. They couldn’t find a single reason for her comatose condition.”

“Yeah, so. What’s your point?”

Marlena shifted from one foot to the other, searching for the right words. “We never had an OB doctor check her.”

Cliff was quiet. He was pondering this statement. He looked straight into Marlena's eyes. "What do you mean an OB doctor? What are you thinking Marlena?"

Again Marlena became nervous. Cliff rose from the chair. He took her shoulders in his hands and looked closely into her face. "Marlena, what are you thinking?"

Marlena could not face Cliff. She turned away and said. "I think we need to have a doctor check Claire for sexual activity."

Cliff's face turned beet red. Fury was building. He almost raised a hand to strike her down. With an intense anger in his voice he asked, "Are you accusing me of
abusing my child?"

Marlena pulled back and shook her head. "No, no Cliff, not you. I never thought that."

The fear was still on his face and now a hatred look appeared. "Who? Who Marlena?"

Marlena was frightened for an instant. She backed up. "I don't know. .. . Well, I hope I'm wrong, but if a doctor confirms, then I am so scared it might have been David."

Marlena never saw Cliff so mad. He started pacing back and forth pounding his fists into his palms. She could here mumbles coming from Cliff. "He's dead. I'm gonna kill him."

"Cliff!" Marlena forcefully spoke.

"What?" he shouted back.

"First, let's make sure. Then if it's true, I'll help you kill him." She thought a second. "No, come sit down and let's figure this out. We're not going to kill anyone. Come on, sit."

Cliff paced a couple minutes more and sat again in the chair next to Claire's bed. Marlena had taken the chair by a window. He took a drink of some water left in a cup on the table by the bed. He looked at Marlena and asked. "OK, what makes you suspect Claire might have been violated and how is David involved?"

Marlena closed her eyes for a second and looked out of the window to gather her thoughts before speaking. "I went to the chapel to pray, like I said. When I left, I was racking my brain to recall what I did the night before you found Claire. I was so messed up that night. So was David." Shyness overcame her and her face reddened. "I do remember that we were going to make love. I couldn't move from the couch and I asked David to go get our protection. It was upstairs in our bedroom. I had no idea Claire was at home. I must have passed out. No I'm sure I did. I don't remember a thing until the next day when you came home. David must have left because I don't recall any sex."

"So what makes you think David might have done anything?"

"I don't know. I just know these memories came into my head that I could never recall before. That was my prayer. That God would give me an understanding of what has happened."

"So now you think God is giving you the answers? Shit, Marlena, that's ridiculous."

"I hope you're right. I don't want my husband to be persecuted needlessly, but think of how she acted when she saw him. Think of how he reacted. Now, what are we going to do for our little girl? Do I request an exam?"

"She's unconscious!" Cliff almost yelled.

"Are we going to wait for how long, Cliff, how long this time before she wakes up? This might be permanent. She may never come out of this. We have to explore all the possibilities."

Cliff hung his head. He sighed and looked at Claire, who appeared to only be sleeping. There was no fear in her expression. "I guess we need to do this. We need an answer."

"Yes, we do!" Marlena said and left the room to find a staff OB doctor.

Cliff wiped the sweat that had formed on his forehead. He reached for Claire's hand and held it in his. He kissed her fingers and said, "We're going to get you back, Tweetie. We're going to make this all better. No one will ever hurt you again, I can promise you that." He laid her limp hand back on the bed and went into the waiting room.

Kim met Cliff half way across the waiting room. Katie and Bill had returned from the cafeteria with Marlena and had explained her suspicions with Kim. She wrapped her arms around Cliff and he buried his head into her shoulder. He softly began to cry, which started tears falling from Kim. She whispered into his ear. "It's going to be alright. The truth will be found and Claire is going to recover. This will all be behind us before you know it." They held each other for several minutes.

Cliff left for a much needed bathroom break and Kim settled back with Bill and Katie. After Cliff returned they discussed all possibilities until Marlena returned to the waiting room. She sat in a seat next to Katie. They all looked to her for an answer. She had been gone for about 45 minutes.

"A Dr. Richman will be down in a few minutes. He's the resident OB on duty today." Marlena told everyone. Katie held Marlena's hand for support. For a while no one could say anything. They only wanted answers.

Cliff looked down the hall from the waiting room. He saw a young man in scrubs walking toward their group. He tapped Kim on the shoulder and said to the group. "Is this our guy?"

Marlena turned. "Yes, that's Dr. Richman." They all rose to greet him.

He was pleasant and antiseptic. “Good afternoon, Charles Richman. How are you? You have the girl I need to see?”

Marlena shook his hand again as did Cliff, Kim and Bill. “She’s in room four. Should I come with you?” Marlena asked.

“You say she’s unconscious?”

“Yes”

“Well, normally I almost never do this sort of exam on girls her age and I surely prefer to do exams with my patient awake. You’re her mother?”

“Yes.”

“Then I need you in the room with me and my nurse. You will need to sign a consent form because she is a minor.”

“No problem. We just need an answer.”

“OK, show me your daughter.” Dr. Richman said and they left for room #4.

Everyone returned to their seats, but Cliff was too nervous. He paced, constantly watching the double doors to the exam rooms. It was only 10 minutes later, but Cliff knew at least an hour had passed. The double doors opened slowly and Marlena walked into the room, head down. She was crying uncontrollably. Cliff ran to her and pulled her face to his. She said nothing; she only nodded and began to cry even harder. Katie had stepped in to hold Marlena and guide her to a seat. Cliff gritted his teeth tightly in his mouth. His eyes were blazing; fists curled. Blood raced furiously through his body pumping the adrenaline throughout his veins. Muscles tensed and without warning he let out a terrifying yell and struck the steel door with his fist. He never felt the pain when the blood gushed out from his knuckles. He began to pace wildly up and down the rows of chairs slapping at the back of seat as he walked by. No other people were waiting at that moment and Katie was relieved. Bill tried to calm Cliff, but he would not listen. He continued to pace and shouted obscenities to himself. Kim stepped in front of Cliff and refused to let him go on.

"Cliff, stop this. Calm down."

She saw a rage and fear in his eyes that she had never seen before. Cliff was always easy going, lovable and under control. He stopped and she took his hands. He looked away and she saw tears forming. Cliff broke down and she wrapped him in her loving arms. He sobbed, "Kim! My baby, my Tweetie, my precious child. I wasn't there to protect her. I let her down."

No one spoke for the next 20 minutes. Everyone was trapped in their own thoughts.

Chapter Nineteen

David had found a cheap motel that was used more by the hour than by the night. The clerk looked suspiciously at him when he asked for a room for the night and he was not accompanied by anyone. The motel room looked as cheap as the nightly rate. The key would barely turn the lock on the unpainted door. There were no curtains on the windows, only a single pull down window shade that was stained with whatever had been thrown at it from previous renters. The walls were wallpapered with stock that appeared to be from the 1950's and it had peeled in many places. There was a double bed covered with a faded blue spread. At the very least the sheets appeared to be in better condition. There was a phone on a night table with a sign indicating all local calls would be 75 cents. No long distance calls were permitted. He found the bathroom in no better condition than the room. At least there was a toilet and it flushed when David pressed the handle. The shower was weak, but the water was warm. No soap could be found. A thin white towel was draped over a silver towel on the wall opposite the toilet. The distinct odor of marijuana, mixed with some cheap sweet perfume lingered throughout the room.

Shaking with uncontrollable fear, David pulled the bottle of Jack he had first opened on the parking lot out of the bag and unscrewed the top. He put the bottle up to his lips, turning it up, he downed a long satisfying drink. He could feel the warmth racing down to ease the pain. After taking another long sip, he placed the bottle on the night stand and he pulled back the spread on the bed to lie down. He reached for his cell phone from the clip on his belt and dialed a memorized number.

There were 3 rings before his call was answered. "Hello?"

David sat up. "Roger? It's David."

"David, my friend, where are you? I think we have some unfinished business." Roger replied with a tone that called up more fear into David.

"I know, I know and I'm gonna pay you. I'm just in a little trouble right now."

"You know, I really don't want to hear this shit. You owe me. I did a job and now you pay. I want my money." Roger said with more force.

"Look, the girl ID'ed me."

"ID'ed you for what?"

"Let's just say I can't be anywhere near there. I need to get out of town, today."

"My friend, I strongly suggest you get me paid before you leave."

David rose from the bed and started to pace. He took another drink for courage. "Hey look, don't threaten me. I'm good for your money."

"Well, that wasn't threat. But you take it as you will. When are you bringing me my $700.00? And don't give me any run around, because the price goes up a hundred a day.

"OK, OK. Let me make a couple more calls. I have your money, but I need more than I have to get out of town. I'll call you back in 20 minutes."

"See that you do or you'll be getting my call and you don't want me to call you." Roger clicked the phone off.

David dropped to the bed and fell back on top of the only pillow. He needed money, and needed it fast. He needed a car too. Roger would have to wait for his money. He would be long gone from Memphis before he could catch up to him. He finished half the bottle and flipped open his cell again. He had one other number to call.

Cliff had seethed and mumbled to himself for more than an hour, occasionally pacing the floor and continuing to take out his frustrations on the furniture in the waiting room. Kim could only watch helplessly. She knew he had to work this out on his own. They could talk later in private. Marlena appeared to be in a daze with her head resting in her palm. Bill and Katie talked quietly together.

Cliff had completed 2 more laps around the room when he stopped in front of the seat Marlena had settled into. Noticing his presence, she looked up with a tear streaked face and swollen bloodshot eyes. The look on his face was one she had never seen before. She reached out for his hand and softly asked, "How're you doing. You OK?"

Cliff pulled back his hand, not allowing her to touch him. There was madness in his eyes and in the tone of his voice when he replied. "You know, this is all your fault! You brought that monster into our house and he has ruined my little girl's life." He raised his voice higher. "You and your drunken passion allowed this to happen. You never cared about Claire. You hated her in fact. You had to be the worst mother in the world."

By this time, Kim had to jump in to calm the waters. She reached for Cliff, but he pulled away. He had had time to contemplate all he wanted to say, now he was letting it all come out. Marlena was crying tears she thought were gone. In a strange way, Marlena agreed with Cliff. She was the one to bring this on her child.
Katie and Bill had moved into the seats next to Marlena, offering protection.

Cliff was relentless at the verbal pounding he was unleashing on Marlena. Finally, Kim stepped in front of him and physically pushed him back and shouted, "Cliff, stop this, right now."

He looked at Kim as if she were someone he had never known before. He stared in confusion at Kim. What had he just done? His mind was reeling with anger and pain. His precious Tweetie was lying in that room, unconscious, maybe forever this time. He covered his eyes and began to cry. Kim led him to a seat opposite Marlena, who continued to cry.

Wiping his eyes on a tissue Kim had provided, Cliff reached to take Marlena's hand. She looked up, but didn't pull away. Their eyes met and in a shaky voice, Cliff offered an apology. "Marlena, I am so sorry. I don't know what came over me. I know you had no control over what happened. I'm just thinking about . . . our little girl in there. She needs to come out of this. She needs to heal and we must be strong for her. All of us." He took Kim's hand in his other hand. "Please forgive me."

Marlena removed another tissue from the box her mother was offering and cleaned her face. The mascara had long since made black streaks down her cheeks. "I know Cliff and thank you. I do feel guilty in many ways, but I wonder how Claire is going to react when she wakes up. I worry she will blame me as well."

"Well, let's just hope that doesn't happen." Katie said.

Just then the double doors to the exam rooms opened and Claire's attending nurse came into the waiting room. Bill cleared his throat and signaled the others of her presence. Cliff turned with a jerk and stood to meet her. "Is Claire OK?"

"She is beginning to stir. I thought you would want to return to the room in case she comes out of the coma."

Marlena jumped from her seat and quickly followed Cliff and the nurse back into the exam room #4. The nurse pulled open the door to the room and went to Claire's bedside. Claire was softly moaning while rocking her head back and forth. Cliff ran to her side and took her hand. Marlena was next to him. He leaned in close to her face. "Claire, can you hear me. It's Daddy." She moaned a little louder. Drool was falling from the side of her lips. Marlena softly said, "Claire, it's Mother. I'm here my sweet little girl."

Claire jerked her head up from the pillow. She snapped her mouth shut and instantly opened her eyes. She was disoriented and confused at the strange room. All the equipment, the lights were strange. The smells were antiseptic. She looked right and saw a woman in a white pant suit with a stethoscope around her neck, smiling down at her. She turned quickly to the left and saw the face of the man she loved so much staring down at her. Behind him she noticed Marlena. The memories rushed back into her mind. The pain and the terror filled her head. All of a sudden she screamed, "Daddy, don't let him hurt me again." She reached up for him and he pulled her close. She was crying. Cliff was crying again, trying to soothe his baby girl. Marlena placed her hand on Claire's arm. Claire looked up at her with vengeance in her eyes. She sneered at her mother, "You get out of here. You're the one who brought that man in my house. I hate you!" She buried her head into Cliff's shoulder and cried even harder.

Marlena was numb. She couldn't cry. The dagger had pierced her heart. The realization of the truth from her daughter had burned into her soul. She hung her head in sorrowful pain and turned slowly for the door and the waiting room. She knew right then that she would have to find David. She needed closure from him. She needed to hear his story, if he had one. She placed her hand on Cliff's shoulder and he turned his head to see the pain and heartbreak in her face. In the last few days he had discovered a new Marlena. He knew now that she would never have let this happen if she had been in control of her own life. Marlena truly loved Claire and Cliff could only offer a look of encouragement. It would all work out, but again, it required time. Marlena was not only back to square one with Claire, she was deep in a trench with little or no way to get out. She would not give up on her relationship with Claire. It would take time to regain her confidence.

Cliff smiled at Marlena and she turned to leave. Claire held tightly to her father, believing the monster was still around and she was afraid. The sights, sounds smells and pain were all fresh again in her mind. She understood with great clarity the events of that night; the night she was attacked. Cliff rocked her in his arms like he had when she was small and scared of the thunder and lightning that came in the night. He stroked her hair and softly hummed a familiar tune close to her ear. Her crying ceased; she felt more at ease. Cliff held her closer and whispered to Claire. "Do you remember now, Tweetie? Can you tell Daddy what happened?"

She cringed in his arms and he lovingly wrapped his arms a little tighter around his baby. After a few seconds, she raised her hand to wipe the tears from her eyes. She buried her face in his arm. She softly said, "I remember. . . . everything."

"Can you tell me, baby? Did David hurt you?"

She only nodded her head. Cliff began to fume inside once again at the confirmation. A million thoughts ran wild in his head; how he was going to punish this monster that hurt his only precious child. He began planning how much he would hurt David; how hard the fists would pound into his face, stomach and groin. This man would not survive his beatings. But, common sense prevailed as it always finally did with Cliff. He knew the police must be contacted and David must be caught and punished by a court of law. Cliff gently pulled Claire from his embrace and looked deeply into her tear-filled eyes. He saw the innocence of his little girl still staring back at him. Searching for the words he said gently, "Claire, I must call the police and tell them what has happened. Do you understand?" She nodded. He continued, "They will want to ask you questions about what happened to you. Will you be able to remember enough to help them."

"I remember everything, Daddy. Will you be here?"

"I'll never leave you, Tweetie."

"I want Kim!"

"OK, you want me to get her."

"No, you stay." She looked at the nurse who was busying herself on the other side of the room. "Can she go?"

"I suppose." Cliff said. He got up from the bed and laid Claire back down on the pillow. He went to the nurse, asked for her help and she complied. In less than a minute, Kim was in the room holding Claire in her arms. Claire told her the whole story about what happened to her that night. Kim cried as she felt the pain Claire endured. Cliff was listening from a distance while he was on the phone calling the local police to report the crime. They assured him someone would be by within the hour. Meanwhile, the nurse had informed the doctor that

Claire was awake and alert. After completing another patient, Doctor 'Doogie' returned to Claire's room and finished assessing her condition.

Kim was with Cliff sitting in the only two chairs in the room. Kim was in a total rage. The emotions Cliff had felt earlier were taking over her thoughts and clouding her judgment. Cliff put his arm around her shoulder and held her hand. She was crying for Claire; crying for the pain this man had brought to this little girl. She felt so helpless that she couldn't do anything. She couldn't make it go away. She couldn't reverse the damage. When she was 16, Kim had found out that her best friend's boyfriend had raped her friend after she broke up with him. For a long time, her friend carried the hurt and pain with her, never telling anyone or reporting the crime. She held it inside and when Kim finally learned, she felt helpless then. There was nothing she could do to ease the suffering her best friend was going through. The boy was never punished for his crime. He probably never considered he had committed a crime. He wouldn't be punished. He got off scot-free. Kim was not going to allow that to happen with David. This man would be punished and he would receive the punishment that fit the crime.

A police detective arrived within the hour after the doctor had released Claire and they were preparing to leave. Detective Sherry Godfrey identified herself to the hospital and was allowed to interrogate Claire in a private room, provided by the staff. Like Cliff had promised, he was right next to her with Kim on the other side. Katie and Bill had left with Marlena earlier to begin the search for David. The police department was informed of the nature of the crime and victim and assigned a female detective to the case. Officer Godfrey was very sensitive to Claire's fragile condition. Her questions were easy and well thought out. She didn't want to frighten Claire, but she managed to get the complete picture as to what events occurred that night. She would need to speak with Marlena as well, and Claire cringed when she heard her mother's name. Cliff provided addresses and phone numbers of all parties of interest for this case, including Janey and Mae. Sherry Godfrey was making notations of each with her own version of shorthand to remind her of the questions she needed to ask.

In a way, Cliff was relieved that the question of what had happened to his baby girl had been answered, yet he was feeling the ache that came because he wasn't there to protect her. He would have to trust the authorities to do their job and locate the man so he could be prosecuted for ruining his child's life. Secretly, he wanted to find David in a closed room. He wanted just a few minutes with him so he might provide some of his own justice.

Katie and Bill had taken Marlena back to their home in Collierville, just 10 miles down Poplar from the hospital. The ride was quiet with Marlena reliving the very last words Claire said to her. *I hate you* resonated in her brain and vibrated throughout her body causing shivers to run up and down her spine. The sheer thought of losing Claire after all they had accomplished together was tearing Marlena apart. The thought of what David had done to her child was also reeling in her mind, and finding him was her utmost priority at this point. The lawyer in her told her that David needed to be apprehended very quickly if any justice was to prevail. If he was allowed to disappear without a trace, then she may never get the answers she needed. David had the rental car, which left Marlena at the mercy of her mother and father to get her around. The car had been rented using Marlena's Hertz Club card and David was listed only as a driver. Marlena decided to take a chance and report the car stolen to Hertz. They would do their job, contacting the police and reporting the theft. Legally, David had the right to drive the car, but if the police do find him, she can explain the complete situation. Then he would be arrested.

Searching through her purse, Marlena located the contacts notebook she had always updated with company clients, acquaintances, friends and family. She supposed David would be calling a few local friends who might be willing to help him out of town. Although her list was not the complete listing of David's known friends and buddies, she would start with the first and call until there were no more. Maybe one would provide additional contact information and possible locations to where David might return.

Marlena had asked to be left alone in Bill's study while she made her calls. Bill decided he would make a few calls of his own. Katie busied herself preparing a quick snack since they had missed Mae's lunch when everything hit the fan. The first call Marlena made was to the

Hertz toll free number. She stated the car was stolen from their hotel parking lot during the night. They would have all the necessary data, license plate number, VIN number, color and make. They made notations and asked if she needed another car delivered to her location. She declined and finished the call.

She studied the names listed under friends with the notations under each name indicating that these were friends of David. She took a deep breath, looked at her watch for the time. It was nearly five thirty and most people would be on the way home or already there. At least most homes have answering machines. She noted the name and number from the list, Steve Palmer. Reaching for the phone, she punched in the number. There were 3 rings before someone answered.

"Hello." Marlena heard the voice of a small child. Maybe no more than five years old.

"Hi, I am trying to reach Steve Palmer. Is he there?" Marlena asked in a tone appropriate for a child.

"Yeah, that's my daddy. DAD, phone!" the child said and then yelled out to his father. Marlena heard the receiver being laid down on a table and the footsteps of the child walking away.

A few seconds later, "Hello, this is Steve."

"Hi, Steve. My name is Marlena Anderson, David's wife. I kinda need help. David is missing and I am a little frantic. I have a list of names and you were the first on the list." She said.

"Yeah, I heard he got married. Sorry I didn't get to come to the wedding. Glad I'm first, but I haven't heard from David in about 9 months. Heard he had moved to Chicago. Guess that was with you, huh?"

"Yeah, it was. So you haven't heard from him at all?" she pleaded.

"No, I have no reason to hide anything from you."

“I know. I apologize. It’s just, well, he’s in some trouble and he took off and I need to find him.”

“What kind of trouble did he get into now?”

“I can’t really say at this time, but do you know of any other friends he might contact for help?” she asked again.

Steve was getting a bit suspicious at this call. He had known David for many years and he never knew of him getting into any trouble, other that a few too many drinks and maybe hitting on the waitress and getting a slap across the face. And who was this women; calling him - claiming to be David’s wife. He had never met her before, never even spoke with her, so how was he to know if this was in fact the wife of David Anderson. For all he knew, this could be some women he made promises to that he couldn’t keep. “Well, Marlena. You did say Marlena?”

“Yes”

“I haven’t heard from David, like I said, and I don’t know of any other friends he might know. Sorry, I couldn’t help.”

“OK, thanks, but would you call one of these numbers if you do hear from him?” she said and gave him her cell and Cliff’s number at home.

Steve jotted the numbers on the notepad by the phone, if only to provide for David, if he ever called, which he doubted. “OK, I got ‘em” he said.

“Thanks, bye,” she told him and hung up the phone.

Marlena spent the next 30 minutes making more calls and pleading her case to the ones she had managed to reach. No one had seen or heard from David. At least, that is what she had been told. She felt a sense of apprehension on the part of several of the men who did talk with her. She was curious as to there actual relationship with David. Were they friends or someone he used when he needed something for himself? Regardless she left the numbers with all the ones she spoke to with a promise that they would call if David showed up or called them. She decided there was little chance she would get a call, but she wanted to hope someone would be compassionate enough to come through with news.

Turning in the chair, she looked out of the big picture window that faced the rear of the house and the beautifully landscaped yard. Lost in deep thought, she didn't hear Katie come into the room.

"Marlena? You OK?" Katie asked.

Marlena snapped around. "Oh, sorry Mom. Just thinking about David. I am so worried what's going to happen to him. To us! He needs to be found so he can tell his side of the story. I'm afraid I won't like it, but he must face the consequences, whatever they might be."

Katie pulled over a padded chair next to her daughter and took her hands in her own. "Sweetheart, I believe everything will work out for the best. Now, at least, we have a better understanding of what happened to Claire. Tragic as it was, we are now getting to the truth. If David must pay for what he did, it shall be done and we can put this all behind us and make sure Claire gets whatever help she needs to have a normal life again."

"I know, Mother, but what about me? What am I going to do? He's my husband. The man I promised to love through everything." Marlena looked away.

"I understand. Your father and I are here for you. We will do whatever you need us to do, no matter what. You will be fine. Claire will be fine." Katie encouraged. "Now, come have a little something to eat."

Katie rose and slid the chair back in place. Marlena followed her into the kitchen where Bill was spooning out some hot chicken noodle soup in some bowls. They had a quiet late afternoon meal together.

Chapter Twenty

David awoke from a 3 hour snooze. Wiping the sleep from his eyes, he rolled over and noticed the bottle of Jack all but drained of its liquid. Then he stared at the clock on the night stand. It was nearly 6:00pm. He quickly jumped from the bed and nearly fell again from the dizziness rolling around in his head. Reaching for the bed, he sat back down on the edge until the swirling stopped. All the while, thoughts were racing back and forth. *Roger is looking for him. He had not made arrangements for any cash. Marlena for sure was looking for him. He needed a car.*

The dizziness had passed and his body became adjusted to an upright position. The effects of the alcohol were still there, circulating throughout his bloodstream, carrying the numbing effects. David went to the bathroom and turned on the cold water in the sink to full force. He splashed handfuls of the cool water on his face. Looking into the mirror, he saw a reflection of a man he had grown to despise over the last several months. He thought he was leaving that man behind, but the reality of his weakness and addiction brought the demon back. Through bloodshot eyes, he could not hold back the tears. His life had changed to the worst life that anyone could have imagined. He was a fugitive, on the run, being chased by everyone who wanted him for different reasons. And, with that reality check, he still managed to succumb to the evil of the bottle. That was his main enemy; the reason he was in this predicament in the first place.

David returned to the bed and sat down hard on the edge. He noticed the nearly empty bottle standing proudly next to the phone. Anger was building inside. He stared at Jack, grabbed the neck of the bottle and flailed it toward the wall, shattering it into thousands of pieces. He could hear the sounds of a frightened couple in the next room. For a moment, David smiled, hoping he had not broken the glass at the wrong time for that couple.

Looking around the room, he spotted his cell phone at the end of the bed. Reaching for the phone, he brought up his name and number list, selected one and pressed the call button. The phone at the other end rang four times before Steve Palmer picked up.

"Hello?"

"Steve, hi, this is David."

"David? David Anderson?"

"Yeah."

"Well, this must be my lucky day. First I get a call from some lady claiming to be your wife and now you call. Could this be a coincidence?"

"Marlena called you? What did you tell her?"

"Nothing, buddy. Cause I don't know a thing. What trouble are you in? She said you were in some kind of trouble."

"I am in trouble. I can't go into it, but I hope you can help me out. I need to get out of town and I need some cash."

"Well, I'm all tapped out of cash."

"I figured that, but can you point me to someone who could. I got a rental car. I'm sure is worth something. Two or three thousand at least. You still have those contacts?"

"I might be able to point you there. So, where are you planning on heading?"

"Texas first, then to Mexico, but that's just between me and you, right?"

"Sure. We go back too far." Steve said as he thumbed through his personal address book. "OK, here's the number. A guy named Roscoe Harris. Now, don't jerk him around. Do your business and leave. Roscoe is no picnic, but he does have contacts to make cars disappear and he makes money too."

David found a pen in the drawer and wrote down the information on the back of a comment card left on the night stand. He thought what a strange thing to leave in a motel like this one; a comment card. What comment would be appropriate? *The sex was good. Hope to get back here soon. Never had a more pleasant stay. You make Motel 6 look like Motel 2.*

David felt a bit more at ease. Not at the prospect of facing a man such as Roscoe, but the fact that his friends were still there for him and were willing to help him out, no questions asked. He said, "Thanks, Steve. You don't know how much this could help me out."

"Just remember this if ever I call you."

"You got it. Talk to you later."

"Alright. Good Luck. You're gonna need it."

"I know, bye" David hung up the phone. He looked at the paper where he had written the number. Summoning the courage, he punched in the number and waited.

Roscoe answered after the first ring. "Yo! What cha' got?"

David stammered, "Uhh, Uhh, Roscoe?"

"Yeah, you got'em. Who the fuck are you?"

"Uhh, my name's David. A friend of mine, Steve Palmer, told me you might be able to help me out."

"Steve? Oh yeah, that prick. He OK though. I suppose you got a ride that's hot?

"Well, not exactly hot. It's a rental car; Mercury Sable, 8000 miles."

"Why the hell you wanta dump a rental?"

"I need money to get out of town. And maybe another car?"

Roscoe thought a few seconds. "I think that can be arranged. Where you at?"

David sighed a breath of relief. This is going to work. He gave Roscoe directions to the motel and assured him that this was no scam after Roscoe promised retaliation if he was not on the up and up. They finished the conversation and David threw the phone back on the bed. He fell back across the bed and stared at the ceiling. No sooner had he closed his eyes, when Jack began to call out to him in his mind. This time, there was no fighting, no delay. He rolled off the bed and pulled the next quart out of the sack that he had left on the small table by the window. He twisted off the cap and took a long soothing drink.

Kim had driven home while Cliff sat in the back seat with Claire tucked safely under his arm. Her arm was wrapped around her father's waist. Mae and Janey were waiting patiently when they pulled into the garage. Katie had called ahead to inform Mae of the events at the ER. Mae was prepared for anything. Amanda, Janey's mother had returned from work and was waiting for Claire's return at Janey's insistence. Mae had not shared many of the details that Katie had provided; only that Claire was much better and her memory was back.

Kim opened the kitchen door to the garage and held it open for Cliff and Claire, who still clung to her dad with her face buried in his chest. For a moment, she felt embarrassed that everyone knew what had happened to her. All eyes would be on her, judging her. Cliff walked her into the great room where they sat on the couch. Claire finally released him and looked through tear-stained eyes at those around her. Everyone was smiling, not sneering and judging her like she thought. Claire felt the love coming from everyone in the room. Janey went to sit next to her on the sofa and Claire was glad.

Mae was the first to speak. "Well, is anyone hungry? I made some spaghetti. It's out there on the stove. Take just a minute to warm up."

Cliff looked up at his loyal friend for so many years. "You know, Mae that sounds pretty good. I am a bit hungry." He looked at Claire. "How 'bout you, Tweetie? You want some of Mae's famous spaghetti?"

With a soft voice she said, "Maybe later Daddy. I think I want to go to my room for a little while."

"You need me to take you?" Cliff asked.

"No, I can make it. Janey can come with me." Claire said.

Janey looked at her mother, "Mom, can I stay a little longer to be with Claire?"

Amanda smiled and stroked her child's head. "I think that will be fine as long as Cliff and Kim say it's alright."

Cliff said, "Sure. Janey's like part of the family anyway."

Janey clapped her hands together for joy and jumped up from the couch. She held out a hand to take Claire's and they went off to her bedroom upstairs. As they approached the top of the stairs, Claire became very nervous. Previously, when she would have the lapses of time and memory, she didn't understand why. Now she did; all too clearly. Her old room was just ahead and she wanted to avoid it. Building up her courage and using Janey for added comfort, she walked boldly down the hall, past the room. But, she had closed her eyes most of the way or looked at the opposite wall. Finally, they reached her bedroom, closed the door and ran to the bed where Claire climbed under the covers and Janey sat cross-legged on top of the comforter. Feeling a sense of safety in this room, Claire decided that she had lots of news to tell her best friend.

Marlena had borrowed one of her parent's automobiles to use until she returned to Chicago, but first she must find David. First stop was her hotel room at the Embassy Suites. David had a magnetic room card key and she needed to see if he had come by there to grab anything before leaving. She parked the car in a spot out front of the hotel near the main entrance. Going through the revolving doors, she noticed many people milling around the lobby. She checked her watched and realized that it was happy hour and many patrons were enjoying the free cocktails and appetizers that Embassy always provided their guests. The temptation to order a drink was strong but she resisted and immediately headed for the elevator to her room on the fourth floor. The room was freshly cleaned and linens changed. All her personal belongings were arranged neatly in the bathroom. Marlena scoured the room for any sign that David had been by for clothes or luggage. Nothing seemed out of place and she surmised that David had not been here. She sat down on the bed and looked around the room. There was such an emptiness she felt; so lost, so abandoned and so heartbroken. She thought of Claire and what she had been subjected to in her young life. Her little girl, the one she rejected all those years; years she couldn't make up. Marlena lay down across the bed and curled into a fetal position. She pulled a pillow from under the comforter and held it close to her chest. She began to cry. What was she going to do? How could David do this? Where was he? She cried some more until all the tears were gone.

Marlena could feel the old sensations and desires coming back to tempt her, to tease her and to coerce her into doing something she had fought so hard to prevent. The tug was strong. She didn't know if she could resist. Too much pain the last 12 hours had brought this on. She had to fight. Her cell phone was in her purse on the bar counter in the other room. She threw off the pillow and hurried to retrieve her phone. Nervously, she found the number in her phone directory and she punched the send button to call Debbie Hawthorne, her AA sponsor in Chicago. Debbie answered after the second ring.

"Debbie? It's Marlena."

Debbie could sense the urgency in her tone. She remembered it when Marlena first came into the program. "Are you OK. Tell me what's up."

Marlena began and told her the complete story as she knew it. Just the sound of Debbie's voice created a sense of calm within Marlena. She would be alright, now. But, Marlena realized that her problem was never going to completely go away. It would be with her for the rest of her life. She will always be an alcoholic and friends like Debbie would have to be there for her. One day, she would be one of those type friends to another, but now she was not strong enough. They talked for almost an hour before Marlena felt at ease with herself.

She went into the bathroom and started a hot bath. This room had a Jacuzzi tub and she planned to take advantage of all the comforts provided. She had some more calls to make, but now was her time.

David was sitting in a chair at the small table by the window, looking out for anyone he could see, when a knock at the door startled him. With caution, he leaned over to pull back the shade a bit to see who was at the door. This man was not the one from the front desk and he looked like a mountain. It must be Roscoe he thought.

Slowly, he went to the door and called out, “Roscoe?”

“Yeah, let me in, sucker.” A booming voice came through the door.

David opened the door and in walked one of the biggest men he had ever seen. Roscoe was at least 6’8” tall and almost as wide as the door opening. He had to be more than 350 pounds and it was all muscle. He reminded David of the huge actor who played in the movie ‘The Green Mile’ with Tom Hanks. Roscoe was bald and wore gold around his neck and large diamond studded earring. His large hands sported enormous gold and diamond rings on every finger. Large bling-bling chains and bracelets adorned his wrists. He wore a solid black T-shirt covered with a leather vest and black leather pants. His shoes were size 14 Nikes.

He closed the door behind him and gave David the once over. David was larger than the average man, but this monster made him look like one of the people from Lilliputian.

Roscoe spoke first. “So, where’s the car?”

A little intimidated, David pointed outside.

"Well, shit man, I know it's outside. Let's go look." He grabbed David by the shoulder and pulled him to the door. David felt like a rag doll.

They walked across the parking lot to an area that was the most hidden spot David could find. There was a hedge of shrubs facing the front of the car and the motel dumpster next to the car. Roscoe was scanning the area, like always, for anything that seemed out of place.

"I called your buddy and mine, Steve, just to check you out. He say you cool. Just in a fix." Roscoe began.

With a relief in his voice David said. "Yeah, I ain't gonna give you no problem. I just need some cash to get out of town and another car. So what can you give me for the car?" he added, reluctantly handing Roscoe the keys. There would be nothing he could do to stop him from taking the car anyway. He just hoped for the best.

Roscoe took the keys and unlocked the door. The seat was all the way back and he managed to get inside. The weight caused the car to lean a little. He cranked the car and looked around at the interior. After a minute, he turned off the motor and got out.

Roscoe looked at the car and then at David, "Alright, we might do some bid' ness. This car be reported?"

"You mean stolen?"

"Yeah, what else?"

"No, I just took off in it today. It's legit, but won't be for long."

"It won't be around for long either. I give ya 3 grand, plus that ride over there." He pointed to a blue,94 Chevy 1500 pickup with some damage to the driver's side door.

David looked at the truck and back at Roscoe. "Is it reported?" he said with a little sarcasm.

"Yeah, what else." David slumped his shoulders and Roscoe added. "But don't be fretting, man. It's been long time ago and they ain't got no all points out on it anymore. Been more than 8 years. I just use it every now and then to haul shit. Figured it bout time I got rid of it."

"Will it make it to Arkansas?"

"Man, that truck will take you to LA and back."

David looked again and then back at Roscoe who had pulled out a wad of bills from his pants pocket. David said. "OK, but I was hoping for more cash, but, hey I take what I can get. Let's go inside and do this. I get nervous out here."

Roscoe laughed. "What you scared of, man. Ain't nobody round here 'cept people like me. They don't give a shit what you doing. Just don't fuck with 'em and they won't fuck with you."

They walked back to the room and completed the deal. Roscoe paid off David with 100 dollar bills and gave him the key to the pickup. David added the cash to his pocket with the remaining money. After Roscoe closed the door, David began gathering what ever he had brought, because he was planning to leave right away. He watched as the rental car turned right onto Airways Blvd. David ran to the truck and opened the door. A thought came into his head. *What if this truck was not Roscoe's and this key wouldn't fit. He was screwed.* David looked at the key. He recognized it as a GM key. He inserted it and it cranked. Relief came over him. He grabbed the quart and took a long swig for the road. He looked down at the gas meter. It read half-full. That would get him far out into Arkansas. He would feel a little safer when he was out of Memphis. He backed out of the parking spot and headed for Airways. He turned left toward I-240. As he approached the proper speed limit, he reached for his phone to make a couple more calls he just had to make before leaving town.

Singing along with some new rap song on the radio, Roscoe turned onto Winchester Rd. heading for his place in Westwood. He looked in the rearview mirror and noticed a police cruiser, in his lane, following; not too close, but close enough that he knew they were watching this car. He looked at the speedometer on the dash; not speeding. He watched for another few seconds; they were following his every move. Suddenly, he saw the blue lights flashing and the cruiser move in closer. "Shit!" he said. He immediately reached for his cell and punched in Steve Palmer's number.

It was nearly 8:00 when Janey and Claire finally finished their talk. Claire told her everything she could remember, leaving no detail unsaid. For the most part, Claire needed to do this just to clarify for herself what had happened that night. Janey had been her best friend for many years and Claire trusted her completely with this story. Janey was not the type to blab gossip and stories to their friends and Claire knew that.

Janey was lying on the bed next to Claire; both were staring at the ceiling of the bedroom, just trying to comprehend this tale of horror Claire had revealed. There was a soft knock on her bedroom door. Claire called out, "Come on in."

Cliff entered carrying his opened cell phone in his hand. He walked to the bed and looked down at the two girls lying there. He remembered the many times as they were growing from kindergarten, how they would have these sleepovers and look so innocent together under the covers. Now, all that had changed a little. A bit of innocence had been removed from his child. He sat on the edge of the bed.

"Claire, your mother is on the phone and would like to talk to you."

Claire tossed him a look that shot daggers. "I ain't talking to her. It's all her fault. I hate her." Then she turned away and pulled the covers up to her face. Janey wrapped her arm around Claire's shoulder.

Cliff left quietly and when he reached the hallway he put the phone back to his ear. “I guess you heard.”

Marlena was crying. “I . .I heard. I had hoped she would have a change of heart, but I guess time will tell. Keep reminding her that I love her and don’t want to give up on what we got started the last few days.”

“I will. She’s just adjusting right now. Has David contacted you?”

“No, not yet. But I did call a few of his friends he had listed here in Memphis. I left my number and yours too, just in case he contacts them.”

“Marlena, he is going to pay and pay hard for this. I just pray the police get him before I do.”

“I know. It’s devastated me. So bad in fact, I almost gave in. But . . . I called my sponsor and we talked for quite a while. I’m better now.”

“Please, don’t get back into that life. You have made such progress. You deserve better now. You deserve better than David.”

“As much as I hate to admit it, I feel the same. But, please continue talking to Claire. I need her in my life.”

“I will. Where are you now?”

“I’m back at Embassy. Dad’s coming by later to take me to a late dinner. I’ll call again tomorrow unless I hear something tonight.”

“OK. Bye.”

“Bye, Cliff. Thanks for everything.” She said and then hung up the phone.

Cliff turned to go back into Claire’s room to have a conversation about Marlena, but he decided to wait until tomorrow. Janey was the best medicine for her right now and they had agreed to allow her to spend the night. Amanda had delivered Janey some clean pajamas, a fresh pair of jeans, shirt and other necessities. He returned to his bedroom, where Kim was preparing herself for bed. After such a trying day, they both decided to get some much needed rest and see what tomorrow would bring. Cliff sat on the linen chest at the foot of their bed and began removing his shoes and socks. "Claire wouldn't have any part of Marlena. I don't know what I'm supposed to do."

Kim turned from her vanity and crossed her legs. "She will come around. I know she will. I think I would feel the same way if I was in her shoes. Marlena will have to wait. Maybe, I can take her out tomorrow, maybe to lunch and we can talk. I'll find a way to bring up Marlena in such a way that won't be threatening to her."

"You would do that? I guess that's one reason I love you so much." Cliff said as he got up and kissed her. "I'm gonna take a quick shower."

"OK, don't be too long." She winked and smiled.

Janey and Claire were continuing their conversations, but the situation of that terrible day was not coming back up. Now they discussed school, the tutor and other friends. Claire felt a twinge of hunger; she had not eaten all day. "Are you hungry? I sure am."

"Yeah, I kinda am. I ain't had anything since Mae's lunch. You want me to fix you something?"

"Would you do that?"

"Sure I would. We're best friends after all. What'd you want?"

"How 'bout a ham sandwich with cheese and some chips." Claire said as she sat up in the bed. "Then we can watch a movie."

The phone rang and startled them both. Janey looked at the phone on Claire's desk. "Should I get that?"

"No, Kim or Daddy will get it their room. It's probably for them anyway." Claire said as the phone quit ringing.

Janey put on her house slippers and robe. Turning to Claire she asked. "Now what if there's no ham? PB and J OK?"

"Sure!" Claire answered and Janey went to the door and out into the hall.

Closing the door behind her, Janey walked slowly down the hallway. Cliff and Kim's bedroom was just ahead and she didn't know if she would be in trouble for fixing her and Claire something to eat. As she approached the door, which was halfway open, she heard Kim's conversation on the phone. She also heard the sound of the shower. Kim's dialog caught her attention. She leaned against the wall and strained her ear to the opening of the door.

Kim was standing by the desk speaking to the caller. "OK, if you're an acquaintance of David's, why can't you tell me who you are?"

". . . . . I understand, but we need to find him. It's of utmost importance."

". . . . Well, why is our concern. . . . OK, OK don't hang up. . . tell me where you think he is. . . . ."

"Do you know what he is driving? . . . . When was the last time you spoke to him . . . . you saw him? . . . . How much did he owe you? . . . . . Did you see the car he was in? . . . . OK, what model truck?" Kim was now seated with pen in hand jotting down all the answers.

". . . . no, we haven't set a reward, but that was thought of. . . . . How long ago was it that you saw David? . . . . Where in West Memphis? . . . Did he mention where he was intending to go? . . . . . well, Texas is big. Any suggestions? . . . . OK thank you so much. I wish you would give me your name. . . . OK, bye"

Kim finished writing some notes on the pad and rushed into the bathroom to inform Cliff of the conversation. Janey had not left her listening post and when she heard Kim enter the bathroom and close the door, she took her chance. She ran into the bedroom and located the pad next to the phone with the notes Kim had jotted down. She scanned the words and tried to memorize everything there and attempted to match up the answers with the questions she overheard from Kim. Quicker than before, she raced out of the room just as Kim came out of the bathroom. Then, Janey ran downstairs and prepared some sandwiches for her and Claire, while storing the information in her brain. She would write it all down later. She was formulating a plan.

While Cliff completed his shower, Kim returned to the room and went directly to the desk and pulled the pad into her hand. She was deep in thought when she lifted the receiver and made a call to a friend she had known for a long time. She had to do something. The police would have this information very soon, but she had a way to help.

Chapter Twenty One

As the sunlight streamed through the window of Claire's bedroom and brightened her face, she rolled over to see her best friend soundly sleeping next to her. Suddenly the memory of the previous day came flooding back into her mind. She pulled the covers up closer against her face for protection. One by one the events of that night flashed in her head, causing her to cringe with fear. She was trying to convince herself that she was safe now; her daddy would be there to watch over her from now on. But, the horrible face of that man, the smell of liquor on his breath and the pain she endured resonated loud within her. She just wanted to forget it all, but she couldn't.

Janey slowly opened her eyes and squinted at the bright sun beaming into the room. After getting her bearings, she realized where she was. Claire was under the covers and Janey saw her friend's eyes staring at her from underneath. "Hey" Janey offered.

"Hi." Claire said in a muffled voice. "I'm glad you stayed last night."

"Me, too. You hungry? I am."

"Kind of. All I've had was that sandwich you made last night."

"Well, that was like, a horrible day for you." Janey said.

"Tell me about it!"

Janey leaned over to look at the time on the clock radio on the night stand. It was nearly ten o'clock. "Wow, it's late. We better get up. No wonder I'm hungry." Janey jumped off the bed and ran to the bathroom. Claire remained under the blankets.

Cliff was in his bedroom when he heard the rustling from down the hall in Claire's room. He slipped on his shoes and walked down the hallway to her door and lightly rapped. "Tweetie, you awake?" he said as he slowly opened the door to peek inside. Claire noticed him entering and waved from under the covers. He went to her and sat on the edge of the bed. "You need to get up baby. I got a call from that lady detective from yesterday. She has few questions to ask me and Kim. She also said there are a couple more questions for you, too." Cliff waited to get a reaction, but received no indication of stress or tension. "You gonna be OK with that?"

"I suppose." Claire said throwing off the covers.

"Good! Like I said, I think this is mostly for other people and I mentioned what Janey had told us about the car, so she wants to talk to her, too. So, ya'll get ready and come on downstairs. She was going to be here in about an hour."

Janey opened the bathroom door and ran to the bed after Cliff left the room. She looked at Claire and said. "Did he say the police wanted to talk to me?"

"Yep!"

"Cool! I've never been part of an investigation before. It's like those cop shows on TV."

Claire sat up in the bed and smiled at Janey. "Well, I guess we need to, like get ready. I'll shower first, OK?"

"Good, I'll watch TV." Janey said as she lay back down on the stack pillows and pulled the remote from the nightstand drawer and pressed the on button.

A loud blast from the air horns from a departing UPS 18-wheeler startled David from an 8 hour sleep in the truck. He had managed to get to the rest stop just outside of Texarkana, Ark. The liquor he was consuming along the way was getting the better of him and he realized that rest was what he needed, but he had only planned to sleep for a couple of hours. Like the many times before when he and Marlena went out on the town, he had little trouble driving while under the influence. Well, that's what he had always thought, but the memory of what he was running from made him understand that getting caught in a DUI offense was the worst that could happen. He was sure that Marlena and Cliff had reported his flight to the police and they would be on the lookout for him as well as notifying other law enforcement agencies around the mid-south. The farther away from Memphis he got, the safer he felt and was thinking that he would not be caught.

Wiping the sleep from his eyes and drool from his mouth, David sat up and looked around the area of the rest stop. He had parked in the farthest spot from the building to avoid travelers looking into the cab of the truck and seeing a man asleep. There were several cars and motor homes parked around the lot with families and singles making their way to and from the welcome center's facilities. He didn't see any cops and he felt comfortable leaving the truck to head for the welcome center's bathroom. He passed a family of four with a boy about 6 and girl close to 12 years old. The girl looked at him in a funny, yet frightening way. He shuddered inside remembering the tragedy that caused all this. But, when he found the men's room and looked into the mirror, he could see the reason the children stared in such disbelief. He looked like the bum you might see on the street corner, begging for loose change for food, when you know all he wanted was money for something to drink. His white shirt was one wrinkle after another and it had been stained with something he ate. He smelled of liquor. David watched his image as tears began to form in his eyes. The reality of it all was now hitting him square in the face. He heard someone in the stall and he quickly turned on the cold water faucet and began splashing water on his face. He wet his hair and slicked it back with his spread out fingers, as best he could. His clothes were in bad shape from a night of sleeping in the truck and this outfit was all he had managed to come away with.

He felt his pocket and was relieved to find the wad of cash he had been carrying was still there. Maybe he should stop at a local Wal-mart or Target and purchase a couple of pair of pants and shirts. Fresh clothing might make him feel a little better; plus a good bath. Hunger pains began to growl deep inside his body and he looked around for the vending machine area. He dropped some coins in the slot and selected a bag of cheese puffs for his breakfast. Later, he would stop for something better, but his thoughts now were getting back on the road and driving deeper into Texas; closer to Mexico and freedom. He walked back to the truck, munching on the cheese puffs. Other people walked passed, giving him a look that told him Wal-mart was definitely his next stop.

When he opened the truck door, he noticed the sack that contained his last bottle of Jack. It was still sealed and he wanted to keep it that way until he stopped for the night. He hesitated for a few seconds, fighting a battle within his mind, one side pushing him to open the bottle, take a drink. It will be OK. The other side, the side that he wanted to be on, called to him to hide the bottle or even throw it in the trash. The bad side was relentless and spoke a good case. The good side spoke to his common sense and suggested to keep the bottle out of sight for now. This was a strange town and he didn't know the streets or the attitude of the cops. The good side won. David took the bottle from the cab of the truck and placed it in the tool box that was left in the bed of the truck. Fortunately the box was not locked. He climbed back into the cab of the truck and fired up the engine. A slight puff of smoke exited the tail pipe, which caught David's attention in the passenger side mirror. Just keep running was all David could think. Putting the transmission into reverse, he backed out of the parking spot and he then pulled back out onto Interstate 30 heading west. Texarkana was 2 miles ahead and Texas was just a few miles more.

As he got up to the speed limit, he noticed a highway patrol unit just ahead of him in the passing lane. He backed off the accelerator and allowed the cruiser to continuing advancing. When he approached the first exit into Texarkana, he noticed a Wal-mart on the left. Immediately, he pushed up the blinker and exited the interstate. There was a McDonald's in the same shopping center and David planned to buy new clothes and change in the restroom. He decided to grab a couple sandwiches to go as well. As he turned into the parking lot, he looked at his gas gauge, which indicated he was half-full. He had filled up in Forrest City the day before and to get on into Texas he would need to buy more. He looked around and saw a Raceway station on the opposite side of the street. He parked the car far out and walked into the store to make his purchase.

Detective Godfrey arrived on time at the Richards home. She also asked a court reporter to document the deposition of those she would interview. When the detective came in the front door, Claire was sitting in the great room with Janey by her side. She had assured her father that she would be alright with the questions, but her nerves were beginning to show. After friendly greetings and introductions, the reporter began to set up at the desk across the room. Claire watched her with curious eyes. Sherry approached Claire who continued to stare at the woman with the strange machine.

"Hello, Claire." Godfrey said and Claire jumped and looked up into a smiling face. "This lady's name is Bonnie Parker." She signaled for Bonnie to come over. "Bonnie this young lady's name is Claire Richards."

Claire extended her hand to shake and Bonnie took it. "It's so nice to meet you, Claire. I guess you're wondering what I'm going to do, huh?" Claire shook her head.

"I am what you would call, a court reporter. Whenever Detective Godfrey or any other officer needs to ask questions of citizens, they sometimes have me come along so I can record every word I hear. It's called a transcript and my machine is called a stenotype. That way, the police department will have a document of all the questions and answers that were given."

Detective Godfrey sat down next to Claire and put her arm around her shoulders. "I tell you what. Why don't I interview your dad first and then you can see how it's done, OK?"

"Sure!" Claire said. She was feeling a little more at ease.

Godfrey looked at Janey and asked. "You must be Janey?"

Janey nodded her head.

"Well, you know, I think I would like to talk to you, too. Is that OK with you?"

Janey smiled and replied. "Cool!"

The detective got up and moved a chair closer to where Bonnie had set up the equipment. She placed another chair opposite the first and she asked Cliff to join her. Cliff sat in the second chair and she sat across from him. Bonnie was comfortably seated, with hands and fingers above her stenotype, ready for the first statements.

Detective Godfrey began while reviewing a paper in her hand, "Tuesday, 30, October, 11:02am. The home of Cliff and Kimberly Richards. Interviewer, Detective Sherry Godfrey, Documenter, Bonnie Parker. " She placed the paper in her lap and looked at Cliff. "Sir, please state your name for the record."

"Clifford S. Richards" Cliff replied.

The interview lasted only 20 minutes and Detective Godfrey decided to continue the questioning with Kim and Claire would follow. Claire and Janey whispered together and watched with intense interest at the proceedings going on in her house. In the middle of the Kim's interview, they were interrupted by a knock at the back door. Mae was waiting for her turn in the chair and busied herself cleaning the last of the breakfast dishes. She answered the door. Cliff went to greet their visitor, while the detective stopped the questions until it could be determined who was there. At the detective's request, Cliff had phoned Marlena and asked that she come by as well during this time for another interview. As they walked into the room, Claire looked into her mother's face and immediately turned away. Marlena felt quite uneasy at being here, but Godfrey had an ulterior motive for bringing them together. She needed to observe Claire's reactions as well as ask detailed questions. Marlena took a seat in the chair against the wall behind the couch where Claire and Janey were sitting. Claire didn't like her being there. She could feel her mother's eyes on the back of her head. It bothered her.

Detective Godfrey completed the questions for Kim and asked Claire to join her. Claire was hesitant at first, but got up and walked slowly to the chair. She turned to see the stares of everyone in the room; especially her mother. Marlena knew she was the object of Claire's anxiety and she got up to join Mae in the kitchen. Sherry began her interview. She was much more sensitive and gentle with Claire than with Cliff or Kim. She needed Claire's confidence and she needed clear answers. Claire was at her best. All the questions were straight to the point and Claire had answers that satisfied Detective Godfrey. Claire's interview lasted almost thirty minutes.

One by one, everyone was questioned and excused. When Marlena took her turn, Claire asked for permission to go upstairs, which she was allowed to do.

David felt so much better after he managed to change clothes in the bathroom stall at McDonalds. He did receive a few stares at Wal-mart and the cashier who rang up his purchase looked him up and down when he presented her with 2 twenties. He was greeted at the order counter with kindness and enthusiasm by a cute blonde teen girl, who sported a mouth full of braces. Obviously, his transformation worked and he was just one of the regular folk of Texarkana. He ordered a two hamburger combination meal with fries and a drink and decided to take a few minutes and eat like a normal person. He paid his bill and took his tray to a seat by the front window, where he could keep an eye on the truck. After all, Jack was out there unprotected in that toolbox. Feeling the cash wad that bulged in his pants pocket, he began to feel a sense of relief that he might have pulled this off. Would he get away? Only time would tell. The border to Mexico was a few hundred miles away from this place and he had to drive the distance. After that, he had no clue what he would do. There were no friends in Mexico waiting for him. He had left his passport in Chicago. For a second, he began to have second thoughts about Mexico. He could barely speak Spanish and an American coming into the country with lots of cash was easily spotted by the locals. Maybe he should try Montana. It was a huge state filled with nothing but land, sky and mountains. He could easily get lost there. Now, the pressure was building inside and the need to rescue Jack from the toolbox was becoming overwhelming. He shook his head to clear the thoughts and he looked out the picture window toward the truck. First, he wanted to finish the meal and get into Texas. After that, he would decide where to go.

The sun was high and a cool breeze started to blow. David had quenched his hunger pain and left the restaurant for the truck. His eye glanced toward the toolbox when he inserted the key to open the door. Jack was calling, but David was determined to resist until the night, after he found a place to stay. As he started to pull away, he noticed an ATM machine in the parking lot. He had already taken out money the day before and he would be allowed to remove the maximum today as well, but his trail could be tracked by these transactions. Should he take the chance? He was in dire need of additional cash since he paid off Roger back in West Memphis. He knew Roger had connections all over the country and if anyone would find him first, it would be Roger. He decided that this was a chance he needed to take. He drove to the ATM and went inside the small enclosed glass building. Nervously, he looked around the area for any sign of trouble. He inserted his card and withdrew the max amount allowed. He knew if Marlena tried to get some money, she would get an over limit message, which would immediately signal her to contact the bank and they would tell her where he was at the time of the transaction. He also withdrew money against his credit card. With a new found energy, he jumped back into the truck and headed for the Raceway gas station to fill up; then on to the interstate.

For a moment, the call of the evil force in the back of the truck was not bothering David. He was almost in a good mood. He turned on the radio and found a local country station. The slowed down traffic was tight and there was a lot of stop and go driving, which did not seem to worry David. His mind was on the music at the moment; off in another world.

The blue lights started to flash in the rear view mirror and David's eyes caught the glow of the flashing lights. He jerked his head around quickly to see a police cruiser right on his bumper. He was already in the far right lane. Traffic was slow ahead and he had no choice but to pull off the interstate into the emergency lane. Slowly, he came to a stop and the cop car pulled in behind him. He wasn't speeding; no one was. David's nerves were shattered. He was obviously shaking in his seat. He watched as a young police officer with dark shades exited his car. He looked like he was just out of the academy.

The officer cautiously approached taking notice of all details of the vehicle. Officer Wilson stopped at the driver's door and signaled David to lower the window, which he did. Immediately, the cop could sense tension in the man in the truck. He was too nervous for a simple traffic stop. The cop's training told him that something was different about this occupant. "May I see your license, please?" Officer Wilson politely asked.

David fumbled with his wallet looking for his driver's license. He remembered that he had just renewed the previous year and the photo was current; a plus in his favor, he thought. His hand trembled when he handed the card to the cop. The officer took the license while continuing to observe David as he reviewed the information on the license.

"Mr. Anderson" the officer started. "Are you OK? You seem a bit frazzled."

David didn't look at him, but kept his face forward as he said. "No, no, I'm alright."

The cop was still convinced there was more to this stop than it appeared. He stared for a few seconds at David, who continued to fidget and shake. "Are you the owner of the vehicle?"

David turned to face him now. "No sir. I borrowed it from a friend in Memphis, just yesterday. Mine broke down and he was kind enough to loan it to me for a few days."

Still curious the cop asked. "So where are you heading, Mr. Anderson?"

"I have some computer equipment to pick up in Dallas." David lied.

"I see." He looked closer into the truck. "Would you mind stepping out of the vehicle, please."

Ohh, shit, David thought to himself as he reached for the handle and opened the door. He walked to the side of the truck bed and leaned against it.

"Do you have any objection if I check out this truck. You know since it isn't yours, I need to make sure you're not unintentionally transporting illegal contraband."

David was petrified. What could he say? Thoughts of Roscoe using this truck to haul drugs filled his brain. With reluctance David offered. "Sure, go ahead."

The cop leaned inside and looked behind the seats and underneath. He walked to the other side of the truck after closing the driver side door, and looked into the glove compartment. He only found a registration slip and a package of condoms. He threw the condoms back inside and studied the registration form. He walked to rear of the truck to compare the license plate; a match. He looked at David and asked. "Who did you say your friend was?"

David looked at the cop, who had completed the circle of the truck and was now standing in front of a very nervous man. David's only hope was that Roscoe had actually done something right and somehow got the truck registered. David stammered when he said. "My friend. . . Roscoe . . . uhh Roscoe Harris."

The cop looked at David and then at the document. Still not convinced, he handed the form to David. He said. "OK, thanks. Uh, what's in the toolbox?"

"Nothing." David said too quickly, all the while knowing Jack was hiding there.

"Mind if I look." He said without waiting for an answer. The lid lifted effortlessly and Officer Wilson peered into the metal box. He noticed a brown paper bag lying on the bottom. He reached in and pulled it out. He looked at David. "Nothing, huh?"

"Well, just that."

The cop looked at the bottle and confirmed the top was still sealed. Obviously, this was the reason for the nervousness. "Well, I guess the toolbox is the best place for this." He said as he placed it back into the toolbox and closed the lid. He also added. "Now, I hope you won't be stopping to try a little of that out while you're driving today."

David felt some relief and began to calm down. “No, for sure, that was for later tonight when I get checked in to a motel in Dallas.”

The cop smiled and said. “Well, I guess you want to know why I stopped you in the first place?” David just nodded his head. “Your right brake light is out. You’ll need to get that fixed real quick. I hear Texas is bad about giving out tickets for such things. I’m just giving you a warning.“

David smiled and said. “Thanks, thank you very much. Can I go now?”

“Sure, and get that bulb replaced soon.” He said and turned to walk back to the patrol car.

“I will.” David said as he opened the driver’s door and got inside. He placed the registration form back into the glove compartment while thinking of what Roscoe had told him about this truck. It wasn’t stolen, because this had to be Roscoe’s personal truck. Or he was a much better forger than David had guessed.

With a better feeling of relief running through his body, David cranked the truck while the patrolman pulled out ahead of him. He eased out into the traffic. He didn’t notice the car with two occupants, who had been observing from a distance. It was on the highway shoulder about 50 meters behind him. After David entered the first lane the white car pulled into the flow of traffic and merged into the same lane as David.

Chapter Twenty Two

The police interrogators completed their questioning by 1:30 and before leaving, informed Cliff they might need further details at a later date. Cliff could not understand what else he could possibly offer, but agreed. He looked at his watch and recalled the appointment for Claire with Dr. Chandler was at 3:00, so he went upstairs to make sure Claire remembered and was properly dressed.

Marlena had left immediately after her questioning was completed with the assurance to the detective that she would be available. She remained emotionally drained after Claire's actions. There was nothing at the moment she could do to change the way her daughter felt. Maybe time will tear down the wall that Claire had erected against her. Marlena was losing David and she needed Claire to remain in her life.

After making arrangements to leave work early, Amanda arrived to pick up Janey. With much reluctance, Janey left. Claire finished dressing for the doctor's visit, while her daddy changed clothes. They both came downstairs together and met with Kim in the kitchen, who was reading some documents from work. Kim called into work to inform her staff and supervisor that she would be working at home for the day.

Kim looked up from the stack of papers laid out across the table. "My, don't you look just beautiful." She whistled at Claire who had dressed in a beautiful white blouse with lace down the front and of course a yellow pleated skirt with a wide belt that was a shade darker yellow than the skirt. It had a large, silver buckle with eyelets trimmed with silver rings. She wore white knee socks and her Nike tennis shoes. Her hair was neatly brushed back into a pony tail with a yellow ribbon tied in back.

Claire smiled at her step-mother and raced to her with open arms. "I'm so glad you're my mom and I love you so much."

Kim could only hold on and fight back the tears that were starting to flow. Cliff was preparing a cup of coffee when he heard Claire's statement. He turned to see a look on Kim's face that told the whole story. From the very first time Claire and Kim met, they bonded immediately and that bond had grown stronger every day. Claire sat at the table next to Kim and Cliff joined them.

David was well into Texas, singing along with John Michael Montgomery on the radio when he spotted a Texas Highway patrol car approaching on the opposite side of Interstate 30. At once, the blown out brake light came to his mind. He must get it fixed. He noticed the exit for Sulfur Springs, TX was only one mile ahead. That would be his stop to locate an auto parts store; maybe they had an AutoZone store. As he approached the exit, he turned on his signal and left the interstate. Continuing to follow, the white Cadillac was about 200 meters back and signaled to exit as well.

Cliff and Claire left for the doctor and Kim continued to work on a presentation she had first started the week before. The Atlanta trip was very successful and this would be the closing sale for this account. She appreciated the quiet of the house. Mae had been given the afternoon off after her testimony, which left Kim all to herself. She got up for a break from the work to fix another cup of coffee. She normally didn't drink coffee, but for some reason the smell of the fresh pot Cliff had made, tempted her. After mixing in a little Equal and creamer, Kim headed for the recliner in the great room to relax and enjoy the solitude. The phone rang.

She set the coffee cup on the desk and picked up the receiver of the phone. "Hello? . . . . Oh, Hi, what have you found out? . . . . . Excellent, when can I expect results? . . . . OK, let me know as soon as you make contact. . . .OK, bye." Kim smiled broadly as she retrieved her cup and went to the recliner.

After driving more than three miles from the interstate, David found an AutoZone store. On one side of the parts store was a fast food restaurant and the other was a gas mini-mart. He pulled into the parking lot of the parts store, parking in a space nearest the restaurant. Then he went inside to purchase the brake light bulb and a screwdriver he would need to remove the lens cover. The men in the white Caddy parked on the far side of the gas station with a clear view of David's vehicle. They watched silently when David returned to the truck and began replacing the light. With the task completed, David got into the truck and checked his pocket again for the only money he had left. He was hungry and he decided to grab a bite to eat; he cranked the engine and headed for the Wendy's next door. He found a parking spot in the back by the dumpster. From across the parking lot an engine fired up in the white car and slowly pulled out of the gas station and into the Wendy's parking lot. They passed David when he was walking to the side entrance; their eyes fixed on him. He never noticed. They parked next to his truck.

Marlena returned to her hotel room at the Embassy Suites. She had been in contact with all of her and David's friends and work associates trying to locate her husband. Her worst fears appeared to be true. David raped her child. The fact that he was drunk at the time was no defense. She had to find him and find him soon. After spending the past hour phoning acquaintances, she was exhausted. Reaching into her purse she took a couple of Excedrin tablets and went into the bedroom of the suite to lay quietly across the bed; a headache was beginning. The lights were off in the room and the curtains were closed, which provided a darkness that would help the pain go away. She was nearly asleep when the ringing phone startled her back into reality. Reaching for the phone on the night stand by the bed, she fell back on the pillows after putting the receiver to her ear. "Hello?"

The man's voice on the other end replied. "Is this Marlena Anderson?"

She didn't recognize his voice, but replied. "Yes it is. Who are you?"

He continued, "You don't know me, but I was given this number to contact you if I had some news about your husband."

Marlena sat bolt upright on the bed. “Yes, yes! Do you know where David is?”

“Sorry, but I can only provide where he’s been.”

“OK, OK tell me what you know. What did you say your name was?”

“I didn’t, but its Clay Sherwood. I’m an old drinking buddy of David. Well, that was before he moved.”

“Thank you Clay for calling. Who gave you this number?”

“Well, actually, I got your number from the bartender at TG’s. Seems some of David’s other buddies came in too and were talking about him skipping out on you, so I suppose they gave your number to Frank. But that’s not what I actually heard. Me and my friend were having a couple at the bar when this guy comes in and sets down a few stools from my friend. He gets to talking to Frank the bartender about some job he just finished. Now I don’t know this guy, but he mentioned David’s name in the conversation. Now, Frank kinda looked in my direction when this guy started talking about David, so I listened close. Seems this guy is a private detective or something and David had hired him to watch someone. Didn’t ever say who. But, he says David was trying to skip out on paying him, but he finally came through. He met up with David over in West Memphis and David paid him what he owed. Now, from what I gather this guy is good at what he does, but he’s also bad news if you don’t pay up. I guess David knew that, too.”

Marlena was alert and tensely sitting on the edge of the bed. “Did he say where David was going?”

“No, not specifically. I did hear him mention Texas, though. So, I guess he might be heading that direction.”

“Did he happen to mention what David was driving?”

“Sorry, didn’t say. How much trouble is he in?”

"Well, we won't really know until he is back here and we get to talk to him. But, it could be pretty bad, so if anyone you know makes contact with David, please call."

"Sure. I suppose that's what Frank had your number for in the first place. After the guy left, Frank asked me to give you a call. Hope you find him."

"Me too. Thank you for calling."

"OK, you take care now. Bye."

"Bye." Marlena said and hung up the phone. She had forgotten about her headache. She lifted the receiver and punched in her father's number.

Bill answered on the first ring.

Excitedly Marlena almost shouted into the phone. "Dad, I think we have a lead on David."

Kim had completed all her notes and documentation for the Atlanta client and cleared the table of business. She was in the great room reading quietly when Cliff and Claire returned home from the doctor visit. Claire ran immediately to Kim and wrapped her arms tightly around her neck. Cliff hung up his light jacket in the entry closet. He came into the room and sat next to Kim on the couch. Claire was on Kim's lap.

Cliff smiled at the sight and said. "Tweetie, why don't you go upstairs and change and come on back down and we can tell Kim all about your visit. And while we do that, we can have some pizza ordered in."

"Yeah!" Claire shouted. She leaned over to give Kim a kiss on the cheek and she jumped up and ran for the stairs. Cliff and Kim watched with love at this child who was now on the road to recovery.

Kim turned to Cliff. “So, did the visit go OK?”

Cliff smiled and said. “Very good. Claire opened up with all she remembered. Dr. Chandler believes she will rebound from this and be able to get on with a perfectly normal life, but he would like to schedule a few more visits during the next 6 months.”

Kim moved a bit closer. “I had a call today. I need to tell you something I put into motion.”

Cliff looked puzzled, but listened intently as Kim began to explain.

The restaurant was quite busy and David had waited for more than 15 minutes just to place his order. Mostly families with kids filled all the tables and booths. David chose a table for two next to the window. Clouds were coming in fast and the sky was darkening rapidly. David looked out the window at the traffic moving on the street. It was late afternoon and the working public was on the way home. He saw no reason to hurry now; just take the time and enjoy the salad, chili and burger. A bright lightning flash illuminated the restaurant and instantly the loud clap of the thunder shook the building. Almost all the children screamed along with a few parents. David jumped with everyone else. Then the sky opened and the rain poured. David opened the straw for his drink and jabbed it into the top of the cup. As he took a sip, he noted the concerned look on many faces around the tables. It was just rain. Then he remembered this part of Texas was right in what they called tornado alley. He took another sip and looked outside at the fast moving clouds.

One by one the family groups left the restaurant, heads covered to ward off the pouring rain. Luckily the thunder and lightning portion of the storm had moved quickly out of the area and all that could be heard was the low rumblings in the distance. As David finished the last bite of burger, he looked out and noticed a clearing in the clouds. It was still dark, but the rain was easing up. He wrapped up all the paper and utensils from his meal and carried it to the trash can. A quick trip to the men’s room and David stepped outside to a light drizzle. Traffic was better, he was refreshed and Dallas was only a couple hours away. A thought crossed his mind as he walked across the lot to the truck. Maybe just one sip of Jack would be good about this time. Just one, no more; he could handle that. The light rain felt good to his face. He walked up to the truck and lifted the tool box lid. He reached inside to grab the last bottle he had. A good stiff drink would do him good about now. As he leaned over looking inside box, he noticed the sack had slid to the other side. He stretched. He didn't see the figure coming up behind him. Suddenly, a sharp pain seared through his head and neck. He saw the bright lights flash in his brain. Then all became dark and David went limp and started to fall. The man dropped the 2x4 into the back of the truck and snatched David under his armpits. His partner reached for David's feet and they carried David in cover of the darkness and rain to the Cadillac with the trunk opened. There was an empty field and an abandoned warehouse that bordered the back of the Wendy's lot. The white car had been backed into the parking space where the trunk could not be seen from the street. David was dumped quickly into the large waiting trunk and the lid was slammed shut. They both scanned the area for any potential witnesses. No one was around. Casually they walked to each side of the car and entered. The taller of the two was the driver. He started the engine and pulled slowly out of the Wendy's parking lot.

Headlights snapped to life on a red Chevrolet Suburban in the AutoZone parking lot. The SUV pulled into the traffic with the white Caddy just ahead. The driver was alone.

The pizza was gone and conversation was sparse. Claire decided to spend the rest of the evening in her room. Maybe she would invite Janey over for a couple of hours; that is unless her mother thought that Janey had spent too much time here already. Kim was clearing away the paper plates, cups and pizza box. Cliff turned on the television to catch the 6:00 o'clock news.

Claire asked her Dad. "Daddy, can I ask Janey to come over for a little while?"

"Sure, but ask her mother first. And no sleep overs, OK?"

"OK." Claire smiled and ran for the phone. Janey's mother agreed and within minutes the two best friends were sitting cross-legged on Claire's bed talking about everything that 11 year olds talk about.

Janey decided to ask. It had never come up since she arrived and she felt Claire wasn't going to offer. "So, how did it go at the doctor's office?"

Claire looked at Janey for a second and then dropped her eyes. Janey thought she had hurt Claire's feelings and said, "Claire, I didn't mean to pry. . ."

Claire immediately responded. "It's OK, Janey. I'll tell you. Anyway, the doctor says I need to talk about it. I guess kinda get it like out of my system."

"So, what did you tell him?"

"Well, you know, it is really all like a dream to me now. I mean, it was so long ago and it happened so fast. I just remember the face and that smell of liquor. I don't think I'll ever want to drink that stuff. He was horrible."

"You mean, David? Your Mom's husband?"

Claire shivered. "Yes."

"So, are you scared he might come back?"

"No, anyway, my dad would probably kill him if he walked through the door right now."

"What about your real mother, Marlena. Are you still mad at her?"

Claire turned from Janey and stared at the other side of her bedroom. Janey repeated. "Claire, what about Marlena?"

"I don't know. She married that bastard."

"You're right, she did, but she didn't make him rape you, you know?"

Claire looked at her. Just to hear those words come out of her best friend's mouth sent chills down her spine. But the realization of the facts was that Marlena was just as innocent as she was in all this. Just hearing those words from Janey made Claire realize what she had done. She was taken back to that wonderful time she spent with her real mother, getting to know her for the first time in her life; making a connection that a mother and daughter should make. Even though she loved Kim with all her heart, she was beginning to love Marlena as well.

Claire's eyes began to tear as she looked into Janey's face. "I have been such a jerk. You're so right. Marlena didn't do this to me and I blamed her for it. I guess she hates me now." Claire started to cry.

Janey reached for her friend and hugged her. "I don't think she's going to hate you. But, I do think you need to makeup with her."

Claire nodded her head and held her friend. They continued to talk until Amanda called for Janey to come home.

Rain was still coming down when David opened his eyes. He could hear the sound beating on the metal roof of the building. He was lying on the floor that smelt of tar and dirt with urine mixed in. David's head ached. As he looked around from his prone position, there was only a faint light that streamed through the cracks from the door frame of the building. Trying to recall what had happen, David searched his mind for the last thing he remembered. *He was eating at Wendy's and it was raining and it's still raining. He went to the truck wanting to get a drink. Did he take that drink and then another and did not stop?* It had happened before.

He tried to get up, but the bindings on his arms and legs prevented him from moving. His mind cleared a little more but still was in great pain; especially at the back of his head. He was lying on his side with his arms bound behind his back. David felt the bindings with his fingers; it was rope. He knew his legs were tied together at the ankles and he assumed that they used rope there as well. Through the throbs of pain, he tried to determine who knocked him out and put him here; wherever this place was. The police wouldn't do this. Still the thought of getting drunk kept coming up again and again. Did he piss someone off? What did he do to get in this predicament? He felt sure no one from Memphis knew of his whereabouts. But he did use his ATM and credit card? Maybe they began tracking. All these thoughts were rolling over and over in his mind.

How long had he been here? Had it been hours or days? And where was here? David fought to turn over and force himself into a seated position but he discovered his captors had secured him to a fixed object in the darkened room. All he could do was lie on the floor. Slowly, his eyesight began to adjust to the darkness in the place of his captivity. The floor was hard and cold; must be concrete covered with dirt. The light from the doorframe was at his feet and David had to fight the pain and strain to lift his head to see. It looked like a garage door; it was wide. There were no windows, or at least none he could make out. There appeared to be one or maybe two tables to his left.

David lifted his legs and jerked them quickly, only to have them snapped back down to the floor. They had been secured to something to his right. David heard a creaking, almost metallic sound give when he pulled up his legs.

The pain in his head was increasing; almost unbearable. His eyes rolled back into his head and he passed out.

Chapter Twenty Three

He didn't know how long he had been locked and bound in this place when he finally woke up. It was still dark inside, but the light from the cracks around the door were brighter. It must be daytime, but which day? He tried to move into another position to relieve the pressure on his body but the bindings were tight. The pain in his head, where he was clubbed, had become less intense, yet was still present. David searched his memory over and over again, trying to figure out who would know where he was. It was obvious someone had been following him. He just didn't consider the possibility. As he lifted his head from the floor, he stretched out his legs. He could not feel his left arm; it had gone to sleep for lack of circulation. He rolled onto his back even though the strain on his shoulders was great. Almost instantly, he could feel some relief in his arms.

The light from the outside, streaming through the cracks of the door, revealed a few more details about his prison. As David maneuvered his body for relief, he could make out the pitch of the roof. He traced the faint outline of the walls where they met the ceiling joists. Best guess was a 15 by 20 foot building. He was sure the walls were just bare studs. He couldn't tell if they were wood or metal. There was a large fixture stationed at the end of his legs. It appeared to be a work bench or table of some sort. It was definitely heavy and made of metal. His ropes were attached to that table.

There were several more objects in the room but too dark for David to discover their identity. The smells told him that the owners of this building used it to store gardening equipment. There was the distinct odor of manure in the air. Mixed with that, David could detect fresh sawdust, like he remembered from when he used to help his father in their workshop back home. That was such a long time ago. The memories flooded his thoughts. The first project he attempted was a magazine rack, which he proudly presented to his mother. His father assisted only with the power saws, but little David built it himself. He was really sad when his father passed away. That was about the time he began to drown his pain in the alcohol. Then less than 2 years later, his mother passed, which drove David deeper into his addiction. This was the first time in years that the memory of his parents persisted in his thoughts. They were happy thoughts but the pain of losing them was there, too.

He rolled back onto his side to relieve more pressure. His arm finally got some blood running through the veins. He wanted a drink, so bad; anything to ease this pain. As he lay there in the dirt and sawdust, he heard the sound of a vehicle approaching far off in the distance. He listened. The turning of wheels on a gravel road got louder and louder. He was sure that someone was coming here. Should he shout out? Could this be someone who could rescue him or were these his captors?

The vehicle began to slow down and then it stopped. He heard the engine clearly and then it shut off. David began to tense up. Maybe the owners of the building were coming to get supplies or to work. He would be rescued. A door on the vehicle opened and then another. David listened. The crunch of boots on the gravel was clear and then the doors slammed shut. Walking; two sets of footsteps were walking toward David's jail. David started to call out, but stopped when he heard the sound of a key being inserted into a lock. Then the door opened and the light flooded the room. David's eyes didn't have time to adjust before the door was closed again. He did notice 2 men had come into the room. One of the men flipped on a light switch by the door. A small overhead bulb came on, filling the room with light.

David squinted at the light and found the 2 men standing and staring down at him crouched on the floor. They were both big African American men, with muscles on top of muscles. David knew at once that these guys were not here to save him. Both were dressed in dark brown leather jackets, black T-shirts and jeans. Bling-bling hung from their necks and wrists with the ball caps turned backwards on their heads. Both men were well over 6 feet tall and at least 250 pounds each.

The taller man spoke first. "Well, sucka, looks like you finally woke up."

David cowered into the best fetal position he could. "What did I do? Please don't hurt me."

The smaller of the men said. "Hurt you? Man you don't know the meaning of hurt." He kicked David in the stomach with his size 13 boot. Doubling up, David yelled out in terrible agony.

"Thought you'd get away with it, didn't ya sucka?" The big man said as he reached down and caught David in the groin with his huge fist. The punch caused David's insides to lock up into one huge cramp and he curled up in tremendous pain; not able to move his arms. He knew he was going to die. For a second he welcomed death.

David felt the rope attached to the table give way. One of the men cut the binding with a switch blade, because he felt the blade glide slowly up his arm. Suddenly, David felt huge hands lifting him by his upper arms. The pain of the last two blows still contorted his body and he couldn't straighten out his legs. David fell back against the chest of the bigger black man. His arms tightly clasped. David opened his eyes just long enough to see the other man lunge a fist at his mid section. A blow so hard it forced the contents of David's stomach out and all over the assailant.

He stopped and looked at his new leather jacket. With hatred in his eyes, he screamed at David. "You fuck! Look what you did to my new jacket!" David was struck hard in his jaw. Two teeth shot from his mouth and bounced off the wall. He was hit again with the man's other fist, this time square in the nose. David's face was covered with blood from his nose and mouth. Pain was indescribable. He wanted to die. Two more blows to his stomach and David slumped over. The smaller man grabbed David's hair with his left hand and lifted his head. He smiled and looked at his partner. He balled his right hand into a fist and a landed a blow onto the side of David's face. David groaned but really never felt it; he had passed out on the last attack.

The man holding David let him go and David's limp body fell to the floor.

"Let's get outta here. That dude ain't gonna make it." The bigger man said.

"Best money I ever made." The smaller of the men said as he kicked David in the back, one last time.

The men left the building, never turning off the light or even closing the lock on the door. They squealed the tires as they turned the big Caddy around tossing gravel into the air.

David lay unconscious in a pool of his own blood.

Cliff and Kim had spent a quiet evening alone for the first time in many weeks. Claire and Janey never came down during the entire evening. After Janey left with her mother, Cliff was turning off lights before following Kim upstairs when the phone rang.

Cliff answered. "Hello?"

"Is this Cliff Richards?" the voice asked.

"Yes, who is this?"

"I'm Sgt. Taggart with Memphis Police. I was asked by Detective Godfrey to give you a call to inform you that the vehicle Mr. Anderson's had used has been confiscated in Texas"

Cliff sat in the chair at the desk. "Do they have David?"

"Sorry, sir, Mr. Anderson was not apprehended. We got a call from the local sheriff's office in Sulfur Springs, TX about a Chevy truck that had been abandoned at a Wendy's restaurant. We faxed over photos of our suspect and he was ID'ed by the clerk at the restaurant. Also he had made a purchase at the parts store next door."

"Who reported the truck?"

"Not clear on that, Mr. Richards. Seems they got an anonymous tip from someone about what went down."

Cliff asked. "Sgt? What went down?"

"Well, the tipster informed the sheriff that they believe our suspect was taken by two other men. They left in a 2000 white Cadillac Seville. The locals have been made aware of our situation. They will be on the lookout for Mr. Anderson as well as the Caddy. We are still assisting Sulfur Springs law enforcement in this investigation. They will contact the surrounding cities for their assistance."

"Do they know who reported it?"

"No sir, just that he was seen with the other men."

"That is good news. Thank you, will you keep me informed?"

"Will do. Good night Mr. Richards. Sorry to have bothered you this late, but we were sure you would want to know."

"You're right, thank you again. Good night." Cliff hung up the phone and raced upstairs to tell Kim the good news. Seems her contact was right on the money.

Claire was lying on her bed with her arms curled up around a pillow. The room was quiet and dark except for the light coming from the hall through the opened door. She had been thinking about the past few days and what her true feelings were. She tried to bury the thought of the man who attacked her, but those memories were the hardest to hide. Marlena continued to fill her thoughts as well. Those few times together that she spent with her mother were good times. They were connecting as mother as daughter; late but still making an effort. Claire wanted that more than anything. She loved Kim very much; she did from the first time she met her. But, the facts were, Marlena came back into her life, trying to make amends for the past. Claire would always remember the way her mother was as she grew up; never there, never a part of her life; leaving Claire feeling rejected and unwanted.

The way Claire screamed at Marlena at the hospital rang in her mind. For the first time, Claire felt remorse for treating her mother that way. Claire finally was realizing that Marlena had nothing to do with the attack; even though she brought the man into their house. Maybe Claire was being unfair. Maybe Marlena deserved a second chance.

Claire's thoughts were broken by the sound of her father running up the stairs calling out to Kim. He sounded very excited about something, so Claire tossed her pillow aside and got out of her bed. Walking slowly toward the open door, she could hear her dad speaking to Kim. Their bedroom door was just down the hall, so Claire quietly made her way to their door. Her heart began to beat faster when she overheard Cliff speaking about David and that his truck had been found. Just the sound of his name and the thoughts that come back to haunt and terrorize her made Claire shiver with fear. She leaned against the wall next to her dad's bedroom door. She allowed her legs to bend as she slid down the wall and sat on the floor in the hall, all the while straining to hear what was being said in the room.

Kim was sitting on the edge of the bed. She had just showered and changed into some blue satin pajamas with her hair still wet. "What kind of truck was it, did they tell you?"

Cliff sat next to Kim. "I think it was an older model Chevy pickup. I suppose David bought it or stole it somewhere; probably here in Memphis. The cop said David was taken away by two other men in a white Cadillac, but they haven't found it. I guess your man lost them too."

"I suppose, but I expect to hear from him soon; maybe tonight after all this. He is pretty thorough and never leaves stones unturned. I'm sure he'll pick up the trail. Where did they say he was?"

"Sulfur Springs, TX is what he said, but I'll bet money he's not there now. If those men took him, they got him somewhere else. I just wonder who else wants him as bad as we do."

"Well, based on what we have found out, David led a pretty calm life; that is for an alcoholic. I guess sometimes he pissed someone off a little too much. Or maybe he owed somebody money here in Memphis and they found out he was back in town. No, that's not it. Anyway, someone wants him, and they got him I guess." Kim said as she wrapped a towel around her head to catch some dripping water.

Claire leaned closer toward the door trying to capture all that was said.

Cliff sat for a couple of seconds without saying a word. He stared blankly at the dresser across from the bed. He looked at Kim and said. "We need to call Marlena. She needs to know this; if she already doesn't."

Kim smiled and took Cliff's hand. "I know I would want to know. Call her. Call her now."

Cliff reached for the phone on the night stand and dialed Marlena's cell phone. Kim returned to the bathroom to finish getting ready for bed. When Marlena answered her phone, Cliff told her everything that he had been told. They agreed to meet in the morning for breakfast with Bill and Kate. Marlena would call her parents as soon as they finished the call.

Claire quietly rose from the floor and walked softly back to her room. She crawled into her bed and pulled the covers up tight. As she lay gently into the pillows, her eyes turned toward the night time lights beaming in from her window. A full moon was rising and she watched it as it made the ascent. Tomorrow would be a better day. She finally drifted off to sleep. She didn't dream any bad dreams or good dreams; just peaceful sleep until morning.

Chapter Twenty Four

Another day brightened the shed where David remained, lying on his side in the dried blood that oozed from his broken nose the night before. David was lucky he didn't bleed to death but maybe death would have been the easy way out. His face was caked with sweat and blood from the pounding he had received. His arms and legs were still tightly bound, David tried to open his eyes, but they had been welded shut with dried blood. He moved his arms a little and pain shot through him like a lightning bolt. His left arm felt like it had been broken. As he forced himself to roll over and take the pain, he managed to open one eye. The door had been left opened and the sun was filling the room with light.

David strained at the brightness and the tears in his eyes finally loosened the tight hold of the dried blood. He bit down hard against the pain coming from his arm and tried to move somewhere, anywhere. His throat was parched; he needed something to drink and for the first time in a long time, he didn't crave the liquor. He straightened out his legs slowly and the pressure eased a bit. As he maneuvered himself to try and sit up, he felt the ropes that were binding his hands loosen. Even with the probable broken left arm, David worked his fingers around the rope, tugging this way and pulling that way. Inch by quarter inch, David worked at the binding until he could free his uninjured right arm. He felt the circulation return to his hand immediately.

With one hand free, he gently pulled the rope off his injured arm and pushed himself up with his good arm. Just to sit felt so wonderful. He wiped his face with the sleeve of his shirt and looked closely at his prison. Only using one hand, David managed to untie the rope around his ankles. He was very concerned that the same men would be back to finish the job. He had to get out before they came and found him like this.

David struggled to push himself to his feet while using only one arm; it proved to be quite difficult. Every part of his body ached and throbbed. Holding on to the heavy table that was used to bind him to the floor, David wobbled on unsteady legs. Twice he almost fell, but managed to hold on with his good arm. He didn't appreciate the ability to walk more than he did now. He took baby steps, just to see if he could. Even those small steps hurt.

There was a chair at the end of the table. David worked himself step by step the few feet away. He wrenched with every step, but at last, he grabbed the back of the metal chair with his good arm. Turning himself slowly, he sat down. For some reason, this felt like a great accomplishment. He was congratulating himself for a job well done. He studied the room for clues and for first aid. This place was obviously a work or storage shed. A few garden tools were hanging from hooks on the walls and scattered across the tables and floor. Stacked below a shuttered window were 40 lb. bags of potting soil and cow manure. A workbench along that wall contained a few empty clay pots and old gallon milk containers filled with something. Maybe they held water. David struggled again but found his strength gaining. He carefully walked to the potting table. He lifted the lid from one of the milk cartons and placed it under his nose. There was no distinct odor; at least no chemical smell. He poured a little out on the table where it would form a small puddle. He dipped one finger into the liquid and touched it to his tongue; it was just plain everyday water. He grabbed the jug and turned it up to his lips and swallowed hard every drop he could. Most rolled down his neck and over his clothes.

David took one final sip of the water and he noticed a paper towel holder hanging above the workbench. He reached for the towels and pulled off several and rolled them in his good hand. He placed the towels on top of the jug of water and tilted the bottle to soak the paper towels. Then he gently washed his face. The sharp pain stabbed him when he rubbed the towel over his nose; it was broken. He stared at the dark red coming off his face onto the towel. As he cleansed his cheeks his eyes scanned the room. He noticed a small mirror hanging on the opposite wall near the door. His legs were weak but David struggled to walk across the room. He wiped a layer of dust from the surface of the mirror. The image that he saw shocked him. The reflection he saw was not familiar. The man he saw was swollen and scarred with open cuts and scratches. Most of the blood had been washed from his face but David began to cry at the sight of his injuries. The pain in his arm suddenly brought him back to reality. He moved the arm slowly. The pain was severe but at least he could move it. With his right arm, he reached around his chest and tore off the sleeve of his shirt. He turned his arm toward the mirror and saw a large 4 inch gash running down his upper left arm. The blood had coagulated in most places, but as he moved the wound would open a little more, allowing more blood to ooze out. He would need to dress this injury, or he might not survive if he started bleeding again. The water and paper towels were all he had to use at the moment. He went back to the table and grabbed the towels and water bottle. He would need a bandage of some sort to cover and wrap the wound. He set the towel and water on the counter under the mirror and spotted some drawers and doors in another cabinet on the other side of the room. Walking was getting easier. He pulled open the first drawer and found only garden tools. The next drawer was empty. Gently bending over, David opened the bottom door of the cabinet. There, next to a bag of potting soil, he saw what he needed; a first aid kit. Pulling the box out of the cabinet, David went back to the mirror. The first aid box contained exactly what he needed; antiseptic, gauze and tape. First he cleaned the area around the wound with a wet paper towel. He had to suffer through the pain. He dried the area as best he could. David's hand shook when he grabbed the antiseptic from the first aid kit. He had always flinched when his mother dressed his cuts and bruises as a child and now he had to do it alone. He unscrewed the top, took a deep breath and lifted the bottle. His hand was shaking so badly he couldn't turn it up. His heart was beating fast now. He knew he had to do this and get out of this place before someone came back to finish the job they started. Summoning up the courage, he turned the open bottle up, lining it above the wound, closed his eyes and with gritted teeth poured the liquid over the open gash. Instantly, the pain engulfed his body. He screamed in agony but almost as fast as it started the pain subsided to a tolerable level. He looked in the mirror at the wound. Most of the dried blood was washing out and down his arm. David grabbed some more towels and cleaned the area again. He struggled with the bandages but managed to close and cover the wound with little pain. He checked the rest of his body for injuries. He cleaned his face one more time and gulped a little more of the water.

Off in the distance a truck horn sounded and at once, he realized that his life might be in danger; he needed to get out of this place. Those two men could return at anytime. David didn't believe he could survive another attack. Staggering to the door, David grabbed the door frame and the full strength of the sunlight blinded him for a few seconds.

After his eyes adjusted to the brightness of the day, he studied the layout of the area. To his right was an empty crop field as far as he could see. To the left was the small parking lot for this building and a row of trees. Straight ahead was the road that left this place for other destinations. Each side of the road was lined with trees as well as high grass, sage brush and gravel. He guessed that he must still be in Texas but he still had no idea what day it was. Suddenly, he remembered his cell phone. It would have the time and day; if it was still active. He reached into his pocket and felt the phone there. When he flipped the receiver open, the day and time appeared in the top half of the display. He stared at the cell phone. He had lost 2 days of his life but he was also thankful he didn't lose his life. Now, he had to get out of this place. For a second he thought of calling Marlena, but why? She knew what he had done. Their relationship was over. The marriage was over. He was just glad his life wasn't over.

David looked around for any sign of the men who beat him. No one was in sight. He made a plan of action in his mind. He would work his way to a highway and attempt to catch a ride. Where, he didn't know. First he had to get away from here. He tore off his shirt that was badly stained with blood. The t-shirt he wore underneath was not so bad; just soiled. He would look like a field hand or normal worker from the area; he hoped. He would tell anyone, who might pick him up, that he cut his arm while working the fields. The strength in his legs was returning more and more. He could move quicker and steadier. He headed for the right side of the road. It offered the most coverage.

The road was empty of traffic, but David could hear the sounds of vehicles off in the distance. A highway must be close by. Where could he be? The thoughts began to run through his mind. Who were those men? Did someone send them? Was Roscoe behind all this? Or was it Roger? It couldn't be Roger. He was paid what he was owed in West Memphis. Yet, he was the last to see David. David was trying to remember if he mentioned Texas to Roger. He was sure that he never told Roscoe. His mind was so foggy right now.

David kept close to the tall grass and brush for cover. The ground was rocky and his ankles were still sore from the rope. He would walk for a few yards before he had to rest. Each time he started back again, he managed to walk a little farther. Suddenly, off in the distance, David spotted a vehicle heading down the road toward him. He dropped to the ground for cover in the tall grass. As the vehicle approached, David watched. It was a red Suburban with two men inside. He couldn't tell if there were more in the back seats. They passed David and never saw him hiding, low in the grass. He didn't know what to do. If those were the men, then they would be looking for him when they discovered the empty building. He couldn't run; he could barely walk. If they were just the men who work there or owned the building, then they would notice someone had been there and report a break-in to the police. Regardless, someone would be searching for him. He stayed low to the ground, waited and listened.

David heard the truck stop at the end of the road next to the building. The men got out. He could hear a conversation, but was too far away to make out what was being said. In no more than 10 seconds, he heard shouts and excitement from the men at the building. The doors to the SUV opened and slammed quickly. The tires spun on the loose gravel as the driver turned back into the road toward David. David tried to drive himself deeper into the soil. He dared not move. With his head lying low and eyes turned toward the oncoming Suburban, he noticed they were driving much slower than before. Oh God, they are looking for him. He watched. They got closer and closer. One man was staring out of the right side window and the driver was watching the opposite side. Suddenly, the man in the passenger seat signaled to the driver and was pointing in David's direction. They had spotted him. The SUV came to a stop and as soon as the doors opened, David struggled to his feet and began to run out toward the fields. He knew it was a hopeless cause, but he had to try. The men were right behind him; they were faster. David passed the last tree and stumbled over an exposed root jutting from the ground. He fell hard, but luckily not on his injured arm. The two men covered him instantly and David felt a cloth cover his face. A strange smell filled his nostrils. It was ether. Seconds later, David was out.

The man with the beard looked David over from head to toe and told the bald man. "He's got some bad cuts and lacerations. Looks like he did his own field dressing. Let's get him back to the room and you make the call. Tell 'em we got him and it looks like someone else got to him first, so we'll need an ambulance to meet us there."

They were careful not to further injure David when they picked him up and carried him to the back of the SUV. The men jumped back into the front seats and sped off down the road. The bald man pulled out his cell phone and dialed a number. After 2 rings his call is answered. The bald man said, "Suspect is in custody. We're expecting ETA in approximately 20 minutes. Contact locals. He'll need medical too." He flashed the phone for a dial tone and made another call.

After the call from Cliff the night before, Marlena was anxious to get to the house. Bill and Katie had planned to pick her up at the hotel and all go together. This was good news, yet was bad news. This nightmare was coming to an end, but Marlena was so afraid that a new one was beginning. The trip over to Cliff's was quiet, even though Bill tried to make light conversation. He felt like he was talking to himself. No one wanted to speculate on the evidence so far. All they knew was that David was thought to be in Texas where he had been seen by someone who reported the abandoned vehicle he had been driving. Maybe Cliff would have more news this morning.

Cliff had been up with Kim since 6:00. Kim managed to get in a run before the guests arrived. Cliff had phoned the detectives assigned to the case and asked them to come by later during the morning to update the family. It was after 8:00 when Claire came into the kitchen. Kim and Cliff were seated at the breakfast table having coffee and juice. Claire slid in the chair next to her father. He put his arm around her shoulders and asked. "Are you OK, Tweetie?"

She shrugged her shoulders and he asked again. "Now, that's not an answer. What's up?"

Kim had poured Claire a glass of orange juice, which she took and downed a long drink. Claire looked up into her dad's eyes and said. "Did they catch that man?"

Cliff looked at Kim.

Claire looked at Kim and then back at Cliff. "I overheard what ya'll were talking about last night. I didn't mean to. I was going to the bathroom when I heard Dad mention his name. So, I kinda listened at the door. You're not mad are you?"

Cliff looked at his sweet daughter's face. The innocence was still there in that smile. "No, Tweetie. We haven't heard anything new. Just that we know where he has been. And that's a long way from here."

Claire took another sip from her glass. "What will they do to him when they catch him?"

Kim said, "He'll go to jail for a long time. What he did to you is one of the worst crimes there is. He'll get what he deserves."

Claire just shook her head and sat there in silence until a knock at the back door startled everyone. Cliff got up and said. "That must be Marlena and her parents." He went to the kitchen door.

Claire suddenly became flustered and nervous. She didn't know why. Her mother was coming in the back door when Claire caught her eye. Marlena smiled at Claire, not knowing what to expect. Thoughts from the night before filled Claire's mind. She thought of the good times she and Marlena were building and the relationship that Claire wanted so much over the years as she grew up. Suddenly, with tears forming in her eyes, Claire jumped from her chair and ran to Marlena. She wrapped her arms around her tightly. Marlena was dumbfounded. What was happening here?

Claire looked up into Marlena's eyes and with a trembling voice she said. "Mother, I'm so sorry for how I treated you. I know now this wasn't your fault and I was wrong to blame you. I still want us to be together. Can we?"

Marlena did not hold back the tears. She fell to her knees and took Claire into her arms. They both cried and held tight to each other. Katie and Kim began to cry with them. Bill had joined Cliff at the table and poured some coffee. He was all smiles at this reunion, yet he had a small tear forming. Kim's cell phone rang.

Kim wiped the tears from her face and grabbed the phone. She went into the great room to take the call.

Marlena finally pulled back and looked into Claire's eyes. She stroked her hair and kissed her on the cheek. Marlena smiled and said, "We will always be together."

Kim returned into the kitchen. Her phone conversation was over. She looked at Cliff and he asked. "Who was that?"

Kim smiled and looked at everyone and stopped at Claire. She said, "They got him!"

Chapter Twenty Five

The ether was not a large dose and David began to come around while the SUV was still in route. He stared at the roof of the truck as he felt the movement of the vehicle. He was lying on his back with his head near the second row seat. He was not bound in any way. He could tell by the movement of the telephone poles zooming by, they were traveling at a good rate of speed. He rolled to his right and lifted his head to see his captors. Both were white men. He lifted his head a little more, rocking with the motion of the SUV. The bald man, who was sitting in the passenger seat, reached underneath his arm and pulled a 9mm Glock from the holster. He pointed the gun directly at David's face.

"I trust you're not going to do anything stupid, Mr. Anderson?" The bald guy asked.

David responded. "No, I'm not. . . Uhh, who are you guys? Are you cops?"

Baldy said, "Let's just say that some interested parties wanted us to find your ass and bring it back."

David, for once, was relieved. At least he wouldn't be killed. Well, not now anyway. He asked. "Where are we going?"

Mr. Bald guy shouldered his weapon and replied. "You'll find out in a couple of minutes."

The driver flipped on the blinker and took the next exit. A few more turns and David felt the vehicle pull into a parking space and the engine turned off. He looked out of the window and noticed a Best Western motel sign. The bald guy exited the passenger seat and walked to the rear. The bearded man met him. Both had weapons drawn and opened the door. David was calm and had no plan to resist. The bearded man assisted David, while the other covered him. David was still groggy from the ether, but he managed to walk to the door of the motel room. At least it was on the bottom floor. David was helped to the bed, where he was allowed to lay down.

Within 5 minutes, there was a knock at the door and bearded man opened the door. David stared at the door. A paramedic entered the room carrying a box of medical supplies. He went to David's bed.

"Mr. Anderson, I'm going to check out your wounds and dress them. Can you take off your t-shirt please." The paramedic said.

David was struggling and the paramedic helped him remove the shirt. He cleaned all his wounds and scratches and re-dressed the left arm. "You're lucky you didn't die." The paramedic told him.

David turned his head and said, "Sometimes, I wish I had."

Another knock at the door and David turned to see 2 sheriff's deputies enter the room. They talked quietly for a few minutes with the bald guy and bearded man while the paramedic finished with David's injuries.

With the medical needs completed and the paramedic packing up, the deputies walked to the bedside. The one with the name badge, *Watson* looked down and smiled at David. "Mr. Anderson, you're under arrest."

Deputy Martin read David his rights and explained why he was being arrested. David didn't need to hear it, because he knew why. They helped him to his feet and assisted putting on his shirt. Then they cuffed his wrists. He was lead to the waiting patrol car outside. David was placed in the back seat with his hands behind his back. At least the paramedic did a better job of treating his wound. He watched in the front of the patrol car as the deputies and the two men who captured him talked. He couldn't make out the words but he did hear Memphis mentioned.

Claire turned and stared at Kim. "They caught him?"

Kim said, "Yes, sweetheart. They got him and he'll never hurt you again."

Marlena stood up and held onto Claire. “Where did they find him, Kim?”

“Texas! Just outside Sulfur Springs.” Kim said.

“I had a man call me yesterday and explain that someone told him that David was going to Texas. Or at least that’s what they thought.” Marlena said.

Cliff jumped in, “What, you knew this yesterday and didn’t call?”

Marlena explained, “Well, it was last night, exactly before you called me. I totally forgot about it until now. Your news only confirmed it.”

Cliff looked at Kim and asked. “OK what’s next? What did they tell you?”

Bill stopped her before she spoke. “By the way, Kim, who are ‘they’?”

Kim sat down while Marlena and Claire pulled up a chair. Kim explained. “I have a couple of good friends who are in the private investigation business. They are tops in their field. Seems they can locate the un-locatable. Anyway, when David took off, I decided to contact them and ask for their help. When I explained what had happened, they told me not to worry, they were on it. And it wasn’t costing a cent. I don’t know how they tracked him but I know the results. The local authorities will take David into custody and prepare extradition papers back to Memphis this morning.”

The patrol car pulled into the local sheriff’s office parking lot. David was quiet and never spoke a word as the deputies escorted him into the office where he was booked and placed in a holding cell awaiting transport to the county jail.

The two private investigator friends of Kim packed their belongings and checked out of the motel.

Within two weeks, David had been arraigned and charged with rape of a child under the age of 13. Papers had been prepared for extradition to Tennessee, which David's appointed lawyer did not dispute. On November 5th, the Grand Jury in Memphis met and indicted David for the rape of Claire Richards. His trial date was set for December 11th. At the prosecutor's request a 1 million dollar bond was set and accepted by the court. David would spend his time in lockup. His wounds were healing slowly.

David was lying on the cot in his cell when a heavy set, African American deputy jailer came to his door. She tapped on the cell door with her club. "Anderson, you got a visitor."

David looked at the deputy in surprise. *A visitor* he thought *but who?* Deputy Castillo leaned over to the microphone attached to her shoulder. She pushed the talk button and requested "C4, open." Within seconds, David's cell door slid into the open position.

David rose and walked to the door. The deputy instructed. "OK, turn around; put your hands behind your back." The deputy placed a yellow plastic tie on David's wrists. David never had a visitor, except his court appointed lawyer. He had no idea who this could be.

He was led down a hall to another room with several armed guards. David saw many booths with prisoners speaking with friends and relatives on the opposite side of the glass. Each prisoner was shackled with yellow ties, just like he was. The escort deputy gave one of the armed guards a piece of paper. He studied the paper and looked at David. The first deputy left and the armed man led David to a chair near the end of the row of booths. As he approached, he saw a face that brought the tears back. Marlena was on the other side of the booth. She was not crying, she was not smiling and for the first time, David saw hatred in her eyes. He sat slowly into the plastic chair which allowed his bound arms to hang uncomfortably in the back.

Marlena noticed the tears but did not react. She watched as he sat down. She started. "David! I just want to know why?"

David bowed his head. There was no reason why. He was under the influence and had no excuse for his actions. He slowly lifted his head, trying to avoid Marlena's gaze. "Marlena. . . . I can only say, I'm sorry. It was all a blur to me. I truly don't remember the details. I just know it happened."

Marlena just stared. In a way she understood the part about not knowing what happened but he had ruined her child's life and caused her such great mental and physical anguish. She turned away for a second.

David watched as her face changed from the hater to the sympathizer. She looked at him again and stated. "You know, you're going to prison."

David said softly. "Yes, I know."

"And you know that we're through? Our marriage is over."

He looked at Marlena with hurt eyes. He knew this was coming, but to hear it now made it all real. He only nodded.

"David, this will probably be the only time I will come to see you, but I will pray for you. I will pray that you are safe where ever you wind up, but you must be punished for what you did to Claire."

He nodded again.

"By the way, what happened to you? Did someone beat you up in there?"

David thought most of the bruises and cuts were healed. He said, "Well, you should have seen me a few weeks ago. Looked much worse. Seems someone else was after me before your guys caught me. They beat the shit out of me."

"I didn't send any guys. That was Cliff's wife, Kim. Who were these other guys?
Did you know them?"

"Two big mothers, black guys, bigger than mountains. Never saw them before."

"Did you tell the cops?"

"What for? They wouldn't do anything."

Marlena looked into David's eyes. For a moment she saw the David she remembered. The David she fell in love with, but now he was the man who raped her daughter. She asked "When is your trial?"

"My lawyer says December sometime. I think he said the 11th or somewhere around there. Will you be there?"

"I suppose I'll be summoned. I haven't heard yet."

"What about Claire?"

"What about her?" Marlena shouted.

"I just hoped she wouldn't be asked to testify. You know."

"What? So she wouldn't have to go through this all over again?"

"Yeah, something like that."

"Well, I was planning to ask that she be deposed and the transcript can be entered into the trial."

"Good." David said turning away to fight the tears again.

Marlena felt his uneasiness and got up from her chair. "I guess I better leave. I'm so sorry, David, that all this came about. I was so looking forward to our life together."

"Me too. At least I haven't had a drink in weeks."

Marlena smiled and spoke her last words to him. "That's great, David. I'll pray for you." Then she turned and walked out of the door while David watched.

The armed guard appeared behind David and helped him to his feet. He was escorted back to his cell to wait for trial.

It was early evening and Claire and Janey had been in Claire's room talking over the day's events when they heard Marlena talking with Cliff downstairs. Claire jumped off her bed and raced downstairs to see her mother. Marlena had been describing her visit with David when the girls ran into the room. At this point, Cliff was not going to hide anything from Claire. The girls sat on the sofa opposite her Dad.

"Marlena was just telling me about her visit." Cliff told Claire.

Marlena looked at Claire. "He doesn't remember, Claire. He knows he did it but it was all a blur."

Claire didn't reply.

"He knows he is going to jail and has accepted that. His trial is in December."

Claire spoke up. "Do I have to go?" She was smart enough to know that victims appear in court against their accuser.

Marlena looked at her. "If the court agrees, then we will have someone from the court come by and type up your story. Kind of like when the detectives came by and questioned everyone."

"Good!" she said.

Marlena turned back to Cliff. "There was one thing though. David was beat up pretty bad. Did Kim's guys do that?"

Cliff looked surprised. “I doubt that her PI’s were involved. How bad was he?”

“Well, most were healing, but from the looks of the scars, I would say they were bad enough to maybe kill him.”

Janey stood up and said. “I guess I need to get home.”

Claire said, “Can’t you stay a little longer?”

“No, I need to go.” Janey said and rushed out the door.

During the weeks before the trial, Claire’s condition improved dramatically and her dreams were finally peaceful and content. Her relationship with Marlena grew to a point it had never been before. Kim was not left out either. Claire loved her more than ever. Claire felt so lucky to have two mothers she could love so much.

Marlena had checked out of the hotel and was staying at her parent’s house in Collierville while she took care of personal business. Her job in Chicago was on hold but she made the decision to move back to Memphis. She located and hired a prominent attorney to handle divorce proceedings.

David was convicted and sentenced to 50 years in prison for the rape of a child. He would be eligible for parole in 30 years. By then Claire would be over 40 and maybe never remember that day.

Marlena flew back to Chicago to sell their house and all the furnishings. She would not bring anything to Memphis except her clothes. Claire was thrilled Marlena would live in Memphis permanently.

Cliff, Kim and Claire had just finished a delicious Saturday lunch that Mae had prepared. Cliff asked Mae to come over and work on Saturday, which was not unusual, but not the norm.

He looked at Claire and said. “Tweetie, how would you like to spend Christmas in the Bahamas?”

"Are you kidding?" she shouted.

Then Kim said "And how about we spend New Year's in Cancun?"

Claire could only sit there with her mouth dropped open.

Cliff said with a big smile "And how about another week in Orlando, Disney World and Universal Studios?"

Claire pretended to faint. She jumped up and ran to her dad. "Are you serious?"

"Serious as can be. Are you ready?"

"You bet, let's go."

"We will. We're leaving Monday." Kim said.

Mae was putting away the last of the fixings for lunch. She came over to the table and smiled at Claire. "Well, my little darling deserves a good vacation. And so do you two."

Claire jumped up from her seat. "Can I go tell Janey?"

"Sure", Cliff said.

Mae sat down and told Cliff. "You sure have done a good thing for that baby, Mr. Cliff."

Cliff took her hand and smiled at his long time friend and employee. "Mae, you remember when you first started working here I told you that if you stayed with me that I would help you out."

"Yeah, I remember, but wasn't sure you did." Mae said with some suspicion.

"Well, come with me, my dear, dear friend." Cliff took her hand and he could feel Mae trembling.

Cliff opened the kitchen door to the garage and he escorted Mae through the garage to the driveway. Kim was following. Sitting proudly in the driveway was a brand new, Ford Expedition SUV. Cliff reached into his pocket and pulled out a set of keys and handed them to Mae.

He said with a smile and a hug. "This is for you, Mae. For all your years of love and caring for me and Claire. I don't know how we could have gotten along without you."

Mae took the keys and with tears streaming down her face, she leaned up to kiss Cliff on his cheek. "Oh, bless you Mr. Cliff. My boys are going to be thrilled."

While Mae inspected her new ride with Cliff and Kim, Claire was running fast to Janey's house next door to tell her the great vacation news. Just as she jumped the hedge like she always did before, she stopped. Should she tell Janey? Would she be glad for her or would she be jealous? She and Janey had been best friends forever. She would be happy.

Claire ran to the door and rapped away. She heard the familiar 'come in' from Janey's mom, so Claire opened the door and went inside. Amanda was doing needlepoint on the couch and she said. "Janey's upstairs, sweetie." Claire ran up the stairs, two at a time.

Janey was lying across her bed. She saw Claire come into the room but turned away. Claire sensed something was wrong and she went to her friend, forgetting about the good news she had to tell.

Claire sat on the bed next to Janey. "What's wrong, Janey? You've been acting weird for weeks now, so what's the deal?"

"Nothing!"

"Now you know we've been friends, like forever. I know when something's wrong just like you know when I'm having a problem."

Janey turned away.

"Come on tell me," Claire insisted.

Janey looked at Claire. "You remember back when your mother was telling us about David at the jail. You know before he went to trial?"

"Yeah, what about it?"

"You remember when she said that he was beat up?"

"Yeah, I was glad."

Janey looked away again and said. "That was my fault."

Claire said, "Your fault? How can it be your fault?"

Janey swallowed hard, took a deep breath and began. "Remember, back when everyone was trying to figure out what happened to you and then you freaked out when David came in the house."

"Yeah"

"Well, I have this uncle who is in the business of finding people, so I called him. I told him what had happened to you and about David and stuff. And I told him about that creep in the car that sat outside all the time. When he heard what David did to you, he told me not to worry. He would take care of things. I think he was really mad at what David did."

"Me, too!"

"Anyway, he has been good at what he does and when Marlena said that David was beat up real bad and Kim's guys didn't do it, then I figured it was my uncle, or someone he hired. I really didn't expect them to hurt him; just find him and bring him back."

"Wait! Is that why you ran home that night?"

"Uhh Huh."

Claire reached over to hug her best friend. "I'm so glad to have you as my best friend. What you did for me was the greatest thing ever. I think even better than what Kim did."

"Really?"

"Really" Claire said. Then she jumped from the bed. "Don't go anywhere, I'll be back in a few minutes, OK?"

"OK?" Janey said as Claire rushed out of the room.

Claire was back within ten minutes and jumped back on the bed next to Janey. Claire looked at her friend. "I got some great news."

"Really, what?" Janey asked as she sat up on the bed.

"My Dad is taking me and Kim on this awesome vacation to the Bahamas, Cancun and Disney World."

"WOW! Great. When do you leave?" Janey asked with excitement.

"Monday!"

"So soon! You're going to bring me back souvenirs aren't you?

"Nope!"

"No, what happened to us being best friends?"

Claire smiled. "Because, best friends are going together! I asked my dad and he said yes and he asked your mom and she said yes. He and Kim are downstairs right now making arrangements with your mom. We're going together, best friend."

Janey started to cry and grabbed Claire in a huge bear hug. They screamed at the top of their lungs. From downstairs Cliff looked up as if he could see through the ceiling. He smiled with great joy because Claire's recovery had finally begun.

Proof

Made in the USA